THE REVIVAL

The Revival

Other Books by Steven C. Smith

The Reversion

The Revival

Book II
of
The Stonemont Series

Steven C. Smith

Copyright © 2018 by Steven C. Smith

All rights reserved. No part of this publication may be reproduced, distributed, or transmitted in any form or by any means, including photocopying, recording, or other electronic or mechanical methods without the prior written permission of the publisher, except in the case of brief quotations embodied in critical reviews and certain other noncommercial uses permitted by copyright law.

Contact the author at: scsmith@integrativepreparedness.com

THE REVIVAL

As before and for always, to my wife and children,
You are the loves of my life and the reasons for my efforts.

THE REVIVAL

From the end spring new beginnings.

Pliny the Elder

THE REVIVAL

A Word of Recommendation

As I said in my recommendation of his first book, *The Reversion – Book I of the Stonemont Series*, Steven "Craig" Smith is a masterful and eloquent storyteller.

Craig has an exciting and accurate knowledge of survival skills, combat skills and mind-set, weapons, military and police tactics, and of 'the good, the bad and the ugly' of when things get 'down and dirty'. He knows and writes about the real stuff – not the 'bull-stuff'. If you want to know what the world would and could be like after a collapse – and how to deal with it - read this book.

The only problem was the same as last time – it kept me awake reading it, and I didn't get much sleep until I finished it. When is number three coming out?

Jim "Ronin" Harrison
Montana, 2018

Called "one of the most dangerous men alive" by Bruce Lee, Jim Harrison is one of the true legends of martial arts, combatives and survivalism. Known for his notorious battles during the "Blood-n-Guts" era of American karate, he has been called the closest thing to a modern samurai the 20th century can produce.

He was 3-time U.S. Karate Champion, 3-time All-American Grand Champion, undefeated U.S. light heavyweight Kickboxing Champion, and coach to the undefeated U.S. Professional Team.

He has trained U.S. Army Special Forces, Rangers, SEALs, Marine Scout-Sniper/Recon and members of First Special Forces Operational Detachment-Delta (Delta Force).

He has provided personal security for Chuck Norris, Linda (Mrs. Bruce) Lee and Prince Mikhail Matijasevic.

He was awarded a Ph.D. (Research, Analysis and Instruction) by Yudanshakai University, and was inducted into the International Karate Hall of Fame with Chuck Norris and Bruce Lee.

He is the founder of Bushidokan, Ronin Jutsu and Sakura Warrior Arts.

THE REVIVAL

This could be the kind of catastrophe that ends civilization, and that's not an exaggeration.

Newt Gingrich
Addressing the Electromagnetic Pulse Caucus

Foreward

In the foreword I wrote for Steven Smith's first book, *The Reversion*, I said that it was destined to become an instant classic in the preparedness/survival/TEOTWAWKI genre. I was right. But the reviews and growing readership proved that it was more. It transcended its original target audience to appeal to many who had no previous interest in survivalism or preparedness as a lifestyle and made the jump to general adventure fiction.

The reasons for this were several. It was well written, expansive in scope yet easy to follow. It told an interesting, compelling, story - intricate in its construction but smooth in its presentation. It introduced well-developed characters who jumped from the pages and spoke to the reader as easily and completely as do those around us, with thoughtful depth and easy humor. The action was swift and gritty, reflecting the author's background in those things most of us have spent our lives trying to avoid, but without being unduly gratuitous. Most importantly, however, it asked, and answered, the seminal questions of our lives: Who are we? What do we believe in? What do we stand for? What will we stand against? And what is it, at our core, that enables ordinary people to accomplish extraordinary things?

Where *The Reversion* left off, *The Revival* picks up. From survival of an existential collapse, we enter the initial stages of the rebuilding of a society - a rebuilding seen through the eyes of those from Stonemont, and, eventually, beyond. As it should, *The Revival* takes us beyond *The Reversion* into a world we do not know, and cannot know, unless and until it happens. In doing so, it addresses unknown and unknowable situations with known and knowable human traits, tactics and strategies in pursuit of the stabilization of a world turned upside down. It is James Wesley, Rawles meets S.M. Stirling with a dash of Louis L'Amour. It is a study of self-reliance, love, fortitude, morality, patriotism and the things that made America great, a critique of what caused the world to crumble, and a blueprint for the revival of those things we feel to be foundational for a people to return to a world of liberty, justice and freedom.

As did *The Reversion*, *The Revival* breathes hope and fresh air into a genre which often, and rightly, concentrates on the devastation of society, and shows us a future world which is, in many ways, more positive than the one in which we currently live. Many readers, in fact, have stated that they prefer the world they have found in the Stonemont series to the one we live in. I can certainly understand why.

The Revival continues the journey *The Reversion* started. It is a journey of life, love, learning and the human spirit. It is a journey you will be glad you are on. I know I am.

John Middleton
Somewhere in America, 2018

Preface

On September 1 and 2, 1859, a solar coronal mass ejection (CME) struck the Earth's magnetosphere causing a geomagnetic storm witnessed around the globe. The northern aurora was seen as far south as southern Mexico and the southern as far north as Australia. Gold miners awakened in the middle of the night to prepare breakfast, thinking it was daytime, and telegraph systems across America and Europe failed, shocking operators and setting papers on fire. Observed and documented by amateur British astronomer Richard Carrington, it was dubbed The Carrington Event.

If a Carrington class CME struck Earth today, it would destroy all electrical grids and electronic components worldwide. We would immediately be back in a world without electricity. A nuclear-induced electromagnetic pulse (EMP) would have the same effect in its target area. In either case, The EMP Commission estimates that 90% of those in affected areas would be dead within one year from starvation, disease, accidents and the violence that accompanies societal collapse.

How probable is this? In their 2012 report, the American Geophysical Union projected a 12% chance that a Carrington class CME would strike the earth within the next decade. The chance of a nuclear-induced EMP attack from one of our global enemies? We have no way to know.

Author's Note

This book is a sequel to *The Reversion* and the second in the Stonemont series. In writing it, I had to decide whether to include enough background material to enable it to stand alone, without the reader having first read *The Reversion*, or to simply continue the story. I decided on the latter, as reading sequels filled with repeated re-introductions of people and situations from previous books has always irritated me and interrupts the natural flow. So, with this in mind, I highly recommend that anyone who has not yet read *The Reversion* do so before starting this one. It will make all the difference.

On a second note, though many of the characters in this book and *The Reversion* are based on real people, I have never included a real person as themselves (except for my wife and kids, who get a kick out of it). In this book, I make an exception. The reference to Jim Harrison is to the real Jim Harrison of Montana (the martial artist, not the writer). While he is not widely known among some of the younger or non-serious martial artists, he is a legend among the elite. Those whose names you know, know him. And, in the spirit of full disclosure, he is a friend of mine.

Although I taught self-defense, defensive tactics, martial arts and combatives for many years, I no longer do so, preferring to write, work in my garden and be with my wife and kids. However, knowing the martial skills can be important, especially in a survival situation, and for those who are interested, Jim Harrison's system, Ronin Jutsu, is the one I would recommend above all others. With the exception of Sakura Warrior Arts in Missoula, Montana, the only place I know of where the complete Ronin Jutsu system is taught is at Kenukan Academy in Olathe, Kansas (my apologies to any others of which I am unaware). The character Travis McKay is based on Travis Boggs, owner and chief instructor of Kenukan, who has studied under both his father, Bob Boggs, and Jim Harrison since he was a child. If you have any interest in learning a real martial system, a google search for these would be well worth your while.

Semper Paratus,

SCS

The Revival

THE REVIVAL

THE REVIVAL

1

Jim Wyatt stood looking out the south window of his den, a steaming cup of coffee in his hand, watching the people walking between the buildings in the common area and looking forward to the Thanksgiving gathering that evening. It had been snowing since early morning and the compound lay under a soft white blanket several inches deep, bringing with it the coziness and joy that always accompanied the first real snow of the season.

The past six months had been a challenge, but things had gone as well as could be expected. Better, really, when the condition of the country at large was taken into account, and, for that, they had a lot to be thankful for.

He took a testing sip from the earthenware mug, a birthday gift from a Stonemont resident-turned-potter that bore the design of a pine tree and the words *An Appeal to Heaven*. The reference was to Washington's naval flag which had been gaining on the Gadsden in popularity among patriots before the collapse, and it seemed particularly appropriate now. Coffee was still one of his greatest pleasures, made even more enjoyable by the slower, simpler life to which they had all become accustomed, and, to him, each sip was a joy unto itself.

His eyes were drawn from the steam of the coffee to the smoke rising from the two chimneys of the main hall, a second massive fireplace having been added to remedy an imbalance he had felt with only one, and he allowed his thoughts to drift with it.

Much had been done over the summer and throughout the fall, and between hard work and the grace of God Stonemont had become a thriving hub of regeneration, not only for its residents, but for the surrounding area as well. Family cabins now ringed the open area referred to as "the commons", each sending up a tendril of smoke from its own chimney as if to announce that a family lived there, and the central hall had been completed in time for Thanksgiving.

School Center was developing well under the leadership of Carol and Jerry Hadley and the protection of rotating squads of Stonemont scouts. Their niece, Naomi, had been a great help, though she seemed to spend as much time at Stonemont as she did at the Center, ostensibly to visit Brin and Tracy

THE REVIVAL

and train with Christian, who always seemed to feel the need to escort her back when she left.

Church Crossing had been secured with the razing of the neighborhoods to its north, and Pasquale Paoli was building a strong community at Redemption, which would most likely be self-sufficient by summer. Hillmont, which they had named Stonemont's outpost at the massive former Family Church complex across from Redemption, had begun operating as a trading post and refugee intake center, providing goods from Stonemont's salvage operations to those with something to trade, and rescue and resettlement for those still escaping the city with little more than the clothes on their backs - a group that was rapidly dwindling and arriving in increasingly bad shape.

The burning of the neighborhoods to the north of the Crossing had been a major undertaking lasting over a month. Each house had been cleared by the scouts, then inventory and loading teams sent in to remove all useful items for transport to Hillmont. Weapons, tools, gasoline, propane, pharmaceuticals and housewares had been designated as priority items, with winter clothing being included on a second tier. Jewelry, family pictures and other valuables had been carefully collected and catalogued by address in case the owners ever returned – a possibility that dwindled as time passed.

Several of the families staying at Redemption were from the neighborhoods being razed and had expressed a desire to return to their homes at a later time if their houses could be spared. While this had presented a challenge, calm weather and the controlled burning of only a few houses at a time had allowed them to save each of those houses, though one deck, one detached garage and a wooden playset had fallen victim to burning embers that had escaped the fire containment teams.

Overall, the operation had been a success, giving Redemption and Hillmont a clear buffer zone of almost half of a mile to the nearest remaining neighborhoods.

He had given the clearance operation to Tom Murphy as a test, and Tom had handled it well. As a retired Marine officer, Tom was experienced in organizing and leading people in critical tasks, and, with the clearance, he had shown a combination of tactical planning and operational commitment that Jim appreciated and respected. That he had put his wife, Patty, in charge of the collection and inventory of valuables, and assigned their teenage son and daughter to help her, showed a respect for his family and their abilities, a respect that had proved to be well deserved.

At Stonemont, family cabins for those staying temporarily in the main hall had been finished by the first week of November, the completion not having

THE REVIVAL

been expected until spring, and the families had been able to move from the temporarily partitioned hall into their own cabins before the weather turned cold. The large number of workers from both School Center and the Hillmont intake had made the construction go much faster than had been anticipated, and although not all of the finishing touches had been completed, all of the cabins were livable, with fireplaces, main rooms and sleeping lofts. The partitions had been removed from the main hall and used in the cabins, and the hall was set up for the gathering tonight.

Yes, he thought to himself, things had gone pretty well.

"What are you thinking about?"

Her voice brought a smile to his face as he turned around. She had always had that effect on him and it seemed the effect was only growing with time. "I was just thinking I'd like a good-looking blonde to come by and keep me company."

Kelly laughed. "Well, will I do?"

His smiled spread to his eyes. "You're exactly what I had in mind."

She walked over to him, snuggled under his arm, and looked out the window at the falling snow. "It's beautiful, isn't it?"

He nodded. "Might be the beautifulest I've ever seen."

She giggled. "Beautifulest? Is that a word?"

He shrugged and smiled again, looking down into her crystal blue eyes. "It ought to be. You're the beautifulest woman I've ever seen."

Her giggle evolved into a laugh. "Well, in that case, 'beautifulest' is a fine word."

They stood together for a minute watching the snow before she looked up at him. "Christian and Naomi have something they want to show us in the barn if you can tear yourself away from this."

He chuckled. "I've seen them going into the barn a lot lately. I'm not sure I want to see what they're doing in there."

She smiled and shook her head. "You have a dirty mind."

"So you keep telling me."

"I keep telling you so that you don't forget."

"Not a chance. Where are the kids?"

"Out organizing a snowball fight – or a snowball *war* by the way Aedan was talking about it. In Brody's terms, it's going to be 'epic'".

He chuckled again. Their two boys were always into something, and usually putting together a project or activity that was going to be the 'biggest' or 'greatest' of whatever it was that had ever been. Their daughter Morgan was rarely far behind. "Okay, give me about ten minutes to finish something up and I'll take you out to the barn."

She slipped out from under his arm and cocked an eyebrow. "Is that a threat?"

"It's a promise," he smiled.

"Good," she laughed, walking to the door. "I'll be in the kitchen."

He turned back to the window, smiling to himself. He was a lucky man, he knew. Kelly and their kids had been his life before the collapse and were even more so now, if that was possible. The new world they found themselves in had stripped away the superfluous, the petty worries and irritations of the past so-called modern world and given them a new life experience in which the simple pleasures and responsibilities had been allowed to again take their rightful place in people's lives.

He thought about life before the collapse, about the constant social stresses of a politically-correct, over-stimulated, over-entertained, over-scheduled and overly-demanding society and knew that, regardless of the dangers and inconveniences, the new world was far better for the human soul and psyche. Once again, people were being allowed to make their own way as their abilities, determination and hard work enabled them, restricted by nothing more than the natural rights of individuals and the mutual agreement of those interacting and doing business with one another. That was the way America's founders had intended it to be, and that was the way he liked it.

He turned and walked to the horseshoe of deep leather couches that faced the stone fireplace and sat down in front of a dark green folder laying on the coffee table. Setting his coffee mug to the side, he opened the folder and flipped through several pages until he found what he was looking for. Picking up a pen and tearing off a piece of scratch paper, he wrote down a couple of lines, folded the paper, laid the pen aside and closed the folder. Standing, he stuffed the paper into his pocket, drained his coffee and headed to the kitchen.

The aroma of freshly baked holiday bread greeted him when he opened the den door and he followed the smell down the hallway, through the great room and into the kitchen where he found Guadalupe, the housekeeper, taking fresh loaves out of the oven and placing them on the island where Kelly was adding a persimmon glaze to the dozen or so loaves already there. He stopped and made a show of taking a deep breath. "I need to put a screen door on my den so I know when to come out."

Kelly laughed, and Guadalupe looked up at him with a beaming smile, her dark eyes sparkling in a round face that looked perpetually jolly. "Good morning, Mr. Wyatt. I was just telling Mrs. Wyatt how I am surprised you are not fat with all the good things she bakes."

Jim chuckled, accepting the thick slice of bread Kelly handed him. "I fully intend to get fat someday, Guadalupe. And don't you think it's time you started calling us Jim and Kelly?"

The woman rubbed the palms of her hands on her apron and shook her head, her face suddenly serious. "No, Mr. Wyatt. I come from a small village of old traditions. You are El Patron. It would be disrespectful for me to call you by your first name." She gave a single and definitive nod of her head. "You are Mr. Wyatt." She turned and nodded at Kelly, smiling. "And your wife is Mrs. Wyatt."

Jim dug a knife into a crock of fresh whipped butter and slathered in on the slice. It smelled of cinnamon and nutmeg and he watched it melt into the bread around the nuts, raisins and bits of fruit. "Well, Guadalupe, that means that in order to be polite we would have to call you Mrs. Hernandez."

Guadalupe shrugged, her smile returning. "It is not necessary, Mr. Wyatt, but as you wish."

Jim chuckled as he carried his cup to the sink, then turned to Kelly. "You ready to go see what they want?"

Kelly finished brushing the loaf she was working on. "I know what they want," she smiled. "Give me a minute."

Jim nodded and grabbed another slice of bread. "I'll get our coats." He walked to the doorway and looked back. "Have a good day, Mrs. Hernandez."

"Thank you, Mr. Wyatt," Guadalupe answered, smiling. "You too."

He walked into the large mud room off the kitchen, stuffing the last of the bread into his mouth. Taking his sheepskin coat off a hook, he slipped it on, then put on his buffalo felt Stetson. Most of the younger people preferred watch caps, which, for some reason he couldn't figure out, they called beanies, and The North Face and Columbia outer gear, which were lighter and less bulky, but he preferred the heavier and bulkier shearling. It made him feel warmer, more separated and encapsulated from the cold.

"I'm ready," said Kelly, coming into the mudroom and accepting her own sheepskin coat from him. Sitting on the bench, she pulled on a pair of fur lined pac boots. "Do you have an idea of what it is they want to show us?"

"Nope," he answered as they stepped outside, "but there's all sorts of things they could be doing in the barn that I don't want to know about. Hope it's something else."

Kelly laughed and shook her head. "Did I tell you that you have a dirty mind?"

"Yep," he said, opening the door. "You bring it out in me."

They welcomed the brisk air as they walked through the falling snow,

THE REVIVAL

greeting those they passed and leaving ankle deep tracks behind them. Unlike the bitter cold that would come in January, November snows in eastern Kansas occurred in the upper twenties and lower thirties, making it invigorating to be outside.

"It's amazing that they finished the cabins in time to get the main hall ready so soon," said Kelly. "I don't think most of the families expected to be in their own places until spring."

Jim shook his head. "I didn't either." He stopped, turned around and looked at the hall, his hands in his pockets. For a moment, he said nothing, then nodded slowly. "It really is amazing how many good people have come to us and how hard they've worked." He looked at her. "Have you noticed how much they're all buying with the credits they're earning?"

She nodded. "Uh, huh. New clothes from our stores here, plus stuff for their homes. It's the same at School Center and Church Crossing. It's almost like before." She looked up at him. "You can feel the energy. People seem to have hope again."

"Good." He kept looking at the hall and the commons for another moment, then turned back around, putting his arm around her shoulders. "Let's go see what they want."

As they walked toward the barn, they looked at the improvements that had been made since the summer. The root cellars had been expanded to hold the unanticipated bumper crop of fruits and vegetables, an additional chicken house had been built and new corrals had been added to accommodate the growing herd of horses, a number of which were standing at feed troughs eating corn and hay, their winter coats coming in to make them look shaggier that usual.

They walked across a large open area and entered the barn through a pedestrian door to a front tack room where they were greeted by the smell of leather, hay and horses. Brushing the snow off his coat, Jim followed Kelly into the main barn and stopped short, transfixed by what he saw.

Standing in front of him were three of the prettiest fillies he had ever seen.

He stood there for a moment, in awe of the beauty of the three horses. Morgans, one black, one bay and one chestnut, each stood straight with its ears up and intelligent eyes focused directly on him. Pushing his hat back, he shook his head slowly as if in disbelief, then looked at Christian and Naomi who stood with the fillies, holding them by their lead ropes. "I've never seen anything more beautiful on four legs," he finally said, realizing his words had come out in a low whisper instead of his normal voice. "Where did you find them?"

"Naomi found them," said Christian, smiling, and nodding at her.

Naomi beamed. "There's a Morgan breeder over east of here that Carol told me about. When Christian said you wanted him to get horses for the kids I told him about it and we went over to take a look."

"The guy said he'd lost a lot of his horses to raiders," said Christian, "but his younger stock is all kept in a central corral complex so we had some to choose from." He nodded his head at the fillies. "These are two-year-olds out of three of his top mares by his top stallion. Pretty, aren't they?"

Jim stepped over to the first one, the black, and offered the back of his hand for it to sniff. "Pretty isn't the word." His words were still coming out in a whisper as the black nuzzled his hand.

Kelly stepped around him to offer her hands to the bay and the chestnut. "They're absolutely beautiful. You two couldn't have done any better. The kids will be ecstatic."

"Yes, they will," said Jim, allowing the black to now nuzzle the palm of his left hand while he smoothed its neck and shoulder with his right. "And when they get older, they'll appreciate the beauty of these girls and the strings they'll get out of them."

"There's more," said Naomi, smiling excitedly.

"More?" Jim asked.

"Yes, over here," Naomi replied, handing the lead rope she was holding to Christian and walking over to a large canvas tarp covering several saw horses. She slowly drew the tarp back, still smiling and watching Jim and Kelly closely.

As she drew back the tarp they saw three saddles, beautifully hand tooled and gleaming with the buttery glow of fine leather. Approaching the saddles, they saw a stylized SM worked into the fenders and the kids' names on the back of each cantle. Jim and Kelly stood for a moment in silence, overcome by the sight.

"Where did you get these?" Jim finally asked, not looking up but stepping forward to trace his fingers slowly over the beautifully worked leather.

Understanding the emotion of the moment, Naomi answered quietly. "There's a man who has a farm over by School Center whose daughter was one of those you rescued. He and his son were in Oklahoma when everything went down and they didn't make it back until after you hung those animals and his daughter was back home. When he heard what happened, and that you wanted horses for the kids, he told me he would take care of the saddles. His wife says he's been in his workshop for the past month doing nothing but working on them. She said sometimes he even slept out there."

Jim kept his fingers in contact with the tooled leather, lightly tracing the intricate patterns, then the names of each of his children. He thought about how the man must have felt while he was trying to make it home to his family, and when he learned what had happened to his daughter while he had not been there to protect her. He thought about how he would feel if it had happened to Morgan, or, for that matter, either of his sons, and an energy seemed to leap out of the leather etchings and jump straight to his heart. He looked up at Naomi. "What is this man's name?"

"Miller," she answered. "Mel Miller."

"Can you take me to see him?"

Naomi nodded. "Sure. When?"

Jim continued to gently stroke the tooled leather as if it was a live being. "Tomorrow."

2

Steam blew from the horses' nostrils as they rode through the woods, the temperature having dropped into the twenties overnight, and the blowing, the sounds of the horses' hooves and the creaking of saddle leather were the only noises that intruded on the silence of the early morning.

The celebration the night before had been everything they had intended it to be. More, really, resembling medieval feasts from the movies combined with the glow and quiet of a true American Thanksgiving. Eschewing the modernity of even the low voltage lighting, the hall had been lit by the two massive fireplaces and hundreds of candles mounted in wall sconces and candelabra on the long tables, filling the hall with the warm light of controlled fire. The tables had groaned under the weight of the turkeys, quail, pheasant, venison, hams and beef roasts, many of which had been cooked in the hall's fireplaces, creating an unbelievable aroma, as well as the squash, potato dishes and vegetables prepared from the yield of the Stonemont gardens and apple, cherry and peach pies from the Stonemont orchards.

The atmosphere had been a combination of joyful celebration and deep thankfulness, as no doubt the first Thanksgiving had been, and the feeling of community had evolved to a palpable level by the time Jim had risen from his chair to speak.

He had stood quietly as he waited for the room to see him and calm to near silence, then reached into his pocket and withdrew the slip of paper on which he had copied some lines from the green folder in his den. He had taken a moment to scan the hall, looking at the faces turned toward him and thinking of what each of them had gone through in the preceding months, then began.

"I was reading through some of our old family history earlier today and came across a passage describing one of our branches who came from Switzerland and settled in Virginia during the early seventeen-hundreds. It struck me that our time is in some ways similar. I think you will see the relevance."

He had put on his glasses and begun to read. "At that time, this section was a wilderness. Deer roamed through the forests and the streams abounded in fish, ducks and geese. Wild and dangerous beasts were plentiful. They were schooled in the hardships of pioneer times. They felled the giant oak and erected their log cabin in the wild woodlands. They preferred such environment in a land dedicated to religious and political freedom rather than to suffer persecution in their native land."

He had paused, taken off his glasses and surveyed the silent faces looking back at him. "We are in a new wilderness, and dangerous beasts are again plentiful, though most of them are two-legged. We are becoming schooled in a new kind of pioneer life and we felled the trees to build our cabins. But more than any of that, we can see the greatest parallel in their preference to live their lives in a land dedicated to religious and political freedom rather than to suffer under persecution in what their native countries had become."

The hall remained quiet and he continued. "Many of us have said that the country we grew up in had ceased to exist long before the collapse. The America that valued liberty, virtue, morality, hard work and self-reliance had devolved into a semi-socialist state of coddled, dependent, incompetent, politically-correct crybabies who were offended by anything with which they disagreed, and who, by their sheer numbers and political influence, were able to stifle and control the producing class which had done most of the work to support them, consequently driving our once-great country into a chaotic decline."

He had paused for a moment, noting the many who nodded in affirmation of what he had said. "The collapse returned us to a reset point, a point from which it may be possible to rebuild the America we once knew. Whether we will be able to do this will depend on a number of things, some of which will be beyond our control, but we must concentrate on and dedicate our efforts to those areas over which we do have control. We must build the future we want our children to live in."

Sounds of approval came from the crowd and he continued.

"Patrick Henry said that virtue, morality and religion are the great pillars of government, and were the armor that made our country invincible in its early days. John Adams said that the U.S. Constitution was made only for a moral and religious people and that it was wholly inadequate for the government of any other.

"There can be no argument that those pillars cracked and crumbled in later years, or that the moral and religious underpinnings of our country dissolved in a culture increasingly consumed with self and celebrity worship. As Abraham Lincoln, Douglas Macarthur and many others warned us, the nation which could not be defeated from without was eventually weakened and defeated from within."

THE REVIVAL

He had paused again, knowing that what he was about to say was perhaps the most important thing he had said at Stonemont - perhaps the most important thing he would ever say.

"With this in mind, and in the belief that the country we grew up in no longer exists, I hereby dedicate and consecrate this Thanksgiving and all subsequent Thanksgivings to God, who blessed the efforts of America's original founders, and who we now ask to bless our own. I further declare Stonemont, from this time forward, to be autonomous, independent and sovereign, apart from all others, subordinate to none, subject only to God and God's laws as we feel them written in our hearts."

He had looked out over the gathering, his gaze encompassing all those in the hall. "I do not know what path other groups or communities will decide to take. I'm sure there will be different ideas and positions. But this is the path we will take. May those who choose to reside at Stonemont, whether here or in any Stonemont community, do so in respect, cooperation and Christian charity. May those who visit Stonemont find it to be a safe harbor and welcoming friend. May those who seek deliverance from oppression find Stonemont a refuge and staunch protector. And may those who seek to victimize or oppress their fellow man find Stonemont to be an unyielding and unwavering foe."

He had taken a moment to allow his words to settle, then spoke more quietly to the silent room. "Stonemont will become a seed of a new American dream. We will leave it to God to determine where that dream leads us."

The room had remained silent for a moment, then a man in the middle of the hall had risen to his feet and stood as if at attention. After a few more seconds, another man rose, then another and another. In a silence marred only by the scuffing of chairs and the shuffling of feet, people rose throughout the hall until every person was standing. Then, a voice in the back had begun to softly sing "America", at first alone in the otherwise silent hall, then slowly joined by others until every voice in the room had become a part of the chorus that sang of a treasured past and hope for the future.

Now, his attention was on the scout on the ridge ahead.

Naomi had brought them through the woods most of the way, but they had reached the open fields that surrounded Mel Miller's property and waited behind the tree line for the scout to wave them forward. Even though this was within what they considered their safe zone they maintained proper security. The lead scout sat his horse just short of the ridgeline so that he could see over the hill without being seen, outriders were at the three and nine o'clock positions, and a fourth scout brought up the rear, remaining about a hundred yards behind them. Naomi sat on the horse next to him, also watching the scout.

After several more minutes the point and outriders gave all-clear signals and they rode out into the open, crossing the snow-covered field and joining the point scout. Their eyes just clearing the ridge, they looked down on the Miller place, a peaceful looking collection of an old farmhouse, a barn with attached corral and several smaller outbuildings. A dog trotted up the drive and a thin trail of smoke rose into the blueing sky.

"Nice looking place," said Jim, then keyed his walkie-talkie. "We'll crest ourselves until they see us. The rest of you stay where you can watch."

Double-clicks told him the scouts acknowledged.

Giving their horses a gentle heel, Jim and Naomi rode up to the crest of the hill where they could be plainly seen from the house and held their position. After several minutes, the dog noticed them and started barking, which soon brought a man to the front door.

"That's Mel," said Naomi. "I'll ride down and wave you in after I tell him who you are."

Jim nodded. "Be careful."

Naomi flashed a smile. "Always."

Jim watched as Naomi slalomed her horse down the hill to the house. The man came out and they talked for a minute, the man looking up the hill, nodding, and she motioned him down.

Jim walked the horse down the hill, following the same slalom method Naomi had used. This had become standard practice, taught in scout training, to make it harder for a concealed gunman to target them in open descents. It wouldn't throw off a skilled shooter but might give an edge against an opportunistic one, so they held to it, especially when approaching buildings or other areas of concealment.

Naomi had dismounted and stood with Miller as Jim walked the horse across the yard and stopped several feet from them.

Jim nodded at the man. "Mr. Miller, I'm Jim Wyatt. I wanted to thank you for the saddles you made for my children. I can't remember the last time I saw anything so beautiful."

Miller took a hesitant step forward, starting to shake his head slowly. "No sir, you don't thank me a bit." His eyes started to redden. "It's me who thanks you," his voice started cracking, "for saving my ba ... my baby, from that ... ," his voice broke and he began trembling, tears now appearing in his eyes.

Naomi put her arm around Miller and Jim stepped down from the saddle, moving toward the man.

Stepping in front of Miller, Jim locked eyes on him, causing the man to focus. "Then we'll just have to agree to thank each other, sir."

He stuck out his hand, which Miller took unsurely. "What's your daughter's name, Mr. Miller?"

Hearing Jim ask about his daughter seemed to further focus Miller. "Sandra."

Jim nodded, continuing to hold Miller's hand while stepping closer and placing his left hand on the man's right arm. "How is Sandra doing?"

At the sound of his daughter's name, Miller seemed to steel himself, straightening a bit, and anger started to replace the tremendous sadness in his eyes. He shook his head. "She's not good." He paused, trying to regain some control over himself. "But she's better than she'd be if you hadn't got her out of there." He shrugged sadly. "She cries ..."

"Mel," called a woman who had come to the door. "Let's have our visitors in out of the cold. Andrew!" she called toward the barn. "Come on out here and take care of these horses!"

A teenage boy emerged from the barn carrying a lever action rifle. "Yes, ma'am," he said, walking to the horses and accepting the reins from Jim and Naomi.

He nodded to Jim. "I'll brush the snow off 'em and give 'em a bit of grain. You want me to loosen the cinches?"

Jim shook his head. "No thanks, son. These days, you've got to stay ready to go."

"That's the truth," the youth nodded knowingly, turning and leading the horses toward the barn.

"Y'all come in," called the woman. "I don't see it warmin' up out there anytime soon."

The interior of the house was surprisingly warm and bright from the large 1930's windows and a fire crackling in the fireplace. The living room furniture reminded Jim of his grandparents' farm, as did the high ceilings and thick woodwork.

"C'mon back in the kitchen like friends," said the woman, turning to lead the way, then turning back to Jim. "My goodness, where are my manners? I'm Kay, the other half of him," she tilted her head toward Mel. "Now let's go sit down. I'm sorry we don't have much to offer you, but I can get you a cup of tomato soup if you'd like."

THE REVIVAL

Jim noticed that Kay had offered a cup of soup, not a bowl, and looked around the kitchen, not seeing evidence of extra food. Mel and Kay both had the gaunt look of hard work and minimal diet, as did the teenage boy who had seen to their horses. He looked at Naomi, who shook her head slowly.

Jim smiled. "Thank you, Kay, but we just ate." He nodded to Mel. "I just wanted to thank Mel for the beautiful saddles. Kelly wanted to come but couldn't get away right now."

"Well, you give her our regards. Excuse me a minute," she said, leaving the kitchen.

"She wants you to meet Sandra," said Mel, "and to have her thank you proper."

Jim lowered his head, then raised it again, looking at Mel. "There's no need for thanks, Mel. I'm sure you would have done the same if the situation was reversed."

Mel nodded. "I'd have tried. But I don't know I coulda' got it done. Anyways, it was you who did it, not me, and we owe you."

"Mr. Wyatt." Kay stood in the doorway, her hand on the back of a teenage girl. The girl was pretty, but had a sad, almost lifeless look about her. "This is our daughter, Sandra." She looked at the girl. "Sandra, this is Mr. Wyatt, and you remember Naomi."

The girl's eyes flitted across Jim and locked on Naomi. "Hi," she said, quietly.

"It's a pleasure to meet you, Sandra," said Jim.

"Thank you," Sandra replied, looking down.

Naomi rose from the table and went to Sandra, wrapping her arms around the girl and holding her tight for a moment before releasing her. "We came to thank your father for the beautiful saddles and to see how you were doing."

The girl looked up at Naomi and gave a small smile. "I'm fine."

"She's been helping me get things organized around here," said Kay, trying to add some energy to the conversation. "Haven't you, honey?"

Sandra smiled again and gave a small shrug. "I guess so."

"Sure, you have," said Kay, patting Sandra's arm. "And it's a good help you are, too. I wouldn't know what to do without you."

Naomi had been watching closely, noticing the near-desperation of the family thinly veiled by a thick layer of pride. She wasn't sure if she should speak up without first checking with Jim, but the unmistakable need of the family drove her to take the chance. "Mel, Kay," she said, "Jim and I wanted to know if you all would do us the honor of being our guests at Stonemont for a few days, maybe through Christmas. That is, if you can leave the farm for a bit." She looked quickly at Jim and saw him nod.

"We could have a couple of our people care for your animals while you're away," said Jim. "We'd like you to be there when we give the kids their horses with your saddles on them."

Mel and Kay looked at each other, seemingly asking each other silently what they should answer. After a moment, Mel started to respond, "Well, I ..."

"Vehicle coming up the road, boss," announced a voice over the walkie-talkie in Jim's pocket. "Looks like an old blue pickup with two occupants."

Jim looked at Mel. "Are there any other farms on this road?"

Mel shook his head. "If they can see them, they're not on a road, they're on our drive."

"Are you expecting anybody? Know anyone with an old blue pickup?"

Mel shook his head. "No."

Jim keyed his mic. "Keep them in your crosshairs, but don't do anything unless we start it, or I say so."

"Roger that," came the reply.

"Dad! Dad!", Andrew yelled as he ran to the house from the barn, shoving open the back door to the kitchen. "There's a truck coming up the drive!"

Mel looked at his son. "Can you tell if it's somebody we know?"

Andrew shook his head. "Can't tell yet."

Mel nodded. "Okay. You get on back up to the loft. Stay out of sight and don't come down until I say."

"But dad, I can stay here and help!" Andrew pleaded.

Mel shook his head. "Do as I say, son. You can help by doing that. If trouble starts, you'll know what to do." He nodded his head toward the door. "Now hurry up, and don't let them see you."

"Okay," a deflated Andrew answered, turning and running back to the barn.

Mel walked to the kitchen counter and opened a drawer, pulling out an old revolver and putting it in the pocket of his barn coat. "I'll go see what they want."

Jim stood up. "We can help if it's needed, Mel. I've got four scouts out there and Naomi and I will side you here."

Mel nodded. "Might need be. We'll see," he said as he walked to the front door.

Cold air blew in the door as Mel opened it, and the blue pickup pulled up in front of the house as he, Jim and Naomi stepped out onto the front porch. Jim's coat was already unbuttoned to allow him quicker access to his pistol and he noticed that Naomi's was too. Coming to the house of a friend, they had left their rifles in their saddle scabbards, a decision he now regretted and made a mental note to correct in the future if he had the chance.

They stood on the porch in silence as the pickup slowly pulled into the yard, stopping about fifty feet from the house.

The truck shut off and two men got out, the driver a large man with a bushy, unkempt beard carrying a deer rifle and the passenger a smaller man wearing a face mask with a skull design on it and carrying a shotgun with a pistol grip instead of a buttstock. Both men shut their doors and started walking slowly toward the house, their weapons laying lazily across their shoulders.

Jim sneaked his right hand inside his coat to release the snap on the cross-draw rig he had taken to wearing and ease the .45 into his hand.

"Howdy," said Mel, watching the men closely. "What can I do for you?"

The men stopped about twenty feet from the porch, the larger one smiling.

"Howdy yourself, farmer John," he said, looking around and taking a deep breath. "Nice day, huh? Makes a man thankful to be alive."

Receiving no response, the man continued. "How 'bout you? Are you thankful to be alive, farmer John?"

"Like I said," replied Mel, "what can I do for you?"

"Hooooweee!" said the large man. "Looks like we got us a hard-ass here, don't it Bones?" He took a couple of steps toward the group.

"That'll do," said Mel, pulling the revolver from his pocket.

"Oh my! Lookee here, Bones. Farmer John's got himself a gun! Oh my, oh my, oh my!" He gave a deep chuckle. "Looks like we've got farmer John, John Wayne and a pretty little thing that I ain't quite got figured out yet."

He motioned to Jim's hat. "I like your hat, John Wayne. Looks like it's just my size." Then he looked Naomi up and down. "And I like your ... well, you know what I like, honey." He looked back and forth. "Which one of these goobers do you belong to, anyway?"

Naomi gave the man a smile. "I don't belong to anyone, lard-ass. Who do you belong to, your skinny little boyfriend here with the scary mask?"

The smile vanished from the man's face as he took a step forward, the rifle coming off of his shoulder. "I'll show you, you bit... "

The bullet from Mel's revolver struck the man in the neck just above his left collarbone, making the man turn to that side slightly and bring his hand to the wound. The first bullet from Jim's .45 struck the man's right pectoral, causing him to drop the rifle, and the second hit just below it. The third, fourth and fifth all struck in the same area, spread a bit by the man's quickly changing position as he fell, and the man collapsed to the ground, twitching, a pool of redness spreading across the snow.

"Don't move!" yelled Naomi at the other man, leveling her pistol at him.

The man stood still.

"Toss your gun!"

The man threw the shotgun about a dozen feet away from him.

"Now, get down and kiss the dirt … snow … whatever. Arms and legs spread out like a snow angel. Palms up. You move after that and you're dead."

The man looked at his partner, then slowly lowered himself to the ground, following Naomi's instructions. He looked up at her as he lay in the snow. "It's cold!"

"You'll warm up in hell about a half a second after you move," she replied, keeping her gun on him. "Your choice."

Jim looked at Mel, who was still holding the gun up and starting to shake a bit. He gently pushed the gun down, keeping his eye on the man they had shot. "Go ahead and put it away, Mel. I'll check him."

Making sure that Mel's gun was down, Jim stepped off of the porch and walked to the downed man, walking around him in order to kick the rifle away and approach him from the back of his head. A sharp kick to the head brought no reaction, and he squatted down to grab a handful of hair and jerk the head back, twisting the neck harshly. The lifeless eyes and slack mouth told him the man was dead, and a large snowflake settling on an unflinching eyeball told him it was snowing again.

Rolling the body onto its back, he opened the coat, took a Taurus 9mm pistol out of the waistband and searched through the pockets. A large pocket knife went into Jim's jacket pocket and a driver's license in the man's wallet said that he had been Alvin Phelps from Rantoul, Kansas.

Standing back up, Jim walked over to the rifle and picked it up. "Mel!" he called. "Do you have a rifle?"

"Yeah," Mel answered. "Got that Marlin Andrew's carrying."

Jim looked at the rifle he had picked up. "We'll, you've got another one now. A good one. Remington 700 in .308. Fair scope on it, too."

He walked back to the porch, where he saw Mel was starting to settle down a bit and handed the rifle to him. "We've got some .308 ammo we can give you."

Mel felt the weight of the rifle, looked at the dead man and then at Jim, shaking his head and trying to hand it back. "You killed him. You should have it."

"You shot him first," said Jim, refusing the rifle. He nodded at the revolver still in Mel's hand. "What have you got there?"

Mel held the gun up for Jim to see. "Thirty-eight. It was my father's."

Jim looked at the gun, smiling. "Smith & Wesson Model 10. That was my first duty weapon. One of the real classics. Can't beat it for dependability." He reached into the pocket of his coat and took out the Taurus he had taken off Phelps. "Here's another one for you. We'll get you some ammo for that, too."

Mel took the pistol and looked at it. "I don't think I know how to work this thing."

Jim shrugged. "We'll teach you." He then stepped closer to Mel so he could speak more quietly. "I need to have a talk with our shivering friend there for a bit. Can I use your barn?"

Mel looked at the masked man still lying face down in the snow. He wondered what Jim had in mind but remembered that this was the man who had rescued his daughter. He nodded. "Whatever you need."

"Thanks," Jim nodded, keying his walkie-talkie. "Scout one, could you come down here?"

Two clicks from the radio told him the scout team leader had acknowledged, and a minute later the man rode into the yard.

"What's up, boss?"

Jim nodded toward the lifeless Phelps. "One dirt-bag we'll need to dispose of here in a bit, but I want to talk to this other one before I decide if it'll be two." He looked at the scout. "You have some zip ties?"

The scout nodded and handed two to Jim.

Jim walked over to the masked man, who now had a light layer of snow on him, and stopped with the toe of his right boot several inches from the man's head. "Hey, snowman, look to your left. That's the toe of the boot that's going to stomp your head if you move in any way I don't like. Got it?"

"I'm f-freezin'!" the man stuttered.

"Well, the lady told you how you could warm up in a hurry. Now, put your right hand in the small of your back."

The man slowly complied, and Jim dropped to a knee, his shin holding the man's neck to the ground, and secured a zip tie around the man's right wrist.

"Now, the other hand."

The man complied again, and Jim ran the second tie through the first and around the man's left wrist. He frisked the man's back, then turned him over and checked his front, finding nothing. Picking up the shotgun the man had dropped, he handed it to the scout then turned back to the man.

"Get up."

THE REVIVAL

The man struggled to get to his feet, the task made more difficult by his bound wrists, the cold and the fear that was growing in him by the minute. "What are you going to do?"

"That depends on you," Jim replied. "Walk to the barn."

The man walked slowly toward the barn, his body starting to shake violently. "It wasn't my idea. I swear. Alvin said we were supposed to come down here and collect taxes from these people. That's all."

Jim grabbed the back of the man's jacket and pushed. "Hurry up."

They reached the barn and Jim shoved the man inside. Remembering that Andrew was still in the barn, he called out, "Andrew! Go on back to the house, son. I need the barn for a while."

Some scuffling came from loft and Andrew came climbing down the ladder, the .30-.30 slung across his back.

"Do you have any duct tape in here?" Jim asked him.

"I imagine," Andrew answered, walking to a workbench in the front of the barn. "Dad has just about everything in here."

He started rummaging around. "Here you go," he said a minute later, handing a large roll of duct tape to Jim.

Jim nodded. "Thanks. You'd better get up to the house now and help your dad keep watch."

"Yes sir," Andrew answered, glancing at the bound man before disappearing out the door.

Jim turned back to the masked man and spoke quietly. "Now, it's just you and me, Mr. Scary. Let's see what you look like."

He pulled the mask off the man's head to see a face covered in tattoos, two teardrops inked under the corner of the left eye.

The man's eyes were slitted and his lips quivered as he sucked in short gulps of air.

Finding two old chairs by the workbench, Jim brought them out and set one next to the man. "Sit."

The man looked at the chair. "Wha ... what are you gonna do?"

Jim looked at him. "I'm not going to tell you again."

The man looked at the chair again, then slowly sat on it.

Jim walked behind the man. "You move and you're dead."

Jim quickly drew out a length of duct tape and threw it around the man's chest, joining it in the back, then wrapped it around the man and the chair two more times. He tore off a shorter length and knelt next to the chair. "Remember what I said."

THE REVIVAL

Grabbing the man's right ankle, he quickly taped it to one of the chair legs, then repeated it with the left.

Returning to the workbench, Jim looked through the tools laying on it and hung in the racks above. Selecting a hammer, some blacksmith tongs and a pair of lineman's pliers, he returned to the man, pulled the other chair over and sat on it facing him, then tossed the tools on the ground between them.

The clang of the tools made the man flinch.

Jim looked at the man, whose eyes were fixed on his own.

"Where did you do time?" Jim asked softly.

The man glared back.

Jim nodded slowly. Picking up the tongs, he swung them backhanded, striking the man in the jaw.

The man gave a grunt as a cut opened on his jaw and blood leaked from his mouth.

"Where did you do time?" Jim asked again.

"Lansing," the man responded with some difficulty, referring to the ancient Kansas State Penitentiary.

"Where else?"

The man looked at the tongs in Jim's hand. "Jeff."

"Jeff City, huh?" said Jim, referring to the notorious Missouri State Penitentiary in Jefferson City. "That's one scary place. How long a stretch?"

The man kept his eyes on the tongs. "Three of five in Lansing. A deuce in Jeff."

Jim nodded. "Good." He tossed the tongs back on the ground with the other tools. He looked the man in the eye. "Before we get started, I need to tell you a few things."

The man looked at Jim, his demeanor now more wary than defiant.

Jim leaned slightly forward, resting his forearms on his knees. "I'm going to tell you something about myself that nobody who knows me now knows anything about."

The man stayed silent.

Jim looked down for a moment, then back at the man. "A long time ago, Uncle Sam spent a lot of money teaching me how to do a lot of things. Some of those things were pretty cool. Others were not so cool. One of the not-so-cool things was how to get people to tell me things they really didn't want to tell me. Do you understand what I'm saying?"

The man nodded slowly, keeping his eyes on Jim's.

"In a minute, I'm going to start asking you some questions. I will know if you lie. Do you understand?"

The man stared at Jim.

Jim leaned over to pick up the tongs again, but the man answered. "Yeah."

"Yeah, what?"

"I understand."

"Good." He tossed the tongs back down on the ground. "Now, this is important. You must tell me the truth. If you lie, I will tape your mouth so that those people out there won't hear the noises you'll make, and I will use these on you for one hour." He nodded at the tools in the floor. "I will remove the tape when you start to puke, so that you don't drown yourself before I'm done, and I will then re-tape your mouth so I can continue. This will probably happen several times. At the end of one hour, I will then un-tape your mouth and ask you again. I can promise you that, when you are able to talk, you will then be truthful about everything I ask you." He looked closely at the man. "But it will be too late for you. If you survive, you will never again be the person you are now. Do you understand?"

The man's eyes had widened as Jim talked, the defiance being replaced with a mixture of fear, resignation and hope.

Jim looked closely at the man. "You have one chance. Do you understand?"

The man gave a jerking nod. "Yes.".

"What's your name?"

"Bart."

"Bart what?"

"Phelps."

Jim cocked his head toward the house. "You related?"

"Yeah. He's my brother."

"Why did you come here?"

"Alvin said we were going to start making collections from anybody we found in the area. He said they were like taxes for living in our area."

"Had you been here before?"

"No."

"How did you find this place?"

"We just drive around looking for places. We thought we were on a road, then saw the house."

"Who came up with this tax idea?"

"Alvin and a couple of the other guys."

"Who are the other guys?"

Bart hesitated, and Jim reached for the duct tape.

"Some friends of ours," the man said hurriedly. He paused for a moment, as if thinking whether to continue. "They had an idea of making this area their own. Like charging people a kind of tax to live here, and they'd be the bosses."

"Who was the leader?"

"Alvin and a guy he did time with."

"What's his name."

Bart shrugged. "Don't know. Just called him Chico."

"How many people have you all "taxed" so far?"

Bart thought for a moment. "About a dozen, I think."

"Do you know where they all are? Can you find them again?"

Bart thought for a second. "I ... I'm not sure. Most of them, probably. Why?"

Jim ignored the question.

"How many guys in your group?"

Bart thought for a moment. "About thirty. It changes some as people come and go."

"Where are these other guys?"

Bart hung his head a bit. "On a farm outside of Lacygne."

"Who's farm?"

Bart hung his head lower. "I don't know. They killed the family and took it."

Jim rose from his chair and looked down at Bart. "It's against my better judgement to let you live, but you're going to take a message back to your friends for us. This area belongs to Grim. He doesn't like it when piss-ants like you two come around acting tough. It irritates him. Then, he sends people like me to come straighten things out, and that usually means that people like you end up in a hole or a cage." He leaned down and looked Bart in the eye. "If I have to come back here, Bart, would you prefer a hole or a cage?"

Bart just stared back, hope growing that he might actually get out of this situation alive.

"That's okay." Jim patted the man on the shoulder. "I'll decide."

Jim carried the tools back to the tool bench and set them down. "Here's the message, Bart," he said, turning back to the man. "You ready?"

Bart nodded.

"Good. You and your group will take no more collections from anyone. Ever. You will find those you have already robbed and return everything you took. Everything. You will cause no more trouble for anyone. Ever. And you will not come north of Lacygne. Ever. If you do any of these, ever, I will be back, and you will be done. Do you have any questions?"

Bart shook his head. "No."

"Good."

3

"The enemy of my enemy is my friend, right?" said Tom Murphy, as they walked across the commons.

Jim shrugged. "I always thought of it more as 'the enemy of my enemy is my tool'."

Tom chuckled. "Yeah, that's more like it."

Yesterday, they had thrown Alvin's body in the back of the pickup and sent Bart to deliver it and Jim's message to the brothers' group. The Millers had agreed to come to visit Stonemont in a few days for the presentation of the horses and saddles to the kids, and two scouts had stayed at their farm to provide security until they did.

Now, Jim was talking to his new intelligence chief about longer term goals.

"We don't know how strong Grim is, but we know he's in Overland Park. We don't know exactly how strong this other group is, but we know they're around Lacygne, which is about fifty miles directly south of Overland Park on 69 Highway. We're a ways west of that line and out of the way, so I figure if we can interest each of them in the other it will be good for us. Let them whittle each other down a bit."

Tom nodded. "It's a classical strategy. We used it with great success until we started arming or training one side or the other. Or both."

"Yeah, I ..." Jim stopped short as a snowball hit him in the back of the neck, some going down inside his coat. "Dam ... ur ... whoa!" He turned around to see a group of kids running back to an elaborate snow fort, giggling and screaming.

Laughing, he opened his coat and shook out as much snow as he could. Then, stooping down, he gathered up a double handful of snow, packed it as hard as he could, and threw it toward the fort. It flew over the fort, missing the kids but drawing another round of screams and giggles from them.

"It's nice to see that again," he said, watching the kids play. "When was the last time you threw something for fun?"

THE REVIVAL

"It's been a while," answered Tom, also watching the kids. "Looks like Aedan is organizing the building of an addition to the fort," he chuckled. "Does he ever slow down?"

Jim shook his head. "Not that I can tell." He looked at Tom. "We need spies. That's what I wanted to talk to you about."

"Spies?"

"Yep." He turned, and they started walking again. "Right now, we're just reacting to things and getting a little information here and there from people who come here or who we run into out in the world. We're doing pretty well, but we don't know the quality of the information we're getting and it's sporadic at best." He looked at Tom. "We now have two organized groups of bad actors that we know of within striking distance, and we know next to nothing about them."

Tom nodded. "What are you thinking?"

"We need to develop the ability to gather our own original information and be able to not only maintain the information flow, but independently corroborate it, regardless of changing situations."

Tom looked at him. "Haven't been thinking about this long, have you?"

Jim shrugged. "We also need disinformation and counterintelligence capabilities."

Tom stopped in his tracks, causing Jim to stop and turn around.

"You were a spook," Tom said with a smile.

Jim looked back at Tom, nothing showing in his eyes. "If I was, I wouldn't tell you, and if I wasn't I might tell you I was just to try to sound cool."

Tom gave Jim a thoughtful look and shook his head. "No, you wouldn't. Who were you with?"

Jim studied Tom for a moment. The man was smart, had done his own time and had become an important part of Stonemont. He deserved some kind of answer. Still, he had never talked about it before and he didn't intend to start now.

"Tom, I started out doing something I believed in. The deeper I got into it, and the more I learned about things, the less I believed in what I was supposed to be doing. I came to despise the things I was doing and the people I was doing it for. So, I stopped."

He took a breath and looked around. "Whoever I was and whatever I did, those days are gone. I don't think about them and don't want to think about them. Today, I'm just Jim Wyatt, husband to Kelly and father to Aedan, Brody and Morgan, and that's all I want to be."

He looked back at Tom, who was watching him closely. "Sometimes, things come back, like they did yesterday, but I don't want them to." His eyes locked on Tom's. "The good Lord saved me from what I had become and put me on a new path. I want to stay on that path, Tom. I imagine you can understand that."

Tom nodded slowly, watching Jim's eyes. "Yeah. There are some dark places, aren't there?"

Jim nodded. "Darker than most people can imagine."

"So, what do you want me to do?"

Jim looked around the compound at the children playing and adults going about their daily lives. "We need to protect this. We need to be able to live our lives with hope, applying ourselves to making life even better, not in fear, and not just trying to survive." He looked back at Tom. "Protecting this means not only being able to defend ourselves but knowing what's going on out in the world before it affects us so that we can be ready."

Tom nodded. "So, what do you want me to do?" he repeated.

"I want you to run our spies and coordinate all intelligence."

Tom nodded again. "Have you given any thought to selection and training?"

"Yep," Jim smiled, "but first we have to build the town."

"Town?" Tom asked.

"We're heading out!" called Christian, as he, Naomi and four scouts approached on horseback.

Jim turned to the group. "Well, I see that you're ready to go at the crack of noon. Hope you got enough sleep."

"Yep," smiled Christian, affecting a stretch. "Kelly told me if I got up too early, I'd end up cranky like you."

"I'm not cranky, youngster, I'm serious."

"Seriously cranky, I'd say. What are you two talking about?"

"Can't tell you."

"Why not?"

"It's a secret."

"I can keep a secret."

"So can I."

Tom and Naomi smiled at the banter between uncle and nephew while the scouts tried to concentrate on anything else, not wanting to seem like they were enjoying the back-and-forth between their leader and their boss.

"So, when do you figure you'll be back?" Jim asked.

THE REVIVAL

Christian looked out over the fields covered with snow, squinting against the glare. "We're going to shoot for tomorrow night. If not then, the next day."

Jim nodded. "Okay, get us a good deal and don't get shot."

Christian chuckled as he clucked and heeled his horse. "I'll try," he said over his shoulder.

"Don't let him get shot," Jim told Naomi as she rode by.

"I'll try," she laughed.

Jim shook his head and gave a half salute to the scouts following them. "Be careful, guys."

"Yes, sir," they said, almost in unison.

Jim watched them for a moment, then turned back to see Tom looking at him.

"Town?" Tom asked again.

4

They rode several miles through unbroken snow before they came to fences that diverted them onto a gravel road that they would follow south and then east. In Kansas, you didn't cut fences unless you wanted to get shot, even if you intended to fix them behind you.

Like the Eddington place to the east of Stonemont, several of the landholdings around them had been abandoned. Whether this was because the residents had left, hadn't been able to make it home after the event or had succumbed to sickness, injury, starvation or violence, they didn't know, but Stonemont had established the area as a protective zone around them, securing the homes and livestock in case the owners returned. In order to make patrolling easier, as well as to have better access to the livestock, they had put gates in at strategic points between the properties, which allowed them to stay off the roads in their immediate area when on horseback. Now, they were more restricted to roadways, except where they could find unfenced areas that they were sure remained unfenced for as far as they needed them to be.

Reaching the gravel road, they broke from their diamond pattern and proceeded single file with about fifty yards between them. As they had been trained, the lead scout watched forward, second and fourth scouts watched the left, third and fifth scouts watched the right, and the sixth, or drag, scout watched the rear. This ensured that every sector had eyes on it at all times. Though all of the scouts had radios with headsets, they practiced hand and verbal communication against the day when either the batteries would be gone or the radios became otherwise inoperable. The lead scout communicated with hand signals, the drag scout verbally, and those between them used both so that information would be passed to those both in front of and behind them.

They made good time on the road, seeing no tracks except for deer and smaller animals in the otherwise unbroken snow, and settled into a comfortable, though watchful pace. The horses blew and whinnied, which were the only sounds except for the occasional scout communications, and by mid-afternoon they were approaching 69 Highway.

THE REVIVAL

The lead scout stopped and raised his hand, bringing the scouts to a halt as it was relayed back through the column.

Christian rode forward from second position to see what the scout had stopped for and saw the white of a concrete bridge about a mile ahead at the top of a hill.

"Looks like a major highway," said the scout. "Is this sixty-nine?"

Christian nodded. He looked at the scout. The kid was good. Serious, smart, hard-working and eager to learn, Alex Cooldale didn't waste time or words. He spoke when he had something to say and listened the rest of the time. At twenty-one, he was the older of two brothers, the nineteen-year-old Aaron now riding drag. Together, they had impressed Mike Carpenter, chief of scouts, and had come to collectively be known as "the Cools".

Christian looked at the position of the sun, judging how much daylight remained. "Looks like we have about an hour and a half before dark. We'll make camp on this side of the highway." He looked at Alex. "I'll take the squad. You go find us a place to set up."

Alex nodded and took off at a trot.

It took the squad about fifteen minutes to reach the bottom of the hill and begin ascending the next when Christian saw Alex sitting his horse just inside the tree line at a natural break. Turning in, the squad followed Alex for a minute as they weaved their way through the trees, finally reaching a small rock outcropping about halfway up the hill.

They stopped, and Christian nodded, though didn't dismount. "Explain your choice."

Alex wheeled his horse to face the rest of the squad, minus Aaron, who had stayed at the trail's entrance from the roadway as a rear guard. Having graduated tied with his brother at the top of the last scout class, he knew this was a test for him, as well as a lesson for the others.

"The wind is coming from the northeast," he began. "These outcroppings allow us to set up on the leeward side and down from the crest of the hill. There are plenty of trees to diffuse the smoke that might emit from the Dakotas, and higher terrain on three sides to keep line-of-sight short for any glow."

He nodded up the hill. "One sentry should post on the crest and the other slightly below camp. Horses picketed below the camp to cover our entry trail. We'll be upwind from a game trail, so anything traveling on it will pick up our scent, but we're not going to be hunting anyway."

Christian nodded. "Good. Send someone to bring Aaron in, then everyone can get started on their preparations for the night."

THE REVIVAL

In addition to the trip having a real-world purpose, Mike had asked Christian to include some training and testing for the newly graduated scouts. Each carried standardized equipment in their field packs that would allow them to survive for an extended amount of time, and when Cody got back with Aaron they all set about their tasks while Christian walked to the crest of the hill to stand guard.

First, was the digging of Dakota fire holes.

After selecting the spot where they would bed down that night, each scout dug a circular hole about twelve inches across and eighteen inches deep, then "belled" the bottom, making it a few inches wider than the top. Then, starting about a foot away from the main hole, they dug a second hole, smaller in diameter, angling it to meet the bottom of the first hole. The design allowed air to be drawn in through the smaller hole by a vacuum caused by the rising heat in the fire hole, thereby providing for a hotter fire using less fuel than a conventional surface-built fire while keeping the flames themselves below ground level.

The second part of the test was to start a fire using flint and steel on the petroleum jelly-coated cotton balls they all carried in their fire kits. As usual, "the Cools" approached the exercise as a contest, getting their holes dug and fires started within seconds of each other and several minutes before the others.

As the fires caught and started to consume the first layer of kindling and small sticks, the scouts added larger sticks and set about constructing their sleeping positions. Each cleared an area of rocks and sticks, then gathered leaves to create a bed about twelve inches thick. Placing a ground sheet over the leaf beds, they secured it to the ground with landscape pegs they carried in their packs. As they worked, they kept feeding larger and larger pieces of wood into the fire holes, the updraft of the growing fires drawing more air into the intake holes, thereby making the fire hotter and more efficient.

Next, each scout tied three sticks together near their ends, two of which were about three feet long and the third about eight feet long. Setting the two shorter sticks up as a bipod close to their fire hole and angling the longer stick away from it, they constructed a frame against which they leaned branches to form a framework for their shelter. Cutting branches from the numerous pine trees around them, they placed the boughs across the framework to make an effective windbreak, then covered the entire structure with ground debris. Once completed, the structures blended in to the surrounding woods.

THE REVIVAL

Continuing to feed larger pieces into their fires to establish a coal bed, each scout began to collect wood to lay up by their shelters for the night, then searched for a flat rock larger than the main hole of their fire pit. Laying the rocks next to the hole, they positioned them with an edge over the edge of the hole, allowing the rocks to begin warming. The rocks would be pulled over the holes when the scouts turned in, subduing the fires and radiating a bit of warmth through the first part of the night. This done, they dug out their mess kits and started preparing their evening meal.

Each scout cut several live branches from a nearby tree and laid them over their pit. The branches would eventually burn through and fall into the hole, but the fact that they were from live trees would allow them to hold up a pot for as long as was necessary. Putting a small pot of water over their fire, they brought it to a boil and added Knorr Pasta Sides packets, the preferred hot field rations of the scouts. While the pots boiled, they collected more wood from deadfalls of a size that could be broken by hand, then larger branches that could be sawn to six-inch lengths to maintain a longer burning fire. By the time this was done, the pots were ready to be removed from the fire and set aside to cool for a few minutes.

Christian spent the time watching the length of 69 Highway, which he could see from his post on the crest of the hill. The divided roadway was smooth with new snow, the only noticeable marks being where a herd of deer had recently crossed. The highway would be a dangerous crossing for them tomorrow, an open gap between the treed hills on each side where they would be plainly visible to anyone else on the long stretch of highway during the time it took them to cross.

He thought for perhaps the thousandth time how beautiful the world was without the intrusion of electricity-based technology. Trying to recall the noise and widespread artificial light of life before the event, he found it difficult to do so, and was awed by the splendor of the world in its natural state.

The sun having set, the near-full moon shined bright on the snow cover, making it almost as easy to see as in the daytime, though the colors of daytime were replaced by the nighttime's shades of gray. He could see clouds coming in from the northeast, bringing snow he could already taste on the wind.

More snow would be both good and bad. Good, that it would help hide their tracks, and bad if they were able to make a deal for some horses and it got deep enough to slow them down on the way back.

THE REVIVAL

It was the highway crossing the next day that concerned him the most. The exposure making the first crossing would be hazardous enough, but fencing and terrain dictated that they cross at the same location on their way back, especially if they were bringing a number of riderless horses with them. This increased the chances of an ambush on their return, but there was little they could do about it.

Mentally sketching their morning route, he saw a figure approaching from the camp.

"We got you set up," Alex said quietly. "What watch rotation do you want?"

Christian nodded his appreciation and approval. "Thanks. I'll go down and eat, then Naomi and I will take first watch. Cody and Blake can take the saddle, and you and Aaron take third."

Alex nodded. "Okay."

Christian woke to the sound of a whisper and the tapping of a stick on his arm. A scout had made the mistake of shaking him awake on a previous exercise and the result had been painful for the scout. Since then, they used a long stick if a whisper alone didn't work.

"Hey, boss," whispered Alex again.

Christian opened his eyes and raised to an elbow. He could tell that it wasn't time to get up yet. "What's up?"

"Sorry to wake you early, but it started snowing a couple of hours ago and it seems to be picking up. I thought you might want to get across the highway before dawn. The snow might cover our tracks before anyone comes along."

Christian sat up and nodded. Alex was smart. He knew what to do but had made it sound like it was Christian's idea. "You're right," he said, giving the credit back to Alex. "Roust the rest of them. Put out the fires but leave the shelters. We might need them on the way back."

Alex nodded and went to wake up the rest of the squad.

The bright moon of earlier was now obscured by heavy clouds and the grey tones of the woods were darker than earlier. Christian could barely make out the individual shelters, now covered in snow, though the dark spots of the warming stones on each fire hole stood out. The snow was now falling heavily in large flakes, an absence of wind making in come straight down, and it was piling up fast.

The scouts now hurried to roll their sleeping bags, put out the remains of their fires, saddle their horses and mount up. Quick starts weren't something anyone enjoyed, but they had had their share during training, so the mechanics were pretty much automatic as their brains shook off the waking-shock.

Christian judged it to be about five o'clock, give or take some. Sunrise this time of year was a little after seven, so they had a couple of hours for the snow to fill in their tracks across the highway if it held up.

Giving the 'go' sign to Aaron, who would be taking the lead on this stretch, he watched as the scouts filed past him, then fell in to take the drag himself.

The darkness and the falling snow made the scouts look like shadows against an only slightly lighter background, and they let the horses have their heads as they weaved along the game trail to return to the road.

At the road, they turned east toward the highway, Aaron moving quickly ahead of the rest to take point while the others adjusted to maintain the normal fifty yards between them.

Reaching the highway several minutes later, Aaron stopped to survey its length in both directions. Falling snow faded into blackness in both directions without interruption and he continued across the highway followed by the others.

Four miles of backroads brought them to a hill overlooking the house, central barn and corral complex of Callahan Morgans. A thin trail of smoke rose from the house chimney, light against the darker sky, and lamplight showed through a window toward the back of the house.

They moved back to just behind the crest of the hill, spreading out to their standard separation, and watched the house and surrounding area. Arriving earlier than they had expected, it was too early to approach the house, and the extra time gave them a chance to watch for a while. Like Jim said, "Watch for a while, and there's no telling what you might see. Don't watch, and there's no telling what you might not."

More lights came on in the house as they watched, a dog barked, and a figure moved between the house and the barn. Soon, another light came on, then another.

A door slammed, and another figure walked from the house to the barn.

A few minutes later, a side door of the barn opened and horses started emerging into a corral, some heading to a covered hay bin and others to the fence rails to look out at the world beyond.

A couple of minutes later, another door opened and more horses spilled into an adjacent corral. This was repeated several more times until the corrals surrounding the barn were filled with horses.

The sound of a hammer breaking ice in the water troughs echoed up the hill, and the barking of dogs being released to take up their daily patrols confirmed that the ranch was awake.

"Let's go," said Christian, heeling his horse to crest, then slaloming down the hill.

They angled toward the road leading to the entry gate, a large structure of stone pillars supporting an iron arch bearing the name 'Callahan Farms' and an iron gate with large 'C's fashioned into the bars. Several large dogs of indeterminate breed met them at the gate, announcing their arrival and daring them to try coming in without an escort.

They waited for several minutes until two men emerged from the barn on horseback and rode slowly toward the gate with rifles in their hands.

"John!" yelled Christian to the approaching men. "It's Christian Bell and Naomi!"

The two men continued to approach until they could see the visitors.

"Howdy Christian, Naomi," nodded John Callahan. "What are you doin' out in this, and who've you got with you?"

"These are some of our scouts and I'd like to see about buying some horses," Christian answered.

Callahan nodded as he moved to open the gate. "Well, you picked a heck of a day for it, but horses I've got." He unlatched the gate from the saddle and swung half of it open. "Come on in. We'll get the horses in the barn and anything that's human under those snowmen into the house."

"I've lost some, but I won't lie to you, without deliveries this year I've got more than I'm going to be able to feed through the winter with the hay I've got."

John Callahan returned to the table with a large coffee pot he had taken off the wood stove. Starting with Naomi, he topped off the cups of those sitting around the large round table. The scouts' hats and coats hung on pegs in the mudroom drying out, and their boots were lined up in front of the fire giving off steam from the snow melting off them. The scouts themselves were warming their hands around the steaming cups of coffee that was warming them from the inside.

"We started off with over a hundred head, including this year's foals," Callahan continued, setting the coffee pot back on the stove. "We're down to sixty-four, but that's still too many, so you've come at the right time."

"How many are you wanting to get rid of?" asked Christian.

Callahan sat back down. "If you could take about half, I could get the others through the winter in good shape and start building up again."

Christian thought for a moment. This was more than he had hoped for, but he was sorry that it was at the expense of someone else's hardship. He looked at Callahan. "What do you want for them?"

Callahan leaned back in his chair and shrugged. "Christian, I know the deal. I'm going to lose most of them anyway. I don't have the hands to protect them beyond the corrals. I don't have the food to feed them all, and, if I cut rations for all of them, they'll all suffer, and I'll probably lose the weaker half anyway." He paused for a minute, shaking his head slowly. "If I pasture them, they'll be stolen or killed for food. If I keep them all barned, half will die. That's just the way it is." He looked back at Christian. "It's best I just give half to you. Best for me, best for you and best for the horses."

Christian watched him closely. The man had spent a lifetime building a dream and was seeing that dream collapse around him, yet there wasn't a hint of self-pity in him and he had welcomed people he thought were going to benefit from his misfortune into his home with the courtesy and grace of years long past.

Christian nodded. "We'll take half, John, if that's what you need to get rid of, but we want to make you a fair trade. You tell us what you need for them and, if we've got it, we'll have a deal."

Callahan looked back at Christian. "You know you could have me over a barrel, don't you? You could have these horses for nothing."

"Is that what you would do?" asked Christian.

Callahan thought for a moment and shook his head. "No."

Christian leaned back in his chair. "You haven't met my uncle, but if you look in the mirror, you'll see him. You pick the half we get, make a list of what you want for them, and, if we can do it and I think it's fair, we'll have a deal."

Callahan nodded slowly. "Okay."

The rest of the day was spent selecting the horses Callahan thought would be best for Stonemont, then making a list of what Callahan Farms would ask in exchange for them. The former consisted of two stallions, two yearling colts, six geldings, twelve mares and eight fillies. The latter contained a wish list of foods, medicines, clothing, fuel and household supplies that John and his wife, Marsha, had worked on together.

Now, Christian sat looking at the list, slowly shaking his head. "It's not enough."

Callahan shrugged. "It's what we need."

Christian looked at him. "John, I don't know what kind of stores you already have, but this list may let you survive through spring. It won't sustain you or give you a strong enough platform to build on." He looked back down at the list. "I don't see any seeds or gardening tools on here. Do you already have a large garden?"

Callahan shrugged again. "Marsha keeps a kitchen garden out back where she grows some things. You know, tomatoes, peppers, lettuce and such."

"Does she grow enough to can and keep you eating through winter and spring?"

Callahan shook his head. "No. Just some odds and ends."

Christian nodded, writing something at the bottom of the list. "You're going to have to become self-sufficient for the long term." He looked back up at Callahan. "How about guns? I don't see guns or ammo on this list."

"We have guns," answered Callahan, then added, "I guess we could use a little more ammo."

Christian made another notation on the sheet of paper. "How about chickens, rabbits, goats or cattle?"

John shook his head. ""We're a horse farm. Never had use or need for the others."

Christian leaned back in his chair. "John, you can still be a horse farm, but now you're going to have to be an everything farm if you're going to make it." He paused, not wanting to offend the other man. "Do you mind if we re-work this list a little bit together? I have some suggestions."

Callahan looked at his wife, then back at Christian and nodded. "Guess it couldn't hurt."

5

"They're back! They're back!"

Aedan, Brody and Morgan came charging across the commons, up the steps, across the veranda and into the kitchen.

"They're back!" Aedan yelled again, his volume assuring that everyone in the house would know.

"And they brought horses!" yelled Brody.

"And ponies!" added Morgan.

"My gracious!" exclaimed Kelly, turning from the oven to set a baking sheet on the island. "Mrs. Hernandez, I think these kids are too excited to care about these cookies we're baking."

She looked at the kids with a smile. "Who's back?"

"Cookies?" asked Brody.

"What kind?" asked Morgan.

"Chocolate chip," said Kelly. "Now, who's back?"

"Christian and the others!" answered Aedan, excitedly. "Can I have one?"

Kelly patted the hand reaching for a cookie. "Let them cool for a few minutes and go tell daddy that Christian's back."

"Yes, ma'am," said Aedan, running off, his minor disappointment giving way to his excitement about the horses.

"Mommy, can I have a pony?" asked Morgan.

Kelly laughed. "Do you think you're big enough, sweetie?"

"Yes," Morgan nodded seriously. "But I want a pink one."

"A pink what, honey?" Jim asked as he followed Aedan into the kitchen.

"Pony," said Morgan seriously.

"Ponies don't come in pink, Morgan," said Brody.

"Yes, they do."

"No, they don't. Only brown."

"I've seen pictures of pink ones."

"Those aren't real, Morgan. They're just pictures."

Morgan turned to Jim. "Daddy, are pink ponies real?"

Jim looked at Kelly, who was looking back at him with a cocked eyebrow and a "What-are-you-going-to-say-to-that?" look on her face.

THE REVIVAL

Jim smiled. "Well, honey, I've never seen a pink pony, but I'll keep an eye out. Would a brown one be okay while we look for a pink one?"

Morgan thought for a moment, then shrugged. "Okay, but I really want a pink one when you find one."

Jim chuckled, leaning over to kiss her on the top of her head. "You bet, sweetie. I'll keep my eyes open."

"Daddy, can we go see the horses?" asked Brody.

Jim nodded, grabbing a cookie off the cooling rack. "Everybody get a cookie and we'll go see what Christian has brought us."

The kids grabbed their cookies and ran out the door.

Jim took another cookie and looked at Kelly. "You want to come see?"

Kelly grabbed a towel to wipe off her hands. "Sure. Guadalupe, can you finish up the cookies?"

"Oh, yes," Guadalupe replied. "You go ahead and see the horses. I'll take care of this."

"Thank you, Guadalupe."

"De´ nada," Guadalupe beamed.

They grabbed their coats in the mud room and stepped out into the bright sunshine, Jim putting on his Stetson.

"Two cookies, huh?" teased Kelly.

Jim held one out to her. "This one's for you," he smiled.

She smiled back at him. "Well, thank you."

He nodded. "No problem. I sleep with the baker."

The scouting party had entered the commons and was making its way toward the main hall, each scout leading a string of several horses. The kids had met the group in the lower field and now accompanied them back, Brody riding behind Christian, Morgan in Naomi's lap, and Aedan walking between the Cools asking about the trip.

"You're late!" yelled Jim as the group approached.

"Yeah?" asked Christian, pulling his horse to a stop. "Late for what?"

"Cookies," replied Jim. "They're all gone. I ate 'em."

Christian laughed as he dismounted. "I don't doubt it. I've been thinking you're about due for a bigger belt."

"I'm the same weight I was in the police academy, smart guy."

Christian winked at Kelly. "That must have been before they had the weight requirements."

Jim chuckled and nodded at the horses. "Looks like you got a good bunch."

Christian nodded. "Yeah, I think so. Callahan is hurting and was glad to get them off his hands. I've got the list of things I agreed we'd trade him in return."

"Good." Jim looked at Naomi. "Did you keep him from gettin' shot?"

Naomi laughed. "So far."

Jim turned to the scouts. "You guys good?"

"Yes, sir," they said, almost in unison.

Jim nodded. "Good."

He looked back at Christian. "Go ahead and get these horses taken care of, then clean up. We're going to meet in the den in a couple of hours to go over some things." He looked at Naomi. "You come too if you like."

6

Jim set his cup of coffee on the table and himself on the couch. "Kelly, why don't you start since you're operations?"

They had rounded up the core while Christian and Naomi took care of the horses and, now, Jim, Kelly, Bill and Ann Garner, Tom and Patty Murphy, Christian, Mike and Naomi sat on the couches and a couple of pulled-up chairs surrounding the large square coffee table in the middle of the den.

Kelly nodded and opened a folder on the table in front of her. "Okay. As always, we have two main categories, people and things. I would say that things are extraordinary in both areas, but I'll start with people."

She took a sheet of paper out of the folder and looked at it. "In the main complex here, we have a total of one hundred and fifty-four people, comprised of twenty-two families with children, fourteen women with children but without men, two men with children but without women, eight single women, three single men, the Hispanic squad, two of the Kansas guys from the national guard and us, including our families. We were able to complete thirty-one small cabins around the compound, in which we have been able to place everyone except the Hispanic squad and the guard guys, who are currently using a section of the main hall as a kind of barracks. It's tight for everyone, but we assigned each family a cabin and folded the others into them where possible and appropriate. It probably can't last for long like this, but it's working out so far."

She put the paper back in the folder. "We have an additional fourteen families and a number of single people at Hillmont. Again, the situation isn't ideal, but it's working for now." She looked up. "I don't know how we can take anyone else in, but I know that we will if they show up, so that's something we need to think about."

She picked up another piece of paper. "The vocational and skills mix has been interesting, with some that can really be helpful." She looked at the sheet of paper. "We have a civil engineer, an electrical engineer, a D.O., a chiropractor, a nurse practitioner, two nurses, two teachers, a veterinarian, an electrician, a retired pastor, and an assortment of other vocations."

She put the paper back in the folder. "As you know, the medical people have set up a kind of clinic in the main hall. It's certainly not like a real emergency room or hospital, but they're helping a lot of people and they say that most maladies don't demand the high-tech stuff that defensive medicine had made necessary before, anyway."

"That's the truth," said Mike.

"And this relieves Mike of having to do double-duty as a medic while also running the scouts."

"That's good," nodded Jim.

"The engineers are working with Ann," Kelly continued, "the teachers are preparing to start a school in the main hall after the first of the year with all of the books the scout teams have brought in, and, of course, the veterinarian has been invaluable. With the new horses, he's going to be even more so."

She closed the folder. "As to the 'things', there's just too much to list. The salvage operations have been unbelievable. We still have the barn full, even though we're also using it as the store. We have eight full trailers parked alongside it, and fourteen more that were taken directly to Hillmont, some of which we haven't been able to inventory yet. I almost feel like saying we shouldn't bring in any more, but I know that's not right.

"As to food production, our yield at harvest was very good. We were able to get four root cellars constructed in time to get most of the produce in them, but we ran out of canning jars so we experimented with some solar drying and dehydrating methods Ann designed and they did very well. We'll build more dehydrators over the summer to be ready for next year.

"The chickens are doing well but egg production went way down for a while, as you egg-lovers know. I thought it was because of colder weather, but the vet says it was because of fewer hours of sunlight so we put some artificial lights in the chicken house and production is coming back.

"We have fifty-seven head of cattle, most of them beef but a few Holstein and Jersey dairy cows including one Jersey bull. Milk production is good, and, with hunting, we've been able to avoid slaughtering any cattle, thereby retaining the breeding herd and letting the younger steers continue to get bigger."

She closed the folder. "That's about it. All-in-all, things are going well."

"How is the general attitude of folks?" asked Jim.

Kelly thought for a moment. "I'd say very good. Everyone has been busy, which is positive for people, and they've transitioned from being refugees to being members of a community. Thanksgiving really brought them together, and, of course, everyone is looking forward to Christmas. I'd say the main concern will be after Christmas when winter really sets in. There will be less to do and, being in such close quarters as most of them are, I can see attitudes changing."

"I agree," said Bill. "Crowded people cooped up with not enough to do is a recipe for problems."

Jim nodded. "I've been thinking about that, too. I think I have a solution, which I'll share with you after the other reports." He looked at Kelly. "Is that all, babe?"

Kelly nodded. "Yep,"

"I object," said Christian, feigning insult. "By calling Kelly 'babe', Jim is obviously showing favoritism to his wife." He looked around at the group. "I demand that he either stop that or address the rest of us with similar terms of endearment."

Jim looked at Christian while the rest of the group laughed. "Okay, sweetie, let's have you give the next report."

Christian nodded. "My pleasure," he said with a self-satisfied smile that brought another round of laughter and some rolled eyes.

"I think our security situation is good. I say 'think', because we haven't been attacked, so our security hasn't been tested."

Mike nodded. "No plan survives contact with the enemy."

"Eisenhower said that plans are useless, but planning is indispensable," added Bill.

"Right," nodded Christian. "That's why we follow the PACE criteria."

"What's pace?" asked Bill.

"It's a multi-tiered planning construct providing for when initial and subsequent plans go south," answered Christian. "It's an acronym for primary, alternate, contingency and emergency. Right now, I'd say we're good through alternative, and are working on the contingency and emergency aspects."

"Is everyone going to drill on these?" asked Bill.

Christian hesitated, looking at both Mike and Tom, but it was Jim who answered.

"Most of that information will be compartmentalized, being shared only within this group and the security/scout squads."

"Shouldn't everyone know what to do if we are attacked?" asked Ann.

Again, it was Jim who answered. "Everyone will be instructed to respond to the commons area if we come under attack, but specifics won't be shared with the general population in case we're infiltrated."

"Infiltrated?" asked Ann.

Christian nodded. "One of our concerns is that an unfriendly group who knows about us will send in people acting as refugees to learn our weaknesses and perhaps try to spread dissent, either as a prelude to an attack or as an attempt to gain control by increasing their numbers within our community. We can't allow that. Look what happened to Europe and our own country before everything went down."

Ann nodded. "I hadn't thought of that."

"Good people rarely do," said Jim. "Being straight-forward themselves, they tend to assume that others are as well. Sadly, that's not always the case."

"So how do we protect against that?" asked Bill.

Jim looked at Tom Murphy. "We're going to address that in a minute, but first I'd like to let Christian finish and Mike give his report." He looked at Christian. "Go ahead."

"Our security zone is pushed out to about five miles now, a bit more to the north where Hillmont is located. That means that scouts and security personnel are able to keep a pretty good eye on things within that perimeter. That doesn't mean, however, that it is necessarily safe - we only consider the compound and Hillmont to be safe zones.

"As you know, a watchtower is being built on the hill. It took a bit of a back seat in the rush to get the cabins finished, but it should be done soon. A similar tower is being constructed at Hillmont, and School Center is thinking about building one as well. Their primary purpose is to surveil the surrounding area of each location, but they should also be able to see signals from each other."

He checked his notes. "A total of forty-six people have completed the basic security program and participate in security zone patrols. Some are scouts and some are not. Interestingly, it's becoming a sought-after assignment, and more younger people are becoming interested in it."

"Are there age requirements?" asked Bill.

Christian nodded. "We allow compound security at fourteen and security zone patrol at seventeen."

"Gosh, that seems awfully young," said Ann.

Christian shrugged. "It's a different world, at least from the recent past when 'growing up' seemed to be something to be postponed or avoided entirely. It's more like a hundred years ago, when young people weren't mind-numbed by video games and social media, and actually wanted to be seen as and treated like adults. We're seeing these kids really stepping up and taking their responsibilities seriously. They're doing a good job."

THE REVIVAL

He looked at a sheet of paper on which he had written some notes. "All lights are up in the compound, chanelling has been completed, and the dog breeding and training program is starting to progress now that Brin is helping with it. She thinks we'll have a few decent guard and sentry dogs by summer. We've already started puppy-training Pink's last litter and are hoping for litters from several of the new dogs this spring or summer."

He looked at Jim. "That's about it."

Jim nodded. "Thanks, cupcake." He turned to Mike. "How about scouts?"

Mike chuckled. "So far, thirty-six have made it through the first two training phases and are considered field-ready. Another five just completed the first phase and nine more are ready to start.

"We're training and forming them up as modular, interchangeable units of four-man pods which can be combined into eight-man squads or twelve-man teams."

"Why is that?" asked Bill.

"To make the best use if manpower," Mike answered. "A four-man unit is sufficient for recon. More would be a waste if we don't anticipate enemy contact. If we need a stronger unit, two pods can be combined to make a squad, or three to make a team."

Bill nodded his understanding.

"We don't have any special weapons," Mike continued, "so there's no need for specialization. Essentially, every scout is a rifleman, though we're starting to train a few on long-range and sniper skill-sets."

He glanced at the notes in front of him. "With thirty-six scouts, we're able to deploy nine pods, four squads, three teams, or any combination therein."

"Where do the scouts come from?" asked Bill.

"Nine are the Hispanics who came with that National Guard unit, two are Kansas Guard guys who decided to stay, and the rest are from those who came here, Redemption or School Center as refugees."

"And is there an age requirement for the scouts?" asked Ann.

Mike nodded. "Minimum age is seventeen. Max is determined by ability." He smiled at Ann and Bill. "By the way, your daughter is one of the best of them."

Bill smiled back proudly, and Ann failed at trying to look pleased.

"All-in-all," Mike concluded, "I think we're doing very well. We'd always like more, but I'm happy with the ones we've got."

"What about the ones who wash out of training?" Jim asked.

Mike shrugged. "Surprisingly, there haven't been that many. A couple came to me, telling me that it wasn't for them, but the rest have folded well into security. So far, no hard feelings."

Jim nodded. "Good. Anything else?"

"Yeah. Our squads are seeing more fires coming from the city, and we occasionally see small groups who run when we spot them. We haven't pursued any of them, so I can't say who or what they are, but they haven't attacked us."

He looked at Jim. "And, as I told you the other day, we came across a house that had been attacked. Before he died, the man said the attackers had taken his wife and kids. Two boys and a girl. He told us the raiders said they were from Grim."

Jim nodded slowly and looked around at the others. "Mike told me this the other day. Apparently, this Grim is raiding closer to us, killing some and taking others. We're going to have to talk about this, but I'd like everyone to think about it on their own before we do."

"Who are they killing?" asked Bill.

Jim waited a moment before answering. "The men."

"And they're taking the women and children?" Ann asked, knowing the answer.

Jim nodded.

The group was silent for a minute as the implication hit each one of them. Finally, Kelly spoke.

"I don't see what there is to think about," she said.

Uncharacteristically, Naomi spoke next. "Neither do I."

"Me neither," said Ann.

Jim looked at each one. "You understand what that means?"

"It means we have to go from a defensive posture to an offensive one," said Bill, "at least situationally. I don't see how we can morally avoid it."

Jim nodded. "It means that we put our own people at risk in order to try to help others. Many of us disagreed with our own country doing that before. How is this different?"

"It's different because we're not doing it to make money and establish a permanent presence, nor create a growing standing military," said Bill.

"Maybe not," said Jim, "but couldn't that be an unintended result?"

"Life is full of imperfect choices," said Tom. "By not acting, we may be condemning countless innocents to a horrible fate. What if it was happening to Aedan, Brody and Morgan? Tommy and Saoirse?" He looked around the table. "And it's going to threaten us eventually. Best to address this when we choose to, not when they choose to force it on us."

Jim looked at those around the table. He had feared that this would eventually happen, that they would be forced to make a decision as to whether to remain primarily defensive or develop a permanent offensive capability. He felt that going after Grim was the right thing to do, as long as there still appeared to be innocent and defenseless people alive in the area, but he wanted everyone to express their opinion.

He got up from the couch and walked to one of the bookcases. "Has anyone read Smedley Butler's 'War is a Racket'?" he asked.

"I have," answered Tom.

"So have I," said Mike.

Jim nodded. "I figured the Marines would have."

He pulled a thin book out of the case. "Butler was an amazing guy. He lied about his age to get into the Marines as a second lieutenant at seventeen years old, then rose to the rank of Major General, the highest Marine rank at the time. When he retired after over thirty years, he was the most highly decorated Marine in history, at that point in time, including two Medals of Honor and one Brevet medal."

He started leafing through the pages. "Butler came to believe that war was mainly a tool of business interests, and that the military was often used improperly to further those interests at the expense of those doing the fighting. Essentially, he came to disagree with any internationally offensive use of the military."

He stopped on the page he had been looking for. "He said, essentially, that he believed in defense at the borders and coastline, and nothing more."

He looked around at the group. "He also addressed what I have long felt to be a major problem when it comes to building a military, or any fighting force. Let me read directly from his book.

He held the book up to read. "'Beautiful ideals were painted for our boys who were sent out to die. This was the 'war to end all wars'. This was the 'war to make the world safe for democracy'. No one told them that dollars and cents were the real reason. No one mentioned to them, as they marched away, that their going and their dying would mean huge war profits. No one told these American soldiers that they might be shot by bullets made by their own brothers here. No one told them that the ships on which they were going to cross might be torpedoed by submarines built with United States patents. They were just told it was to be a "glorious adventure'. Thus, having stuffed patriotism down their throats, it was decided to make them help pay for the war, too. So, we gave them the large salary of $30 a month! All they had to do for this munificent sum was to leave their dear ones behind, give up their jobs, lie in swampy trenches, eat canned willy (when they could get it) and kill and kill and kill ... and be killed"."

He looked around the group. "Some of us here know how easily young men can be made to think that war and violent interaction is exciting and something to be pursued. It appeals to our sense of adventure and our inherent need to prove ourselves in great causes – to save the damsel and the world, so to speak. Eventually, if it doesn't destroy us physically, it becomes addictive and threatens to destroy us mentally, even morally."

He tossed the book on the table. "I got out of that business years ago and swore I'd never get back into it. But now, here we are."

He paused again, thinking. "I will not be a part of convincing fine young people to sacrifice their lives or their well-being under the guise of adventure or heroic deeds. Yet, I can't stand by and allow innocent people to suffer unbelievable horrors because of my refusal to act."

"Edmund Burke said that all that was necessary for evil to triumph was for good men to do nothing," said Bill.

"Yep," Jim answered, "and whenever I heard that quote I said that men who would do nothing in the face of evil were not good men. Now, that comes home."

"I don't think there's any choice," said Bill, "and I think we are all agreed on that."

"What if Christian and Mike had decided to not get involved when we were attacked?" asked Ann.

"Or if you all had done nothing when you learned about Barnes taking over the school?" added Naomi. "It seems to me that this is just on a bigger scale."

"Agreed," said Mike.

Jim nodded and looked around the group. "Does anyone disagree or have any reservations?"

Everyone shook their heads.

Jim waited another moment and nodded. "Okay. Then that's settled. We have a couple of other things." He looked at Ann. "Ann, anything to share about engineering?"

"Just a couple," said Ann, glancing at her notes. "First, our solar power production has declined as the days have gotten shorter, but we anticipated that, and the additional wind turbines have taken up the slack. Also, the volume of the creek has fallen as the weather has gotten colder and precipitation has decreased, not to mention some ice forming, but it has still been enough to run the ram pumps and keep the tanks on the hill full. The winter solstice is just a few weeks away, and after that the days will gradually become longer again, so we will start to see increased solar production."

She looked at Jim. "I think we should increase our water storage capacity in case of drought, and also build protection around the tanks. Being above ground like they are right now, they are vulnerable to being punctured in an attack, and also to freezing. We need to keep them on the hill in order to provide adequate pressure, but I ran some numbers, and, if we bury them with the bottoms about four feet underground and build berms on top of them, they will be protected from puncture and freezing and still maintain the elevation needed to preserve an adequate flow rate."

"How many more gallons of storage do think we need?"

Ann shrugged. "I started trying to figure that out but came to the realization that the answer is simply 'as much as we can'. Everything depends on water – crops, animals, people. Without water, everything dies, so the only smart answer is as much as possible. I know that we have several ponds, and that the smaller creek and one pond are spring-fed, but I still think we should store as much as we can – not only for normal use, but for fire suppression if necessary."

Jim looked at Mike. "Okay, start bringing in as many large containers as you can find."

Mike nodded.

"Anything else?" Jim asked Ann

Ann nodded. "As Kelly mentioned, we built some solar dehydrators that seemed to be working well." She smiled. "We got the idea from one of the *Mother Earth News* flash drives you have. We're going to build quite a few more so that we can preserve more like that. Not only is it a good storage method for normal circumstances, but we can provide much lighter rations for the scouts."

"Good deal," said Jim. "Anything else?"

Ann shook her head "Nope, that's it."

Jim nodded and got up from the couch, walking to the bookcase and retrieving a roll of paper and returning to the table. "Tom, I'm going to step on your time a bit because your report will fit into this well."

He unrolled the paper on the tabletop, revealing a map of the area. "We're going to build a town."

"A town?" said Bill, his eyebrows raised.

THE REVIVAL

Jim nodded. "Yep. Right here," he put his finger on a spot north of Stonemont.

"Why?" asked Bill, still showing his surprise.

"A number of reasons," answered Jim, "several of which have been mentioned in the last few minutes."

He looked around at the group. "We feel at home here because it is our home. Hopefully, you do too. But I'm sure the others don't. It's good that they've transitioned from refugees to members of a community, but they will never be able to feel like autonomous family units as long as they're living on someone else's property, and a strong community is made up of strong family units."

Tom Murphy leaned toward the table as he studied the large diagram in front of him. "Why not just start the town at Church Crossing? We already have Hillmont there, with Redemption close by."

"A couple of reasons," Jim answered. "First, that would put the town on the edge of our secure area. There would be no buffer between it and the rest of the world. I want Hillmont to be that buffer. By building the town at this crossroads, it puts it about a mile and a half north of the contact gate, which makes it two miles from our entrance and about five miles south of Church Crossing, well inside our security zone." His finger traced a wavy line on the diagram. "Also, it puts it on a large creek, a year-round water source."

Tom nodded. "That's going to be quite a job. We'll be starting from nothing."

Jim nodded. "That's the other reason. By starting from scratch, we can lay things out exactly as we want them with considerations for security as well as aesthetics, sustainability and energy independence."

"Sustainability?" asked Christian. "Are you becoming a tree-hugger, Jim?"

Jim squinted at him. "Tell me something, dear-heart, what were modern houses built with?"

Christian shrugged. "Regular building materials. Wood, drywall, shingles and stuff."

"That's right," Jim smirked. "And now that we've exhausted your knowledge of construction, I'll continue."

He looked around at the others, most of whom were smiling at the exchange. "For the last two hundred years, most houses thought of as modern have been built with wood frames sheathed with boards, plaster or drywall. The walls in most of them were too thin to contain much insulation, so, recently, they were artificially heated and cooled with high energy-draw mechanical systems. Those systems were expensive to install, run and repair, played havoc with the internal humidity, and created an unhealthy living environment because all of the air was being recirculated through a closed system, often through dirty air ducts. We're going to build a better way - an older way."

"You're going to show us how you built the pyramids?" chuckled Christian.

Jim looked at Christian. "Maybe I'll show the rest of them that. I think I'll show you how I built the first outhouse."

"I already know how to dig a hole."

Jim nodded. "As you're proving right now."

Christian and the others laughed.

Jim looked around. "Now, if Christian is done with his attempted humor at the expense of his wiser and better-looking uncle, maybe we can get back to the business at hand. We're going to build with cob."

Most of the others looked at each other in confusion. Finally, Mike asked "What's cob?"

"Cob is a mixture of clay, sand and straw," answered Jim. "It's similar to adobe but applied differently. It's placed in layers, then essentially sculpted, as opposed to being formed and laid like bricks as adobe is."

"We're going to build with mud?" asked Kelly.

Jim nodded. "Kind of. Let me show you something."

He went to one of the large bookcases and withdrew a book, then returned to the table and handed the book to Kelly. "Take a look and pass it around."

Kelly took the book and looked at the house on the cover. It looked like a modern two-story timber and stucco house. "Nice," she said, looking up at Jim. "This is made with cob?"

Jim nodded. "Cob structures have been built for thousands of years, and usually last for hundreds of years. Many are built without timber support, being load-bearing themselves, and only use other materials for flooring and roofing. We will build some that way and others using timber frame."

He took the book and flipped to a pre-marked page. "Traditionally, cob walls are anywhere from eighteen inches to two-feet thick." He handed the book back to Kelly. "This makes them thermal masses themselves, making them cool in the summer and easy to heat in the winter."

"How are they heated?" asked Kelly, passing the book to Ann.

"Many are just heated with fireplaces," answered Jim, "but we're going to go a step beyond that and also build rocket mass heaters in them."

"What are those?" asked Bill.

Jim turned to Ann. "Would you like to explain that, Ann?"

Ann nodded. "A rocket mass heater is, essentially, a rocket stove embedded in a thermal mass – in our case, cob, which it warms up to provide radiant heat to an area."

Bill cleared his throat. "At the risk of redundancy, what's a rocket stove, and why haven't you ever told me about this?"

Ann laughed. "A rocket stove is a stove constructed with any number of materials with a small separate air intake that causes a strong draft in the firebox, resulting in a hotter, much more efficient fire. The updraft can sound like a rocket, hence its name, and it uses up to ninety percent less fuel that a standard fireplace or wood stove. Essentially, it runs on twigs and sticks instead of logs." She smiled at Bill. "I just learned about it from Jim's *Mother Earth News* flash drive."

Bill nodded. "So, we have maximally-insulated buildings paired with minimal-consumption heaters. Why weren't we building like this before?"

"Some were," said Jim. "Minimalists and the back-to-nature crowd were really starting to build a movement, especially up in the Northwest. Also, a lot of homesteaders were starting to build this way." He shrugged. "The rest of us didn't know much, if anything, about it."

"There's a lot of adobe out in west Texas," said Naomi, "but I thought it was only good for drier climates."

Jim shook his head. "They say that cob stands up well in wetter climates, as is shown by the growing movement in the Northwest and older buildings in Europe. They claim that the oldest cob structure is over ten thousand years old. As long as there is a good foundation and a good roof, the structure seems to easily outlast the builder."

"What all are we going to have in the town?" asked Kelly.

Jim pulled back the map, revealing a second sheet bearing a town plat. "As you can see," he said, pointing to the center of the diagram, "a main hall will be at the center, like in the old town squares. It will provide a main meeting place for the town, as well as a fortified defense position and watchtower. Since it will be several stories high, it will be timber-framed to support the load."

He scribed his finger around the central portion, indicating squares surrounding the hall. "And just like the old town squares, buildings for businesses will form a square around the hall." He pointed at the four corners of the square. "Where streets come into the square from the neighborhoods, gates will be installed which can be quickly closed in order to allow the entire square to be turned into a fortress if necessary."

"What kind of businesses are you thinking about?" asked Ann.

"Pretty much anything that anyone would like to try to make a go at," said Jim, "but there are a few things that I think are essential, like a general store, an inn with a restaurant and rooms for travelers to stay in, a bakery, a barber shop and some kind of medical aid station. Other than that, it's up to people's individual entrepreneurial spirit."

He saw that everyone was studying the diagram, so he continued, moving his finger outside the town square. "Then, surrounding the square will be individual houses on large enough lots to enable each family to have their own large gardens, and even chickens if they like." He looked around the table. "The goal is for each family to be as autonomous and self-sufficient as possible."

Bill was studying the diagram and nodding his head. "It will give each family a feeling of being an integral part of a united community." He looked up at Jim. "Do they buy their homes, rent them or what?"

"It will take workers to build the town," said Jim. "Stonemont will pay the workers in credits, as usual, then those who want to can rent the homes from us in order for us to recoup the cost. Stonemont will retain ownership of the buildings and the land, as well as the hall, which will serve the community, the shops around the square, for which tenants will pay rent, and the ground on which they sit."

Bill nodded his head, thoughtfully. "What if people want to buy the homes?"

Jim shook his head. "I thought about that." He looked around at the group. "We all know how people can be. Right now, they are still on their best behavior because they are still close to the time they lost everything. As time passes and things get better, some will forget and start to have different ideas about how things should be run. These will be the same people who weren't prepared in the first place and had to come to us for help, but they won't remember that. They'll just think that they should have a say in how things are done. Next thing you know, some 'citizens committee' will show up demanding one thing or another and we'll be right back at the start of what brought America down in the first place – those who can't, won't and didn't trying to tell those who can, will and did what to do."

Jim turned to look out the window at the commons. "Most of the people out there are good folks and are going to be an important part of building something new and worthwhile. But odds tell us that there are a few trouble makers in the mix. We don't know who they are yet, but we will, eventually, and I don't want them having any say in what we do."

He turned back to the group. "If anybody wants to build their own house and develop their own place outside the town, more power to them. I hope they all do, eventually, and we will help them all we can. But the town will remain under our control – for our safety, our future, and for the safety and future of our families."

Those at the table nodded their agreement.

"Okay. Does anybody have any comments or questions?"

"When do we start?" asked Kelly.

"Well," Jim shrugged, "you said that you expected people to start having some problems after Christmas, so let's start on January first. It will give everyone something to do, to think about and to plan for."

He looked around at the group. "It will be a New Year, and a new start for a new life."

THE REVIVAL

7

The excitement was palpable as the residents of Stonemont gathered in the commons to make their first trip to see the new townsite.

The month of December had been busy, with everyone making improvements on their hastily-prepared living arrangements and taking care of chores and tasks that just took longer in the cold and snow.

The snow-cover had remained through Christmas, a new snowfall arriving on Christmas eve to add a freshness and beauty to the celebrations, and the annual 'January thaw' had arrived several days later to begin the melt. Hard winter hadn't hit yet, but the brief respite of the temporary warmer weather had lifted moods and attitudes to recharge for what was coming and people took advantage of it to open their cabins to some fresh air and spend more time outside in the sunshine.

The Miller family had arrived with their scout guard several days after Christian had returned with the horses from Callahan's and the presentation of the horses and saddles to the Wyatt children had been an emotional experience for everyone, a combination of joy with the recognition of the sadness that had precipitated the tooling of the beautiful saddles.

The new horses were a source of constant interest and entertainment for everyone, especially the children, who spent hours each day hanging on the rails of the corrals watching Naomi and Becky, who often came over from the Samuals' place, take them through training.

Above everything else was the eagerness everyone felt at the announcement of the creation of the town.

The safety of Stonemont had been a blessing for all who had come there, and, through work and cooperation, each person had come to feel as if they were part of a close community. But things were getting tight as more and more people came in, and the crowding was starting to cause occasional friction where people rubbed up too closely against one another.

The town had been the subject of most conversations since Jim had announced it, and, while some were nervous about leaving the safety of Stonemont to live in a more exposed location, most were anticipating it with a measure that gave new energy to everything they did. Talk was about gardens, how they would make the homes feel like their own, and which newly-made friends would live next to each other. Some felt that they would stay as tenants in the homes that would be built by Stonemont, while others intended to use the homes as a stepping-off point to build their own places as soon as they could. Still others had asked if they could stay at Stonemont, something that had surprised Jim, and about which he was considering the ramifications.

Now, they were gathered in the commons, children running around yelling and laughing while adults talked to each other about the day's trip and the hope it brought.

One of the box trucks sat just inside the gate, loaded with supplies that a scout pod would be taking on to Callahan's after dropping off tools at the townsite. Three dirt bikes leaned on their stands in front of the truck awaiting the scouts who would ride them as point guard, a fourth being secured in the box of the truck for the driver in case it was necessary for him to join the other three of his pod on two wheels. The club cab pickup sat behind the truck to carry a rapid-response squad.

Excitement mounted as Mike and Tom approached, leading two scout squads, one of which would relieve the squad at Hillmont, which would rotate back to Stonemont, and the other to continue on an assignment that hadn't been shared with the general population. The crowd got louder as Jim and Kelly came out of the main house with Bill and Ann to join the group.

Jim smiled and gave a wave. "Everybody ready?" he shouted.

A mixture of cheers and applause arose, much of the noise coming from the kids who saw this as a great adventure.

Jim laughed. "Well, let's go!"

The rapid response squad loaded into their vehicle and the point guard kick-started their bikes, adding the bumblebee sound of the small-displacement engines to the noise. The truck started up, its deeper-throated rumble seeming to give the final signal.

Sentries opened both ends of the entry gates and the assemblage started moving slowly through them and onto the road.

If the group had been excited in the compound, they were even more-so as they spilled out into the expanse of the world outside the gate. Many had not ventured beyond the safety of the enclosure for several months, and those who had had not done so with the purpose of starting a life outside of it. An energy filled the group as adults talked with one another and children ran into the fields chasing and being chased by each other.

Within twenty minutes they streamed through the contact gate and within another hour arrived at a crossroads where the scouts halted the column.

THE REVIVAL

Fields and gentle hills surrounded them, rising like waves, and a tree line several hundred yards to the west marked the large stream that would provide not only the town's water, but energy as well.

The people looked around, commenting to each other about different features of the land and picturing in their minds how it might look in the future, a year from now, two years, ten years.

The sound of the box truck's rolling door opening drew their attention and Jim climbed up into the rear of the box.

"Folks, welcome to town!" He waved his arm to indicate the surrounding area. "It may not look like much now, except as a beautiful piece of God's creation, but we're going to make it into something special – a place where everyone can build the life they want and prosper according to their interests, talents, determination and hard work."

He looked around the crowd. He knew it was important to turn the unfocused excitement into directed purpose, "We won't really be able to start building until it warms up a bit and we're able to work the cob mixture, but there's a lot of work to be done to prepare for that." He waved his arm again. "These fields are all wheat which was planted last spring but was never cut because of the collapse. It's going to be our straw for the cob, so all of it has to be cut and stacked at the mixing area." He chuckled. "That should keep everybody busy for a while."

The crowd laughed good-naturedly.

"Ann Garner will be leading the engineering team in laying out the streets and property plats, as well as the individual building sites, so they will be marking the areas that need to be cleared first. Also, we have a surprise that we haven't shared with you." He motioned to Ann. "Ann, would you come up here and tell them about it?"

Ann walked through the crowd and climbed up into the truck. "Does anybody here miss electricity?" she yelled out over the crowd.

"I sure do!" came a voice from the middle of the crowd.

"Me too!" yelled another.

"Nah," drawled a voice farther back, drawing laughter from others.

Ann smiled. "Well, we're going to see if we can bring some old-school, consistent electricity to this town."

She pointed over toward the tree line. "Right inside those trees is a stream that is kind of a rarity around here. It has the volume and the vertical drop that we believe will be able to generate enough constant electricity for over a hundred families. After we finish laying out the town plats, the other engineers and I are going to start working on a power generating plant that will serve the town."

"But electricity doesn't work anymore," said a man in the crowd.

Ann shook her head. "Wrong. The EMP, if that's what it was, fried all existing, unprotected electronic circuits. Our electricity was supplied through systems that were dependent on those circuits and supplied appliances which were run by electronic circuits. Electricity can still be generated like it has always been and delivered like it was before the systems became circuit-dependent."

"How do you make electricity?" asked a woman.

Ann nodded. "Good question. Electricity can be generated in several ways, but in our situation, we will do it by using the water flow to rotate magnets around conductive materials, namely, loops of copper wire."

"You mean like a dam does?" asked a man.

"Exactly," Ann answered. "The large dams used massive turbines to produce enough electricity for whole sections of the country. We'll be using the same principle for our town, just on a smaller scale."

"How are you going to get the electricity from the generator at the creek to the town?" asked another man.

"The same way they did it before," answered Ann. "Through transmission lines."

"How long will it take?" asked a woman at the front of the crowd.

Ann smiled down at the woman holding a baby in one arm and the hand of a toddler in the other. "When you move into your new home, you'll be able to read bedtime stories to them by electric light."

"Well then," yelled a man, "what are we waiting for?"

"Just waiting for you to come up and get your shovel!" Jim yelled back.

"Well," said the man, pushing through the crowd, "if you're waiting for me, you're falling behind!"

Two men from the crowd climbed into the truck to help Jim and Ann hand down tools to the crowd. Shovels, rakes, weed cutters and anything else they had been able to get from the gardening centers were dispersed to waiting hands, and everyone soon had something to work with.

Ann handed down spools of twine and mason's line to the other engineers for laying out the plats, then looked out over the crowd. "Everybody ready?" she yelled.

This time, a cheer went up, probably due to the reality the tools in hand gave the people.

"Good! Let's get started!"

8

Mike jumped down out of the rear of the box truck, followed by Tracy and the rest of the scout squad he would be leading, then the squad that would be rotating into Hillmont. He watched as they took their defensive positions, then walked over to where Tom was talking with the leader of the squad that was being relieved.

"He says they've been getting some sniping and seen an increasing number of fires from the north," said Tom at Mike's approach. "Also, they had a couple of people disappear yesterday."

"Who were they?" asked Mike.

"A couple of kids," answered the squad leader. "Boy, seventeen, and a girl, sixteen. Their parents said they were kind of a thing and had been going off together. This time, they haven't come back"

"Any chance they just ran away?" asked Tom.

The squad leader shook his head. "Doubt it. Everyone here has a pretty good idea of the dangers out there, and there really aren't the kind of stresses here that used to make kids run off. I think they just went off for some privacy and something happened."

"Do you have any idea which direction they went?" asked Mike.

The squad leader nodded. "Folks said they usually went toward Redemption, but one of the women said she saw them walk off to the north this time. We tracked them to just over that first rise and found signs of a tussle."

"Between the two of them?" asked Mike.

The squad leader shook his head. "Nope. Them and several others. We followed the tracks to the next rise where we found traces of a camp just over the crest. Looks like they had been watching us. We followed the tracks from there but lost them when they got to the neighborhoods."

"Any idea how many there were?" asked Tom.

The scout shook his head. "By the look of the camp, I'd say four or five, but they walked single file and it's pretty dusty."

Mike looked at Tom. "Looks like they're taking them somewhere."

Tom nodded. "Looks like they're headed in the direction you're going anyway. Can you include this in your objective?"

Mike nodded. "Yep, as a priority. It wouldn't surprise me if this somehow leads to the other, anyway." He looked at the squad leader. "Anything else you can tell us?"

"The boy's name is Josh. He's got brown hair and was wearing jeans and a blue work shirt with a brown Carhartt jacket. The girl's name is Hannah. She's blonde and was wearing black leggings and a white jacket - one of those puffy ones. Neither of them has been any trouble. They're both good kids."

"Do you know what kind of shoes or boots they were wearing?"

The squad leader shook his head. "No."

"That's something to pay attention to, okay?"

The scout nodded, looking slightly ashamed. "Yeah. Sorry."

"Don't be sorry, just be better."

The scout nodded.

"Okay," Mike said, seeing that his squad had their equipment on. "We'll see what we can find out." He looked at Tom. "We'll be out of radio range, but we'll pop a flare if we need the cavalry."

Tom gave a small smile. "Come back whole."

"What do you think?" asked Tracy.

They had found the spot where Josh and Hannah had been taken by the group, then the group's camp. From there, they had been able to find bits of tracks leading them to the first fringes of neighborhoods beyond the razed area. The tracks had been lost as the group started walking on paved streets, and they had spent the rest of the day making their way through neighborhoods as quickly as they could, the abandoned houses and cars giving an eerie feeling as they went.

Now, Mike watched the wide expanse of a major street they were about to cross, looking for any movement or sign of life. "I think they were watching Hillmont and took the kids when the kids gave themselves up as targets of opportunity." He dug his binoculars out of a side pouch of his pack. "I think they're taking them somewhere."

Tracy thought for a moment. "You think they're taking them somewhere specific?"

"Yeah."

"Why do you think that?"

Mike scanned the area with the binoculars. "They were moving single file in a manner that indicates they have a specific destination in mind. There are about six or seven in the group, though it's hard to know for sure because the tracks of the last ones blot out the tracks of the first. It looks like Josh and Hannah are toward the rear of the group."

"How can you tell that?"

"I was able to see what tracks they left before they were taken, so I can distinguish them from the rest. I've seen quite a few of theirs, which means they're not toward the front."

Tracy nodded. "Can you teach the rest of us how to track like that?"

"Yeah, that's coming up in another phase, but we have to move too fast for me to teach everybody right now."

"I know." Tracy watched him scan the neighborhood. "You know a lot of stuff."

He shrugged. "Just stuff they taught me."

"Cool."

He took the binoculars away from his eyes and looked at her. Her eyes were wide with the golden flecks reflecting the sun. He realized that he was staring at her and turned back to the street.

Squelch broke on the radio and a voice said, "Position three, boss."

Mike panned the binoculars to the two o'clock position where the number three scout would be. "What have you got?"

"Looks like one down in the street."

"Recent?"

"Can't tell."

"Any movement?"

"Negative."

Mike thought for a moment and looked at the sky, then keyed his mic. "Okay, everybody, we've got about an hour left of daylight. Stay put and keep an eye out. We'll move after dark."

Mic clicks let him know that everybody had copied and he turned to Tracy. You stay here. I'm going to go take a look."

"Okay," she answered, smiling at his retreating form, knowing that he didn't know she had understood his staring at her.

He swung to the right, staying low as he approached the scout who had eyes on the downed figured. "Coming up," he said, quietly.

"Come ahead," answered the scout.

He cleared the final ten yards and dropped into a depression from which the scout was observing the street ahead. A small strip mall dominated by a large chain grocery store stood on the opposite side of the street, and a major cross street ran about fifty yards to the east. Beyond that was a Sam's Club and Home Depot with the usual outlying businesses around them.

Mike brought his binoculars to his eyes and studied the body lying in the street – a man wearing jeans and a denim work jacket lay face-down in the street.

Crossing the wide street was too risky in daylight, as the buildings on the other side provided plenty of places for a shooter to wait in hiding. He looked to the west and, seeing that the sun was touching the treetops, figured it would be dark in an hour. He keyed his mike. "Everybody stay put. Converge on position three after dark with NVGs on my call."

Seven double clicks told him everyone had acknowledged.

He put his head up a bit and looked around. The tall uncut grass was good concealment for the scouts as long as they weren't moving, and he could imagine similar operations almost two hundred years before as Kansa and Osage Indians used the grass to cover their approach on a herd of bison or a group of settlers, or three hundred years before that against Coronado.

"Seen anything else?" he asked the scout.

"I thought I saw some movement down by the Home Depot a few minutes ago," answered the scout. "Could have just been a piece of paper blowing around, though."

"What color?"

"White."

Mike thought for a minute. The girl had been wearing a white jacket, but he had expected them to be farther ahead. Plus, where the body lay in the road ahead of them and the Home Depot were not on the same line going from Hillmont to where they thought Grim's headquarters was. Still, they were only offset by about a quarter of a mile, and he didn't know everything the group had been doing. They would wait.

Dusk slowly turned into night, and he withdrew a small FLIR thermal imaging device from his pack. Powering it on, he scanned the area around him. The scouts were the only things that showed up, other than the body in street, which emitted a faint post-mortem signature. Putting the FLIR in his pocket, he keyed his mike. "Everybody NVG?"

Double clicks gave him affirmatives.

"Okay, everybody prairie dog."

Heads rose out of the grass and scanned the area around them.

Mike gave them a minute, then asked, "Anybody have anything?"

Silence told him no one had seen anything.

"Meet at position three."

Within a minute, all eight scouts were gathered in the depression.

"Everybody good?" Mike asked.

THE REVIVAL

Nods and "goods" told him that all were.

"Okay, I'm going out to check the body. You and you," he indicated two scouts, "on my wings. Ready?"

Both scouts nodded.

"Let's go."

Stepping out of the depression, Mike walked through the grass at a half-crouch and onto the street, keeping his rifle trained on the body while the wing scouts covered the area around him. Thermal had told him the man was dead, but careful was careful. Arriving at the face-down body, he squatted next to it and put his fingers on the side of the neck. No pulse and cool.

Talking a length of paracord from a side pouch, he formed a loop and put it around one of the corpse's wrists, cinched it tight, then walked back to the grass and lay flat on the ground. "On the deck, guys," he said.

He waited until both wing scouts were flat on the ground, then pulled the cord hard.

The body rolled toward him, settling on its back with its legs twisted and ankles crossed.

"Okay, guys, looks like he's clean."

He got to his feet and walked back to the body. He hadn't really expected a booby trap, but the body just lying in the middle of the street had seemed a bit odd to him, like bait, and he wasn't taking any chances.

Squatting next to the body, he determined it to be a man in his twenties. There were several slashes on the man's arms and in the front of his denim jacket, the fabric darker where it was wet. He unbuttoned the jacket to find a thermal undershirt covered in blood.

Taking a small flashlight out of his pocket, he cupped it in his hand and risked two seconds of light to see the wounds. From the pattern on the shirt, it appeared that three major punctures had been made in the man's abdomen. The wounds seemed to have been made with a large, heavy blade and the bleeding had been profuse. One of the gashes exposed a loop of intestine.

Looking around at the blood pattern, it looked like the man had been stabbed several feet away before collapsing where he now lay, dying fairly quickly, though not immediately.

He made a check of the man's pockets and clothing, finding nothing but a pocket knife and a half-filled plastic bottle of murky water.

"Back to the squad," he said, and returned to the depression with both of the wing scouts.

"Okay," he said, looking around at the scouts, "the guy was killed with a big-ass knife or something. Not long ago, maybe a couple of hours, and from the front, which means he was facing his attacker and at arm's length. No telling whether it was a robbery or an argument, and no way to know if it tells us anything."

He nodded down the street toward the Home Depot. "We don't really have any idea where to go from here, but Bobby thought he saw something down there, and we haven't checked that one anyway, so we'll head down there."

He saw the scouts nodding and continued. "I'll take point with the FLIR. Tracy, stay on my six with the rest of your pod behind you. We'll cross both roadways and walk in the ditch on the other side."

He looked at the other pod leader. "You take your guys into the median and stay even with Tracy's. That will keep all of us in a depression in case someone pops up on us."

The pod leader nodded.

"I'll check the areas with thermal, but give a heads up if you see anything I don't," Christian continued. "We don't want to waste time, but we don't want to be stupid. Our first goal is to find those kids." He looked around. "Any questions?"

No one said anything.

"Everybody good?"

Everyone nodded.

"Okay, let's go."

They left the depression and crossed the roadway at a half-crouch trot, Bravo pod dropping off in the median and Alpha following Mike to the far shoulder ditch. Turning east, they passed the grocery store and a free-standing bank, then crossed the cross street to pass an Aldi, a Culver's, another bank and a party store before reaching a side street that ran in front of the Home Depot. Forming back into a single file squad, they crossed the side street and took cover behind a row of sample sheds in the store's parking lot.

Mike scanned the expansive parking lot with the FLIR, seeing nothing on the first pass. Scanning again, a hot spot appeared at the far end of the lot near a line of trees. He kept the device focused on the spot, not sure if it was a dog or other animal, when the spot suddenly got brighter, moved to the left, remained stationary for a minute, returned to its original spot and disappeared.

Putting the thermal device back in his pocket, he switched back to night vision. The parking lot was full of cars, more densely arranged in the middle of the lot and more sparsely toward the edges. Pallets of mulch, dirt and concrete pavers filled a large area at the far end of the lot, beyond which stood three more sheds lined up in front of the trees. As he watched, the door of the

THE REVIVAL

middle shed opened and a man emerged, walked a few feet away and relieved himself on the concrete before turning and going back into the shed.

Mike thought for a minute while looking at the layout of the parking lot, then whispered into his mic. "Looks like we have somebody in a shed at the far side of the lot. Bravo, approach from the front and get as close as you can to it while staying behind cover. Alpha, follow me to set up a line at a right angle to Bravo on the west side. Nobody fire unless I say so."

The scouts acknowledged numerically and Mike said "Go."

Bravo filtered through the cars, eventually taking positions behind the landscaping pallets about fifty yards from the sheds, while Alpha followed Mike to a line-position perpendicular to Bravo and about fifty yards to the west of the sheds.

Seeing that everyone was in position, Mike again whispered into his radio. "Everybody hold position. I'm going around the back to try to get closer. Radio silence from here on. I might transmit, but don't answer or acknowledge. And remember, nobody fire unless I give the order or they shoot me - in which case light 'em up."

Giving Tracy a thumbs-up, he took off at a half-crouch trot, entering the tree line.

The tree line turned out to be the fringe of a larger treed area following a shallow ravine with a creek flowing at the bottom. Moving farther into the trees, he advanced toward the sheds and saw light coming through a crack of the middle one. Stepping carefully through the brush, he edged closer to the shed until he heard voices.

"How long you figure till we get back?" asked a man's voice.

Another man grunted, answering in a gruff voice. "Should'a been back today. Would'a been if Fingers hadn't 'a wanted to go past those apartments he used to live in." He paused. "We'll get there tomorrow."

"Fingers seemed like a good guy," said the first voice. "Why'd you have to kill him?"

"Fingers was a dumbass," answered the second voice. "Everybody knows the rules. Everything goes to Grim first, no matter what. Fingers tried to take a piece for himself first and it got him killed."

"Can't hardly blame him. She's cute."

"Cute don't matter. Everything goes to Grim first. If we'd brought her back used, or took off with her, he'd have us on the spit instead of porkchop, here."

A heavy thud was followed by a grunt and a groan.

"Please, stop hurting him," a girl's voice pleaded.

THE REVIVAL

The sound of a scuffle and the girl gasping for breath preceded the gruff voice. "Shut up, bitch. Just because I can't hurt you in some ways doesn't mean I won't hurt you in others."

"Leave her alone," rasped a boy's voice.

Mike heard the sound of something heavy being dropped on the floor, the girl gasping, and another heavy thud followed by another grunt and half-scream.

"You need some more tenderizin', porkchop?" asked the gruff voice.

"Why do you keep calling him porkchop?" asked the first man.

"Because that's what he's gonna to taste like," answered the gruff voice.

A moment passed before the first voice asked, "What are you talking about?"

The gruff voice laughed. "What the hell you think you been eatin' since you showed up?"

Another short pause passed before the first voice asked, tentatively, "Pig?"

The gruff voice laughed louder. "Pig? Yeah, long-pig!"

"What's long pig?" the first voice asked.

"Man meat, dumb-ass! Tastes like pork!" The man kept laughing. "You've seen what we do with the women. What did you think we do with the men?" He stopped laughing abruptly. "And junior here looks like he'll taste real good. How 'bout you, goldilocks, you think your boy's gonna be too hot, too cold or just right?"

Mike moved around to the front of the shed as he heard the sounds of wretching and crying, now knowing what the situation was. He let his rifle hang as he drew his pistol, a more appropriate weapon for the small shed, and started to reach for the door shed handle when the door burst open and a man stumbled out vomiting. The man felt to the pavement and the lantern light in the shed was just enough to allow Mike to stitch three shots from sternum to throat on the large man still standing in the shed holding a machete and laughing.

Tracy made her way through the trees and squatted next to Mike. She looked at the prisoner sitting on the ground with his hands tied behind his back, then back at Mike. "They're both still so scared they can hardly talk. I think she's okay physically, but she can't stop shaking and crying so I'm not sure. How's the boy?"

"He's got some cracked ribs and a broken nose. He'll be okay. We're going to have to keep them with us until we finish this, but our new friend here

THE REVIVAL

might be able to help us with that." He looked at the man. "How about it, new friend? Want to help us?"

The man nodded jerkily. "Yeah, sure."

"Yeah, sure?" asked Mike. "Pretty easy to convince, aren't you?"

The man nodded. "I figure you'll kill me if I don't."

Mike nodded thoughtfully. "Yep, might." He paused, watching the man closely. "So, been eating your fellow man, huh?"

The man started shaking his head, then started wretching again in dry heaves.

Mike waited until the man stopped heaving. "Didn't know it, huh?"

The man shook his head again, started another heave, but was able to catch himself. "No."

"I'm going to ask you some questions," said Mike. "They will be simple questions to which I want simple answers. Understand?"

The man nodded. "Yeah."

"Who runs the place you came from?"

"A guy named Grim."

"How long have you been with him?"

"About a month."

"Where did you come from?"

"Independence."

"Alone?"

"No."

"Who'd you come with?"

"Some friends."

"How many?"

The man thought for a moment. "Seven."

"Why did you come over here?"

"Things were getting sparse in Missouri. We figured we'd come over to where the rich people lived."

"How'd you end up with Grim?"

"He surrounded our camp one night. Gave us a choice of joining him or dying."

"How many people does he have?"

The man thought for a moment. "About a hundred, I think."

"Men and women?"

The man shook his head. "Just men."

"Where do they get the people?"

"Raiding. Sometimes people come by looking for help."

"There are still people around there?"

The man nodded. "Yeah, some. Not as many as there used to be."

"So, they eat the men?"

The man started to shake but got himself under control. "Guess so. Yeah."

"What do they do with the women?"

"Use them."

"For what?"

The man's head slumped. "Everything."

"How about children?"

The man shook his head. "I don't know."

"You don't know?"

The man closed his eyes. "I saw some young girls with the women, but I don't know about the rest."

"Why were you watching our place?"

"Things are getting thin. Grim sends us out to look for new places and people."

"Where is his place?"

"Several miles from here. North."

"What's between here and there?"

"Not much. Bunch of houses with dead people in them."

Mike stood up, followed by Tracy. "We've got most of the night left. Tell everybody to be ready to go in five minutes. It's going to be rough on the kids, but they'll just have to tough it out."

They stayed on the main streets to make the best time, Mike walking point and sweeping with the FLIR while Tracy escorted the bound prisoner twenty feet behind. The rest of the squad followed in a staggered line with similar separation.

An eeriness settled around them as they progressed farther into the city, the moon flitting behind the clouds and casting unnatural looking shadows on the empty hulls of houses and large apartment complexes. Trash and other items strewn across yards and drives gave testament to the gradual abandonment of hope, property and finally life itself by the past inhabitants, and the scouts imagined the horrors and despair that must have permeated the minds of each as the decline moved inexorably toward the final collapse. Occasional heat signatures registered on the FLIR, showing dogs and other animals on their nightly hunts, but they encountered no other humans.

Several hours of cautious walking brought them to the I-435 overpass, under which Metcalf Avenue continued to run to the north.

THE REVIVAL

Giving the signal for the squad to hold position, Mike turned to the prisoner. "Where from here?"

The man lifted his chin to indicate Grim's camp was up ahead. "'Bout a mile up on the right. An old Lowe's."

Mike looked up the road. "What's between here and there?"

The man shrugged. "Couple of strip malls and a big church." He looked at Mike. "What are you going to do with me?"

Mike looked at the man. "If you continue to cooperate, I'm going to let you go. If you cause trouble, I'll kill you. Does he post lookouts?"

The man nodded. "There's usually a couple of burn barrels going and a couple of guys at each one."

"Okay," said Mike. "Remember what I said."

The man nodded.

They went under the overpass, then got off the main roadway and made their way north, travelling behind the strip malls and through stands of trees that ran between the roadway and the neighborhoods to the east.

The clouds were getting thicker and Mike could taste the threat of snow in the air.

A faint glow grew gradually brighter as they got closer to where the prisoner had said the Lowe's was, and they soon came to the edge of a tree line through which they could see the Lowe's parking lot. Two burn barrels were in the parking lot, flames dancing from their open tops and illuminating the sentries huddled around them.

Mike watched for a few minutes, studying the layout. Both main entrances had been fortified with concrete blocks and bags of dirt, constructed to provide fighting positions and effective barricades against a ramming attack. A poorly constructed run of cyclone fence spanned the entire front of the building, presumably to provide a first layer of obstruction to unwanted visitors. Just as with the Home Depot, a number of abandoned cars dotted the parking lot and pallets of landscaping materials sat at the far end, though most of the dirt and concrete blocks had been taken to fortify the doorways. A steep hill rose on the right.

Mike motioned to Tracy, who quickly joined him.

"Take your guys and do a three-sixty on this place. The guards are looking into their fires, so they're night-blind, plus they're cold, sleepy and bored, but don't take any chances. We need to get information at this point, not get into a fight."

Tracy nodded, signaled her pod to follow her and took off.

They moved slowly behind the tree line to the right, watching both the parking lot to their left and the rear of the houses whose yards they walked through on their right. The houses were dark and quiet, as was the parking lot, and they began to ascend the hill when they got to the corner.

The hill rose gradually until, at its high point, it was above the roof of the massive store, giving them an excellent view of the area around it. Fencing supplies and sheds were arranged along the side of the building and a semi-trailer was backed up to a dock door in the rear. Another truck looked like it was in line to off-load next.

Walking just below the ridge of the hill, Tracy scanned the area beyond the store as well as the building and parking lot. Nothing moved except for an occasional piece of trash blowing in the breeze and she realized she was feeling snowflakes against her cheek. Raising her gaze, she saw that the clouds had moved in to the point where it was difficult to see the difference between earth and sky and the snow was starting to come down harder.

Coming even with the far corner of the building, she began to descend the slope of the embankment to the west side of the store, the side that included a large fenced-in garden center. The increasing snow made the slope more precarious in the dark and she moved slowly, checking the scouts behind her to ensure they were as well.

Reaching the level concrete of the parking lot, she looked back to check the squad once more, then turned back to see a man staring at her through the bars of the gardening enclosure.

Her breath caught at the shock and her rifle came up before her brain processed what she saw. The face in her sights was bland. A man. Holding onto the bars on each side of his drawn face.

She put her finger on the trigger and kept the rifle pressed tightly to her shoulder as she raised her left hand for the scouts to stop.

The scouts held their positions, turning and raising their rifles to cover both flanks and the rear as Tracy moved closer to the fence.

She looked to the left and right, then took several cautious steps toward the fence while keeping her eyes and rifle on the man.

"Please help us," said the man in a dry, raspy voice.

Tracy looked left and right again, assuring herself that no one else was near, then took several more careful steps toward the man - not close enough for him to reach her, but close enough for her to see him better and speak quietly.

"Who are you?" she asked.

"Russell," the man answered. "Please, can you help us?"

Tracy flipped her NVGs up so that she could see the man's face without the artificial assistance. The man was gaunt and unshaven, his eyes lifeless. His clothes were dirty and hung on his frame as if they belonged to a much larger man. His fingers were almost black with grime.

She looked past him into the shadows. "Are you alone?" she asked.

"No," the man said, shaking his head slowly, as if in a dream. "My son," he said, slowly turning to look behind him. "Others."

Tracy flipped the NVGs back down and looked behind the man. A mass of bodies lay together in a pile surrounded by bags of mulch. She couldn't tell if they were alive or dead. "How many are there of you?"

The man had started to turn back toward her but her question made him stop midway and turn back. Finally, he turned back to her, his mouth trembling. "Not sure," his voice caught. "Please. My son." Tears formed in his eyes.

Tracy thought quickly. If they tried to rescue this group, they would expose themselves and possibly become involved in a gunfight. Their primary objective of quiet intelligence gathering would be blown. But they couldn't leave these people here, knowing their fate.

"Are you the army?" the man asked.

"No." She looked again at the mass of bodies. "How many are alive? Can they walk?"

The conversation seemed to be having a rejuvenating effect on the man and he answered more quickly this time. "They can walk." Again, he looked behind him tentatively, then back at Tracy. "Please, can you get us out?"

Tracy was still weighing the options and signaled the second scout to come to her position. "I don't know," she answered the man. "Is there a guard?"

The man shook his head. "Guards are out front."

Tracy turned to the scout who had come to her side. "See if there's a way in here," she whispered.

The scout took off and was back in less than a minute. "There's a gate secured with a medium chain and padlock. No problem."

Tracy nodded, still thinking. Each scout pod carried a set of bolt cutters for their salvage operations, so the chain was no obstacle. Still, taking the men out could be a big mess and make their departure more difficult. "I'll be back," she told the man. "Wake them up and get them all on their feet, ready to go. And keep them quiet."

Mike nodded. "Tracy's right. We can't leave them there."

THE REVIVAL

Tracy had returned with her pod and explained the situation quickly and concisely, including her reasons for wanting to liberate the imprisoned men. It would compromise their primary objective, but reality often got in the way of plans, and morality required that they act. The question was how to maximize the chance of success while minimizing the chances of casualties in the squad.

He looked around at the squad, all of whom had heard Tracy give her report a second time for their benefit. "This is going to be tricky, and it's not something we came prepared for, but it may be possible to do this with zero casualties if everyone does what they're supposed to, is careful, nobody takes chances and we have a little luck. Okay?"

All heads nodded.

"We're going to have to walk them back. That's going to be tough because of the shape they're probably in. We have two basic choices, loud or quiet. We're going to try quiet. We can get loud later if we have to."

He looked at the Bravo pod leader. "You guys will form up on a line along the top of the incline on the west side overlooking the area where the men are being held. Your job will be to overwatch and support, if necessary, the initial extraction by Alpha, then deny pursuit to the best of your ability. I will be with you."

He looked at Tracy. "Alpha will extricate the captives, lead them up and over the embankment out of sight of the lookouts, down the other side to the road and then south."

Tracy nodded.

He looked back at the others. "Alpha may be moving slowly and need time to get some distance, so Bravo will hold their position for an hour if no enemy contact is made and as long as we can if we get in a fight. We will then catch up to Alpha and provide rear watch and defense."

He looked around the group. "Everybody with me?"

All heads nodded.

He looked back at Tracy. "When you cut the chain, make sure you don't let it drop and take it with you. A missing chain will make them wonder more than one laying in the ground and we want them to wonder as much as possible."

Tracy nodded.

"When you get them over the hill, give each of them a drink of water," Mike continued. "Don't let them drink too much, just a few sips, and let them all share the same bottles. They're already cross-contaminated, and if there are any health issues we don't want it passed to us. Give each of them a protein bar and tell them to eat it slowly. Then hit the road and go as fast as you can. If there's no pursuit, we'll stop in a couple of miles and take stock."

"What if there is pursuit?" asked the Bravo leader.

"If we haven't been able to contain them at their base, we'll go to plan B, C or D."

"What are those?" asked the Bravo leader.

"You'll know when I tell you," Mike smiled. He looked around the group. "Any more questions?"

Everyone shook their heads.

"Very good." He looked up and saw that the snow was falling faster. "No time like the present. Let's go."

Tracy held the chain in both hands as another scout made the first cut, then cupped her hands under the link to catch the pieces as they separated. The scout made the second cut and the link came loose, half falling into her cupped hands and the other half landing to balance precariously on the heel of her hand. Leaning over, she secured the half-link between her lips, dropped it into her hand with the other and stuffed the links, chain and lock into her pocket.

The men had lined up at the gate with a silence that was almost eerie, Russell at the front of the line with his arm wrapped protectively around a thin young boy. One body remained on the ground, the man apparently having died during the night.

She had explained the plan to the men, and the importance of remaining quiet, and now slowly opened the gate.

One by one, the men filed out of the enclosure, some listless from malnutrition and exposure, others almost feral in their desire to escape. As they exited, the scouts guided them across the short stretch of parking lot to the bottom of the hill where they carefully started climbing the incline.

Tracy counted the men as they came out, then went in to check the dead man. She knelt to check the body for signs of life and, finding none, started to rise when she saw another man sitting a few feet away staring at the door to the main building. "Come on, we have to go," she said, as quietly as she could.

The man shook his head.

"You have to get out of here," she said, more urgently. "Come on."

The man turned toward her and shook his head again. "My wife and daughter are here."

THE REVIVAL

The implication of the man's statement hit Tracy as she thought it through. "You know what will happen if you stay?"

The man turned to her with tears in his eyes and nodded. "Maybe I can keep them alive a little longer."

The horror of what the man was saying threatened to twist her reality and she fought to find a response. "Do you think that's what they would want?"

He shook his head. "No. But maybe they won't know." The man's eyes seemed to suddenly clear and his chin lifted. "Where there is life there is hope, and they will have each other."

Tracy stood in silence, transfixed by the enormity of what the man was doing. She could think of nothing to say. Nothing in her life or imagination had prepared her to come face to face with a knowing sacrifice of such magnitude. Nothing she could say could even approach being suitable or meaningful to someone in the man's position. She felt small, useless, even meaningless in the seemingly greater life the man was exhibiting and she realized that she was totally unprepared to fully deal with it.

Finally, she reached out and put her hand on the man's shoulder. "God be with you," she whispered.

The man didn't turn, but he smiled as if seeing something he loved and lifted his hand to gently pat hers. "He is."

9

The group sat around the table in silence, digesting the information Mike and Tracy had shared in their reports and allowing it to filter through layers of normalcy to collect in a lower, darker pool of reality. The initial shock some of them had felt had given way to disgust, then sadness and finally anger. The thought that the world they once knew had so quickly devolved to this was almost more than they could comprehend, but they knew they must face it squarely on if they were to be able to deal with it.

Finally, it was Jim who spoke in a low and quiet voice. "Everyone who gave much thought to a collapse predicted this. I knew it had to be happening, but we've been able to insulate ourselves from it." He looked at the others around the table. "Now, it's come to us, and we're going to have to deal with it."

"Isn't that going a bit beyond our area of responsibility?" asked Bill.

Jim looked at Bill for a minute, surprised at his apparent change of heart. "If a young kid from down the block had come to your door before the collapse and said men were beating his mother and sister, what would you have done?"

Bill nodded. "I understand where you're headed. There are no police. But this is quite a distance from us. Is it our responsibility?"

"Is responsibility determined by distance?" Jim asked.

Bill shook his head. "No, but aren't we risking a lot going out so far? What if Stonemont is attacked while much of our fighting force is gone? What if they have more people than we think they do and we get wiped out?"

"What if we don't go?" asked Jim, pointedly.

"That's not who we are," said Kelly.

"No, it's not," said Christian.

Mike and Tom nodded, as did Tracy.

"I just wish there was another way," said Bill.

Jim nodded. "So do I, but sometimes there's not."

"So, what's the plan?" asked Tom.

Jim got up from the couch and walked to the window, looking out at the commons. "We're going to see if we can buy the women, kids and whatever men are left from Grim. Then we're going to make sure he never does it again."

He turned back to the group. "Christian, I want you to go to Mason. Tell him what we've got going on and see if any of his people would like to go with us. Then come back here. You'll be staying here with a scout squad to keep Stonemont secure."

As Christian started to argue, Jim cut him off. "I'll be leading this deal, 'cause I want to look this bastard in the eye. I need you and Kelly here to take care of things."

"Why? In case something happens to you?" Kelly asked quietly.

"Until I get back," Jim answered.

He looked at Mike. "Mike, we'll be taking all of the scouts except for the squad Christian will be keeping here and four we'll leave at Hillmont. Get them ready and tuned up. Full gear and plenty of ammo. If we have to hit them, I want it to be as hard as we can."

He looked at Tom. "I'd rather have you stay here, but I know you probably want to go. Your call."

Tom nodded. "I'll come."

"Okay." Jim looked at Kelly. "I need one of the box trucks filled with food. Make sure a lot of good stuff shows when we open it up, including plenty of beer and booze." He had another thought. "Also, throw in a bunch of clothes for the women. Just sweats and stuff. We don't know how many there are or what kind of shape they'll be in, but I can imagine. So, pack plenty and don't put it where it can be easily seen."

Kelly nodded.

"What can we do?" asked Ann.

"We need to keep the work going on the town platting, so just keep that on track, Ann. Bill, I'd like you to come with us."

Ann nodded and Bill look surprised. "Okay, Jim," he said, "though I don't know how much good I'll be."

"Every gun will help," answered Jim.

"When do we go?" asked Tom.

Jim thought for a moment. "Day after tomorrow. We'll leave about midnight that night, 'cause I want be there before sun-up."

The group broke up, each person heading back to their responsibilities or going to prepare for the trip.

Following Kelly into the kitchen, Jim poured a cup of coffee from the pot on the stovetop and walked over to look out the window.

Once again, reality had broken through the fragile cocoon in which he had hoped to shelter his family. He had to admit to himself that he had always been afraid this would happen. More honestly, he had always known it would happen. That's why he had prepared for it. Still, he wished he could have held it off a little longer.

Kelly's voice and soft touch on his back brought him back to the present. "Bill was surprised that you wanted him to go with you."

Jim nodded. "Bill is a good man, but he's sliding back into a due process, play-it-safe frame of mind because things have been fairly peaceful. That time may come again, I hope it does, but it hasn't come yet."

He took a sip of his coffee, still staring out the window. "He told me once that he felt his biggest weakness was that he didn't always recognize trouble in time. A lot of people are like that, maybe most people. Normal people. Failing to fully recognize and understand problems in time, they form committees, have meetings and think up so-called mitigation strategies that relieve them of individual responsibility rather than stepping up and actually solving the problem. I want Bill to see the problem in person. He can be a tremendous asset if he can be made to see the potential horrors that we may have to deal with. If not, I'm afraid his 'devil's advocate' positions may start to do more harm than good."

Kelly rubbed his back gently, allowing the uncharacteristic silence to last for a minute. When it seemed that Jim wasn't going to say anything more, she quietly asked "What are you thinking about?"

He was silent for a moment, then set his coffee cup down. "You didn't know me in my previous life. You may not have wanted to."

"I don't believe that," she said softly, looking up at him.

He turned toward her. "That's because you don't know everything about me."

He looked at her for a moment before continuing, not wanting to say what he knew he had to, not wanting to allow even the words of his past to taint his present life.

"Long before I met you, I did a kind of work that made it necessary for those of us who did it to suspend normal human feelings and many moral constraints. It was beyond what normal people could understand, and the psychic cost to those who did it was very high."

He turned to look out the window again, staring into the distance as if into another dimension. "I reached a point where human life meant very little to me, including my own, and I finally broke and asked a God I could barely remember to either cure me or kill me because a life without feeling was not worth living."

He paused a moment before continuing. "Apparently, he thought I was worth curing, because I slowly started to feel again. It took fifteen long years before I was able to really function again in what people call polite society. I cut all ties to my previous life, essentially disappeared from everyone who had known me, and slowly learned how to live again in a world I had forgotten how to understand." He shook his head. "To be honest, I never was able to fully reintegrate, though I did become able to function in society again."

He turned back to her and saw that she was listening to him intently. "Over the next five years, I rediscovered the principles and values I had been raised with and came to better understand their worth and importance because of the years I had spent ignoring and violating them. Then I met you."

He smiled. "At first, I tried to deny it, but, when I realized that I loved you, and you apparently loved me, I figured that God had yet another strange plan that I didn't understand so I'd better go along with it. Since then, I've had a more wonderful life than I ever could have imagined. I want you to know that. You and the kids are everything to me, and the idea that the man I was thirty years ago could someday have the life I have now is unbelievable to me."

Kelly started to say something, but he stopped her.

"Wait," he said, putting his finger to her lips. "The reason I'm telling you this is because you asked me what I was thinking, and I want you to know. In order for me to do what I have to do to keep us safe, I'm worried that some of that man is going to come back. I don't want him to, but I'm afraid he might, and I'm worried that it's going to affect how you and the kids feel about me."

He looked at her intently. "I don't want to lose any part of you and the kids, but I know that to ensure your safety I might. That's what I'm thinking about."

Kelly looked up at him, waiting to see if he was done. When he didn't continue, she stretched up and kissed him, then held his face between her hands. "Whatever you do, whatever you have to do, you will never lose any part of me or the kids. And if I had known you back then, I would have loved you back then too."

He looked at her, studying her, then nodded. "You're alright, you know that?"

She kissed him again, longer this time, then pulled away and smiled. "Yeah. So are you."

10

Jim stood on the steps of the main hall and looked out over the crowd of those who would be going with them. Twenty scouts made up the core of the group, along with himself, Mike, Tom and Bill. Mason Booker had brought over thirty Vikings, Naomi had brought about two dozen men from School Center and about twenty more had come from Hillmont and Redemption. It was more than he had anticipated - much more.

He watched the crowd as it started to quiet and thought about what must be going through their minds right now. The Vikings had a code of brotherhood and honor that had brought them to join Stonemont in what they felt to be a just cause. Ever since they had brought Mason and Bonnie's son Austin to be treated for his knife wound, the Vikings had been like family. Some of the men whose daughters, sisters and girlfriends had been victimized at the school by Elvin Barnes and his men had also been eager to come, their own experience causing them to feel a responsibility to others in need, as well as their feeling of indebtedness to Stonemont for freeing their loved ones. Those from Redemption and Hillmont felt a similar indebtedness.

As the crowd quieted, he picked out individual faces. Regardless of the motivations off the different groups, he knew that each person had their own reasons, their own story, their own fears and their own hopes for what lay ahead. At this moment, those differences were put aside and a common purpose melded them into a unified force that would attempt to satisfy the personal desires by serving the common need. Such, he knew, was the genesis of many great endeavors, and not a few defeats, throughout history. The result of this union would be known soon enough, even if it's longer term manifestation might not be seen for some time, and he felt a need to implant the moment in his mind.

Seeing the crowd now quiet and looking at him, he spoke with a voice loud enough to carry to those at the farthest fringe.

"Welcome, friends!" he shouted, and was answered with applause and a few yells.

"Thanks for coming!"

THE REVIVAL

A louder round of applause came in answer.

"We've been together before, helping each other through some tough times, and have emerged as a community of communities dedicated to mutual assistance and support."

A still louder round of applause filled the commons.

"Now, a group outside our circle needs our help. You all know the situation. If we are to be able to establish a safe area in which to live and raise our families, we need to meet and defeat these threats as they come. Beyond that, humanity and morality demand that we take action in this case.

"Your leaders have given you the details of the situation and will give you details of the operation before we make our final approach in the morning. Right now, I want to tell you the basics."

He paused, seeing that everyone was paying attention, then continued.

"We have about two hours of daylight left, during which we will travel to a position about a mile from our objective. We will be travelling quickly on the main streets in order to get there by sundown and outrun any of their recon teams that may see us. We know that their recon is on foot and normally do not operate at night. Sucks for them, good for us.

"Once we reach the staging area, we will deploy a rear sentry line to detect and secure any of their recon who might have seen us and are trying to get back to warn their main body. Sentries will rotate so that everyone can get some sleep.

"About two hours before sunrise, a squad of our scouts, along with those of you from school center, will advance to the objective and assume positions on the hills overlooking the building. You will have clear fields of fire on both sides and the rear of the building. The squad leader will report the situation back to us by radio.

"At the same time, a full scout team, reinforced with some of you from Hillmont and Redemption, will advance to positions in the tree line across from the front entrances of the building. They will hold at this point and the team leader will keep us apprised of the situation by radio."

He looked around the crowd. "Everybody with me so far?"

Nods and "yos" told him they were.

"Very good. The rest of us, including the Vikings, will drive to the objective, arriving at the front of the building at first light. We will be loud and we will move fast, attempting to provide a bit of confusion to the hopefully sleepy and sleeping defenders.

THE REVIVAL

"Your group leaders will provide specifics to you regarding your particular role and function. Make sure you understand and ask questions if you need to. Any questions for me now?"

Silence told him there were none.

"Alright, let's mount up."

They loaded into the vehicles that would be taking them to their objective, scouts on dirt bikes taking point followed by two older club cab pickups carrying more scouts, Jim's Excursion with Mike, Tom, Bill, Tracy and Naomi, a box truck, a semi parked outside of the entry gate and the Vikings bringing up the rear, the thunder of their Harleys starting up almost shaking the ground.

Slowly, the convoy snaked through the gate and onto the approach road, the eagerness of those in it to get underway balanced by the trepidation of their families who waved and shouted words of love and support as they passed.

As the semi pulled into place, the column moved up the road, slalomed through the bollards at the contact gate and gathered speed.

They passed the town-site, then Church Crossing several minutes later, turned east to 69 Highway, then north towards the city.

The countryside looked peaceful in the evening light, the fresh snow making the fields look like sugared cereal and the darker grey of houses, barns and trees standing out starkly against it.

Having been mostly blown off the elevated roadway by the wind, the light dusting of snow that remained gave little hindrance to the vehicles and within half an hour they were entering the suburbs.

The scout bikes on point increased their lead distance ahead of the main body of the convoy as they entered the more congested area and they were soon approaching their staging area, a large church on a hill commanding a view of the area approaching their objective.

As the lead scouts ascended the road to the church, the pickups dropped additional scouts off to approach and clear the church on foot. The semi stopped on the main street and off-loaded the volunteers from School Center, Hillmont and Redemption, who also made their way up the hill on foot.

It took less than ten minutes for the scouts to clear the church and the leader to signal for the remaining vehicles to approach, and another ten to dispatch sentries. Scouts and volunteers assembled in the sanctuary, breaking out cold meals and readying sleeping positions while Jim led Mike, Tom, Bill, Mason and Tracy into what appeared to have been the minister's office.

THE REVIVAL

Closing the shutters on the window, Jim took a small LED light out of his pocket, turned it on and set it on the desk. The small light cast macabre shadows and made the group look like resistance partisans in an old movie. "Let's all grab a seat," he said.

They had talked little on the way, the gravity of their mission precluding small talk, but each had been thinking about the situation privately. Now, sitting as a group and waiting to move on their target, their individual thoughts again returned to concentration on a common purpose.

"Anybody have any last-minute questions, comments or suggestions?" Jim asked.

The group was silent for a moment, until Mike spoke. "Yeah. Why not let me take point on this one, Jim? This thing could go south in a hurry and you've got young kids."

"I agree," said Tom. "Mike's fully capable. Or me, for that matter."

Jim shook his head, looking at Mike. "I know you are, but not this time." He looked at Tom. "You both have a military bearing. If he's former military like they say, he's going to feel comfortable with that. It might also put him on higher alert. I don't want him to feel comfortable. If anything, I want him to feel superior so his finger will be off the trigger, so to speak. But thanks."

Both men remained silent, not liking it but knowing that further discussion was pointless.

Jim turned to Bill. "You asked me why I wanted you to come."

Bill nodded.

"You are going to be the judge."

"The judge?" Bill asked, seeming confused.

Jim nodded. "We're not marauders, and we're not conquerors. Our actions will be just, as well as guided by moral obligation. We don't know exactly what we're going to find when we get there, though I think we have a pretty good idea. And we don't know if they'll just hand over all the captives or not." He paused, looking around the group. "If they don't put up a fight, or if they do and some survive, they'll have to answer for what they've done."

He looked back at Bill. "Their crimes may include kidnapping, false imprisonment, rape, torture, premeditated murder and cannibalism. I want you to decide sentencing."

Bill looked at Jim, stunned. Although he had executed two men who had attacked his family shortly after the collapse, his function since arriving at Stonemont had mostly been to assist others as he could. His expertise as a lawyer and judge had almost been forgotten in favor of his simple ability to help others in their jobs. Now, he was being called upon to decide the fates of people who may have committed the most heinous crimes imaginable.

The months at Stonemont made his legal career seem far in the distant past, obscured by the more recent and far more basic life of rebuilding a livable community. Additionally, it had been Jim who had addressed any problems and dispensed what justice needed to be handed out. Now, Jim was asking him to return to his former role of judge - to determine the guilt or innocence of his fellow man and decide the punishment for the crimes of those found guilty.

He thought back to the day he had executed the men who had attacked him and his family, to his realization that he had lived by and relied on a legal system that he knew had become corrupt and to his personal shame that he had been a part of the legal mechanism which had repeatedly turned out men like those who had tried to destroy his family because that was simply the way the system had come to work. It had been a comfortable, if occasionally frustrating, existence, resting in the legal hammock of precedents and judicial restrictions that so often insulated him from the responsibility of personal judgement in cases of horrible actions. Yet, that was the way the justice system had been designed in order to provide the impartiality that was necessary to ensure equality under the law.

Or had it? Had it been designed that way, or had it devolved from its original design in order to accommodate a gradual yet continual decline in societal standards of behavior and expectation?

Suddenly, he remembered something he had asked his first-year law students to do on their first day - to describe Lady Justice. Almost all mentioned her blindfold. Most mentioned the scales she held. Very few, however, mentioned the sword she also held, the symbol of her authority and the promise that her justice could be swift and final.

He admitted to himself that, in the years before the collapse, he had often seen the blindfold askew, the scales unbalanced and the sword either withheld or improperly applied. The corruption of the old world had made that possible. The promise of a new world made that anathema.

He nodded solemnly. "Okay."

Jim nodded back. "Good. Now, let's all get some sleep."

11

Jim stood looking out the window when the sentry came in to wake them. He had never been able to sleep before a major operation and had never envied those who could. Major tasks often brought major changes in situations and people, and wakefulness was his way to fully prepare for and experience both the task and the transition.

He wasn't looking toward their objective to the north, but to the south, toward Stonemont. He thought about Kelly, Aedan, Brody and Morgan, hopefully fast asleep and snuggled warmly in their beds, dreaming of things far removed from the dangers of the world around them.

He imagined them suffering the horrors of a situation like the one he and the others would deal with today, and the thought inflamed him, focusing his mind on the job ahead with new intensity. The evil that men were capable of had once amazed him. That amazement was eventually tempered to acceptance, and his amazement came to be directed at the willingness of people to overlook and ignore the atrocities happening all around them unless it touched them personally. Man's inhumanity to man had become a social norm masked with a smiley face.

"We're ready, Jim," said Tom, coming up behind him.

He remained still, holding on to the thoughts of those he loved most in the world for just a moment longer, knowing that this might be the last time he would be able to think of them without a new layer of horror clouding his mind. He held them hard in his mind for a moment longer, then allowed them to retreat back to their dreams of a safer world and turned. "Okay, let's go."

He didn't know that Kelly had just awakened to the sound of his voice calling her name.

Kelly startled to wakefulness at the sound of Jim's voice. "Are you back already?" she asked sleepily, turning over toward his side of the bed. "Is something wrong?"

He didn't answer, so she reached out to touch him but found he wasn't there.

"Honey?" she said, fumbling for the light on her side. "Is everything alright?"

Her fingers found the switch and turned on the lamp. "What's wrong?" she asked, again turning toward his side.

The empty room confused her. He had just spoken to her, calling her by name, but the blanket on his side was undisturbed and no other light was on.

She swung her feet to the floor, a developing sense of dread causing her to move more quickly and clumsily than normal as she got to her feet and walked around the bed toward the master bathroom. No lights were on, and when she flipped the light switch she saw he wasn't there.

Not wanting to wake the kids, she picked up the flashlight Jim always kept on his side of the bed and walked to the bedroom door. Opening it quietly, she stepped out into the hallway and shined the flashlight down the hallway.

Nothing.

Making her way down the hall, she came to the stairway and descended to the family room. The nightlights in each of the first-floor rooms gave off a soft glow, allowing her to see without the flashlight, so she turned it off.

"Honey?" she called quietly, walking into the empty kitchen.

"Is everything okay, mom?" Aedan asked from behind her.

Kelly's breath caught and her heart raced at the surprise of Aedan's voice. She turned to see him standing at the door of the kitchen, a flashlight in one hand and his rifle in the other. He had grown so much he almost looked like a man standing there. The sight of the rifle in his hand gave her a mixed feeling of pride and regret - pride that he was growing into such a strong, responsible young man and regret that his childhood years were slipping away so quickly. She nodded. "I thought I heard daddy's voice."

Aedan walked into the kitchen and over to the windows looking out over the commons. It had started snowing again and the roof of the central hall was starting to turn white. "Dad said he'd be back in a couple of days. You must have been dreaming."

Kelly gave a small nod and joined him at the window looking out at the snow. "Maybe."

"You know what this reminds me of?" asked Aedan.

"What?" she asked, putting her arm around his shoulders.

"The first campout we went on with Brody's Cub Scout pack. Remember?"

Kelly groaned and gave a shiver. "Oh, it was so cold."

Aedan chuckled. "And you and dad didn't get any sleep at all and still drove us to Iowa the next day to get the kittens."

Kelly smiled. "Yes, I remember."

"I always wondered, why did dad always call it BF Iowa?"

Kelly gave a small laugh. "I'll tell you when you're older. Or maybe daddy will."

Aedan looked her sideways. "Are you keeping a list?"

"Of what?"

"Of all those things you're going to tell me when I'm older. I'm afraid you're going to forget some."

Kelly smiled. "Don't worry, you're going to know everything soon enough." She paused and sighed. "And then you'll know too much."

"Dad says I already know too much."

She glanced over at him, noticing something different. "That's not your rifle."

Aedan looked down at the AR-15 in his hand. "Dad gave it to me before he left. He said I'd earned it and had shown I could handle it."

She nodded slowly, then looked back at his face, realizing for the first time that she was looking slightly up at him instead of down. "When did you start calling us mom and dad instead of mommy and daddy?"

He smiled a bit self-consciously. "Just now, I guess. I hadn't noticed."

Kelly quickly pressed her fingers against her mouth, stifling a sound that threatened to announce the tears that had suddenly sprung to her eyes.

Aedan looked at her. "Dad's going to be okay, mom. He can take care of himself."

Kelly tried to reply, but her clamped teeth wouldn't relax and her tears blurred her vision of him. She nodded jerkily.

"Do you want to go back upstairs?" Aedan asked.

Still unable to speak, she shook her head.

Aedan nodded, set the flashlight on the counter and put his arm around her. "Okay. I'll stay here with you."

12

Dalton Coates wasn't sure what the noise was at first. Months without mechanical noise had sharpened his hearing but made him forget what certain sounds were, so it took him a couple of minutes for him to identify it. Motorcycles.

"Hooter!" he called to his partner who was returning from a large pile of lumber carrying scraps for the barrel. "You hear that?"

The other man grunted, throwing a chunk of lumber into the barrel. "What?"

"Sounds like motorcycles."

Hooter grunted again. "You're hearin' things."

Dalton cocked his head. "Yeah, I'm hearin' bikes."

"Bull. You ain't hearin' ..." he paused as he heard the sound himself and looked around. "Hogs."

"Sounds like a few of them," said Dalton.

Hooter nodded his head, trying to determine the direction of the sound. "Yeah, quite a few."

"Where do you think they are? Do you think they're coming here?"

"Shut up."

"Maybe it's some of your club. Maybe they can get us out of here."

"I said shut up." Hooter walked away from the barrel and looked out into the dark grey light of pre-dawn. He wished it was some of his old club, but he could hardly hope for that. Still, if it was a similar group, maybe he could latch onto them and get away from this bunch of psychos. Of course, depending on what kind of group it was, he might find himself in the middle of a turf war, never good if you were the one standing in the middle of a parking lot being lit up by a fire barrel and holding an old shotgun with only two shells in it. He'd have to be careful.

The sound of the engines got louder and he saw the flicker of what looked like headlights turning a corner toward them several hundred yards away.

"Hooter!" called Dalton. "Should I go tell Grim?"

THE REVIVAL

"Shut up and stay put," Hooter growled. If there were enough bikes to stand against Grim, and he could talk to them before Grim came out, he just might jump teams before the game started.

More headlights turned the corner following the first two. He counted ten. Not enough.

"Go tell Grim," he said over his shoulder. He'd stay with the biggest team, at least for now.

Dalton left the barrel and ran to the barricaded entrance. "Motorcycles coming down the road!" he yelled to the guards behind the barricade.

"We see 'em, asshole," replied a guard.

"We gotta tell Grim!" shouted Dalton.

The guard scoffed at Dalton. "We'll tell Grim. You get back to your barrel."

"We're sittin' ducks out here," yelled Dalton. "We gotta come in there with you!"

The guard levelled his rifle at Dalton. "You're a sittin' duck for me right now. Now get back to your barrel. I ain't gonna tell you again."

Dalton stood still. He had long suspected it would come to this, being hung out to dry by Grim's inner circle, but he had never had the guts to call them on it or leave and try to make it on his own. Being with Grim, even as a lower-level member, had at least been safe. And he had eaten, even if he didn't like to think about some of the things he ate. Now, he was standing in the parking lot, exposed and lit up by the burn barrel, holding a .22 rifle with six cartridges in it and being denied the safety of the barricade just a few feet away. He, Hooter and the other pair of sentries were SOL for sure if trouble started and *'sucks to be me'* ran through his head as he turned back to see the motorcycles coming closer, led by a box truck.

Jim drove the truck slowly toward the building, not wanting to invite fire by coming in too fast and wanting to give the sentries time to get Grim to the door to control his side of things. By coming in slow, they would avoid looking like an attacking force and more like traders, if bikers on Harleys could look like traders. But they were the first display of muscle to open the gambit, and this play and the subsequent moves would determine how it turned out.

He realized that his old focus had returned, that unusual hyper-awareness that manifested in the almost three-hundred-sixty-degree organic consciousness he had always gotten at the beginning of an operation. All thoughts outside the immediate situation were gone as he turned the truck toward the building, flashed his lights in what was meant to seem a friendly arrival signal, then button-hooked the truck to expose the back of it to the building and stopped about a hundred feet out from the west entrance - the entrance outside which Dalton and Hooter were positioned. Coming to a stop, he turned off the lights and shut off the engine.

"Ready?" he asked, watching the sentries and entrance in the driver side mirror.

"Ready," answered Mason, watching the same scene in his mirror.

"Let's go."

Both opened their doors and stepped out of the truck as the Harleys pulled in to bracket them, five on each side and spaced about five yards apart. The bikes shut down and the ensuing silence seemed to be even more complete than before they arrived.

Dalton and Hooter watched as a massive biker and a man wearing a cowboy hat walked to the back of the truck. The biker unlatched the rear door and rolled it up, revealing boxes stacked to the ceiling. They expected the biker to say something, but, surprisingly, it was the man in the hat who spoke.

"Howdy," said Jim.

Dalton looked at Hooter, who was studying the two men at the truck and the other bikers. They were a hard-looking bunch, but none of them looked familiar and they weren't wearing colors.

"Hey," answered Hooter.

"Grim around?" asked Jim.

"I imagine he's comin'," answered Hooter. "Wha-du-ya got in there?"

Jim turned toward the boxes in the truck, making sure his flashlight lit up the cases of beer and whisky. "Well, we've got beans, corn, Spam, spaghetti and cans of just about anything you'd want. Oh yeah, and some beer and liquor."

"You bringin' it to us?" Dalton asked excitedly.

Jim shrugged. "Well, we're bringin' it here. Whether we're bringin' it to you depends."

Something didn't feel right about this to Hooter. Why would these guys just show up from out of nowhere with a truck full if food and booze? And why so early in the morning. It didn't make sense. "Depends on what?" he asked.

"On whether you have what we want in return," Jim answered.

"What do you want?"

"Women."

Hooter looked at Dalton, then at Jim and then at Mason. "Who are you?"

THE REVIVAL

"Just guys looking for women," answered Mason.

Hooter shook his head. "What club are you? You ain't showing colors, but I can tell."

"Vikings," Mason answered.

Hooter nodded slowly. "Yeah, I heard of you."

"Do you have women?" asked Mason pointedly.

Hooter looked up and down the row of bikes. "Is this all there is of you?"

"Why? You think we need more?"

"We got some women," said Dalton. "Maybe Grim would let you have a few for this truck."

"Shut up, asshole," said Hooter as he watched Jim and Mason warily.

"Stand down!" yelled a voice from the entrance as several men emerged from behind the barricade.

Jim watched as the men approached. The man leading the way was big. Not as big as Mason, but impressive none-the-less. A long black beard hung below a hard face with cold eyes set in a shaved head. Lightning bolt tattoos showed on each side of his scalp, with an open eye in the middle of his forehead. A long black leather coat hung from his wide shoulders, huge tattooed hands emerging from the sleeves.

The man moved toward them, bracketed by two men on each side of him with rifles. His eyes shifted between Jim and Mason, finally settling on Jim.

"Who are you?" he demanded in a low, gravelly voice.

Jim looked into the cold eyes. The man was a killer, but smart. He had hoped the man would focus more on Mason because of Mason's size, but the man had correctly identified Jim as the leader. "I'm Jim Wyatt. Who are you?"

The man raised his chin a bit, his lips moving into a half-sneer. "I'm Grim. What do you want?"

Jim looked at him calmly. "Women. I hear you have some."

Grim looked at Jim coldy, glanced at Mason, then looked back at Jim. "What's with the hat?"

Jim smiled. "It's my hat. I like it."

"I don't like it."

Jim knew this game well. "Then I won't make you wear it."

Grim's eyes narrowed at the response. He scanned the Vikings sitting on their bikes. "This all you got?"

"No. Do you have women or not?"

Grim looked at Jim, then at the back of the truck, ignoring the question. "What'a ya got in there?"

"Food and liquor to trade for women," Jim answered. "What have you got?"

Grim looked at Jim. "I've got some women. Maybe I'll let you borrow a couple in exchange for what you got in the truck."

Jim shook his head. "I'm not interested in borrowing. I'm buying."

Grim rolled his head as if loosening up his neck. "You ain't got the guys to be callin' shots. I'll take what I want and you'll take what I give you. I figure I'll let you borrow a couple of the older ones for what you've brought me. Say, for a week."

"Mason?" Jim said, continuing to watch Grim.

Mason raised his left arm straight up and the sound of motorcycles starting up came from the corner around which the first ones had arrived. In a few seconds, the first headlight appeared, then another and another. Within a minute, twenty more motorcycles had entered the large parking lot forming a half-circle around the front of the building and the men standing in front of it. As each motorcycle reached its position, its rider swung it broadside to the men, shut of the engine and dismounted, taking position behind it and training a rifle on Grim and his men. The original ten riders followed suit.

Grim looked around at the ring of rifles pointing at him. His eyes flickered and the muscle in his jaw jumped. "I got more guys inside. More guys than you. You're exposed out here."

"So are you."

Grim looked at Jim. The guy didn't have the animalistic look that most people did lately. In fact, it looked like he had been living pretty well. Probably soft, though he didn't seem scared. Maybe he could take the truck from this cowboy, but a lot of people might get hurt, including him. It would be easier to make a trade. "I'll give you two women for what's in the truck."

Jim acted like he was considering the offer, then shook his head. "No, I want them all."

Grim's brow furrowed as if he wasn't sure he'd heard right. "What do you mean you want them all?"

"I want them all," Jim repeated. "Every last one of them. And I want you to have your people bring them out to me. Right now."

Grim's eyes widened and he started to say something when Jim raised his left arm straight in the air.

Without taking his eyes off Grim, Jim spoke to the man on Grim's right. "You in the purple jacket. Tell your boss what you see on the right side of his head."

THE REVIVAL

The man looked at Grim. "There's a red dot kinda' dancin' around on your head, general."

"General?" Jim chuckled. "You call yourself general, huh? I knew a couple of generals, and you don't look much like them. I'd say more like general population. Right?"

Grim glared at him but remained silent, trying to think what his play should be.

"That's one of our snipers putting that dot on your head, General Population," said Jim. "I've seen him shoot, and he can knock the freckles off a flea." With his right hand, he pointed to the man on Grim's immediate left. "Your turn. Tell General Population what you see on the other side of his head."

"Same here, gen..., er, boss," the man said, recognizing a change in things. "There's a little red dot flittin' around your ear."

"That's another sniper," said Jim. "I think he's better than the first, but that's just my opinion. They argue about it. If my arm comes down quickly, whether by me dropping it or me falling, your head will explode. Then, your men will start dropping where they stand, and then we will go in and kill the rest and take what we want. The alternative is that your men here start unloading this truck and some of your other men bring the women out to us. All of them. Now."

Grim's building rage at the cowboy's disrespect and demands was beginning to make his head hot and his body tremble. The same mind-body separation that used to happen to him in the yard when there was work to be done began, and, though it made him feel invincible, it kept him from noticing the cowboy's right hand slip inside his coat.

Jim could see the rage building in Grim as the big man's fists started clenching. The man was beyond talking, and his eyes held a bloodlust Jim had seen before.

Jim raised the .45 government model in his right hand and aimed it at Grim's chest. "You other men," he said loudly. "I think your boss is about to make me kill him. When I do, you can either raise your weapons and die or keep your weapons down and live a little longer. Your choice."

Mason brought his AR to his shoulder, slowly sweeping the men behind Grim.

Grim's mind was becoming non-functional. He was a boss, beholden to no one. He ruled harshly and enjoyed the fear, even terror, he instilled in those under his control. There was nothing he could not do, nothing he could not have. And now this punk in a cowboy hat thought he was going to take it from him. He knew he could get to the man before the snipers could react and fire. And he knew that he would kill the man. What would happen after that they would just have to see.

The mental separation complete, his rage exploded beyond control and he launched himself forward. His movement was so fast neither sniper would have been able to hit him, but the flame coming out of the gun in the man's hand preceded a punch he felt in his chest. Then another and another. And another and another.

He had only taken a few steps, but he was suddenly tired, his legs were weak and it was hard to breath. He stopped, feeling heavy, his head spinning like it did after a night of drinking. Something was pulling him down and he felt one of his knees touch the ground. He suddenly felt cold and he wasn't able to raise his arms. A thought flashed across his mind of a dog running across a yard. Then a woman's face. Then he fell forward into the darkness.

Jim caught the whiff of expended gunpowder as he shifted the pistol to the man standing to Grim's left and now added his second hand for a better grip. He only had three rounds left, but he knew that Mason was also covering them and they were aware of the snipers on both flanks. "Your choice," he said, his words sounding muffled and hollow to him after the concussive effect of the gunfire on his eardrums.

The men had not raised their rifles, and now the one at whom Jim was aiming slowly lowered his to the ground, stepping away from it. The other three followed suit.

"You men at the barrels!" Jim shouted. "Lay your weapons on the ground, take five steps forward and get face down on the ground."

The sentries complied. They weren't sure what was happening, but Grim was down, maybe dead, and, since the intruders didn't continue to fire, the vacuum of leadership didn't lend itself to further individual resistance.

Jim pumped his left arm twice and the scouts moved down from the embankments led by Mike and Tom, a pre-determined number of volunteers remaining on the hills to continue surveillance of the surrounding area. A wave of his arm then brought the volunteers forward from the tree line to set up a perimeter as the scouts prepared to enter the building.

With Mason covering the sentries, Jim removed the partially expended magazine from his pistol, replaced it with a full magazine and re-holstered. He returned to the truck, pulled out his AR and returned to Mason as Mike and Tom approached.

"How many more inside?" Jim asked the sentries.

THE REVIVAL

When none of them answered, Jim leveled his rifle at the one he had previously pointed his pistol at. "You're next. How many?"

The sentry glanced at another sentry then looked back at Jim. "I'm not sure. About twenty."

Jim shifted his rifle to the sentry the first one had glanced at. "That right?"

The second sentry hesitated. "Yeah," he said, glancing at the first. "About that."

Jim kept his rifle on the sentry. "You're staking your life on it. If we go in there and find more, you're both going to die. You want to change your answer?"

The sentry glanced furtively around. "Maybe thirty, I'm not sure."

"We heard there were more of you."

"Some of our guys went out a couple of days ago," said the first sentry. "They haven't come back."

Jim watched them for a minute, then lowered his rifle. "You and you," he pointed at the two sentries he hadn't spoken to, "start unloading this truck. Put everything on the ground except the beer and liquor. That stays in the truck."

The two sentries got up, walked to the truck and started unloading it while being watched by Mason. Scouts picked up their weapons along with the weapons of the first two and the barrel guards, frisking each for more weapons and finding none.

"Now, you two" Jim pointed at the sentries he had spoken to before, "are going to lead us into the building. You are going to call the rest of your people out, telling them that Grim is dead and there's a truckload of food out here for them."

The sentries looked at each other.

"You seem to be checking with each other," said Jim, raising his rifle again. "Bad idea. You do what I tell you, when I tell you, or I don't need you. Decide fast."

One nodded and the other said "Okay."

"Good," said Jim, motioning toward the building with the muzzle if his rifle. "Let's go."

"Jim," said Mike.

Jim lowered his rifle and turned toward Mike.

Mike cocked his head to the side. "A minute?"

Jim nodded and walked several yards away with Mike.

"Let me do this," said Mike, quietly. "I've done it a hundred times. It's what I'm trained for."

101

"He's right, Jim," Tom said as he walked up to them. "He's your head of scouts and the right man for the job." He thought for a moment before continuing. "You can't keep taking point."

Jim gave a wry smile. "You think I'm getting too old?"

Tom shook his head. "It's not that. Things can happen. You've got young kids. They need you." He paused for a moment. "We need you. Mike can do this job, but he can't do all the other things you do and neither can the rest of us. You've got to start protecting yourself, for everyone's sake."

Jim looked at Tom, then at Mike, then back to Tom. He knew they were right. He had stayed in the action because he wanted to, because he enjoyed it. Hell, he was starting to love it again, just like he had thirty years before. But that was selfish. He thought again of Kelly and the kids. The kids needed him around longer, and, like Tom had said, things happen. He slowly nodded his head, knowing they were right and knowing that his next words would close one chapter of his life and open a new one. "Okay." He looked at Mike. "It's all yours, buddy. Show us how it's done."

Mike nodded, turned away and gave a whistle and rally sign for the scouts to form on him.

"Sucks, doesn't it?" said Tom, remembering when he had been pulled out of the field and into an office.

Jim smiled and gave a small nod. "It's the way of the world. I was getting to like this stuff too much again, anyway. Need to let the young studs have their day." He turned to Tom. "Guess I'll just stand here and watch you guys do all the work."

Tom chuckled. "Whatever you say, boss," he said, walking away to prepare to either back Mike up or receive more prisoners.

Mike looked around at the scouts and volunteers around him. "Okay, you know the deal. We'll give them a chance to come to us. That's the easiest and safest way. After we think everyone's out who's going to come out, we'll go in. We'll consider it a rescue with active resistance because we can't trust that they will all come forward - if any come forward at all.

"Scouts will be entering the east door while volunteers remain outside the west door to meet any who try to exit there. Volunteers are already at the back doors."

He looked at the different leaders. "I'm assuming this is set up like their other stores. We'll be going in with four pods. Alpha and Bravo combine to go down the center toward the back. Charlie, take the left wall, and Delta take the right, staying one aisle behind Alpha and Bravo as they move toward the back so that you won't be in line of any shots they have to take."

The scouts nodded in understanding.

"ROE?" asked one pod leader.

Mike nodded. "Rules of engagement. Take out anyone who fires or points a weapon at you. Anyone holding a weapon, order them to drop it. If they don't immediately comply, drop them."

"What if they surrender?" asked another pod leader.

"Put them on the floor, secure their weapon and zip-tie them. Some of the intelligence people will be behind you to take them out."

He paused to see if there were any more questions, but the group was silent. "Okay, now the big one - captives. We don't know what we're going to find, what shape they'll be in or how they'll respond to us. Don't expect them to recognize us as rescuers at first. They will be in all kinds of psychological shape and will probably see us as just another group of predators they need to fear. Do not approach them until we establish a secure area and Tracy has had a chance to talk to them first. If you do approach them later, do so gently but carefully. There's no way to know what their reaction will be. Other than that, we're entering a big black hole of unknowns. Stay alert and be careful. Any questions?"

Silence told him there were none.

"You first," Mike pointed to the sentries who had been selected to enter the building, then at the entrance.

The fact that they had received no fire since Jim had killed Grim seemed to indicate that those who remained inside were not anxious to fight. That figured. Grim didn't seem the kind of man that inspired loyalty out of respect, and those who followed out of fear rarely continued the fight when the source of their fear was gone.

"Why us?" asked one of the guards.

Mike brought his rifle to his shoulder. "If you don't want to go, I'll pick two who want to live."

"No!" yelled the other. "We'll go. We'll go!"

Mike nodded. "Then go."

Mike followed the sentries through the entrance and into the building, followed by Alpha and Bravo pods, which fanned out behind him. The sun had just cleared the horizon and the indirect light through the numerous skylights gave the inside of the building a grey look. The place was a mess. An acrid, nauseating smell permeated the air and he avoided thinking about its source. "Go ahead," he said. "Make your announcement."

One of the sentries looked back at Mike, then turned back to the interior of the building. "Rocco!" he yelled. "It's Dog! Can you hear me?"

A moment passed before a hollow sounding voice from the rear of the building answered. "I hear you."

"Grim's dead! There's a bunch of guys out here with good weapons, not shit like we got. They brought a truckload of food to trade for the women."

There was no response.

"Rocco! You hear me?"

Another moment passed. "I hear you. We're talkin'."

"There's not much to talk about!" yelled Dog. "They say if everybody doesn't come out they're going to come in and kill everyone! And they can do it, Rocco, I promise you!"

"How are you so sure they'll give us the food, then?"

"Our guys are already unloadin' the truck!"

Another moment passed before Rocco asked, "And they just want the women?"

"Yeah!" yelled Dog. "And you ought to see the food, man!"

"Why do they want the women?" Rocco asked.

"Hell, Rocco, why do you think? Haven't we used them enough? They ain't worth much anymore! But you ought to see the food, man! And liquor!"

Another moment passed as Rocco thought about it. Things hadn't been that good with Grim. They might have been surviving, but the man had been a psycho, and surviving his way had been nothing like Rocco would ever have imagined before. If this new bunch had already taken Grim out, maybe they had their shit together and Rocco could latch on for a better ride. He had been able to work his way into other groups. Maybe he could do it again "What do they want us to do?" he asked.

Mike stepped up. "All of you come to the middle aisle of the store and line up on your knees. Leave all of your weapons where you are. Anyone found with a weapon of any kind will be killed."

"Who are you?" asked Rocco.

Mike shook his head. Why did people always ask that? "I'm the guy who's going to feed you if you come out or kill you if you don't. Don't keep me waiting. My boss is not a patient man."

A minute passed before Rocco yelled "Okay, we're comin'."

"Remember what I said," yelled Mike. "Anyone found with any kind of weapon will be shot. And one more thing. You better bring everybody out. If we come in and find anyone but the women still in here, we'll come back out and kill you all. Got it?"

"Okay. We're comin'."

At Mike's signal, Charlie and Delta pods entered the building and went to their assigned side aisles, holding in the front corners to await the next move.

The sound of shuffling footsteps reached the scouts and men slowly began to appear in the center aisle.

"Hands on top of your heads and on your knees!" Mike ordered.

The men complied, though slowly. They were a rag-tag group, dirty and disheveled. Their clothes hung from them loosely and sunken eyes showed a feral combination of fear and ferocity. Several moved with a jerkiness and uncoordination that could have been the result of injuries and malnutrition, but also resembled the effects of kuru, a disease Mike had seen on a rotation through New Guinea where cannibalism was still practiced. The bad smell increased with the arrival of the group.

Mike counted twenty-six. "This all of you?"

"Yeah," answered a man in front with the voice of Rocco.

Mike leveled his rifle at him. "You sure? Think real hard."

The man nodded his head.

"Okay," said Mike, "you know what happens if you're lying." He swept the group with rifle. "Everybody listen real good. Do exactly as I say, when I say it. Everybody lean forward, lay on the ground, cross your wrists behind your back and cross your ankles."

It took a minute for the group to get down and positioned because of the cramped space in the aisle.

"Now, look away from me and stay that way. Do not talk. If you move or try to communicate with each other I will assume you are trying to organize an escape and I will shoot you. If you understand, remain quiet."

The group remained silent.

"Outstanding. One by one, you will be flex-cuffed and taken outside for processing. Remain quiet and be cooperative. If you don't, you will be shot."

Mike stepped back as scouts from Alpha started working from the outside of the group, flex-cuffing the prisoners, getting them on their feet and handing them off to Bravo to take to the intelligence people at the front. Within fifteen minutes, all of the prisoners had been taken outside and the scouts were formed up to check the building.

Thoughts of what they were going to find was foremost in their minds and adrenaline mixed with dread caused an odd combination off anticipation and reluctance in many.

"Okay, everybody ready," said Mike. "Charlie and Delta, remember to stay one aisle back. Let's go."

THE REVIVAL

Alpha and Bravo pods started down the center aisle, clearing each side aisle as they moved. The floors were littered with things that had fallen or been knocked from their shelves and not replaced, some aisles made impassable by large items that had purposefully been thrown off of higher shelves. As they advanced farther into the building the stench increased and some of the scouts pulled their shirts up over their mouths and noses. The more experienced took out bandanas coated with menthol rub and tied them around their faces.

As they neared the rear of the store, the Charlie pod leader spoke into his mic. "We're comin' up on it."

"Any sign of life?" asked Mike.

"Not so far," responded Charlie leader.

"Okay," Mike answered. "We're coming your way. Delta, come over on our six."

"Okay, boss," responded Delta leader.

They moved carefully across the back of the store through the electrical and plumbing sections. The stench was becoming almost unbearable and a scout in Charlie pod wretched.

"Steady, everybody," said Mike. "We knew this wasn't going to be any fun."

The words were barely out of his mouth when he rounded the last shelves and stopped in his tracks.

The back corner of the building had been cleared of the normal displays, and furniture had been moved into the area. Some of it was patio furniture from the store and some of it had obviously been brought in from outside, possibly from surrounding homes. Mattresses were strewn around the area in no apparent order with blankets rolled on some and left in piles on others. A fire burned in a make-shift grill pit constructed of concrete blocks and rebar in the corner, casting heat into the room and a hellish glow up the soot-blackened walls.

Mike moved forward, scanning the mess as he approached the pit. Tools lay on the side of the pit, saws for cutting boards to feed the fire, and hatchets, pliers and smaller saws to deal with other things. A long bone devoid of meat lay on the grill, smoking as it charred from the fire beneath it, and, looking closely into the pit, he saw a metallic piece he recognized as a knee replacement device.

Turning, he saw the scouts behind him moving slowly toward the pit, looks of disbelief and horror on their faces. He let them all come closer to get

THE REVIVAL

a good look before walking over to a storage shed that had been placed against the back wall.

Carefully opening the door, he looked inside to see a mattress on the floor and personal effects neatly aligned on shelves. A lantern hung from the ceiling, illuminating the interior and a pornographic book lay opened and upside down on the unmade bed. The space was tidy and organized, obviously that of someone used to living in a small space. Grim.

"Mike!" called a scout from a row of four other sheds along the other wall.

Mike walked over to the sheds, noticing that many of the scouts were still standing at the pit. What have you got?"

"Noise from inside this one."

Mike withdrew a piece of rebar than had been placed through the pull handles and slowly opened the door. "Tracy," he said quietly, after seeing what was inside.

Tracy, still trying to process what she had seen at the pit, walked over to Mike and looked in the door he was holding open. She lifted a trembling hand to her mouth. "Oh, my god."

Billy Newton had been almost back when he heard the motorcycles. He had been coming through the houses like he always did when returning from "going out" and had just made it to the last row when he saw the truck and motorcycles turn off of the road and into the parking lot.

The rest of his crew was either dead or missing after their attack on what they had mistakenly thought was a small group of families camped together in a park had gone wrong. What they thought was going to be an easy raid had turned into a rout, then a slaughter when a group of men on horseback had descended on them out of the dark screaming and shooting. The crew had scrambled to get away from the onslaught and he had ducked into some bushes next to a small bridge where he had waited shivering until daylight when he started back to "the fort". None of the rest of the crew had shown up, and he was trying to figure out how to explain it to Duane. He was still trying to figure that out when he saw the truck and motorcycles turn into the parking lot and park, and he was starting to move through the backyard of a house toward the trees that separated the residences from the parking lot when he saw movement in the trees. People. Quite a few of them.

Billy turned around and went to the front of the house, which he entered through the front door. They had used the house as a get-away when Duane let them take one of the women to be alone. He had brought a girl named Debra here several times before Jax had taken her and killed her by mistake.

THE REVIVAL

Billy went up the stairs to the room where he had taken Debra, knowing that no one would be there because it was too cold. It had been a girl's room, and he knew Debra had liked it by the way she had looked at things and picked things up. One time, he had let her take a strip of cloth with a prayer and embroidered angels on it. She had been holding it every time he saw her after that and they had found it in her hand after Jax killed her.

He moved to a window overlooking the parking lot and saw Duane walking out, followed by some of his bodyguards. He watched as Duane talked to the men at the truck, then saw him go for the man in the cowboy hat. He heard several sharp sounds and Duane went to a knee and collapsed.

He watched, stunned, as Duane lay unmoving on the ground. His mind went blank, unable to process what had happened. Duane Hodgekins, known to others as Grim, was invincible. Nothing and nobody could stand up to him. Yet, now, he lay unmoving on the ground.

Billy turned and sat down hard on the floor. He was trembling and his breathing had become choking gasps. His mind fought for something to hold onto and he remembered the first time he had met Duane.

He had been in processing for two weeks and was being taken to population, his fear obvious to those who watched him being led to his cell by the guard. The taunts echoed in his ears and he felt his knees might give out as the guard stopped at a cell and motioned him in. The most fearsome looking man he had ever seen lay on the bottom bunk watching him.

He wanted to scream and run, but when the door clanged shut behind him the man said, "Don't worry. You're with me. Nobody will mess with you. Take the top bunk," and closed his eyes.

Duane had protected him for the next fourteen months and had never asked anything of him. He never knew why and had never asked. When the power went out and they had eventually released everyone except those on death row, he had just naturally gone with Duane, the closest thing he had ever had to an older brother and the closest he had come to loving another human being since his mother had died when he was thirteen.

Now, Duane was gone and he was alone again. Alone, confused and afraid.

He got back to knees and looked again at the parking lot. As he watched, more people came down from the hills on each side of the building, talked with the man in the cowboy hat, and took a couple of the guards inside.

He continued watching, and eventually people started coming back out. He couldn't make out who they were, then remembered the scope on his rifle. Bringing the rifle to his shoulder, he looked through the scope as saw the strangers bringing out the crew one by one, sitting them down in two rows facing away from each other. It took a while and he kept watching until he felt that all of them were out.

He kept watching as the man in the cowboy hat walked over to the crew, leaving Duane laying alone on the ground. Tears came to his eyes as he looked at Duane through the scope on the rifle Duane had given him and his hands squeezed the stock and foregrip. Duane had given him the rifle because he was a good shot. He couldn't do much else, but he could shoot.

Suddenly, he knew what he had to do. Wiping the tears from his eyes, he brought his eye down to the scope and scanned the parking lot for the man in the cowboy hat. He saw the man walking toward one of the entrances where he was met by a man and a woman.

Billy opened the window. He slowed his breathing and tried to calm himself. This was for Duane. This was for his big brother.

He found the man again and placed the cross-hairs on the man's head, but he wasn't steady enough to hold it on target. He lowered his aim to the middle of the man's upper back and held steady. His finger began putting pressure on the trigger as he pulled the rifle into his shoulder. He took a breath and let it out slowly, then another. On the third breath, he let out half, held it and pulled the trigger.

The recoil made him temporarily lose sight acquisition of the man, but he quickly regained it to see the man lying on the ground, the man and woman he had been talking to kneeling next to him and the cowboy hat rocking on the pavement several feet away.

He remembered someone saying that you should always shoot someone twice, so he brought his eye back to the scope.

It was more difficult to hold the rifle steady this time. His breathing had become ragged and his hands were trembling. He couldn't hold the scope on the man and he was crying again. Then, something Duane had told him about doing work in the yard came to him - take your shot and move away.

Somehow, remembering Duane's instruction calmed him and gave his mind the direction it needed. Taking one more look at Duane, then at the unmoving man on the ground, he rose to his feet, turned, left the house and ran.

13

Bill Garner stood at the intersection of Cob Road and West Street, his hands in his pockets, enjoying the warmth of the sun and the sound of workers preparing for the opening of the Jamestown Inn.

Cob Road had received its name because it was the road made by the trucks coming from the cob pit near the creek, and West Street from the fact that it was the street on the west side of the town square. North, South and East streets, named for which sides of the square they ran on, were still delineated by little more than wooden stakes and yellow mason line but West street was covered with newly spread pea gravel in preparation for the night's event.

The months since the raid on Grim had been tough. Kelly had become the public face of Stonemont and had held together well. He and Christian, with a lot of help from Naomi, had kept the necessary daily functions going while Mike and Tom had been working to further strengthen the security area around the Stonemont satellite communities and increase intelligence activities in the surrounding areas. Ann and the other engineers had been busy platting the town, constructing the hydroelectric plant at the creek, running the transmission lines to the town and overseeing the construction of the first building. A lot had been done, but, without Jim around, the energy was gone. People still did their jobs, but the feeling of hope and a sense of purpose had dissipated and now they seemed to work just to survive rather than grow.

He thought again how strange it was that one person could make such a difference and realized with surprise that he was having a hard time recalling the vitality, excitement and even joy of only a few months ago. He felt as if he, too, was just going through the motions, doing his best to carry out his responsibilities, but without the previous vigor that was driven by the belief that the efforts of each day were important and integral parts of a promising future. Still, life went on and it was important to keep things going, and he, like everyone else, was doing his best.

"You look like you're getting a lot accomplished, standing around with your hands in your pockets."

THE REVIVAL

Bill turned around to see Tom walking toward him. He nodded. "I was just wishing Jim was here to see this."

Tom stopped next to him, shifting his rifle from the front to hang at his right side. He looked at the scene Bill had been watching. "Yeah, me too."

"Would you ever have thought we'd be building a town?" Bill asked.

Tom gave a small smile and shook his head. "Nope. But then, I wouldn't have thought a lot of things that have happened in the last year." He paused. "Makes sense, though."

He looked at Bill. "Good thing we have your wife around to get things done while you stand around with your hands in your pockets."

Bill smiled. Ever since the raid, he and Tom, the scholar and the warrior, had been experiencing a growing friendship. The horror of what they had found, especially the condition of the women and children, had impacted everyone, but Bill's stunning sentence of death to all who had been involved in Grim's operation and Tom's direction of its implementation had created a bond between the two that transcended their former social and professional differences. "We each must do what we do best."

Tom chuckled. "I agree. Which is why I'm ready to eat."

"Did Patty tell you what's on the menu?"

Tom shook his head. "She wouldn't tell me. Said it's going to be a surprise."

Bill looked at him skeptically. "You mean that the head of our intelligence operations can't get a simple menu out of the woman he sleeps with? Why do I suddenly feel less secure than I did a minute ago?"

Tom shrugged. "She's a tough nut. But don't worry, I'm better with bad men than I am with good women."

"What about good women?" Christian asked, walking up to the pair.

"We were just wondering when you were going to find a good woman and settle down," said Tom.

"I think he's already found one but just won't admit it," said Bill.

Christian just shook his head, remaining silent.

"Actually, we were just wishing your uncle was able to be here tonight," said Bill.

"He's coming," answered Christian. "He says if he stays in the house one more day he may as well be dead, and that's not part of his plan right now."

Bill looked surprised. "Should he be out and about yet? I mean, it will be great to have him here, but is he strong enough?"

Christian shrugged. "Aedan told me that he's been exercising in secret for a while, getting his strength back. He said he's been lifting weights, walks up and down the stairs at night and has lost about twenty pounds."

"So, he's been sandbagging," said Tom, shaking his head in amusement.

Christian nodded. "Apparently. Aedan says he's been in great shape for a while but continued to use his cane and act slow when we were around."

Bill started laughing. "And Aedan told you all this?"

"Yep," Christian chuckled.

Bill looked at Tom, still laughing. "See how it's done, colonel? Maybe Christian could help you with intelligence."

"Why would he do that?" asked Tom. "Why would he play an invalid if he's back in shape?"

Christian paused, looking down for a moment then back up at the other men with a wry smile. "I know my uncle pretty well and I can guess. He wanted to see how we would do without him."

"He was testing us?" Bill asked, incredulous.

Christian nodded. "I'd say more watching than testing, but yeah, that's my guess."

Bill looked at Tom again. "And you didn't know this either, colonel?"

Tom shook his head again, amusement showing in his eyes. "I'll be darned."

14

Kelly dried her hands on a dish towel and used a wooden spoon to check the whisky sauce one last time. The bread pudding with Jim's favorite sauce was going to be a surprise for him when they got back, and she had been trying to keep him out of the kitchen all day. She knew that he had smelled it baking, but his sense of smell was pretty much limited to *smells good* and *doesn't smell good,* so when he had asked what smelled so good she had simply said 'something for tonight' and left him thinking it was for the opening of the Jamestown Inn.

She took the pan off the stove and placed it in a warming drawer with the bread pudding, left the kitchen and went upstairs to their bedroom.

Walking down the hallway, she heard him whistling, a habit she had noticed when they had first spoken to each other, when she had said 'You sound happy' and he had smiled and replied 'I was born happy'.

"Whistling a little Air Supply?" she asked as she walked into the room, engaging in a long-running joke between them.

"It's Journey, and you know it," he replied. "Or maybe Foreigner. I could never keep those two straight."

She walked over to him, watching him brush his hair in front of the mirror. His shirt was off and she could see that his recent diet and secret workouts had done him good. She reached out and gently touched the puckered entry wound scar on his upper back. "Does it still hurt?"

He turned around, capturing her in a bear hug. "Nice try, pretending to care about my wound to cover your burning desire to touch my magnificent body."

Kelly rolled her eyes and fake-struggled to get away. "Not too full of ourselves, are we?"

He kissed her on her forehead. "Only my unbelievable humility keeps me from continuing to admire my reflection." He smiled. "That, and the fact that I'd rather look at you, anyway."

She wiggled out of his loosening grasp and raised to her toes, kissing him quickly on the lips. "Well, when you can tear yourself away, the kids are almost ready to head to Jamestown."

Jim grimaced. "Can't we get them to name the town something else?"

Kelly cocked her head and looked at him sternly. "We've been through this. We didn't think you were going to make it and they wanted to honor you. Besides, Jamestown was the name of the first permanent English settlement in North America - the new world. This is the first town built in this new world, at least around here. Plus, John Smith was an ancestor of yours. It just makes sense."

He frowned. "Yeah, well, I'm fine now and people are going to think I named it after myself. And John Smith wasn't an ancestor of mine. He didn't have any kids. He was an off-shoot of somebody or other."

She smiled. "The explanation has already been taken care of. You'll see. And if that doesn't satisfy people, I'm sure you'll explain it to them in your usual tactful way."

He curled his lip but remained silent.

She kissed him again. "We'll be ready downstairs."

He watched her walk away, then turned back to the mirror. The exit wound scar on the left side of his chest was larger and angrier looking than the entry wound, but it had closed nicely and, though it had kept him from doing some exercises with his left arm until a few weeks ago, Doc had said he was out of the woods and could return to whatever activities he felt he was up to.

He had been lucky, and he knew it. The wound had been a through-and-through, missing the ribs and scapula but not missing his left lung. Had Mike not been there to seal the wound then get him back to Doc, he wouldn't have made it.

The recuperation had given him time to do some thinking, and he had done a lot of it. He hadn't had to rely on other people since he was a kid, and the experience had given him a new perspective and appreciation for the people and things around him. He had come to recognize Kelly's every ministration as not just the acts of a dutiful wife, but as acts of love. Each visit from members of the core, as well as other Stonemont residents, took on a deeper meaning, and each minute with the kids was an irreplaceable lifetime in itself that he cherished in the moment and re-lived in his memory later. When Doc had told him how close he had come to not making it, he realized how many more things he wanted to tell them, show them and teach them - and how much he just wanted to keep being with them.

He looked at the scar in the mirror, recognizing it as evidence that someone had tried to take him from everything he loved most in the world. Evidence that evil truly did exist. Evidence of the reality of the new world.

THE REVIVAL

He finished brushing his hair, put on a shirt and slid his .45 into its holster. The familiar action felt good, both a sign and a statement that he was back in the mix, ready to contribute again.

"The kids were hoping you'd ride over and they want to go with you," Kelly said over her shoulder as he entered the kitchen. "They have a surprise for you and they're waiting outside."

"Okay," he said, coming up behind her. "What are you making?"

"Nothing," she said, throwing a dish towel over the baking dish. "Just something for tonight."

"It smells good. Can I have a bite?"

"You can have as many bites as you want when it's time to eat it," she said, turning and play-pushing him back. "Now go outside. The kids want to escort you to town and they're champing at the bit."

"Are you coming with us?"

"I'll be driving over with Patty and Saoirse in a little bit."

"Alright," he said, taking a large biscuit off a platter on the island. "Did Mrs. Hernandez make these?"

"Uh huh. She brought them over earlier as a farewell gift."

He took a bite. Cheese, onion, sage, rosemary, basil and cilantro all fought to dominate the flavor but combined to create a taste that made him moan, "Boy, I'm going to miss her."

Kelly laughed. "You'll just have to go eat at the Jamestown Inn occasionally. She said these are going to be the signature biscuits on her menu."

"Okay," he said, taking another biscuit, "you'll know where to find me."

"You'll get fat."

"Been meaning to," he chuckled as he grabbed a rifle out of the rack and walked out onto veranda.

"Hi daddy!" yelled Brody and Morgan in unison.

"Hi dad," said Aedan, seriously.

Jim looked at his kids as he crossed the veranda. They were sitting on their horses, side-by-side, Brody and Morgan beaming huge smiles and Aedan looking serious and watchful. Aedan had his AR slung over his shoulder, the rifle hanging down his right side behind his leg. Ever since Jim had been shot, Aedan had stayed as close as he could to him and always had his rifle. Not to be outdone, Brody had his pellet rifle slung over his shoulder and Morgan had her pink BB gun over hers.

"Well, it looks like I've got a top-tier security detail," Jim laughed. "You guys look great!"

"You have to stay between us all the time till we get there!" yelled Morgan.

"And if we're attacked, you have to do what we tell you while we save you," said Brody. "That's what Christian said."

Jim chuckled. "Well, I sure do feel safe." He looked at Aedan. "I take it you're the head of this detail. How do we line up?"

Aedan nodded. "I'll take point, Morgan will be next, then you, then Brody."

Jim smiled. Aedan sounded so serious that it made him proud and sad at the same time. "What have you got there?" he asked, nodding his head at a large dapple-grey horse with a flowing mane and tail, the reins of which Aedan held in his left hand.

Aedan smiled for the first time, his eyes dancing with excitement. "He's for you," he said, holding the reins toward Jim.

Jim stepped off of the veranda and walked to Aedan, suddenly choked with emotion. Somehow, the simple words *he's for you* conjured up the dynamic spectrum of love and giving. The standard relationship of him, as father, giving to his children had been turned around and the children were now giving to him, not hand-traced turkeys on construction paper or plaster-of-paris hand-prints, but something in the adult realm. He looked up at his son, took the reins from his hand and looked at the horse.

The horse was beautiful. Fifteen hands, at least, with a well-sculpted head and intelligent eyes, its dappling was dark, which set off its lighter mane and tail. A dark brown hornless saddle covered its back and a matching bridle encased its head.

He held the reins in his left hand, offering that palm to the horse's muzzle while gently stroking its neck with his right. The horse nuzzled his hand, blew softly, then raised its head to look directly at him.

Jim looked up at Aedan again. "Where did you get him?"

"Naomi found him in a barn," Morgan exclaimed before Aedan could answer. "He couldn't get out and she saved him."

"We don't know what his name is," said Brody. "I think you should call him Ghost, 'cause he looks kind of like a ghost, especially at night."

Jim nodded, smiling. "Ghost sounds like a fine name." He looked back at Aedan. "How long have you had him?"

"We got him right after you got shot," answered Morgan.

THE REVIVAL

"Morgan," Aedan looked at his sister sternly, clearly irritated that she had answered a question directed at him.

"Soorrry," Morgan replied, her eyes rolling in a grimace face.

Aedan looked back at Jim. "A few days after you came back." He avoided mentioning Jim being shot, "Mike took a scout team back up to look around Grim's old place. They found a farm that still had some animals around. The house had been burned and some horses and cows were in the field, but Ghost was in the barn by himself. Naomi got him out and she and Becky have been working with him ever since, waiting to give him to you." He took a breath. "They say he's a great horse."

Jim nodded, smiling and stroking the horse's neck again. "He looks like a great horse." He looked at the saddle. "Where did you get the saddle?"

"From Australia," answered Morgan.

"Australia?"

"They found it in the barn with Ghost," said Brody. "Becky says it's an Australian saddle."

Jim nodded and looked back up at Aedan. "Are you guys ready to go?"

"Yep. Mike and Tracy and some scouts are going with us. They're waiting for us at the gate."

"Alright, then, best not keep them waiting." Jim passed the right rein around the horse's neck and took it in his right hand along with the left rein, then took both in his left hand as he grabbed the pommel with it and the cantle with his right. Putting his left foot in the stirrup, he swung up into the saddle, feeling a brief twinge in his left shoulder.

He immediately noticed the different feel of the saddle, the higher pommel and cantle holding him more securely than an American western saddle. The knee pads added to the feeling of stability and the more forward position of the stirrups felt more comfortable. Even the lack of a saddle horn felt more comfortable as he rested his left hand on the rounded pommel.

He looked around the commons, thinking how good it felt to be involved again and heading to the new town-site. The fact that the new inn was opening was exciting and he realized how much he had missed. Swinging Ghost toward the gate, he gave the horse a cluck, only to be stopped by Morgan.

"Daddy!"

He stopped and looked at her to see what she wanted.

"You have to be behind me. Did you forget? You're our protector."

"Protectee," corrected Brody.

"Whatever," she said as she heeled her horse ahead of Jim to take her rightful position behind Aedan and flashed a smile back at her daddy.

THE REVIVAL

They rode through the gate, Mike and Tracy taking the lead followed by two more scouts, Jim and his 'security detail' in the middle and four more scouts bringing up the rear.

The day was beautiful, with a blue sky dotted with whispy white clouds and the trees in full leaf. The gentle rocking of the horse beneath him was relaxing, as was the quiet conversation of the scouts and the kids, and Jim found the peacefulness a welcome balance to the hyper-awareness he felt after being cooped up for so long.

He had extended his recuperation beyond what was necessary, purposefully keeping himself out of his normal leadership role in order to see what would happen without him at the helm. For the most part, things had gone well. The core continued to do their jobs, maintaining their focus as always, and progress on the town had been steady. Mike had continued the development of the scouts, adding more training classes and pushing recon patrols farther out to the north, east and south. Tom had worked closely with Mike, training the scouts in intelligence gathering, development and tactical analysis. Bill had been steady, as always, but with an added gravity that grew from his part in the sentencing of Grim's crew. The surprise had been Christian.

The joking, happy-go-lucky nephew he had known had disappeared after the raid, replaced by a more sober, incredibly focused leader and protector. He had re-doubled his efforts to ensure the security of Stonemont, spent every moment he could with the kids, watched protectively over Kelly and, at night, spent hours talking with Jim. Sometimes, they talked around the kitchen table with Kelly and the kids, sometimes they talked on the veranda with others of the core, and sometimes they talked in the privacy of the den where they spoke of things they did not want to speak about in front of others.

Those times had been important for both of them. They had come to know and respect each other on a much deeper level, and each had shared things they had never shared with another person before. Jim came away knowing that he could count on Christian to step into the main leadership role if necessary. Christian came away with an education.

"You heal up real quick," said Mike, having dropped back from point to ride beside Jim.

Jim chuckled. "Well, if you call four months real quick, I must have been in worse shape than you told me."

Mike looked at him out of the corner of his eye. "I call two days real quick. The day before yesterday you could barely make it up the stairs. Today, you look like you've been well for a while."

Jim smiled. Mike was quiet, but he was smart. "Yep, it's a wonder what a good night's sleep can do." He looked at his chief of scouts. "How are things coming along with your training program?"

Mike gave a thoughtful nod. "Pretty well. We've had quite a few new recruits coming in from all over. I think a lot of them are those who were able to take care of themselves for a while but were coming to the end of their rope. Others are from some of the surrounding towns and communities and see it as more interesting than farming or whatever else they were doing at home. Kind of like the old military."

"How many do you have now?"

"Over three hundred, and more coming in all the time."

Jim looked at him, surprise showing on his face. "That many? Are you able to handle them all?"

Mike shrugged. "So far. Over a hundred have completed first phase since you've been out of commission. About half of those have completed second phase, about half are still in it, and a few have been diverted to other assignments. Another hundred are currently in first phase and another hundred or so will be starting in about two weeks."

Jim nodded. He had done a lot of thinking during his self-imposed sabbatical and he knew they were going to have to increase both their defensive and offensive capabilities if they were going to remain secure. Thinking about that, he realized he had missed something Mike said.

"I'm sorry, what did you say?"

"We've added a couple of special phases that I'd like to show you after the meeting tomorrow. Not every scout will be able to master them, but some will, and I think it will greatly enhance their capabilities. Even those who can't master them will be improved."

"What are they?"

Mike hesitated, then shrugged. "It would be better if you just saw them." He looked at Jim. "If you don't mind."

Jim chuckled. "I don't mind. Must be good."

They rode on, speaking briefly with the sentries as they passed through the contact gate, then followed the roads to Jamestown. Cows dotted the fields around them, chewing lazily on grass or cud and occasionally turning to watch them with disinterested eyes.

"It's amazing how different things are," said Jim. "It's been just about a year."

Mike nodded. "I was just thinking that the other day. Seems a lot longer."

"Yeah, it does. You going to try to get back to your family now?"

THE REVIVAL

Mike was silent for a minute. "I've been thinking about that, too. We've got a lot going on right now and I thought maybe I should stay a little longer if you think you can use me."

Jim smiled. "We can more than use you, buddy. You know that. But I wouldn't want that to stop you going back your family if that's what you want to do."

Mike nodded. "I think about them and would like to see them, but it just doesn't seem like the right time. That trip would be a task and a half right now. A thousand miles of rough country and rougher people, not to mention having to cross the Mississippi and other rivers where I imagine there are tolls or checkpoints by the locals." He paused again and shrugged. "I think I'll give it a little more time for things to shake out. I'm sure they're fine, and they know I am - mom has a way of knowing. Maybe another year or so. I'll know when the time is right."

Jim nodded. "Sounds like you've thought it through, as always. I'm glad to have you stay for as long as you want." He looked over at Mike and smiled. "I'm sure others are, too."

It took them another hour before they topped the rise of a small hill overlooking Jamestown. The cross-hatch of newly-graded streets made the town-site look like a checkerboard and a large, u-shaped timber-frame building with a large courtyard dominated the west side of the square, strings of multi-colored flags trailing from its second-floor roof to tall poles on the opposite side of the street. Rectangles in the street in front of the building revealed themselves to be tables as they rode closer, and people scurried about with obvious purpose.

They descended from the hill and swung onto South Street, riding past West Street and around the building to enter the enclosed stable at the rear of the building, the coolness surprising after the warmth of the sunshine.

"Buenos dias, Senorita Tracy, Senor Mike and Senor Wyatt!" exclaimed a smiling man who approached them from the side office. "Welcome, amigos," he said to the rest, then, seeing Morgan, "and muchacha!" He turned to the interior of the stable. "Oscar! Graciano! Come take our guests horses!"

Two smiling boys came forward, obviously excited at the arrival of their first customers.

Tracy swung down from the saddle, handing her reins to one of the boys with a smile and turned to the man. "Hi Cesar. I want to introduce you to Jim Wyatt and his children, Aedan, Brody and Morgan." She turned to Jim and the kids. "Guys, this is Cesar."

THE REVIVAL

"Cesar Velez Mejorada," said the man, smiling broadly. "At your service!"

Jim stuck out his hand. "Good to meet you, Cesar."

Cesar took the hand, still smiling. "You as well, Senor Wyatt."

Jim smiled. "How did you know who I was?"

Cesar shrugged. "Mike and Tracy said they would be bringing you today and everyone says you wear a cowboy hat. Who else could you be?"

Jim laughed. "Well, it's good to meet you. You run this place?"

Cesar nodded. "I sub-lease the livery from Mrs. Hernandez. She says more people are going to start riding horses, so I thought why not give it a try? It's kind of like the movies, you know?"

The boys came back to take the rest of the horses and Cesar spoke to them. "Give them some grain and a good brushing. Make them happy and shiny so they'll want to come back."

"Okay, papa," the boys said in unison as they led the horses away.

"Can we go through to the inn from here?" Jim asked.

Cesar nodded. "You can, but I think Mrs. Hernandez would like you to come in the front so you can see it."

Jim smiled and nodded. "Of course." He turned to the others, who had dismounted and handed their horses over to Oscar and Graciano. "Everybody ready?"

Nods told him they were.

"Okay, let's go. Thanks, Cesar."

"You're welcome. Enjoy the party!"

They left the stable and walked around to the front of the building, its mass now apparent as they walked beside it. It was timber-framed with smoothed cob between the posts and beams and looked like a combination between an old English manor and a Spanish hacienda. There were windows on the second floor but none on the first, a design feature speaking to its potential use as a fortress.

They walked through an iron gate into a large stone-paved courtyard, the walls of which were three feet thick and six feet high. Timber posts, rails and balusters framed the second-floor balcony overlooking the courtyard, the roof providing shade and shelter to the balcony and building beneath it. Baskets of flowers hung from hooks set into the pillars and walls, and a fountain splashed in the center. Two steps led to a porch that ran the span of the front entrance wall and two massive wooden doors which now opened.

"Mr. Wyatt!" exclaimed Mrs. Hernandez, hurrying out the door and down the steps to greet the group. "You are here!"

Stepping past Jim's out-stretched hand, she flung her arms around his waist and pressed her cheek into his chest.

Surprised, Jim laughed and returned the hug, to the amusement of the others. "Mrs. Hernandez, between your biscuits and that hug, I think I may be coming here a lot."

Mrs. Hernandez disengaged herself and self-consciously smoothed imaginary wrinkles from the front of her embroidered dress. "We have been waiting for you. Please," she stepped back and made a welcoming gesture with her arm, "please come in. I want to show you everything!"

They mounted the steps and passed through the doorway into a short hallway which led to a large, high-ceilinged room. Like the outside, a balcony ran around the second floor. Timber posts supported wrought iron railings which framed numerous doors on all sides of the room, and baskets of flowers hung from the railings and sat in the middle of the numerous tables that filled the room. Just as it had in the stable, the coolness of the room was almost shocking after stepping in from the outside.

"It feels like you have air conditioning, Mrs. Hernandez," said Tracy.

"That's the cob," said Ann, entering the room from the kitchen and wiping her hands on a cloth. "Your final water hookup is done," she told Mrs. Hernandez, then turned to the rest, smiling. "So, what do you think?"

"It's amazing, mom!" exclaimed Tracy. "How did you get everything done so fast?"

"We had a lot of help," replied Ann. "Once we got started, it went very quickly. As a matter of fact, we almost had too many people working on it, but we wanted to get this building done so we held back on others till we finished here." She looked around the large room. "It really did turn out well." She looked at Mrs. Hernandez. "Should we give them a tour?"

"Si´, yes," Mrs. Hernandez said, smiling. "They must see everything."

They spent the next hour touring the inn, Mrs. Hernandez proudly showing them the different rooms and Ann explaining the engineering of the building itself, the kitchen and the reverse osmosis water system. By the time they returned to the main room, many others had arrived and were milling around the room and the outside courtyard where a group of musicians were starting to set up.

"There's mommy!" said Morgan, pointing to the courtyard gate where Kelly was entering with Patty and Saoirse. "Can I go over there, daddy?"

Jim waved to his wife and patted his daughter on the shoulder. "Sure, honey. You go on, but stay with mommy."

"I will!" she said, handing him her BB gun and disappearing into the growing crowd.

"Can we go look around, dad?" Aedan asked.

"Yeah, can we?" Brody added excitedly.

Jim smiled. "Sure, guys. But first you need to put up your rifles. Sidearms are an acceptable part of a man's social dress, but rifles make you look a little too aggressive." He looked at Mrs. Hernandez. "Is there a place where our people can put their rifles, Mrs. Hernandez?"

"Certainly, Mr. Wyatt," she answered with a broad smile. "We have a gun room behind the service bar. I'll show them on my way back to the kitchen, if you'll excuse me."

Jim watched as Aedan and Brody went to rack their rifles with the scouts, then stepped out onto the porch to watch the crowd.

He recognized many of the people but was surprised at how many new faces there were. He had been shot at the beginning of the hard winter, the time they expected would start the final die-off of those who had been able to hang on through the milder months but were too compromised by health issues or lack of resources to survive the harsher ones. Obviously, many had finally been driven to seek out places to try to survive or had been discovered by Stonemont scouts on their widening patrols and reconnaissance probes.

The recent arrivals had greatly increased their numbers, which, while increasing their ability to accomplish work, had also increased the societal problems that invariably accompanied a growing population. The construction of the inn had been accomplished in remarkable time and, by the looks of things, the rest of the town was developing quickly as well. So far, problems had been minor and infrequent, probably for the same reason things had gone fairly smoothly right after the collapse - people who had most recently been fearful of starving to death or being killed or enslaved by marauders felt a sense of relief and gratitude when offered a safe place to live, work to do and a community to be a part of. Still, he knew that the facade of civility could often be shallow, and that a small scratch could quickly reveal the less attractive aspects of human nature lying beneath the surface.

"Well, I feel safer already!"

Jim turned to see Christian coming out of the doorway, nodding at the pink BB gun in Jim's hand.

"I was going to surprise you," he answered, "but you caught me before I could wrap it."

Christian smiled and looked out over the crowd with Jim. "Quite a deal, huh?"

THE REVIVAL

Jim nodded. "It is. You've accomplished a lot since I've been out of commission." He looked at his nephew. "You've done a good job."

Christian shrugged. "Everybody has worked hard and pulled together."

"Yeah, but you led. That's the difference."

"So did Kelly. She'd make a good war chief. Like Boudica."

Jim chuckled. "I know, but I'd like to keep her as a wife. You'll have to do."

He looked around to make sure no one was within ear-shot, then looked back at his nephew. "You know, sometimes when you get too close to something you can't see the whole thing. I've spent the last several months listening and watching instead of talking and doing, and I've learned a lot."

He looked out over the crowd. "I've realized that this is going to continue to grow. There's no stopping it. Therefore, it must be controlled. I'm sure this is happening all over the country, maybe all over the world. We can't be that special."

Christian nodded. "Yeah, I think you're right. So, what's the plan?"

"You think I have a plan?"

"I know you have a plan. You always have a plan. I'm just waiting for you to tell me."

Jim smiled. "Let's go somewhere a little more private."

People kept arriving throughout the afternoon, the small crowd milling around the inn and its courtyard becoming a large one that spilled out into the street, and the soft murmur of voices in conversation growing to a happy cacophony of laughter, shouts and the shrieks of children playing.

As the sun fell lower in the sky, workers spread cloths on the outside tables and set up a serving line in the courtyard. Platters of beef, pork, venison, fruits, vegetables, pastas, breads, pies and cakes covered the tables that ran the southern length of the courtyard, and carvers and servers took their stations waiting for Mrs. Hernandez. Noticing the activity, the crowd slowly migrated into the courtyard until it was full, eagerly awaiting the start of the meal.

After several minutes, Mrs. Hernandez stepped out onto the veranda, smiling and clutching her hands together in front of her. "Welcome, friends," she said, her voice light and airy with excitement.

A smattering of applause rippled through the crowd.

"Welcome to the opening of the Jamestown Inn," she said louder, her voice gaining strength with increased assurance.

THE REVIVAL

Another round of applause was louder and more prolonged, punctuated by a young boy's voice yelling, "When can we eat!"

Mrs. Hernandez laughed along with many others. "Pretty soon, little one, pretty soon. First I want to thank you all for coming." She straightened her back as if to prepare herself for something.

"Today is a dream for me, a dream I never thought would happen." She paused, looking around the crowd as if wanting to include each person in her special moment. "We have all been through so much. We have all lost much. But we are here today starting a new future - one that we will build with our own hands and our own will."

She turned to where Jim and Kelly were standing off to the side. "I thank God for this opportunity, and I also thank the Wyatts. They took us into their home like family, just like they welcomed so many of you, and helped us in getting set up in this beautiful new inn." She nodded at Jim and Kelly. "Thank you, Mr. Wyatt. Thank you, Mrs. Wyatt."

Jim and Kelly nodded and smiled in return.

Mrs. Hernandez turned back to the crowd. "What you see around you will soon be a town. Perhaps it will be one of the first new towns built in this new America. It will be where we live and raise our families and teach our children the values we believe in. One day, hopefully, it will be what our children call their hometown, the place where they grew up, the place they are from."

She paused and took a deep breath. "I did not know this, but Jamestown was the first permanent English settlement in what became known as America. It was the seed from which the greatest country in the history of the world grew. This new Jamestown, named to honor Mr. Wyatt, although I am told he doesn't like that, is also a seed. What it grows into depends on us, our strength, our perseverance and our faith. We must ask God to direct us, and we must always heed his direction."

A smattering of applause again ran through the crowd.

She continued. "A book Mr. Wyatt gave me said that Captain John Smith, the leader of the first Jamestown, said that those who did not work would not eat. Actually, he took that from the Bible, and a sign with those words will soon be erected in this square."

She spread her arms wide. "But tonight, there is no work. There is just eating and celebrating. Thank you, and welcome to Jamestown and the Jamestown Inn!"

15

The entire core was waiting when Jim walked into the den, evidence to his having overslept and an obvious cause of humor for some.

"Thanks for coming, Jim," said Christian with a smile. "There's coffee on the table if you feel you're up to it."

Jim stopped the retort that came to mind and took a seat on a couch next to Kelly. "Sorry to keep you all waiting. The second and third helping of Kelly's surprise last night put me out and kept me under."

"Uh, Jim, I don't think we should talk about things like that in front of everybody," said Christian, a glint in his eye. "Especially so early in the morning."

"I'm talking about her bread pudding with whisky sauce, wise-guy," said Jim, reaching for the carafe of coffee.

"Oh, is that what you call it?" Christian chuckled. "Cute."

Jim stopped with his hand holding the carafe over his cup and looked at his nephew. "I'd tell you to get your mind out of the gutter but the gutter would be a step up." He poured coffee into his pine tree mug and set the carafe aside, looking around at the group. "Is he getting worse or is it just my imagination?"

Bill laughed. "You certainly seem to bring it out in him."

"Pot and kettle," said Kelly.

Christian stood up. "Before we let you re-assume command, we have something for you."

He walked to a bookcase and picked up a slim wooden box, returned to the table and set it down in front of Jim. "Here. It's no bread pudding, but we hope you like it."

Jim looked warily at the polished wooden box in front of him. "Is something going to jump out at me?"

Christian shrugged and sat back down. "You never know."

Jim squared the box toward himself, putting his hand on the latch and looking around at the group. "Is everybody in on this? I just want to know who to blame."

"If you don't want it, I'll take it," said Tom.

"I found it," said Mike.

"But I'm your favorite nephew," said Christian.

Jim looked at his nephew. "You sure?"

"Well, I'm your only nephew."

"Yeah, still ..."

Looking back at the box, he opened the latch and slowly raised the lid. A large revolver rested in the red velvet-lined interior, its polished mahogany grips shining almost as much as the blued finished.

"Are you kidding me?" he asked, stunned, as he realized what it was.

"Smith & Wesson Model 57," said Christian, smiling. ".41 magnum. Six inch barrel."

Jim looked at his nephew, then back at the gun. "Where in the world did you find this?"

"Mike found it when they were clearing houses east of here. I saw it on the inventory list and remembered you telling me it was your favorite handgun of all time."

Jim nodded slowly, picking up the revolver almost tenderly. "It is," he said, opening the cylinder and testing the smoothness if its rotation. "Mine was stolen from my house in the eighties when I lived in Kansas City. I never replaced it and never thought I'd see another one."

"What's so special about it, Jim?" asked Bill.

Jim closed the cylinder and laid the gun back in its box. He shrugged. "All guns are tools, but revolvers are works of art. The .41 mag is between the .357 and the .44 magnum. More powerful than the .357 and almost equal to a .44 magnum but a bit easier to handle. In my opinion, the perfect handgun." He looked at Christian. "Do we have any ammo for it?"

Christian nodded. "We already had some, but Mike found a bunch of it with the gun."

"It's called cowboy loads or something," said Mike. "Semi-wadcutter stuff. It sounds like what Christian told me you used to use."

Jim shook his head again slowly. "I can't thank you enough, but thanks."

"There's one more thing," said Kelly, getting up from the couch.

"I don't think you should be giving him any more bread pudding," said Christian, "at least not right here in front of us."

Kelly snapped a look at Christian. "Christian, I'm going to wash your mind out with soap. Does Naomi know what's rolling around in that head of yours?"

Christian laughed. "She's starting to."

THE REVIVAL

She picked up an old paper grocery sack from behind the couch and returned to the table. "Well, I hope she sticks around when she sees the whole deal." She handed the sack to Jim. "It's from Mel Miller, but I wrapped it."

Jim took the sack from her. "Very nice. I hope you didn't spend too much time on it."

"Nope," she smiled, sitting back down on the couch next to him.

Tentatively opening the bag, he looked inside, then opened it fully to withdraw a leather gun belt. The belt was thick, yet beautifully tanned and buttery smooth, holding a cross-draw holster on the left side. Twelve bullet loops were sewn onto each side and JAW was engraved across the back.

"What does JAW stand for?" asked Christian.

"My initials, wise guy. You know that."

"I just realized that I don't know your middle name."

"I don't have a middle name."

"You don't have a middle name?"

"No."

"Why not?"

"My parents couldn't afford one."

Christian laughed. "Raise of hands for everyone who's surprised Jim's initials are JAW!"

Several chuckled

"Put it on," said Kelly.

He hesitated, still overcome by the surprise of the gifts, but stood up, took off the gun belt he was wearing and threw the new one around his waist. Cinching it tight, he buckled it, took the revolver out if its box and slid it into the holster, snapping the retention strap over the hammer.

"It looks good," said Kelly. "How does it feel?"

Jim smiled. "It feels great."

"Well," said Christian, "I think we can all agree that Jim looks good and feels great. How about we start with the meeting?" He paused for a moment and looked a Jim. "Seriously, it's good to have you back."

Jim looked at Christian and nodded, then sat down. "It's good to be back."

He looked around at the group. "Before we start, I want to say a couple of things. First, everyone has done a remarkable job over the last few months. Everyone. I've been paying attention, and I couldn't be happier or more encouraged by what I have seen. Thank you all for everything you've done to keep us moving in the right direction.

"Secondly, we are about to enter into a new phase of our evolution." He looked around at the group. "Our population has exploded, and I expect the same thing has happened in other fortified communities for the same reason."

"Why do you think that is?" asked Bill.

Jim looked at Tom. "First, let's see what our chief of intelligence thinks."

Tom nodded. "I think the cold winter made the last of the small groups understand that they can't survive in this new world outside of a community. Our entry interviews indicate that most had come to the end of their resources and realized they had no good plan for going forward. Coming to an established working community was their only viable option. Like you said, I imagine the same is happening everywhere there is an established community."

"What kind of people are in these groups?" asked Jim.

"All sorts," said Tom. "Cul-de-sac neighbors, extended families, church groups, Boy Scout troops, soccer clubs, you name it. I think we've seen everything but a bowling team."

"Any problems?"

Tom shrugged. "With people come problems, but nothing major"

Jim nodded. "Okay, we'll get into that more when you're up." He looked at Kelly. "Okay, puddin', start us off."

Kelly rolled her eyes. "As always, it's people and things." She opened a folder and glanced at a column of numbers. "We now have three hundred and sixteen people at Stonemont and two hundred forty-seven at Hillmont. Redemption fluctuates, but usually has around a hundred. School crossing also fluctuates but usually runs about two-fifty."

"Why do those places fluctuate?" asked Ann.

"I wondered about that myself," Kelly answered. "I think it might be that Stonemont, and Hillmont as part of Stonemont, have established economies with jobs available to support families as well as security. School Center has a bit of that, but not nearly like Stonemont, and Redemption is really more like a temporary way station since it doesn't have much permanent housing available."

"So, that's around nine hundred people and three hundred are scouts?" said Jim. "That ratio seems pretty high."

Kelly shook her head. "That's not counting scouts. They're separate."

Jim raised his eyebrows in surprise. "Twelve hundred people?"

Kelly nodded. "Almost a thousand of them under Stonemont directly, not counting the satellites."

"How did ... " he started, then paused, raising his hand as if to stop his question. "Never mind. Go ahead."

"That many people coming in that fast has really stretched us," Kelly continued, "especially with housing. Some of the newer arrivals are doubling up in the cabins with older ones, we're using the main hall to house people again and we even have some staying over at the Eddington place."

"How about feeding that many people?" asked Jim.

"Supply is no problem but logistics is a challenge. Most of the adults are working on the town, so we set up a buffet line in the main hall for breakfast, another one in town for lunch and a third in the main hall for dinner. It was tough at first, but everyone has gotten used to the routine and things have smoothed out and it's working pretty well.

"I don't have a breakdown as to number of men, women, families and such - there are just too many - but it seems like a normal community mix."

"Who's doing all the meals?"

"Mostly it's the wives of the men building the town. The younger kids help, as do a few men who can't work on the town. A lot of the older kids and a few women work on building the town."

"And they're all being paid with Stonemont credits?"

"Yes, on a set scale for each different job."

Jim nodded. "Good. What's wrong with the men who can't work on the town?"

"One has COPD, one had a stroke and doesn't function too well, and one has a bad back."

"A bad back?"

Kelly nodded. "That's what he said."

"What's wrong with his back?"

She shrugged. "He says it goes out on him."

"Goes out on him, huh? Like mine does but I keep on working?"

"Yep."

"So, what does he do?"

"He mostly helps with serving the food."

Jim looked at Christian, who nodded his understanding that he was to check the man out.

Jim looked back at Kelly. "Sorry. Go ahead."

"As far as the building of Jamestown, we are adjusting our building schedule to put housing on the same time-track as the hall. That means they should all be done about the same time with the hall being finished later than planned but the houses earlier."

Jim nodded his agreement. "When do you figure it will all be done?"

"Ann and I were just discussing this yesterday and we figure around the first of August."

Jim looked surprised. "That's only three months. Are things really going that fast?"

Kelly nodded. "With this many people working and this kind of construction, it's amazing how fast it goes. But that's when we think everything will be done. Now that the Jamestown Inn is finished we're splitting the work crews with half working on the hall and half on the homes. The houses will all be the same design, so it should go pretty quickly, and we expect to complete four a week. We'll start moving people into them as soon as they're ready, so that will start alleviating the housing problem right away."

"How many are you planning to build?" asked Bill.

"We've platted fifty to start," answered Kelly, "which should get everybody out of temporary housing. If more people show up, we'll just keep building."

"How big will each house and lot be?" asked Tracy.

"Each house is one story with a main room which includes living and kitchen areas, two bedrooms and a bathroom, and each will have about two acres. That will give each family enough space to grow large gardens and keep some chickens, goats and even a couple of cows or horses if they want to. A real step toward self-sufficiency."

"Each house will have electricity and running water," Ann interjected. "There is no waste system, though, so each house will have a compost toilet in the bathroom."

"Where does the water come from?" asked Bill.

"It's pumped from the creek through a main line to a central water tower, treated, then gravity-fed through underground pipes, just like before," answered Ann.

"Will there be showers?"

Ann nodded. "Each house will have a solar heated water tank to provide hot water to the kitchen and bath."

"Where does the wastewater go?"

"It goes to a holding tank in the ground away from the house where its allowed to drain slowly back into the ground.

"Couldn't that water be used to water the gardens?" asked Tracy.

Ann shook her head. "No, that water is called grey water and it will contain soap and other contaminants. You don't want to introduce that into food production."

THE REVIVAL

Kelly waited so see if there were any more questions, and, seeing that there were none, continued.

"The population mixture is a good variety, pretty much what you would expect if you threw a net over any suburban area." She glanced down at her notes. "A couple of doctors, several lawyers, a building contractor, a couple of electricians, a plumber, two police officers, a firefighter, another teacher, another paramedic and a whole bunch of IT people and middle-to-senior managers and executives. One of the lawyers and several of the managers were in the military, so they have been directed to Mike and Tom. The other managers and IT people are fitting in where they can, most of them working in construction."

She checked that subject off her list. "School is out for the year and planting is well underway. We estimate we'll have about eighty acres in crops this year and the gardening manager from School Center is showing us how to take cuttings from our fruit trees to increase the orchards. That's a long-term project, but it should start paying off in four or five years.

"Salvage operations remain strong and we are bringing in more than we can inventory. Still, I don't think we should let up. The answer to the old question 'how much is enough?' is always 'we don't know', and I think we need to secure as much of everything as we can while we can. There's no way to know how things may change in the future and we don't have manufacturing, so if we may need it we'd better get it now."

"Anything special you have in mind?" asked Mike.

Kelly nodded. "Clothes. We don't have any way to make good clothes or even fabric, so when what we have wears out we're going to need replacements. Right now, there are stores full of clothes, but those buildings will start to deteriorate in the next year or so and the clothes will be ruined. We need to get what we need now and keep them in storage."

"How much should we get?"

"All we can. And for this, let's stay away from Walmart. We need good quality clothes that will hold up. Get all the Carhardt, North Face, Columbia and similar brands you can, plus underwear, socks, gloves, shoes and boots."

"Bass Pro, Cabela's, REI, Scheels and Academy," suggested Jim. "Also, Menards and Tractor Supply."

Mike nodded.

Kelly checked her list and looked up. "That's it for me."

Jim nodded and turned to Ann. "Engineering?"

THE REVIVAL

Ann opened her folder. "Like Kelly said, we're making unbelievable progress on Jamestown. I jotted down some questions people asked me last night, so I'll start with those.

"First, electricity. Yes, the town will have electricity. The source is a rudimentary hydro-electric plant we constructed on the stream which we believe will serve up to one hundred buildings with basic service. It won't look like Times Square, but it will look like civilization."

"What happens if we end up building more than a hundred buildings?" asked Tom.

"We've already identified another spot on the stream where we can build a second plant," answered Ann. "After that, we'll either have to limit building or develop an additional energy source, which brings me to my next item."

She looked at her folder, finding what she was looking for with the tip of her finger. "We've been figuring our gasoline and diesel will be going bad in another year or two," she looked up and around at the group, "so we'll start making more."

"Making more?" asked Christian.

Ann nodded. "Kansas has good-sized oil and natural gas fields. The big ones are farther west, but we've found producing wells just southeast of here. Actually, Mike found them. We figured we'd keep it a secret and surprise you today."

Jim leaned forward. "Producing?"

Ann nodded. "We've opened the valves on six and each one showed production capability. We have no reason to believe the others won't."

"How many are there?" asked Christian.

"Over forty that we've found so far," Mike answered.

"How much oil or gas are we talking about," asked Jim. "How long will it last?"

Ann paused before answering. "I almost hesitate to say this, but, for us, probably indefinitely."

"We can process it to use?" asked Jim.

"Yes," answered Ann. "Natural gas, diesel and gasoline."

The group stared at Ann, stunned. Finally, Jim broke the silence. "What do you need to get started?"

"Your okay."

Jim nodded, still stunned. "Yeah, well, okay."

Ann smiled and nodded. "We'll get started."

"Anything else? Maybe we have a gold mine too?"

Ann shook her head. "Sorry."

Jim looked around at the group. "Who wants to try to follow that?"

No one spoke, so Jim said "Let's go with you, Mike."

Mike looked around the group. "Like I told Jim yesterday, we have about three hundred scouts either trained or in the pipeline. The overall quality is pretty good, but, as would be expected with a group that large, there is a pretty wide spectrum of talents and abilities. Therefore, we've developed an assessment and selection process through which we filter recruits in order to determine how each should be assigned for maximum effectiveness.

"I've been happy with the results and consider even the basic level scout to be effective within the standard requirements and tasks of the unit. That's the good news. The better news is that we have some who far exceed the standard level in both physical and mental abilities. They routinely exceed all requirements and expectations and push themselves and each other to increasingly difficult training levels."

He looked at Jim. "In my opinion, this group would justify our considering the formation of some type of special unit within the larger scout structure."

Jim looked at him thoughtfully. "What do you have in mind?"

Mike glanced at Christian and Tom, then looked back at Jim. "I don't mean to get ahead of things, but the rate of our expansion, including the new gas and oil fields we're going to have to secure, tells me we're going to need to not only increase the size of our defense force but have a force capable of, and perhaps specifically trained for, taking direct action against an enemy if necessary."

Jim nodded. "I agree." He paused for a moment. "This essentially means the creation of a standing army," he smiled and nodded to Mike and Tom, "no offense to you Marines. I had hoped to avoid this, but we can't. I have no doubt other groups will be doing this, so we'll have to in order to be able to defend ourselves. What are you thinking in the way of a special unit?"

"Well, it wouldn't be on the order of military special ops. For one thing, the technology we used isn't available, nor is the massive support structure. I'm thinking more along the lines of Rogers Rangers and Francis Marion - a unit of highly motivated, highly trained, highly adaptive scouts who are able to travel light, travel fast and either operate covertly or deliver an inordinate amount of force when needed."

Jim started to ask what types of special training Mike had in mind but decided against it. There would be time for that later, and many aspects of the training should probably not be discussed in a general meeting. "Okay. We'll talk details later but go ahead with it."

"Okay," Mike nodded. "Finally, there are a couple of things that I mentioned to you yesterday I'd like to show you when we're done here." He looked around the table. "Everyone's welcome. I think you all might enjoy it."

"Okay," Jim answered then looked at Christian, Tom and Bill. "Unless any of you have something that can't wait I'm going to ask you to hold it until we can talk later. I have a couple of requests that you might want to consider and include in your next report."

All three men nodded.

"Good." He looked at Bill. "It looks like we can't escape becoming some kind of political entity, whether that be a city, a state or whatever. We need some system of justice beyond my say-so. I'd like you to develop the judicial arm of Stonemont, whatever it becomes. You will create our legal and justice system and adjudicate all complaints and disputes. I have just one caveat - that the entirety of laws, ordinances, processes and penalties must be no longer than ten written pages and easily understood by any adult of normal intelligence. What do you say?"

Bill stared at Jim as if he couldn't believe what he had just heard. He was being asked to create the structure and administration of an entire legal system from scratch.

During his career, he had often thought about how the system had evolved into a monster that was too complicated for anyone to understand, and it had been a common joke that no one could make it until lunch without committing a felony they knew nothing about. After the Ten Commandments and the Code of Hammurabi, laws had been written to empower the wealthy and those who made their money administering them. Even the laws of the United States, ostensibly written to make all men equal under the law, had become a morass of politically motivated intricacies nobody could navigate themselves. The idea of creating a system from scratch, one that all could understand and in which all could represent themselves, was irresistible yet daunting.

"Ten pages?" he asked, raising an eyebrow.

"Ten and a half if absolutely necessary," Jim said, smiling, then looked serious. "Some years back, I put together a small fighting organization. The purpose was to let fighters fight in as close to a real-life environment as possible."

"Like cage fighting?" asked Tom.

"Sort of," answered Jim. "It was called pankration, taken from the Greek words *pan*, meaning 'all', and *kratos*, meaning 'strengths' or 'powers'. It had been the king of events in the ancient Olympics and they were trying to get it back into the modern games. Anyway, we had a bunch of fighters who were

THE REVIVAL

anxious to participate until they saw the rules. The referees and rules committee made the rules so complex that they made the referees the most important part of the competition rather than the fighters. The fighters hated it, the spectators hated it and I hated it. I did away with most of the rules, the referees left, and we started having great competitions that everybody liked. In short, it is those who actually participate, whether in a fight or the normal fabric of human life, who are the important ones. Laws and rules should set the broad parameters of those interactions, not dictate the minutiae of them, and referees and judges should simply enforce the rules, not become active participants in the conflict by constructing rules that are unnecessarily complex, favor certain groups over others or by inserting their own personal bias or interpretations."

"I quite agree," said Bill.

"So, is this for you?"

Bill smiled and nodded. "I'll do my best."

"Good."

Jim turned to Christian. "We're going to need formalized law enforcement. I don't want it to be like it had become before all this happened, where a lot of cops spent their time trying to catch people doing something wrong so that they could impose their authority and raise money for the politicians. That's wrong and always creates an adversarial relationship between the police and the community they are supposed the be serving. Our new model will be the old model of the American west, peace officers who will enforce the law impartially, and serve and protect the residents of their jurisdiction within the framework of their commissioned responsibility. You're the one for this if you think it's for you. Is it?"

For once, Christian answered seriously. "It is."

Jim nodded. "Good. Pick two people to be deputies and about a dozen more to deputize as reserves. Pick people who will take the responsibility of their job seriously and won't let authority go to their heads. The people must respect them, and they must respect the people." He nodded toward Bill. "You might work with Bill and give him your input as he puts together the statutes."

Christian nodded, as did Bill.

Jim looked around the group. "As head of intelligence, Tom is responsible for obtaining, analyzing and, in some cases, disseminating information for the safety and security of Stonemont. In traditional situations, intelligence keeps much of that information, as well as sources and methods, contained within a close group of people on a so-called need-to-know basis. We are going to consider this group," he nodded around the table, "as need-to-know. To restrict information from anyone here would not only be an insult but counterproductive. We need everyone's ideas and expertise. Sometimes those with the least experience come up with ideas we so-called experts wouldn't think of."

He turned to Tom. "You're up."

Tom leaned forward and looked around the group. "There is something about the town that we haven't shared with everybody. Jim has asked me to tell you today. In addition to being a place for people to establish homes, Jamestown is designed to be a financial engine and an intelligence gathering community. By providing goods and services that people want, it will draw people from surrounding areas bringing both economic growth and information about the areas they came from and through which they passed. That will allow us to gain an understanding about the world around us that simply sending out patrols can't.

"Each person who comes to Jim wanting to open a business in Jamestown goes through a process to determine its suitability and chance of success. When Jim has reached a tentative decision, the final step is that we explain the information gathering aspect of each business to the new prospect. If they agree, they are granted a lease."

"What if they don't agree?" asked Bill.

"Then a lease isn't granted."

"Isn't that illegal?" asked Tracy. "I mean, isn't that discrimination, to refuse to do business with somebody because they think differently than you?"

Bill leaned forward. "First off, this is private property. Jim owns all of it because he paid other people to secure and develop it, and he's offering leases, not sales, thereby retaining ownership and ownership rights of the property. He can decide to do business or not do business with anyone he wants for whatever reason he wants."

"But the Supreme Court repeatedly ruled against prejudicial treatment on the basis of any number of things, including personal opinions. Aren't we denying someone the right to make a living based solely on their refusal to collect information for us?"

Bill shrugged. "Those decisions were usually close votes and swung depending on the changing dynamics of the court. They were never universally held and were often seen as infringements on the rights of property owners."

"Tracy, do you believe in slavery?" asked Jim.

"Of course not," Tracy answered with surprise.

"But I'm sure you're familiar with the Dred Scott decision."

"Yes, but everyone knows slavery is wrong."

"So, the court was wrong in Dred Scott?"

"They simply said that he had no standing before the court."

"Because he was not a U.S. citizen?"

Tracy nodded. "Yes."

"Because those whose ancestors were imported from Africa and sold as slaves could not be American citizens?"

Tracy hesitated. "Yes, that's what the court said."

"Do you think the court was right?"

"No."

"So, the court was wrong?"

Tracy nodded. "Yes."

"So, the Supreme Court can be wrong?"

Tracy nodded again and smiled. "I see what you're saying, and I get it."

Jim nodded in return. "We're not forcing anybody to do anything. If they want to set up a business outside our area of control, they're perfectly free to do so without our help or interference. It's just that if they want to live or do business here, they have to do it our way."

"And as far as what's lawful," said Bill, "there are no laws except what we make, and those must always support the basic concept of the sanctity of private property."

"So, Caesar and Mrs. Hernandez agreed to be spies?" she asked.

"We call them information contacts," answered Tom. "They know that our success and security depend on watching out for each other and they're doing their part."

"Sun Tzu said to use spies for every kind of business," Jim said. "We intend that our information gathering be woven into the fabric of our community so completely that it will be indistinguishable from normal daily life. We all depend on it so we must all participate in it." He paused, looking at Tracy. "It's like a family. Everyone must look out for everyone else. Good news is passed on from one person to the others, and so is bad news and warnings. It helps protect the family and each individual in it."

Jim looked around the group. "Does anyone have anything else?"

The head shakes told him than none did, so he looked at Mike. "Okay, buddy, we're all yours. Where to?"

Mike stood up. "They're training at the Eddington place today. We can walk it."

THE REVIVAL

16

The day was warming up and Jim was glad he had switched from his felt Stetson to a straw Resistol.

It had been many years since he had worn a real gun belt, having succumbed to the nylon and plastic holsters which had become popular as the tactical movement had grown, and the feel of the wide leather belt felt good and substantial, easily supporting the weight of the large revolver and the twenty-four rounds he had placed in the cartridge loops. It was heavy, but a comfortable heavy.

The number of people walking around the commons was fairly small, with most of the men and some of the women away working on Jamestown, but he was surprised that he only recognized about half of those he saw. Almost all were women, most of whom had kids buzzing around them, though he did see two men, one older man and one middle-aged, at the door of the hall where the day's lunch items were being loaded into the bed of an old pickup. The older man was taking plastic bins from women bringing them out of the hall and carrying them to the truck while the younger man kept up a running chatter, pointing to where the older man should put the next bin and making a show of straightening them once they were loaded. He noticed that the younger man was overweight, his red t-shirt stretched across a large belly.

"How about you, Jim?"

Jim looked over to see Bill looking at him expectantly.

"I'm sorry, what?"

"We were talking about what we regretted not doing before the collapse that we now won't be able to. Kelly said see the Swiss Alps, Ann said visit the Da Vinci museum in Florence and I said attend a session of the Supreme Court. How about you?"

Jim thought for a minute and chuckled. "Well, I always thought it would've been fun to drive coast to coast with my blinker on."

Bill laughed.

"You think he's kidding," said Kelly. "He tried a couple of times, but I caught him."

Jim chuckled. It had been funny, but Bill's question was a good one. What had he always wanted to do before the collapse? He took a few steps before he realized that the answer had immediately come to his mind. "This," he said.

"What?" asked Bill.

"This," he repeated, looking around and indicating their surroundings with his hands.

"You wanted the world to fall apart?"

Jim shook his head. "No, but I wanted a simpler, more meaningful life for my family. I wanted more time for us to spend together working on common goals. I wanted peaceful and happy mornings, days of honest, meaningful work that brought us into closer alignment with nature and God's purpose for us, relaxing evenings to contemplate the day just lived and the day to come, more time to just watch, listen to, teach and hug my kids, and to live that life in a community of good, like-minded people." He looked around again and smiled. "If it took the world falling apart, so be it."

They walked several more steps before Kelly said, "Me too."

"Me three," said Ann.

Bill smiled. "Yeah, I guess the Supreme Court doesn't measure up to that."

They entered the tree line, feeling the coolness envelope them as they followed the trail to the Eddington property. The family had not returned and, accepting that they probably wouldn't, the scouts had begun using the property for housing and training. The dog breeding and training program, run by Brin, had also been moved there, as had part of the horse training program because of the large barn and corrals.

Making their way through the trees, they began hearing the dogs, then the voices of Naomi and Becky working the horses in a near-side corral.

Exiting the trees, they walked across the open space between the house and the barn, waving to Brin, Naomi and Becky, then followed a path to where a large obstacle course had been built. About a hundred scouts sat on a berm overlooking the course, some leaning back on their rucksacks, watching several other scouts run a series of logs, barrels, boxes, low walls, high walls, windows and ropes. An instructor stood off to the side, watching.

"I hope you're not wanting us to do this," chuckled Bill.

Mike shook his head. "Nope, but I want you to see something." He turned and walked the short distance to the instructor where he talked for minute, then returned to the group.

THE REVIVAL

He handed a stop watch to Jim. "We're going to have two guys run the course, one after the other. I'd like you to time them," he looked around the group, "and I'd like everyone to watch."

They all nodded and murmured their okays.

Mike turned to the instructor and gave a thumbs-up.

The instructor nodded and motioned a scout out of the training group.

The scout got to his feet and jogged to the starting point of the course.

"Get ready," Mike told Jim as the instructor raised his arm.

The instructor dropped his arm, the scout took off and Jim started the watch.

The scout ran quickly to a series if three logs mounted horizontally across his path, approximately six feet apart and at graduating heights of three, four and five feet. He vaulted over the first, vaulted over the second and jumped to put his hands on top of the third to leg over it.

Landing after the third log, the scout shuffled across a twelve-foot log, jumped to grab a large rope, climbed the rope to the cross-beam from which it hung, muscled over the cross-beam and slid back down the rope.

Running to a ten-foot wall, he grabbed a rope attached to the top and crabbed to the top, then over, landing with a roll on the opposite side.

Approaching a series of staggered log ends embedded end-up in the ground, he stepped from one to the next until he had traversed all twenty-four.

Jumping off the last one, he sprinted to a structure simulating a window in a wall, climbed through, then ran to another wall with a window on the second floor, climbed a ladder, crawled through the window and descended to the ground by a rope hanging from the other side.

They watched as the scout continued through the rest of the course and Jim hit the stop when the scout crossed the finish line.

"What did he get?" asked Mike.

"Three minutes and forty-two seconds," Jim replied.

Mike nodded. "That's good. He's one of our fastest. We consider four minutes thirty seconds acceptable and under four minutes exceptional."

He turned to the scouts and waved another one over. A lanky scout popped up as if lifted by a spring and jogged to the starting line.

Mike turned back to the group. "Now, watch this." He looked at Jim. "Ready?"

Jim re-set the watch and nodded.

Mike raised his arm, paused for a moment, the dropped it. Jim started the stop watch as the scout took off.

THE REVIVAL

The scout ran smoothly, his strides longer than those of the first, and he reached the logs quickly. As he approached them, he jumped up, landing on the first one with his right foot, continued the momentum to the second log, landing on his left foot, then bounded to the third, landing on his right, and leaped to the ground, landing in a roll from which he smoothly came up to run to the twelve- foot log, which he traversed in four long steps.

Running to the rope, he ascended it quickly using only his hands, swung over the bar and came down twice as fast, again using only his hands. Running to the ten-foot wall, he ran straight at it, not slowing down, jumped from his left foot to plant his right three feet up the wall and launched himself to grab the top of the wall, chinned himself to the top and swung over to drop to the ground on the other side, immediately running to the embedded log ends.

Rather than step on each one, he leaped over every other one, not breaking stride, and completed the series in twelve steps.

Jumping from the final log, he ran to the window structure and dove through it head-first, tucking into a roll when his hands touched the ground and bouncing back to his feet to run to the second-floor window obstacle.

Several long strides took him to the structure, but instead of running to the ladder he repeated the same movement he had used to scale the wall, leaping to plant his foot several feet up on the wall then launching himself up to grasp the sill of the window, chinning and muscling his way up and through, then dropping lightly to the ground on the other side.

The scout continued through the course using similar techniques, seeming to bounce and sail his way through with far less effort than had the first.

Jim stopped the watch as the scout crossed the finish line and looked at it.

"What did he get?" Mike asked, smiling as if he knew the answer.

"Two minutes twenty-four," Jim answered, looking up at Mike. "What the heck was that?"

Mike chuckled and waved at the scout, who jogged over to them.

"Mr. Wyatt wants to know what that was," Mike told the scout.

"Parkour, sir," the scout answered.

Jim looked at the scout, then at Mike, then back at the scout. "What's that?"

"It's a method of seeing and moving across obstacles in a different way, sir, of taking the most direct route from one point to another by using obstacles in the course rather than being impeded by them."

Jim looked at the scout thoughtfully. He well understood how the training could not only improve the scouts' physical abilities but be useful in practical application as well. "Can you teach the other scouts to do this?" he asked.

The scout shrugged. "I can teach everybody something and I can teach a lot to some. It depends on each individual's physical abilities and desire to learn."

Jim nodded, looking from the scout to Mike, who smiled, then back to the scout. "What's your name, son?"

"Nathaniel, sir."

"Well, Nathaniel, consider that your new job. Any way you can up the physical skills of the scouts will no doubt be helpful in the future."

"Yes, sir."

Jim turned to Mike and nodded. "Exceptional."

Mike nodded and spoke to the scout. "Nathanial, would you go form everybody in a circle and tell Travis he's up?"

The scout nodded and trotted back to the group.

Mike looked at Jim. "Christian told me you taught him how to fight."

Jim smiled. "That was a long time ago."

Mike shrugged. "Well, he showed me some of your stuff and it was brutal. I liked it. It was beyond what we got."

Jim remained silent, waiting to see where Mike was headed.

"I figure you don't want to teach anymore and Christian has enough on his plate, but I think our scouts should learn some real hand-to-hand."

Jim nodded. "It can come in handy."

"I think I found a solution." He cocked his head toward the scouts who were now forming a circle. "Let me show you."

They walked to the group of scouts who stepped aside to let them enter the interior of the circle where a slim young man was tossing a training knife from one hand to the other.

"Jim, this is Travis McKay," Mike said. "Travis, this is Jim Wyatt."

"Howdy, Travis," said Jim.

"Hello, Mr. Wyatt," Travis answered with a friendly smile.

"Travis, do you think any of these guys can stick that knife in you?" asked Mike.

Travis smiled. "I guess we can find out."

Mike chuckled. "Guess we can." He turned to the scouts. "Who's first? Who wants to try to stick Travis and win a prize?"

Hesitant murmurs ran through the crowd. "What's the prize?" asked a voice from the other side.

"You get to say you stuck him!" answered Mike.

More murmurs ran around the circle.

"They don't seem to be too anxious," observed Jim.

"Travis tends to teach very realistically," answered Mike. "Most of them are already nursing a boo-boo or two from his lessons."

"I'll do it!" shouted a large scout with a U.S. Navy tattoo on his bicep as he stepped into the circle.

"You healed up from last time, Quinn?" Mike asked.

The scout shook his head. "Almost, but I've got him figured out."

"You do, huh?"

"Yep," Quinn nodded confidently. "I'm gonna get him this time."

"You ready?" Mike asked Travis, who was smearing something red on the blade of the training knife.

"Let's go," said the scout. "I'm gonna kiss you this time."

"Okay," Travis replied and tossed the knife to Quinn.

"Kiss him?" Jim asked, raising an eyebrow.

"Travis rubs lipstick on the knife blade. That way, there won't be a question as to whether the blade makes contact. If it does, they call it a kiss."

"Lipstick and kisses?" Jim asked, raising the other eyebrow to match the first.

Mike chuckled.

They watched as Quinn began to circle Travis, making small feints and switching between Latin and Russian grips. Travis moved smoothly, cutting the area to make Quinn do most of the work.

Quinn reversed direction, now circling clockwise and holding the knife out in front of him, flicking and probing like the tongue of a snake. Taking a quick step forward, he executed a reverse slash from left to right, quickly reversing to slash right to left.

Travis avoided both slashes easily, shooting a front kick into Quinn's ribs as the second slash flashed by.

Letting out a grunt, Quinn involuntarily dropped his elbow to cover his injured ribs, backing away for a moment to catch his breath.

Travis watched.

Sucking in a deep breath and wincing at the pain, Quinn settled into a partial crouch, attempting to minimize targets on his own body while extending his knife arm out to fend off any more kicks. He reversed direction again, now circling counter-clockwise. He suddenly stopped, acted as if he was standing up to stop the exercise, then lunged, the knife shooting out at Travis.

Travis smoothly stepped outside the lunge, catching Quinn's wrist and locking it to his hip, then drove his right knee into Quinn's ribs twice. Quinn grunted and dropped to his knees, posting his left arm to try to stay off the ground, but Travis stepped back with his right foot, pulling Quinn's arm out straight and taking him down on his stomach. Stripping the knife from Quinn's grasp, he drew a red line of lipstick across the larger man's throat.

Mike looked at the broad smile on Jim's face. "You look like you just saw the birth if your first son."

Jim nodded. "Outstanding. Have him come over here."

"Travis! Come on over!"

Travis nodded and helped the groggy Quinn to his feet, then walked over.

"That was nice," said Jim, his smile growing wider. "Where did you learn that?"

"I've trained since I was a kid, sir," Travis answered. "I came up under my dad at Kenukan, our dojo in Olathe, and then under Jim Harrison."

Jim's eyes narrowed. "Jim Harrison of Bushidokan?"

"Yes, sir."

"Up in Montana?"

Travis nodded. "You know him, sir?"

"I know *of* him. Hell, everyone knows *of* him. I've heard a lot about him but never met him or any of his people before." He raised his head as if pointing to the ring of scouts with his chin. "That his stuff?"

"Yes, sir. It's his system, Ronin Jutsu."

Jim nodded in recognition. "Skills of the masterless samurai."

"Yes, sir."

"You know more than what you just did there?"

"I know the whole system, sir."

"What does it include?"

"Everything, sir."

"Would you like to be our hand-to-hand combat instructor?"

Travis nodded. "I'd be happy to, sir."

"Good, then you are." Jim held out his hand. "Welcome to Stonemont."

Travis took the hand and smiled. "Thank you, sir."

Jim started to say something else but looked up at the sound of a dirt bike coming out of the trees. The bike blasted through the buildings and down the hill, skidding to a stop in front of him and throwing dirt over the feet of the three men.

The scout on the bike lifted his goggles. "Sheriff Freelove is at the front gate, Jim. Christian said to come get you."

THE REVIVAL

THE REVIVAL

17

Sheriff Freelove pushed the white straw Stetson back on his head and took a long drink. "How the hell is it that you have cold beer?"

Jim sat down on the couch across from him and took a drink from his own glass, smiling. "God loves me."

"Yeah? God loves me too, but he hasn't given me cold beer."

Jim chuckled. "Did you ever watch much YouTube before everything crashed?"

Freelove shrugged. "Sure, whenever my kids weren't watching kittens or people eating weird stuff."

Jim laughed. "Well, I used to watch a lot of the prepper stuff and there was a guy on there, an engineer, who made a lot of videos about gasifiers, ram pumps, heating and cooling and refrigeration and stuff in a grid down situation." He took another drink. "I've got some engineers here and I didn't see any reason why the world collapsing should keep me from having a cold beer."

Freelove shook his head and laughed. "You sure got it figured."

"How about you?" Jim asked. "How are things out your way?"

Freelove cocked his head thoughtfully. "Not bad. Pretty good, really. We've had a higher survival rate than the ten percent they projected. I'd say more like sixty percent. A lot of that is probably due to everybody pulling together from the beginning and the farms around us. It's probably lower than ten percent in Topeka and bigger cities."

Jim nodded. "We've made a few probes into the suburbs of Kansas City and haven't found many since winter. I hate to think what's in there."

"Me too. I don't even want to go into Topeka, but we're going to have to eventually."

"I've been thinking about that myself. How long do we go before we go into Kansas City. Or do we go in at all? Maybe it's better to just leave it be." He took a drink and set his glass on the table. "Anyway, what brings you here?"

Freelove drained his glass, leaned forward with his elbows on his knees and looked at Jim. "Riley's opened its gates."

Jim nodded thoughtfully. "Is that good or bad?"

Freelove shook his head. "Don't know. Can't tell yet." He leaned back into the couch. "They have some working vehicles and are starting to make patrols around the area. They're courteous but not friendly."

"Have they offered any help?"

"The commanding general, a guy named Braddock, has issued an invitation to all community leaders to come into Riley. He says it's to discuss securing the area and arrange assistance to surviving communities."

Jim thought for a moment. "What do you think?"

Freelove shrugged. "I don't know. It makes sense, at least from a government perspective."

"Remember what Reagan said? 'The most terrifying words in the English language are 'I'm from the government and I'm here to help'?"

Freelove chuckled. "Yeah, that's the truth."

"If they wanted to help," Jim continued, "why didn't they come out and offer it before winter when they might have actually saved some people?"

Freelove nodded. "I thought that myself. So did McGregor and Dehmer," he said, referring to the Sheriff of Coffey County and the Highway Patrol lieutenant who had attended the conference at Stonemont with him.

"So, what do you think?"

"I think like McGregor said, the army's got a plan for takin' a shit in a sandstorm, so this is part of a plan. We just don't know what the plan is yet."

"You guys start drinking without me?" Tom asked as he walked in.

Jim waved him in. "Grab a beer and sit down. This is ..." he paused, looking at Freelove. "What's your first name, anyway?"

Freelove smiled. "Mark."

"Tom, this is Mark Freelove, Sheriff of Osage County out west of here. Mark, this is Tom Murphy, our chief of intelligence."

The men nodded to each other as Tom took a beer from the bucket, skipped a glass and sat down on the third couch.

"Tom, Mark says that Fort Riley has come out of its gates. He says they've started making patrols in the area and are inviting area leaders to a meeting to discuss assistance. What do you think?"

Tom took a pull from the bottle and leaned back. "Have they offered any assistance during the crises?"

Freelove shook his head. "Nope."

"Are they offering any now?"

THE REVIVAL

"No, just saying they want to meet with leaders to talk about it."

"How far out are they going with their patrols?"

"Not far. They started with just the highway, then slowly started going into town. They're moving carefully and withdrawing at the first sign of aggressive contact."

"By aggressive, do you mean citizens attacking the patrols?"

Freelove shook his head. "No, just asking for help a little too loudly, I guess."

"How many vehicles in a patrol?"

"I'm not sure, but I got the impression it was only a few."

"What town is it?"

"Junction City."

Tom thought for a moment. "Do you have any idea how many soldiers and dependents stayed in or came back to base after the crash?"

Freelove shook his head again. "Not really. I know the sheriff there and he would know. A lot of the soldiers live off base and they maintain an awareness."

Tom nodded and looked at Jim. "The pattern of their probes would suggest to me that they don't have eyes in the sky. No drones, no satellite feed. That means their technical abilities are compromised. To what extent, we don't know.

"Sending only a few vehicles on graduated probes makes me think their operating vehicles are limited. Not surprising, since most current stuff relies heavily on electronics.

"The fact that they are trying to contact community leaders but withdrawing when people push for help might mean that they are qualifying the cohesion and leadership in different areas and groups, or it could mean that their own leadership is weak."

He turned to Freelove. "Have they set a date for the meeting?"

Freelove shook his head. "Not yet. They're still trying to contact leaders."

"How did you hear about it?"

"From the Geary County sheriff. He heard it from some of the people who were contacted by a patrol."

"Are you going to go?"

Freelove nodded. "Yeah, I'll go. So will McGregor and some of the other sheriffs. We want to know what's going on."

Tom nodded and looked at Jim. "The meeting will have two main purposes. First, to try to establish themselves as the area authority. Second, to

150

identify leaders and begin to construct an association matrix. They need to know who is out here and how everybody fits."

"You think we should go?" asked Jim.

Tom shook his head. "No. I think I should go, and you stay under the radar."

Jim nodded slowly. "Tell me your reasoning."

"It's been a year since the event. We have had no contact from any government entity. We have seen no aircraft. We have heard nothing on shortwave or ham that indicates any government is functioning anywhere."

"Glen's a Ham and he said the same thing," Freelove said.

Tom nodded. "All we've heard is a grapevine message about some soldiers driving around in a few vehicles wanting to have a meeting. That does not sound like a well-planned, well-led, well executed operation."

"So, what are you thinking?" asked Jim.

Tom paused, looking from Jim to Freelove and back. "I hesitate to say this, but I think there may be no government left at all."

"You mean in the whole country?" Freelove asked incredulously.

Tom shrugged. "Maybe somewhere, but not around here."

18

Naomi swung her feet to the floor and stretched. She had awakened halfway through the night and the old cot combined with thoughts of the task ahead had kept her from getting back to sleep. Still, it had given her time to think.

Pushing herself up, she walked to the shower stall, peeling off the old Haskell t-shirt she slept in. Hanging it on a nail, she stepped into the stall under the showerhead and turned on the spigot.

Water cascaded over her as she closed her eyes, remembering when the old barn had been a refuge after the attack on their farm. It had been her refuge again last night, offering her a place to hide from all the things around her except her thoughts, and just as it had served its purpose the first time it had done so again.

She stood for a moment, her face turned up into the spray, feeling its thousand little pin-pricks and hearing the rushing in her ears, then took a bar of soap off the shelf and started to wash.

Bits and pieces of the past year kept flickering in her mind, disobedient to her attempts to organize them, and she realized they were presenting themselves according to importance rather than chronology, so she let them have their way and tried to see what they were telling her. The attack. Killing the men. Christian. Carol and Jerry. Christian. Stonemont. Her parents. Christian.

Putting the soap back, she stood under the water to rinse off, not wanting to leave the space or the moment, then reluctantly turned the spigot closed, grabbed a towel and dried off.

She dressed quickly, strapped on her gun belt and saddled the Arabian, the beautiful filly Jim had given her. Sliding her rifle into the scabbard, she made a final check of things, led the horse out of the barn, closed the door, mounted up and headed west.

What a difference a year had made. Was she the same person she had been before? The startling answer was yes. While the catastrophe had changed most of the people it had not killed, it had simply made her more of who she already was. The world had changed to become one she understood better and appreciated more than the world that had collapsed. Like it had for Jim Wyatt. Like it had for Christian. Like she was sure it had for her father.

Glancing behind her she saw the first feint line of daybreak on the eastern horizon, telling her that sunrise was about an hour away, exactly when she wanted to arrive at Stonemont.

She entered the trees and followed the path she had walked so many times, first to escape Elvin Barnes' men after the attack, and then with Jerry to take supplies from the house to the barn on countless midnight trips. That seemed so long ago. Another world, another lifetime. A time when her only two goals had been to help Carol, Jerry and the kids survive, then get back to Texas.

She thought of her mother and father, the two pillars of her life. They had given her the solid foundation of a family she knew would always be behind her, no matter what. She had been wild and willful and seemed fearless to others, but she knew that her confidence and apparent fearlessness came from her knowledge that, no matter where she was or what she was doing, she was supported by those two pillars. Now, she wasn't even sure if they were still alive. Nor, if they were, were they sure she was.

She brought their faces to mind, almost shocked at the effect it had on her. How often did they think of her? Would they approve of what she was about to do? Would they ever even know? The thought grabbed at her heart and she realized she was crying.

The realization brought a brief feeling of loneliness. Embarrassed at the feeling, she straightened in the saddle and consciously adopted a stern, almost fierce look on her face. Her father had taught her that most people allowed their feelings and emotions to affect the look on their face, but that it was also possible to affect your feelings and emotions by simply controlling or changing the look on your face. He called it 'going Comanche'. She immediately felt strong, focused and almost invulnerable, contemptuous of her momentary weakness, and rode on.

She passed by Carol and Jerry's house, then the school, now called School Center, and entered the tract of woods that ran to within a mile of Stonemont. The trees had leafed, keeping it dark beneath the canopy through which she could now see a lightening of the morning sky.

She passed the spot where Brin and the other girl had been found and soon exited the trees at the edge of the lower field of Stonemont. There, she stopped.

The sun had just broken the horizon and the sky graduated from a medium blue in the east to darker blue in the west. Stars still shone from directly overhead westward and she saw the central hall and the main house silhouetted against them. A light shone from a window of the house.

The filly's ears pricked up as it recognized the area and its nostrils flared slightly as it caught familiar scents. Giving the horse a cluck and a gentle heel, she started across the field and crossed the commons, soon passing the hall and approaching the house.

"You're up early," said the voice, and it was only when he stood up that she saw him.

"Jim?"

He chuckled. "Nobody else around here crazy enough to be up this early," he paused, "except you, I guess. What's up?"

"I wanted to talk to you." She slid off the filly and led it to a post at the corner of the veranda, tying it up with a highwayman's hitch.

"Must be important to get you up so early to ride over here."

"Yeah, kinda." She stepped up onto the veranda and could now see him studying her face.

"Early morning talk needs coffee," he said. "I haven't started the pot for the rest of them yet, but I can make you a Folgers instant like I drink if you want."

She smiled. "Just like my dad."

He chuckled. "Every time you say something about him I like him more." He gestured to the table. "Sit down. I'll bring it to you."

She sat down and looked around. She had only been coming here for a matter of months but somehow it felt like home to her. She looked down the long table and thought about the many meals and celebrations she had been a part of here. She could picture each person sitting at their regular seat.

"Here you go," he set a cup in front of her.

"Thank you," she said, picking up the cup and taking a sip. Another reminder of home.

He returned to his chair and sat down. "You look like a girl with something on her mind."

She took another sip, wondering how to start, then decided to just lay it out. "Christian asked me to marry him."

He nodded. "And being the intelligent girl that you are, you naturally said no."

She smiled, feeling her tension lessening at his usual humor. "No, I said yes."

He shook his head in mock consternation. "And now you want me to talk you out of it, right?"

She smiled again, almost laughing. "No. I love him. I want to marry him."

He smiled. "Good. Don't tell him I said this, but you couldn't find a better man."

She nodded, her smile thoughtful. "I know."

He waited, and she took another sip before setting the cup down and looking at him.

"I had meant to try to make it home in the spring, but then this happened." She paused. "I've thought about it a lot. I'd like to go to Texas. I want to see my parents and I feel bad about getting married without letting them know first, but that's taking a big chance right now." She picked up her cup and took another sip. "It's funny. A year ago, I wouldn't have given a second thought to heading out by myself. Now, I don't want to take the chance of something happening to me, or to Christian, while I'm gone. Now, we have too much to lose."

He leaned back in his chair and nodded. "Francis Bacon said, 'He that hath wife and child hath given hostages to fortune, for they are impediments to great enterprise.' When we have others in our life who we truly love, other things diminish in their relative importance and we begin to judge them according to how they threaten the ones we love or our life with them. We stop looking for excitement and adventure, both of which are really attempts to fill voids within us, and we start cherishing our time with those who really do fill those voids." He paused and looked at her. "Have you two talked about him going to Texas with you?"

She shook her head. "No. He needs to stay here. You need him here."

He shrugged. "I want him here and can sure use him, but it's not my say as to what he does, and it wouldn't be right for me to try. He has to do what's right for him, and now for you and the family you'll hopefully have."

She smiled at the thought but shook her head again. "It's more than that. This is where he should be. I see how important he is to you and everybody else, but I also see how important you all are to him. This is Wyatt land, family land. This is where he needs to be and should be to ensure the safety and prosperity of the family into the future."

She paused, looking down at her coffee cup, then back at him. "I have a strong family and brothers who will continue its legacy in Texas. I want to be the wife who helps Christian continue his family's legacy here. I want to be a part of your family and have children who will benefit and further strengthen it."

Tears came to her eyes. "Since my dad can't be here, I came to ask if you would stand in his place."

He sat quietly, seeing the tears in her eyes and hoping she did not see the ones that had suddenly sprung to his own. He swallowed and cleared his throat. "I'd be proud to honey."

"You'd be proud to what?" asked Kelly as she came out the door.

Jim wiped his eyes as if he was still sleepy. "This beautiful, talented and otherwise intelligent girl wants to marry Christian."

Kelly smiled. "I've been waiting for that."

She walked around the table and wrapped her arms around Naomi's shoulders. "Good for you, sweetie. And Jim will be proud to stay out of your hair and stop razzing Christian, right?"

"I asked him to stand in for my dad."

Kelly stopped in mid-hug, realizing the solemnity of the situation she had walked into. She tightened the hug. "Oh honey, I'm sorry. Of course."

"You all are like family to me, and ..." her voice trailed off.

Jim got up and walked to the edge of the veranda, looking at the sunrise and thinking. After a moment, he turned back around. "If Morgan were getting married, Kelly and I would want to know about it and be there. Knowing the daughter they raised, I bet your parents feel the same. Why don't you write a long letter to them, letting them know you're safe and inviting them up for the wedding?"

Naomi looked confused. "But we can't mail a letter."

Jim nodded. "True, but we can send a scout team with it."

Naomi looked at him, stunned. "You would do that?"

He nodded again. "For my future niece-in-law? You bet. This is a once-in-a-lifetime deal. You should have your folks with you if they can make it. Besides, we need to find out what's out there and it will give the scouts some good experience."

Naomi began trembling. The sudden thought that she could write to her parents, telling them she was alive and well, then inviting them to her wedding was more than she was able to process. Emotions she had held deep inside were rushing to the surface, threatening to erupt. She tried to say something, but realized she was only breathing rapidly.

Jim walked to the women, putting a hand on a shoulder of each. "I'm going to make Naomi and myself another cup of coffee. Then we're going to take her down in the bunker. I have an even better idea."

Leading a confused Naomi into the house and down to the currently-unused basement apartment, they walked to the closet in the rear and opened the door.

"Watch your head and don't spill your coffee," Jim said, shoving a bunch of clothes aside and sliding a false rear wall to reveal a door behind it. Unlocking the door and flipping a light switch, he stepped into the bunker followed by Kelly and Naomi.

Naomi looked around the large room. "Wow."

"See anything you like?" asked Jim.

The second cup of coffee and surprise of the bunker had given her mind a chance to reset and she now felt more in control of herself. She kept looking around. "Everything?"

"Come on back here. You're going to like this."

He led them into the back room reserved for electronics and started opening cabinets. "You should still write a letter, but you should also make a video for them."

"How can I do that if electronics don't work?"

"Most don't. These do. This bunker is essentially a Faraday room."

"He did all this mainly so he could always watch John Wayne movies," said Kelly.

Jim chuckled. "There are worse reasons."

He laid a digital action camera on the counter, then opened a smaller bin and extracted two Micro-SD cards. "Here. These hold thirty-two gigs each. Ought to be enough for a start." He looked at her. "Make them a movie. Tell them about what you've been doing. Show them where you live. Let Carol, Jerry and the kids talk to them. Show them Stonemont and introduce Christian to them. Show them anything and everything you want. If sixty-four gigs isn't enough, I've got more. The scouts will take your letter, your movie, a tablet to play it on and a solar charger to your folks."

He smiled. "And don't forget to invite them to your wedding."

19

The following two weeks were busy. Sheriff Freelove and his men stayed for two more days while he and Jim discussed the situation at Fort Riley. Work continued at a somewhat slower pace on Jamestown as more people were needed for spring planting of the expanded fields. Scout teams pushed out farther into surrounding areas, securing them as a buffer for Stonemont, contacting small communities that had made it through the winter and still bringing in occasional groups or individuals who had somehow survived without being a part of a larger community. The thing that was central on everyone's mind, though, was Naomi's video project and preparations for the scout team to leave for Texas.

She had tried to start a letter, but the excitement and thought of making the video wouldn't let her settle down enough to get far so she decided to do the video first.

Her energy was overflowing and it seemed like she was everywhere, no one being safe from her camera. Not that they wanted to be, of course.

Naturally, she started with herself. It was tough at first and she had to start over several times to be able to do it without crying. She told them about what had happened after the collapse - though leaving out the worst parts, about the re-building of School Center, about Stonemont and, finally, about Christian.

She shot video of School Center, the barn they had hidden in, Stonemont, Jamestown and everything in-between. She had interviewed Carol, Jerry and the kids, Jim, Kelly, Bill and Ann Garner, Tom and Patty Murphy, Mike, and finally Christian.

The last had been the most difficult to start, introducing him to her parents on video, and she could imagine how surreal it might be for them to first see him like this, but Christian had been his usual calm self, being serious when necessary and interjecting humor when needed, and it had soon become fun.

When she was finished with the video and told Jim with some concern that it was three-and-a-half hours long, he had simply smiled and said, "They'll wish it was four."

Jim, Mike and Tom spent the time preparing the scout team for the trip. Twelve of the top scouts were selected, to be led by "The Cools", Alex and Aaron. Weapons and equipment loads were standardized so that each scout would know the equipment of every other scout and Mike gave them an intensive course in combat first aid and basic lifesaving.

They decided the team would travel on horseback, as vehicles would be loud, would require a large amount of fuel, would be subject to breakdown and would not be able to cross all terrain if necessary. While they would keep to the roads in order to avoid cutting fences or crossing potentially inhabited private property, horses didn't have the same limitations. Studying a Rand McNally atlas, they chose a route that would keep the team as far from the major population centers as possible. Calculating the distance at about seven hundred miles and daily travel at forty miles, they estimated the trip would take about eighteen days if nothing went wrong - longer if Murphy showed up. The difficulty of crossing three major rivers, the Arkansas, the Canadian and the Red, would depend on how high the water was when the team arrived at them and whether crossings were blockaded.

Each scout would take an extra horse, which they would lead individually as opposed to running in a remuda, each carrying fifty days of food for the scout along with other equipment not carried in the regular pack he kept on his back or in his saddlebags. An action camera was given to Alex, along with extra batteries and SD cards, with instructions to document the trip and any situations of interest along the way. Naomi's letter and video, the tablet and charger were placed in a padded water-proof pouch and given to Aaron for safekeeping. Jim had included a letter of his own to Naomi's parents.

The morning the scouts were to leave was clear with a soft breeze and cloud whisps dotting the sky.

An aura of excitement surrounded them as they formed up at the main gate, double-checking their equipment, and a crowd soon formed to see them off and give words of encouragement. Other scouts, those who were not going, spent time with their friends who were, talking about things that those who share a common bond only discuss with each other.

Starting with a couple of people, then more and more, the crowd turned to see Naomi walking toward them accompanied by Christian, Jim, Kelly, Mike and Pasquale Paoli who had come the night before to conduct a special service in preparation for the scouts' task.

Naomi walked with her head up and her jaw tight as she approached the group of men who were about to take her message to her parents. Her emotions were close to the surface after two weeks of preparation and anticipation and she guarded against breaking down from exhaustion and the building pressure of her hope.

Christian reached out and took her hand and she seemed to calm as they reached the crowd, then made their way through it to the scout team.

The crowd quieted, cognizant of the gravity of the situation, and silence fell over the group as Naomi came face-to-face with the team.

She stood staring at the men, feeling responsible that they were about to risk their lives for her, not to save hers but simply to take her message to her mother and father. She looked at each scout individually, knowing that any or all of them might die in the attempt. Those who loved them might never see them again. They might die quickly or in prolonged agony, never growing older to have families of their own, wives to love, sons to teach and daughters to cherish. She didn't know what to say. There were no words for this. Suddenly, she broke, tears long held in flowing down her cheeks. She shook her head. She couldn't let them do this. Not for her. "No," she shook her head. "No ... no ..."

Alex stepped forward, putting his hands in her upper arms and looking hard into her eyes. "We'll get through. Don't worry." He smiled. "But you have to name your first kid Alex."

The joke brought her out of her emotional ditch and she flung her arms around Alex's neck, hugging him until he blushed.

"Or Aaron," said Aaron, smiling and opening his arms for a hug.

"Or Justin," said another scout.

"Or Sam!"

"Or Josh!"

Naomi went down the line of scouts as they offered their names, hugging each tightly. Finally reaching the end, she turned to all of them. "Thank you doesn't do it, but that's all I can say. Thank you." She folded her hands in front of her chest as if she was praying. "Be careful. Please be careful and come back safe."

"Yes ma'am," said a scout who had identified himself as Ryan, touching the brim of his hat and smiling. "Mike already gave us that order, but it sounded a lot nicer coming from you."

"Mount up!" called Alex as he stepped into the saddle and turned toward Jim, Christian and Mike. "See you soon," he said with a half salute and, with that, he wheeled his horse toward the gate followed by the rest of the team.

The crowd watched as they left, dwindling as they got further away until only Christian and Naomi remained, watching them until they were out of sight.

20

Declan Moore straightened up from the pump where he had been rinsing off his hands and stretched his back. Saddle broncs and Texas Tech football had taken their toll even before going on the Amarillo PD and then on to DPS and the Rangers, and his body often sounded like a bowl of Rice Krispies when he didn't stay stretched out. A cloud of dust was headed his way and he waited, pulling his sleeves back down and buttoning the cuffs, watching until he could make out the vehicle causing it. A red pickup. Pres Walker. Driving faster than usual.

Declan walked to the house, entered the back door and called to his wife. "Cilla! Pres is comin' down the road in a hurry."

"Okay," came a voice from a back bedroom, "I'll be out in a minute. I have to give him that cake pan to take back to Cindy."

Declan stepped out onto the front porch and looked around with hidden disappointment. It had been even dryer than usual and the garden he was trying to keep going with well water was not looking promising. The drought was getting worse. He'd have to pump more. He watched as Walker slowed down for the turn, then sped up again as he came up the drive, finally scattering a group of chickens as he slid to a stop in front of the house.

"Declan," Walker said as soon as he stepped out of the truck, "there's some boys down at the station who say they're from Kansas." He held out an envelope as he mounted the four steps to the porch. "They brought this."

Declan took the thick manila envelope and looked at it. His whole body seemed to flush when he read *Mom and Dad* in his daughter's handwriting and he suddenly felt short of breath.

"Hi, Pres," said Cilla as she stepped out the door. "Could you take Cindy's cake pan back to her?" She stopped, looking at the men's faces. "What's wrong?"

Declan looked his wife in the eyes and held the envelope up for her to see.

She felt her heart jump, reaching out to grab his arm with one hand and help him hold the envelope with the other. Her eyes darted from the envelope to her husband to Pres.

"Some boys from Kansas brought it," Pres said.

THE REVIVAL

Trying to keep his hands from trembling, Declan reached into his pocket and took out a folding knife which he flicked open. Carefully placing the tip under the flap, he slowly slit the envelope open, being careful not to damage it or its contents. Methodically folding the knife and putting back in his pocket, he reached two fingers into the envelope and withdrew the thick sheaf of paper within. Unfolding the paper, he noticed several smaller pieces fall out onto the floor which Cilla stooped down to pick up.

Dear Mom and Dad, started the letter, *I am alive and safe*.

"Dec," said Cilla, standing back up and staring at the papers in her hand.

He looked. A picture of Naomi, smiling, standing in front of a fireplace.

With trembling fingers, Cilla went through the pictures. Naomi with Carol, Jerry and the kids. Naomi on a beautiful grey horse. Naomi with a tall dark-haired man. Naomi sitting at a long outdoor dinner table with a group of smiling people. She looked up at her husband, tears welling in her eyes. "She's okay."

Declan nodded, not sure whether to trust his voice.

"The Kansas boys say they've got a video she made for you, too," Pres said. "I wasn't sure it was legit, but I guess it is. You want me to go get it?"

Declan was still staring at the pictures and shrugged. "We don't have anything to play it on but bring them on out."

"Okay. They're on horseback so it'll be a bit."

Declan nodded absently and took Cilla's arm. "Come on. Let's go sit down."

He led her to the kitchen table where they pulled two chairs together. Cilla spread the pictures on the table in front of them while Declan began to read.

"Dear Mom and Dad," he began, "I am alive and safe. I pray you are too. I have so much to tell you."

They read page after page, all twenty-three pages, constantly looking at her pictures on the table in front of them. Then, they read it again.

They were silent, each lost in their own thoughts, until Cilla asked, "Do you think we can go up there?"

Declan nodded, his silence having covered the plans he was already starting to make in his head. "Yep, we'll go." He looked at his wife. "It sounds like she's in a good place."

Cilla nodded. "And getting married." She paused. "I had hoped ...," her voice trailed off.

"He sounds like a good man," said Declan.

Cilla smiled. "He sounds like her father."

"You want to read it again?" he asked.

She nodded.

He handed the letter to her. "Read it aloud. I want to hear her words in your voice."

She had read the letter and he had listened, hearing his daughter speak to him over the miles and months, and they were sitting at the table in silence holding each other's hands when they heard Pres's truck come back up the drive.

They got up from the table and walked out onto the porch, still holding hands. Pres was just coming to a stop in front if the house and they could see a group of riders just turning off the road and into the drive. Behind the riders trailed two pickups owned by other Rangers.

"Brought some back-up, I see," said Declan as Pres stepped out of his truck.

Pres shrugged. "You never know."

Declan nodded. "What do you think?"

"Seem like good boys. You'd think they were from Texas."

Declan smiled. That was high praise from Pres.

They waited in the shade of the porch while the riders made their way up the long drive, finally stepping down and walking out to meet the group in the yard beyond Pres's truck. The riders had the hard, lean look of men who spent most of their time outdoors and the squint of those who were used to looking into the sun. Each sat their horse comfortably and was leading another, the last one leading two. He counted eleven men.

"Howdy," said Declan, nodding at the riders.

"Howdy", nodded the lead rider. "Are you Mr. Moore?"

"I am," answered Declan. "And you're scouts from Stonemont?"

"We are," Alex nodded. "Naomi must have told you about us in her letter."

The sound of his daughter's name coming from this man he had never met felt strange, but somehow reassuring of her safety. He nodded. "She did."

"I'm Alex. We have some more things for you."

Declan nodded again. "You can corral your horses in back and stow your gear in the barn. There's a pump out there where you can wash up." He nodded at the four Rangers getting out of the pickups. "The boys will help you. I'll go see if Mrs. Moore can whip up something for you to eat."

He looked up and down the line of scouts. "Welcome to Texas."

THE REVIVAL

21

"We lost one crossing the Canadian up in Oklahoma," said Aaron. "His horse slipped, might have stepped in a hole, and came down on him against a rock. We did everything we could, but he died the next morning. Had to shoot the horse."

The group of scouts and Rangers sat around a large fire pit in the back yard of the Moore's house, sitting on chairs, benches and old tree stumps. Declan and Cilla had read Jim's personal letter to them telling them of the love and respect everyone at Stonemont had for their daughter, assuring them of her safety and inviting them to stay at Stonemont if they were able to come to the wedding. Afterwards, they watched the video Naomi had made from start to finish. Now, Declan was laying strips of steak on the grill from a steer they had just butchered while Cilla brought out a pot of beans, jars of salsa and a plate of tortillas. It was a simple meal that the Rangers had established as a tradition whenever a large group gathered at the major's house so as not to put Cilla to too much work. Each man would take a strip of meat off the grill when it was done to his liking and put in on a tortilla slathered with beans and salsa. When he finished eating it, he made another one and continued until he was full.

More Rangers had shown up as the word got out about the scouts' arrival and now the groups were about even.

"That's tough," said a Ranger. "There are lot of things out there that can kill a man."

"What did you find for the most part?" asked another Ranger.

"A lot of pretty country," said Alex. "Mostly empty, but with some small towns, farms and ranches with people in them."

"How were the people?" asked Pres. "Did you talk to any of them?"

Alex nodded. "We talked to quite a few. Most towns have sentries or checkpoints on their main roads. We talked with most of them, but we didn't want to stop too long and most of them didn't seem too thrilled about us hanging around anyway, though they were glad to hear news from the outside."

Pres nodded. "Understandable."

"The only real problem we had was at a bridge over the Canadian," said Aaron. "A bunch of guys had it blockaded and wouldn't let us through unless we paid a toll."

"What did they want?"

"Some of our horses and food."

"Did you give it to them?"

"Hell, no. It kind of stuck in our craw not to have it out with them right there, but Jim gave us strict orders to avoid trouble if possible and we probably would have lost a few."

"We went down river a couple of miles," said Alex. "Found a low spot in the river with some rocks and sand bars to make a crossing. That's where Dave's horse fell on him."

"As far as I'm concerned," said Aaron, "those guys at the bridge killed him. If they had let us pass, Dave would still be alive."

"That's how I'd look at it," nodded a Ranger.

"When are you headed back?" asked another.

"We'd like to have a day or two out of the saddle if the Moores don't mind us sleeping in their barn for a couple of nights. Then, we'll head back."

"You have enough food?" asked Pres.

Alex nodded. "We're good."

"You all seem pretty well set up."

Alex nodded again. "Jim's a planner and he's got good people with him. We're set up pretty good."

"That's the truth," said Declan to the Rangers. "If any if you guys want to see the video Naomi made, I can bring the tablet out here. Cilla and I already watched it and this Stonemont where these guys are from looks like a pretty tight outfit." He paused and looked at Alex. "You guys think you'll be ready to head back in a couple of days?"

"Yes, sir. And we brought a camera in case you and Mrs. Moore would like to make a video to send back to Naomi."

Declan thought for a moment. "I appreciate that, but Cilla and I have been talking and we think we might just go back up with you."

"I'll go with you," said Pres. "I haven't been to Kansas in a while."

Declan shook his head. "You need to stay here and take care of things while I'm gone."

Pres spit in the fire. "Hell, Dec, what needs doin' around here? The bad boys we didn't shoot have pretty much killed each other off. Things around here are about as exciting as a mashed-potato sandwich. Besides, Manny will be comin' by tomorrow," referring to the Amarillo lieutenant. "He can run things just fine."

Declan considered it. Pres was right. Nothing important had been happening since winter. Lubbock PD and the Lubbock County Sheriff's Office were the main law enforcement in the area, as were other sheriffs and police departments in their jurisdictions, and they had a good handle on things. The Rangers mainly assisted with their special units and in major cases, so the temporary absence of a few Rangers shouldn't make much of a difference.

"How long did it take y'all to get down here?" Pres asked Alex.

"Twenty days," Alex answered. "Shoulda' been nineteen, but we lost a day at the Canadian."

Pres looked at Declan. "If just you and Cilla go, it's gonna take you twenty days, maybe longer, to get up there. Then, what are you gonna do when it's time to come back, do it all by your lonesomes?" He looked around at the other Rangers. "I say some of us come along and we trailer these boys' horses on back up there. Should be there in two, three days. Then, when it gets time to come back, you've got the guns to get you back. We've got enough running vehicles and can get the trailers."

"I'm for that," said a Ranger.

"Me too," said another.

Pres nodded and looked around. "How many think that's a good idea and want to go?"

All of the Rangers raised their hands.

Declan thought about it. He had seventeen Rangers in addition to himself and the two lieutenants, and there really wasn't enough work for them to do in the new situation. He had talked with most of the other company commanders and, though they had lost contact with the companies in El Paso and Weslaco due to cartel and border violence, those in Garland and Waco were mainly driving around showing the flag, just like they were doing here in Lubbock. Pres's idea made sense, but leaving the area without telling headquarters first went against the grain for him. Still, it had been a while since he had received direct communications from Austin and he had gotten the feeling that statewide Ranger operations had become more of an informal personal effort depending on each company's manpower and local needs. Lord knows they hadn't been paid since everything went to hell. Not that that mattered - a Ranger was a Ranger, and the Rangers had a foundational history of working for free.

THE REVIVAL

Even though the Rangers weren't a democracy, every one of them was an experienced man and lawman, and he valued their opinions. He nodded slowly. "Okay." He looked at Pres. "You and seven others come with us." He looked around at the other Rangers. "You all figure out among you who's comin'. Take tomorrow to get the trucks, trailers and yourselves ready. We'll leave the morning after tomorrow."

THE REVIVAL

22

The trucks and trailers started arriving shortly after four o'clock and the gear and horses were loaded by the time the sun broke the eastern horizon.

The previous day had been a day of rest for the scouts but was one of preparation for the rest - Declan, Pres and the selected Rangers getting equipment ready and Cilla going around to friends making a video to take to Naomi. Naomi's brothers, Eamon and Noel, both Rangers, were coming, Pres and three other Rangers were bringing their wives, and another was bringing his two grown sons, making the trip seem more like a holiday than a police operation and the excitement was palpable when Declan gave the order to get underway.

Alex and Aaron watched as the rest of the scouts dispersed into the trucks behind them, then loaded into the back seat of Declan's pickup, securing their rifles between them. After a minute, Declan saw a wave from the drag vehicle and put his truck in gear with a wave to the convoy to move out.

They drove down the drive slowly, making sure all vehicles were in line before turning east on the gravel road and heading into the sun.

Aaron looked out the side window to see the line of vehicles coming down the driveway and turning in behind them. "How do you have so many trucks running?"

Declan looked at his right mirror to check the progress of those still coming out the drive. "This is west Texas. We never fell for that cash-for-clunkers bull they were trying to shovel us. We've got more old pickups out here than we've got rattlesnakes." He smiled. "Well, almost. Anyway, we've got plenty."

He saw the last truck pull onto the road and pulled his visor down to block the sun. "Here we go."

By mid-morning they had reached the Caprock Escarpment and descended from the Llano Estacado to see the landscape change from that of the high plains to the tall grasses of the western great plains. They swung north to avoid Wichita Falls and by noon they had crossed into Oklahoma.

Conversation was sporadic with each lost in their own thoughts, Alex and Aaron enjoying the trip but eager to get home and Declan and Cilla thinking about their daughter.

The roads were good and unimpeded, and they made good time, though kept their speed around sixty because of the trailers. They occasionally passed other people in cars and trucks with whom they exchanged waves and passed through several small towns where they waved acknowledgement to stares that ranged from curious to hostile.

Stopping to refuel from cans they carried on board, Declan walked to where Alex and Aaron were stretching their legs. "Pretty country," he said.

Alex nodded and Aaron answered, "Yeah, it is."

Declan handed the map they were following to the brothers. "We'll be coming up on the Canadian in a while. Show me where the blockaded bridge is."

They looked at the map for a moment and Aaron pointed at a spot. "Right here."

"Are you going to go around it?" Alex asked.

Declan shook his head. "Nope. We're going to have a chat with those boys."

Aaron smiled and nodded.

Seeing that all the trucks were refueled, Declan gave a rally signal and waited for the other Rangers to join him. When they were all there, he spread the map on the hood of his truck.

He indicated a spot on the map with his finger. "Here's the bridge the scouts say is blockaded. It's on highway 33, not that that matters, and is between the towns of Thomas on this side and Fay on the other." He looked around at his men. "No way to know which town the blockaders are from, or if they're just highwaymen who have laid a claim to that bridge. People are usually a little easier-going in the morning, so we'll stop this side of Thomas for the night and head in in the morning."

"Are we going in hard or soft?" asked Pres.

"Soft. We'll just go in like regular folks passing through till we see what the deal is." He thought for a minute. "But keep your badges on."

They continued on, passing through Custer City where they got waves and horn honks from a group at a Kwik Shop, then stopped at Deer Creek where they watered and picketed the horses and slept in the trucks, rotating sentries through the night.

THE REVIVAL

It rained throughout the night, but morning broke with a sunrise of purples and oranges shining in a sky that looked like it had been washed clean of yesterday's dust.

Breakfast was protein bars and water as they loaded the horses back into the trailers and circled around Declan to get the plan of the day. Shirts were wrinkled, and hats sat farther back on heads than they would later, but eyes had begun to un-blur and truck-sleeping kinks were starting to shake out.

Declan looked around at the group. "We'll be getting to Thomas in a bit, then we'll see what's what."

"Who do we act like we are?" asked a Ranger.

"We are who we are," answered Declan. "Texas Rangers and Kansas scouts, coming from where we were to where we're going."

"ROE?" asked another.

"You're Texas Rangers. You shoot anybody who shoots at you or looks like they're about to. Or anybody who looks like they're getting ready to shoot anybody else who you think shouldn't be shot." He looked at Alex and Aaron. "I imagine you boys have a similar policy."

Alex smiled. "Word for word."

Declan nodded. "Well, this day isn't getting any longer. Let's move out."

Moving back onto the highway, they headed northeast. The landscape was broken by hills and tributary streams feeding the Canadian River and they enjoyed the scenery while remaining watchful at side roads and ranch drives. Soon, they were passing scattered houses on the fringe of Thomas.

The houses were closer together as they entered the town and soon gave way to businesses lining the road on both sides. Several people stared at them as they passed, some returning their waves, and a tractor crossed the road two blocks ahead.

They passed a Dollar General on their left, then went through a block of brick buildings of the old downtown. A Family Dollar and a gas station on their right looked closed but secure and kids played in a city park on their left.

"It looks like a nice little town," said Cilla.

"Looks like," Declan answered.

Seeing a patrol car parked in the driveway of a two-story frame house on the left, Declan pulled over and parked on the right shoulder, getting out as the other trucks pulled over and parked behind him.

Declan crossed the street to the house. The patrol car was covered with dust and the tires were almost flat. The graphics showed Custer County Sheriff Department. Walking up the sidewalk, he mounted the steps to the front stoop and rang the bell.

No one answered, so he waited a minute and rang again.

"Bell don't work," said a man in a white straw Stetson walking around the corner of the house. The man seemed in his fifties and wore a khaki shirt with a gold sheriff badge on it.

Declan stepped back off of the stoop. "I'm Declan Moore from Lubbock, sheriff," he said, extending his hand.

"Homer Frisbee," the man said, taking Declan's hand. "The sheriff's down at Dead Woman's Crossing. You're a ways from home."

Declan nodded. "We're heading up to around Kansas City. My daughter got caught up there."

Frisbee shook his head. "Sounds like a bad place to be." He looked at the caravan of trucks and trailers. "Looks like you brought your troops."

Declan nodded. "We didn't know what to expect, so better more than less. How are things around here?"

Frisbee pushed his hat back on his head. "Quiet enough. Lost some people after it happened, but we're gettin' along. Slower pace suits me fine. How 'bout down your way?"

"About the same. We're livin' the life our great-grandparents did. Suits me, too." He looked up the road to the east. "I see a bridge up ahead on the map. Is it passable."

Frisbee looked up the highway as if envisioning it. "It is, and it isn't. The bridge is in good shape but there's some boys from Fay that have set up a toll on it." He looked at the caravan. "They're gonna ask for some stuff to let you pass."

"What if we refuse?"

Frisbee shrugged. "Guess you'll be in for a fight."

"Have you tried to clear them out?"

"Me?" Frisbee scoffed. "Not hardly. I've got a wife, a daughter and two grandkids I'm tryin' to keep alive. We've got about forty men left in this town, with an average age of me. That bridge don't make no never-mind to us and we're not gonna get killed tryin' to roust those boys. Best advice I could give you would be just give 'em something and be on your way."

Declan thought for a minute, then nodded and held out his hand again. "Thank you, Homer. Guess we'll get goin'."

Frisbee took the hand. "Okay. You take care of yourselves."

"You too."

Returning to his truck, Declan waved the convoy forward, then stopped again a couple of miles out of town, got out and gave the rally sign.

THE REVIVAL

As the Rangers and scouts joined him, he looked up the road then back at the group. "The bridge should be a couple of miles up. Now, this isn't Texas or Kansas, but a deal like these boys are running is wrong no matter where it is."

"The way things are now, Dec, who's to say what's Texas and what isn't?" expressed a Ranger.

Dec chuckled. "Got a point." He looked at the scouts. "Would you boys be willing to make another river crossing? If we come from this direction and you come from the other, we can have them between us."

Alex and Aaron looked at each other, then at the other scouts, all of whom nodded. "Sure," they said in unison.

Declan nodded. "Good. Let's unload you here and let you saddle up. Head over to cross where they can't see you from the bridge, then come up around them so you're coming down the road like you did before. Set a fire, a big one so we can see the smoke, then get to the bridge thirty minutes later. You got stuff to start a fire?"

"Yep," said Alex

"How do we know when thirty minutes is?" asked Aaron.

Declan looked around on the ground and picked up a stick. Squatting down, he pushed it into the dirt. "Set a stick in the ground, then put a pebble or something two fingers from where the shadow falls." He put his fingers on the ground and placed a small stone next to them. He looked up at the scouts. "Make sure you put your marker on the side the shadow is moving towards. When the shadow touches your marker, call it time."

Aaron smiled and nodded. "Pretty slick."

The scouts headed southeast to reach the river out of sight of the bridge. The terrain was mostly flat with occasional rises and draws, which they made use of as they worked their way along. Most of the land was open and they only encountered one fence which they cut and repaired behind them.

They arrived at the river, its bank a gentle slope to the riverbed which showed mostly wet sand and pebble bars separated by narrow and shallow runs of water, the thirsty, drought-ravaged ground having soaked up the previous night's rain. Mindful of Dave's accident, they dismounted and led their horses across, allowing them to drink their fill, then remounting only when they reached the solid ground beyond.

Continuing east, they came to a road which they took north, arriving at the highway about a mile east of the bridge and around a long curve that hid them from it.

They dismounted and walked their horses into a stand of trees, picketing them, then started gathering wood for a fire.

The trees were old growth, not having been cut or thinned for many years, and deadfall was plentiful. Not bothering with the folding saws they carried, they dragged large limbs and logs out onto the roadside until they had a fairly large brush pile.

Starting three fires at the edges of the pile, they soon had a roaring blaze onto which they threw leaf-covered branches they had cut from live trees in order to create a large amount of smoke. The smoke billowed straight up into the still morning air and Alex stuck a stick in the ground, placing a small stone two fingers-width away from the tip of its shadow.

"There it is," said Pres, putting a pebble two fingers-width from the tip of their own.

When the shadow touched the pebble, the scouts led their horses out of the trees and mounted up. Taking to the shoulder of the road, they soon rounded the curve to see the bridge ahead. Vehicles blocked it as they had before and thay could see a number of men milling around.

They made it to within a hundred yards of the bridge before several of the men sauntered out into the middle if the road, waiting for them.

"Looks like you're back!" one of the men yelled when they came within earshot.

The scouts continued their approach without responding.

"Guess you figured out it was better to pay the toll, huh?" the man yelled, looking more closely. "Where are the rest of your horses?"

The scouts continued without responding.

"Hey, dipshit!" yelled the man, "I said where are the rest of your horses?"

The scouts stopped about fifty feet from the man. "They're comin'," said Alex.

"They're comin'?" laughed the man. "What do you mean, they're comin'?"

The scouts sat silently.

The man looked around. "I s'pose you want across our bridge now?"

Alex shook his head. "Nope."

The man squinted at the scouts. "Nope? What the hell you doin' here, then?"

"Came to see you," answered Aaron.

"Came to see me? Well, you see me. You think I'm pretty or somethin'?"

Aaron looked at the other men who were walking to the bridge to back up their leader. "Came to see all of you."

The man spread his arms and looked around at his men, another dozen or so having joined him on the bridge. "Well, howdy-doo. He came to see all of us. Ain't that nice?"

"Yeah, that's real nice," said one of the men, spitting a stream of tobacco juice to the side.

The scouts sat silently.

Emboldened by their silence, the man smiled. "Now, you may not be aware, but this isn't just our bridge, this is our road. And you know what? It's a toll road." He turned to smile at his men. "Ain't that right?"

"That's right," said one of the men.

"That's a fact," said another.

The man turned back to Alex and Aaron, his smile bigger. "So, you see, it don't matter if you don't want to go across our bridge. You're already on our road. And like I said, it's a toll road."

Alex nodded as if he was thinking. "Guess we'll just wait, then."

"Wait? Wait for what?"

Alex pointed across the bridge behind the man. "Them."

The man turned to look behind him to see a white pickup truck coming towards him. The pickup was towing a horse trailer and there were more vehicles behind him. "So, who the hell is that?" he demanded, his voice losing some of its certainty.

"That's who we were going to see when you wouldn't let us cross the bridge," said Alex.

"One of our friends died because you wouldn't let us cross," said Aaron.

"Died?" the man asked, confused. "Why did he die?"

"We had to make a river crossing because you wouldn't let us cross the bridge. His horse slipped and fell on him."

The man shrugged, his bravado slipping with the arrival of the trucks. "That's tough luck, but I don't see how that's our fault."

"You don't have to see," said Aaron. "I see. That's enough."

The sound of a truck door slamming made the man look around again to see Declan walking toward him with a rifle in his hand. Several other men were walking up behind him, also carrying rifles.

The man looked back at the scouts to see them dismounting and walking their horses to the side of the road, swinging their rifles from their sides to ready positions.

"You men clear the bridge!" Declan called.

The men looked back and forth between the scouts and the Rangers. "Who are you?" the leader asked Declan.

"I'm Major Declan Moore of the Texas Rangers and these are my men." Declan stopped about fifty feet from the men. "Those men," he said, indicating the scouts, "are Kansas scouts who were under orders from their commander not to engage you on their way down but are probably itching to blow you off this bridge in a minute."

The man's bravado was slipping at the sudden command of and threat from Declan, and his voice carried a bit of a whine. "This ain't Texas or Kansas. You all got no authority here."

Declan shouldered his rifle, as did the Rangers behind him and the scouts. "Let me tell you where you are, boy. You're nowhere. You're not in Texas, you're not in Kansas and you're not in Oklahoma. You're in the sights of twenty rifles and about two seconds from a hole in the ground if I don't see those vehicles moving real quick."

The man held up his hands as if to ward off what Declan was saying. "Wait, wait, wait ..."

"Who's your second in command?" demanded Declan.

"What? Why?"

"So I know who to talk to after I shoot you."

"Okay, okay, okay!" The man's fear exposed his lack of experience and he started backing up. "Okay, we'll get 'em moved!" He turned to the other men around him, trying to regain some of the authority he knew the exchange had cost him. "Let's move these trucks for the Rangers! Let's go!"

Two men moved out of the group and walked slowly toward the two pickups blocking the bridge, looking askance at their leader. Getting in the vehicles, they slowly backed them off the bridge and onto the shoulder of the road, shutting them off and getting out.

"You got 'em?" Declan asked Alex and Aaron.

"Yep," said Alex as Aaron nodded.

Holding his rifle in one hand while he led his horse with the other, Alex led the scouts across the road so that the men wouldn't be blocked from them when the caravan went through. He pointed his rifle at the leader. "You all back up twenty steps and sit down."

The men complied, and Alex gave the sign for the convoy to pass.

"What are you going to do?" asked the leader.

Alex looked at him, then up and down the line of seated men. "We're going to let most of you live."

The trucks and trailers passed behind them.

"What do you mean, most of us?"

The trucks and trailers stopped.

"You," Alex pointed at the man, "stand up."

The man hesitantly stood up.

Alex swept the group with his rifle. "Listen closely. You may have wondered why we haven't shaken you down for weapons. It's because we don't want to shoot unarmed men. My brother is going to take him," he nodded toward the leader, "out on the bridge. He has some business with him because he laughed at making us cross the river where our friend died. He has to pay. The rest of you stay still. If you try to intervene or make a move on us we will kill you." He paused. "You might get a couple of us, but we will get all of you. Does anyone not understand?"

No one said anything.

"Good. Now stay relaxed."

Aaron motioned at the leader with his rifle. "Go."

Trying his best to maintain his composure, the man walked to the bridge and then out onto it.

"Keep going," Aaron said when the man stopped after several steps. "Walk till I tell you to stop."

The man started again, his steps short and his legs beginning to tremble. They walked until Aaron saw that they were over the thin ribbon of shallow water beneath the bridge.

"Stop. Face the side. Look at the river."

"Please, mister." The man's voice was shaking. "I've got kids."

"Step up on the railing."

The man tried to turn around, but Aaron jabbed him hard with the muzzle of his rifle. "If you don't step up, I'll shoot you and throw you over."

The man put his hands on the low concrete side rail, his whole body now shaking, a sudden stench indicating that he had lost control of his bowels. He struggled onto the rail, slowly standing up.

"Look at the river. What are your kids' names?"

"Cheyenne and Dakota."

"How old are they?"

"Sev... seven and five."

"Look at the sky. Do you love Cheyenne and Dakota?"

The man was crying now. "Yes."

"Our friend's name was Dave. He didn't have kids yet. He wanted kids. Now, he never will. He had a girl he was going to marry. Now, he never will. What do you think Cheyenne and Dakota are doing right now?"

THE REVIVAL

The man shook his head. "I .. I don't know. They're home."

"Do you think they'll miss you? Will they wonder why their daddy felt it was more important to go bully people and get himself killed than stay at home to love them and raise them?"

The man was falling apart. "Oh god, oh god ..."

"What would you say to them right now if they could hear you?"

"Oh god, I love them so much. I'm so, so sorry."

Aaron waited for a minute, then stepped back. "Listen closely. You're not gonna die today, at least not by me. You have another chance to be a father and love and raise your kids instead of coming out here to harass and hurt other people. You understand?"

The man was choking. "Y ... yes."

"I'm going to leave. You stay there until someone comes and tells you to get down. You understand?"

"Yes."

"If you get down before someone comes and tells you to, I'll figure you didn't understand any of this and I'll come back and kill you. Understand?"

The man nodded feebly. "Yes."

"If you guys are at this bridge when I come back through, I'll kill you for not taking the opportunity I'm giving you today. Understand?"

"Yes."

Aaron looked at the man for a minute, then turned and walked back to the group where Declan and the scouts were still watching the other men.

"You gonna let him live?" asked Alex.

Aaron nodded. "For now."

Alex looked at Declan. "Okay, we're ready."

Declan looked at the men on the ground. "We'll be coming through here again. Your job from now on is to keep this bridge open and safe for travelers. If I see you don't do that, if you try to run your little game again, we'll kill you."

Declan walked back to his truck and the scouts mounted up.

Aaron wheeled his horse to face the men. "If anyone takes a shot at us, we'll come back and kill you all." He nodded toward the bridge. "When we're out of sight, you can go tell your boss out there he can get down."

23

"They're back! They're back!"

Aedan raced his horse from the gate to the house. Running a horse in the commons was a definite no-no but the excitement of the news he had was enough to risk an admonition from his mom and a stern look from his dad.

He reined the horse in at the hitching ring next to the veranda, jumped off, tied the reins to the ring with the highwayman's hitch Naomi had taught him and ran into the house.

"They're back!" he yelled again to his mom who was in the kitchen chopping herbs to put in the dough for the next day's bread.

"Who's back?" Kelly asked, wiping her hands on a kitchen towel.

"The scouts! Where's dad?!"

Kelly frowned. Something must be wrong. They couldn't have made it to Texas and back so quickly. "He's in his den with Mike and Tom."

Aedan ran out of the kitchen and down the hall to the den. "Dad! Dad! They're back!"

"Who's back?" Jim asked as Aedan exploded into the room.

"The scouts! And they've got a bunch of Texas Rangers with them!"

Jim looked at Mike and Tom, then back at Aedan. "Where are they?"

"Coming up to the main gate by now, I guess." He was trying to catch his breath. "I was at the contact gate when they got to it and the guards told me to come let you know! They're in trucks pulling trailers!"

Jim smiled. "Well, let's go welcome them."

Declan concentrated as he snaked the truck and trailer through the gate complex. It wouldn't have been a problem with a standard two-horse trailer, but they were all pulling four-horse trailers and he figured they would be lucky to all get through without leaving some paint on the walls.

The top of the walls came up to the top of his cab and all he could see was what was straight ahead of him and the trees and sky above. He felt claustrophobic and vulnerable, knowing that he would not be able to see an approaching attack or have room to maneuver if he needed to.

THE REVIVAL

The final turn brought him to the exit and Stonemont sprawled in front of him. A large stone and timber house sat on top of the hill ahead and a large building that looked like a cross between a church and a Viking longhouse sat beyond it to the left. As he drove up the hill he saw cabins ringing the large open area and a man directing him toward the house where three men and a woman were standing. One man wore a cowboy hat, another wore a coyote tan ball cap and the third was bare headed. The woman was blonde. As he pulled toward the house, the man in the cowboy hat gave a welcoming wave.

He pulled up beside the house, checked his mirrors to see the other trucks clearing the gate, put the truck in park and looked at his wife, taking her hand. "Here we are. You ready?"

Cilla nodded, looking at the people waiting for them. She gave his hand a squeeze. "Yes."

He shut off the truck and got out, walking around to meet Cilla.

The man in the hat came toward them, smiling. "Mr. and Mrs. Moore?"

"Mr. Wyatt?" Declan responded.

Jim walked to them, followed by the others, and stuck out his hand. "Jim Wyatt."

Declan took Jim's hand in a solid grip. "Declan Moore." He turned to his wife. "This is my wife, Cilla."

Jim took Cilla's hand. "Cilla, it's very nice to meet you and have you here."

He turned to Kelly. "This is my wife, Kelly."

Kelly shook Declan's hand and gave Cilla a hug. "This is a wonderful surprise! I'm so glad you could make it up!"

"This is Mike Carpenter, our chief of scouts, in the ball cap," said Jim, turning to the other men, "and Tom Murphy, our head of intelligence, in the Marine haircut."

The men shook hands, with Mike and Tom nodding "Ma'am" to Cilla.

"Looks like you brought some boys," said Jim, nodding at the Rangers who were helping the scouts un-trailer their horses.

"Yessir," said Declan, making it one word with one and a half syllables. "We figured it'd be best to have some of our own firepower on the way back."

"Well," said Jim, "as glad as I am to finally not be the only one around here wearing a cowboy hat, I think you're wanting to see your daughter right away. She's over at a town we're building a few miles northwest of here. We could send a scout to let her know you're here, but I bet you don't want to wait, and if you're up to gettin' on a horse we can saddle some of these up and go over right now." He looked at Declan and Cilla. "I bet the sight of you coming over the hill to her is something she'll never forget."

Declan looked at his wife, then back at Jim, smiled and nodded. "We're from Texas. Horseback sounds just fine."

Naomi took a drink from her canteen, poured a trickle over her head, then drenched the bandana that she re-tied around her neck. "It's amazing how fast this is going."

Christian nodded, looking around at the progress being made on the homes and central hall. Over twenty houses had been completed, with twelve already occupied by families, and work was beginning on the second floor of the hall. "I keep wondering why things are moving so fast and then I remember that no time is being spent texting, shopping or watching TV or online videos. It's amazing how much work gets done when people actually work."

A wagon went past carrying a new load of cobb from where it was mixed near the creek to the houses that were currently being built. "You want to eat at the Inn tonight?" he asked.

"Sure. Do you mind if I take a shower at your place first and change my clothes? I'm not sure Mrs. Hernandez would let me in the way I am."

He looked at her and smiled. "You look good to me."

She laughed. "You're prejudiced."

She looked up the hill where a group of riders had just crested and begun their descent. "Looks like the scouts must have scored a bunch of cowboy hats."

She shielded her eyes from the sun and kept looking, feeling a vague sense of familiarity at the white hats and white shirts coming toward her. When the sun flashed off of a silver badge on one of the rider's shirts, her hands flew to her mouth. "Oh, my god! Oh, my god!"

She ran to her horse, her trembling hands barely able to snap loose the hitch and her eyes barely able to see through the tears that had suddenly flooded them.

"What's wrong?" Christian asked, worried at what he didn't know.

"My dad!" she cried, her foot missing the stirrup in her haste. "That's my dad!" She got her foot in the stirrup on the second try, swung herself into the saddle and set her horse down the street at a gallop.

They saw the rider headed down the street and then angle into the field at the bottom of the hill, not slowing down as they started up the incline.

"It's her, Cilla," Declan said, recognizing how his daughter sat a horse. His voice sounded choked and gravelly. "We'd better get off these horses before she knocks us off."

By the time he got his second foot on the ground she had skidded her horse to a stop, dropped the reins and launched herself at him, taking both of them to the ground.

24

"We've kept in touch with other Ranger companies, so we had an idea what to expect, but to come this far seeing such a scarcity of people was still a bit of a surprise." Declan held up his sweating bottle of Budweiser. "How is it that you have cold beer?"

The reunion of Naomi and her parents had been emotional and long, the first half-hour occurring on the hillside overlooking Jamestown, then continuing as the group made their way back to Stonemont to get Declan and Cilla situated in the basement apartment of the house and the Rangers in two of the cabins that had been vacated when their occupants moved to their finished houses in the town.

Now, the Rangers stood around the fire pit with Jim, Christian, Mike, Bill and Tom drinking beer and watching a hog roast on a spit while Kelly, Ann, Tracy, Patty and Naomi folded Cilla and the other Ranger wives into their group as they prepared the rest of the meal.

"Well," Jim laughed, "Bill and his wife came along right after this thing happened. When I found out that Ann was an engineer and Bill liked cold beer I knew they were the perfect couple to have around."

Declan looked from Jim to Bill. "You mean you have refrigeration?"

Bill nodded. "Not the first summer. We were a bit busy trying to get accustomed to the new way of living. But during the down time over the winter Ann came up with some very innovative solutions for some things."

"How did she do it?" asked Pres. "Maybe we can do it at home."

Bill shrugged. "Beats me, I'm a lawyer. It could be magic for all I know, but it gives me cold beer." He smiled, holding up his bottle.

"She'll be happy to tell you," said Jim. "We'll probably be out of the commercial stuff in a few months, but one of our people had a micro-brewery and is working on coming up with a way for us to produce our own." He shrugged. "We'll see. How are things in Texas?"

Declan took a drink. "Mixed. The border is like a war zone. The cartels took advantage of things and wiped out all of the ranchers and some of the smaller towns from El Paso to the gulf. They're pretty much in control of everything fifty miles into the U.S. except Fort Bliss, which, from what I hear, is like a big Alamo now. I don't know how long they can hold out, but I hear nothin's gettin' in and nothin's gettin' out. Hell, they might be gone already."

"Do you know if they had any operable armor or air support?" asked Tom.

Declan shook his head. "I don't know. We haven't received any communications from our El Paso guys since it happened. There were a couple of major intel units at Bliss, one DOD and the other run by the feds. If there was any way to get information out I'd think they'd have the capability, but I haven't heard anything."

"How about the rest of the state?" asked Christian.

"The big cities are gone," replied Declan, "or might as well be. Fires, violence and starvation pretty much took care of those who weren't able to get out. Those who could get to family or a community who would take them in the first couple of weeks are okay. The gangbangers and dirtbags who tried to come out into the country found out who really had all the guns and they're fertilizing the landscape now.

"In addition to the southern border incursion we're gettin' pressure from the reconquistas in New Mexico," he added.

"What's that?" asked Bill.

"There are a lot of Mexicans and Mexican-Americans who think a large part of the southwest was stolen by the United States and want to see it returned to Mexico. They refer to it as the Reconquista."

"But they ceded that to the U.S. when they lost the Mexican-American war," said Bill.

"That doesn't matter to a lot of them," said Pres. "There's a lot of anti-American hatred down there and they think they should have it back. They've been working at it politically and through immigration for a long time. With the collapse, they see an opportunity."

"Are you all going to be able to hold?" ask Jim.

Declan nodded. "We'll hold, but I'm not sure where. The militias and a lot of mags have deployed to a line running roughly from around Midland to Corpus Christi. There's talk of re-establishing the Texas Republic, re-structuring a government and forming our own military."

"At the risk of being the only one asking stupid questions, what's a mag?" asked Bill.

"A mutual assistance group," answered Declan, "referred to by the acronym. It's a group of people who have formally banded together to help each other in emergency situations. Texas is full of them, as is the rest of the country from what I here. They have a lot of active and former military and law enforcement, as well as just regular guys, and run from the ridiculous to the very good with most of them toward the good end. They've been responsible for securing a lot of our areas and helping a lot of folks. They're going to be a very important part of whatever happens."

The door to the kitchen opened and Kelly came out followed by the other women carrying bowls of slaw, baked beans, sweet potatoes and fresh biscuits. "Are you guys hungry?" she asked, setting her bowl on the side table.

"Ma'am, I'm as hungry as the first man who ate an oyster," said a Ranger.

Kelly stopped, taking a moment to process that, then laughed. "My, you *are* hungry!"

"We have a tradition that we made up a while back called 'first cut'," said Jim, moving next to the sizzling hog. "It means that when we have a special guest, they get the first slice and first go at the rest of the food." He looked around at the group. "Tonight, we have more than one."

"Declan and Cilla," he looked at the couple, "we can't tell you how glad we are to have you here and about the reason for it. Our home is your home."

He looked at the Rangers. "To you Rangers, we have high standards here for people - standards that we feel are important and reflect the values upon which good families and good communities are based. The reputation of your organization precedes you, as I'm sure it does everywhere you go, and I have no doubt that each one of you is worthy of it." He nodded to them. "It is an honor to have you here with us."

He turned to Naomi. "And to the one who is responsible for all of this, you have become like a member of our own family and that is exactly how we think of you, but this is the first time in a long time you've been able to be with your own family, so we include you in the honor of tonight's first cut."

He pulled his bowie knife out of its sheath. "So, if our eleven honored guests would each grab a plate and line up, I've got some cutting to do and you've got some eating to do!"

THE REVIVAL

25

Jim woke earlier than usual, with only thin lines of grey appearing along the bottom of the window shades. He looked over at Kelly, but it was still too dark to see her face, so he quietly got out of bed, got dressed and went downstairs. Stopping in the kitchen, he sat in a chair to put on his boots then stood back up to buckle the gun belt around his waist.

He filled the enamel coffee pot with water from the Berkey and carried it out onto the veranda where he set it on the side table and started a fire in one of the concrete rocket stoves they had constructed right after the event. When the fire got the draft sounding right he placed the pot on it and walked to the end of the veranda to watch the sky.

Like he did so often, he wondered what the day would bring. Though less hectic, days in the new world were more interesting and fulfilling than before and he knew that it was because average life issues were now of more importance than the superficial drama that had previously filled the waking hours of so many. He was thankful that he and Kelly were now able to spend their days teaching their children about the important things in life rather than spending half of their time trying to catch and correct questionable things the kids picked up at school and in the general world around them. And he realized with some surprise that he actually enjoyed being with and dealing with people now that they concerned themselves with the practicalities of actually building something rather than the trivialities of the constant consumption of gossip and entertainment. A great catastrophe had destroyed a devalued world of worthless pass-times and given birth to a new one focused on value and worth. He liked it.

The arrival of Naomi's parents and the Rangers had been a surprise in that it had happened so quickly with a minimal amount of trouble. It was a sign that traveling distances was possible, but he couldn't help but wonder whether subsequent attempts would be as successful or if they had just been lucky.

The sound of the coffee pot boiling made him turn around just in time to see Declan stepping through the door putting on his hat.

"Mornin'," he said.

"Mornin' back," said Declan. "Hope I'm not prowlin' around too early."

Jim shook his head. "Not a bit. I was just fixin' a cup of coffee. You ready? It's Folgers instant."

Declan nodded and smiled. "I'm ready and it's what I drink."

"Have a sit. What do you take?"

"Black, thanks."

Declan sat down at the table and looked out over the commons and the lower field. "You've got a nice place here."

Jim took two mugs from a shelf and scooped some coffee into each. "Thanks. We worked on it for quite a while." He poured water from the pot into the cups, gave them a quick stir and set one down in front of Declan. "It's really grown in the last year."

"Thanks," said Declan, accepting the cup. "It's amazing what you've done."

Jim shrugged. "We just did what needed doin'."

Declan looked at Jim. "I want to thank you for everything you've done for Naomi. Somehow, we knew she was alright, but if I'd known she had hooked up with you folks I wouldn't have worried so much. We're in your debt."

Jim shook his head. "She's done as much for us as we've done for her. You raised a heck of a girl."

Declan nodded and smiled. "Thanks." He took a sip of his coffee. "It looks like you've got some good ones yourself."

Jim nodded. "I was just thinking how glad I am to be raising them now, the way things are, rather than how things were."

"Yep, things were gettin' crazy."

Jim took a sip of his coffee. "You seem to have pretty good communication between your Ranger companies."

Declan nodded. "When this thing started, one of our top priorities was establishing and maintaining contact between all the DPS units. Some of the guys had a pretty good idea what had happened right away, but everybody was on board within about a week, so we put together kind of a pony express deal running between stations. We had plenty of old trucks and fuel, so we ran a pretty consistant circuit giving us all a good idea of what was happening state-wide. We lost a couple of guys, but then we started running three-truck convoys with two guys in each and didn't have any more trouble except down south." He took a sip. "We lost guys going to El Paso and Weslaco, then lost the guys we sent to find them. Then we sent recon teams and found out the cartels had taken over."

The sun had cracked the horizon enough for them to recognize Tom walking toward them.

"You're late!" yelled Jim. "Declan and I already drank all the coffee."

"I'm never late," Tom answered. "The sun is early." He walked up onto the veranda, took a mug down and filled it from the pot. "You missed some."

Jim chuckled. "Sit down. Declan just told me something very interesting. Something we need to start here."

Tom sat down and nodded to Declan then looked at Jim. "What's that?"

"They've set up a vehicular communications system between their stations giving them a handle on what's going on around their state." He looked at Declan. "Is it regular routes and schedules?"

Declan nodded. "Pretty much. We have regular routes between DPS stations. Each of those stations has a network of secondary locations like sheriff's offices, police departments or militia units they have routes with. So, say, if somebody in Amarillo wants to send a message to their brother in Beaumont, their letter would be sent to our office in Lubbock, which would send it to Company B in Garland, which would send it to Company A in Houston, which would send it out to Beaumont. Any answer would just come back the opposite way."

Jim looked at him, stunned. "I thought you were just talking about official communications. You mean you run mail too?"

Declan nodded. "Within reason. We don't haul cargo or deliver grandma's fruit cake, but personal letters are fine."

"How long does it take?"

"The scenario I just gave would take three days."

Jim looked at Tom. " I'm ashamed that I didn't think of that myself."

Tom nodded. "It's a good idea."

"Yes, it is. It won't just help to bring the area together, it will be another intelligence generator. We'll use scouts on our end and set up some main routes, then try to get the second-tier satellite locations to use their own people to feed them." He thought for a moment. "We'll go over this with Christian and Mike a little later." He looked at Declan. "Are you going over to see Carol and Jerry today?"

Declan nodded. "Naomi and Christian are going to take us over after breakfast." He smiled. "It'll be a good way to start getting to know my future son-in-law. Are his folks around?"

Jim shook his head. "They were killed by a drunk driver his senior year of high school. His mom was my younger sister. She and Chris were both good people."

"Tough luck," said Declan.

Jim nodded. "He lived with us until he joined the sheriff's department when he turned twenty-one and kind of followed the same path I did. He's a good man. I'm glad to have him with us."

"You talkin' about me?" asked Christian as he came around the corner.

"Yep. Telling your future father-in-law how you're always late. Plus, you're sneaky. You should wear a bell around your neck so I can hear when you're trying to sneak up on me."

Christian laughed as he poured himself a cup of coffee. "My uncle won't admit he's getting hard of hearing."

"What?"

"See?" Christian said, sitting down at the table.

Jim chuckled. "How long are you going to be staying over at School Center?"

Christian shrugged. "That's up to Declan and them. We'll come back whenever they want."

"Okay, Declan just gave me an idea that I want to jump on. It's going to add a whole new dimension to what we're doing."

They talked through the rising of the sun and another pot of coffee as others arrived, then had a breakfast of bacon, eggs, hash browns and biscuits before the group going to School Center left.

Watching the horses disappear into the tree line, Jim turned around and entered the kitchen where he found Kelly trying a new braid in Morgan's hair. "What's on your agenda today?" he asked.

She was biting the corner of her lip, trying to remember the exact order of the strands. "If I ever get this figured out I thought I'd go over and see Ann before she heads over to town, then come back here and fold some clothes. What are you doing?"

He leaned against the counter, crossing his arms. "I was going to go watch the scout training and talk to Mike about something, but I've got a better idea."

"What's that?"

"Let's take the kids for a ride over to town and see how it's going. Maybe have lunch at the Inn."

"Really?" she smiled.

"Yeah, we've been too busy. Let's take a day off." He looked at Morgan. "Would you like to ride over to town, Morgie?"

"On our horses?"

"Uh huh."

THE REVIVAL

"Can I take my BB gun?"

"Sure," he laughed.

She thought for a moment, scrunching her eyes in thought. "Can mommy finish braiding my hair first?"

"Yes," he answered seriously.

"Okay," she said smiling.

"Good," he smiled, pushing himself off the counter. "The boys and I will saddle the horses and we'll be around in a bit."

The sun had risen into a clear eastern sky with storm clouds on the southwest horizon and they rode at a relaxed pace, enjoying the early summer warmth. Sentries at the main and contact gates had greeted them and had complimented the kids on their horses, saddles and rifles, wishing them a good day and thanking them for their wishes in return.

They stayed on the road rather than riding cross-country and saw the additional fields that had been planted in beans, peas, corn, tomatoes, cucumbers, beets, broccoli, potatoes and wheat. Workers waved as they passed, then returned to their duties as children ran up and down the rows playing.

"How many acres do we have planted now?" Jim asked.

"Our last estimate is about eighty," Kelly answered. "There are about fifty here and thirty on the original site east of the commons. We have a few more acres on the eastern slope of the hill where we have grapes, blackberries, blueberries and elderberries."

"How are the elderberries coming along?"

"Pretty well. We're not expecting any fruit from the first-generation plants until next year, but they're growing strong and our propagation efforts look like they're working."

He nodded. "Good. Let's concentrate on planting more, even encouraging people around the town to put some in themselves. There's no better natural medicine."

She nodded. "Okay, and speaking of natural medicine, we've doubled the size of the herb garden and are building green houses to keep them growing through the winter."

He smiled. Kelly had always been big on natural healing, and it had really payed off. He had been amazed at the health and medicinal benefits of many of the herbs and oils she had told him about, not to mention minerals like silver and diatomaceous earth. In some ways, she reminded him of his grandmother who would heat up turpentine and lard in a jar lid and put in on his throat and chest when he was sick as a child. It had worked much better than the commercial menthol rubs that came around later. Sometimes, the old ways really were the best ways.

"Daddy, can we race?" asked Brody.

Jim turned in the saddle to look at Brody and Morgan riding side-by-side behind them and Aedan bringing up the rear, carefully watching the area around them with his rifle across his pommel. "Not here, buddy. It's not good to run horses on hardtop, and you guys need a little more experience in the saddle before I want you running them." He looked back at Aedan. "Everything okay, buddy? See anything?"

Aedan shook his head seriously. "Nope."

"How come you call Aedan buddy and Brody buddy but not me?" asked Morgan with a half-pout."

Jim smiled. "Because I call you honey, honey. Would you rather I called you buddy."

She thought for a moment and shook her head. "That sounds like a name for a dog."

Jim laughed and turned back around. It seemed like the kids were becoming new people every day, their personalities expanding in ways he never could have imagined. He looked over at Kelly. "I wish I'd met you sooner, so we could have had about ten of these," he side-nodded his head back at the kids.

"Ten?!" she asked in mock shock. "I'd be a worn out old hag after ten." She smiled. "How about seven?"

He acted like he was thinking, then nodded. "Yeah, you may be right. You got better looking after each kid. You'd be far too good-looking after ten. Seven it is." He smiled. "We can start tonight."

He turned back to the kids. "Hey, would you guys like to have a baby brother or sister?"

"Yeah!" yelled Brody.

Aedan shrugged. "I guess so."

"I'd rather have a bunny," said Morgan.

"I see it!" yelled Brody. "There's the town!"

Jim turned around again. "You want to lead us in, Aedan?"

Aedan smiled and trotted his horse ahead of them, swinging his rifle muzzle up and resting the butt on his thigh like Christian had taught him to do when on horseback in populated areas.

The could hear the voices of the workers as they approached the building sites, happy and energetic with an occasional shout. People who had come through the trials of the past year found fulfillment in working toward a common purpose, and many had said how much happier they were doing the physical labor of building than they had been in the office jobs of their previous lives. They had become stronger, had lost any extra weight they had had, slept better and had twice as much energy as they did before.

Aedan turned to those behind him. "Ann's waving at us to come over there," he pointed slightly to the left.

Jim nodded. "Okay, buddy, take us in."

They passed the first few plots, with stone foundations already in place, then angled off to the left toward a house that was underway. As they reached the site and dismounted, Ann came toward them wiping her mud-covered hands on a piece of burlap which she then stuck in her back pocket.

"Got the whole tribe out?" she smiled

Jim nodded. "I figured we'd come to town for lunch." He paused and smiled. "That sounds kind of nice, doesn't it?"

Ann nodded. "Yes, it does."

"We also wanted to show the kids how the buildings were being built," said Kelly.

"Great. Here comes a truck with a new load of cob," said Ann, pointing down the road. "Tie up your horses and we'll get this load dropped, then I'll give you a guided tour."

They led their horses to a rail where they tied them and turned to watch an old dump truck back up to the site. The truck stopped and its bed inclined, dumping a large brown mass of cob on the ground.

Kelly raised an eyebrow at Brody and Morgan, who were giggling. "Don't say it."

"Don't say what, mommy?" asked Morgan, giggling louder, her mischievous eyes dancing.

"You know what," Kelly answered sternly. "Now, come on."

The two younger ones continued giggling while Aedan rolled his eyes.

"I think I know what they'll like," said Ann, helping Kelly get the kids' minds off of the joke they weren't being allowed to tell. She looked at the kids. "Who would like to take off their shoes and finish stomping on this big ball of mud?"

"I would!" both of the younger ones yelled in unison.

"Can we, mommy?" asked Morgan.

Kelly looked at Jim, who smiled and nodded. "Okay. Take of your shoes and socks and try not to fall down."

THE REVIVAL

"Yay!" they cheered, immediately sitting down on the ground to pull off their shoes and socks."

Ann turned to Aedan. "Now that we have them occupied, would you like to see how we build these houses?"

Aedan grinned. "Yes, ma'am."

"He's so polite," Ann smiled at Kelly and Jim, then waved Aedan to follow her. "Let's go take a look."

"We start by digging holes for the posts we set to provide a framework for the house," she explained as they walked over to the wall of the house being constructed. "We dig the hole four feet deep, set the post, check for plumb, then ram clay from sub-soil around them." She took them to a post. "We started with posts we got from lumber yards, but now we're using trees which we cut and de-bark."

"How come?" asked Kelly.

"We have an abundance of trees that are either of the right circumference or that can be cut to provide several posts of the right size. The shape doesn't really matter - they can be round, square or half-moon. They don't even have to be perfectly straight. Their function is to provide stability for the walls and to support the weight of the roof. That lets us use the milled lumber for beams that need to be straight."

She pointed to the top of the post. "We cut them in fourteen-foot lengths, which allows for four feet in the ground and ten feet to the top of the walls, then secure beams on top of them to support the ceiling joists and rafters."

She took them to a spot where several men were laying a wide row of stone between two posts. "The next step is to lay a wall foundation of stone so that the cob doesn't rest directly on the ground." She smiled. "There's an old saying that a cob house can last forever if it has a good hat and good boots, meaning a good roof and good foundation."

"How long can it really last?" asked Kelly.

"There's a claim that the oldest standing cob structure is about ten thousand years old, but I doubt that's true. I did see in some of Jim's stuff that there are many cob structures several hundred years old that are still being lived in."

She pointed back to the men laying the stones. "The foundation is three feet wide. When it's set, two walls of cob, one interior and one exterior, are built on the foundation. Each wall is about fourteen inches thick and the space between them is filled with rubble. This provides amazing insulation. In order to provide even greater strength and stability, long pieces of iron or stone are

THE REVIVAL

laid across the entire width of the wall at regular intervals to lock them together."

"What about doors and windows?" asked Aedan.

"He's the engineer in the family," smiled Kelly.

Ann nodded. "Good question. See those men over there placing stones on the wall?"

Aedan nodded.

"When the cob reaches to where the windows should start, they lay stone to form the sill, then stack them up as they build the wall to form the window frame, incorporating the frame into the wall as they go. It creates a seamless integration of the building's different elements which adds to the strength and integrity of the building. When they reach the top of the window, they lay timbers across the opening to continue building on. Same thing with doors."

"Will a bullet go through the walls?" Aedan asked.

Ann looked at Jim. "I'll leave that one to your dad."

Jim shook his head. "It only takes a few inches of dirt to stop most handgun rounds, and only a few more to stop most rifle rounds. About one and a half sandbags or buckets of dirt will stop a fifty cal. These walls will stop anything short of a canon."

"What about the roof?"

"Traditional cob houses have thatch roofs," said Ann, "but we're layering metal and cob in order to keep it essentially fire-proof. We put on a metal roof, over which we put about eight inches of cob for insulation, then another layer of metal to protect the cob from the weather. So, in addition to being bullet-proof and fire-proof, it will be so well insulated it will feel like it's air conditioned in the summer and you can heat it with just the fireplace and the rocket stoves in the kitchen in the winter."

"That's amazing," said Kelly.

Ann nodded. "It really is. We went from natural building with earth and stone to so-called modern building that took unbelievable amounts of energy to heat and cool, and now we're back to natural building again. It's like we've come full circle, and to tell you the truth, I think this way makes more sense."

Jim looked out across the fields at the homes dotting the landscape, some finished and some still in the process of construction. "How many are occupied do far?"

"Two families are moving in today," answered Kelly. "That puts us at twenty-three. Over half way done."

Jim turned to see Brody and Morgan still stomping in the large pile of cob. "Well, it shouldn't take more than an hour to clean them up." He looked back at Ann. "We're headed over to Mrs. Hernandez's for lunch. Want to join us?"

She checked the position of the sun and nodded. "Sounds good."

They ate lunch at the Jamestown Inn and spent the rest of the day touring the community hall and the homes that families had moved into.

Work was going quickly on the hall, the large number of crews having completed the first floor and half of the second. Being built for defensibility as well as function as a community center, it was being constructed with thicker walls and a stronger support structure than the homes and buildings designed for business. Massive forty-foot logs were placed into eight-foot holes at the corners and every twelve feet of the outside walls, which were four feet thick and reinforced with rebar and welded wire. Interior walls in the first floor were two feet thick to support the floors above, and second floor walls were constructed directly over the first to carry the load from the third floor directly to the ground. Windows were more numerous on the second floor than the first, a tactical design for defense.

The area of finished homes looked like a new housing development, though with larger lots, and with all the activity that comes with new residents excited to start their lives in a new neighborhood. Younger children ran around squealing as they played their games while older children helped mothers turn the soil and plant new gardens with seeds from Stonemont's heirloom plants, for which Stonemont would receive ten percent of the yield. Only one man was around, all the others occupied working on the hall or unfinished homes.

They stopped at a number of the properties, chatting with the women while the kids played with new friends, accepting drinks of water and going inside several of the houses to see and compliment the families' new homes.

By the end of the day, the younger kids were worn out, and they rode home with Jim holding a sleeping Morgan on the saddle in front of him while Kelly led her horse.

When they got home, Jim carried Morgan upstairs, tucked her into bed and quietly turned to leave.

"Daddy?" her small, sleepy voice came from behind him.

He turned and walked back to the bed, kneeling beside it and stroking her hair. "I thought you were asleep, honey."

"Daddy, why does Melissa's daddy hit her?"

THE REVIVAL

Surprised by the question, he tried to remember who Melissa was. "Who's Melissa, honey?"

"My friend I met today. She said it makes her sad. He hits her mommy, too. Why does he hit them, daddy?"

He stroked her hair a few more times before answering. "I don't know, honey, but he won't anymore. I'll go over tomorrow and tell him not to. Okay?"

"Okay," she said, and turned over to fall asleep.

26

Jim and Kelly were just finishing their breakfast of ham, eggs, biscuits and gravy when Christian and Mike walked up to the veranda with two of the Rangers.

"You're too late," Jim called. "We ate it all, and it was good."

"You guys come up here," laughed Kelly as she got up. "There's plenty of ham, biscuits and gravy, and I'll have eggs ready before you get your coffee poured."

The men stepped up onto the veranda and began filling their cups from the pot.

"We don't want to put you out, ma'am," said one of the Rangers.

"Oh, it's no bother," Kelly smiled. "You sit down, and I'll have it out in a jiffy."

"Thank you, ma'am," nodded the other Ranger.

"That's more 'ma'ams' than she's used to hearing in a week," said Jim, "and you two got 'em in before breakfast. Settin' the bar kinda' high, aren't you?"

The Rangers smiled as they took off their hats and sat down. "Our dad might still switch us if we didn't," said one.

"I've got a surprise for you, Jim," said Christian as he sat down at the table. "Eamon and Noel, here," he nodded at the Rangers, pronouncing the second name 'Nole', "are Naomi's brothers."

Jim sat back and looked at the Rangers, then at Christian. He nodded. "Stayed on the down-low to find out what kind of ne'er-do-well their sister was hitchin' up with. Don't blame 'em a bit."

He looked back at the Rangers. "We'll, since none of you have shot each other, I assume you're on friendly terms so far?"

Eamon chuckled. "He may not be from Texas, but she could do worse."

"Gotta' get him a hat, though," said Noel.

Jim nodded solemnly. "I agree."

He looked at Christian. "You and I have a little business in town after breakfast."

"What's that?"

"A man has apparently been knocking his wife and daughter around. We'll go see what's what, then talk to him about it."

"Talk to him?"

Jim shrugged. "We'll start off talking."

"Mind if we come along?" asked Eamon.

Jim nodded. "Happy to have you."

"You want me to come, Jim?" asked Mike.

Jim shook his head. "I've got something else for you. I want you to send scouts to Church Crossing, School Center, Mason and Sheriff Freelove. Have the scouts tell them it's the beginning of a regular messaging service, daily to Church Crossing and School Center, and weekly to Mason and Freelove. We'll carry mail and small packages back and forth."

"How about people?" asked Christian. "People might like to catch a ride to visit friends if they didn't have to make the trip alone. It could be like the old stagecoaches."

Jim looked at his nephew. "That's the second good idea you've had, the first being to ask Naomi to marry you. She's obviously improving your mind." He nodded. "We'll do it. I should have thought of all this a long time ago. I'd kick my own butt if I could get my foot up there."

"I could help you with that," Christian smiled.

"Careful, youngster. You just might ... "

"Here you go, guys!" Kelly came out carrying platters of sliced ham and eggs. "Get your plates and I'll be right back with the biscuits and gravy."

It was mid-morning when they rode up to the house Morgan had described as Melissa's. A woman was working out back in the garden and a little girl was helping her. Seeing no place to tie their horses, they dismounted and led them back toward where the woman was working.

As they drew closer, Jim remembered the woman and little girl. They had both seemed reserved during the visit and the woman had seemed nervous. The husband had not been at home as he was working on the town hall.

"Good morning, ma'am," Jim said.

The woman looked up as if startled, though he was sure she had seen them approaching.

"Hello," she said, straightening up and shielding her eyes from the sun with her hand. "You're Mr. Wyatt." She looked at the other men. "Have we done something wrong?"

Jim shook his head. "No ma'am. We just stopped by to make sure you all were okay." He smiled. "I'm afraid I don't remember your name from yesterday. I'm bad with names."

"Jenny," the woman said. "And your wife's name is Kelly?"

"Yes, ma'am." He looked at the little girl. "Our daughter Morgan was talking about Melissa when we got home last night. She was hoping Melissa could come over and play sometime."

Jenny started to smile, then stopped herself, a worried look returning to her face. "Well, I ... I don't know. That's nice of you, but I'd have to check with Carl."

"Is that your husband?"

She nodded quickly, looking down and away.

"That's quite a shiner you've got there, Jenny. What happened? The hoe come up and hit you in the eye?"

She quickly brought her hand to her face, a combination of feeling the injury and and trying to hide the bruise. "Yeah, I guess. I'm not really sure."

He looked over at the little girl who was picking dandelions. "Is that the same hoe that whupped the back of Melissa's legs?"

Jenny's hand moved from her eye to her mouth as she stared at the ground. "We don't want any trouble, Mr. Wyatt. We just want to be able to stay here."

Jim looked at her. "Jenny, is Carl your husband?" he asked softly.

Tears filled her eyes and she shook her head.

"Is he Melissa's father?"

She shook her head again, closing her eyes. "No. He said we had to act like it so we could get a house."

Jim nodded. "Where is he?"

She took a deep breath and looked up at him. "What's going to happen to us?"

He smiled. "Carl will be leaving. You and Melissa will be coming to live in a cabin at Stonemont where you'll be safe. Now, where is he?"

She looked up at him hopefully and took another deep breath. "He's over working on the hall."

Jim looked over toward the hall and nodded, then turned back to Jenny. "Is there anything in the house that belongs to him?"

She nodded. "Some clothes and things."

"Go wrap them up in a sheet or something. We'll take them to him and be back to get you in a little bit." He put his hand on her shoulder. "Don't worry. You and Melissa will have everything you need."

THE REVIVAL

The work crews were just breaking for lunch when they arrived at the hall. The lunch servers from Stonemont were laying out sandwiches, cups and coolers of lemonade while the workers washed up and made their way toward the serving tables.

Jim watched as the women and older girls laid everything out quickly and neatly, chatting lightly with the men as they lined up. One overweight man worked with the women, joking with them while ignoring the workers who also ignored him.

Jim dismounted and walked his horse to a post where he tied it. The others followed.

"You want me to handle this?" asked Christian.

Jim smiled. "You think I'm getting too old?"

Christian shrugged. "No, but it's really my job."

Jim nodded. "You're right, but let me do this one."

He started walking toward the crowd of men gathered at the table, looking around for something to use. Construction sites always had good stuff laying around. Seeing a broken piece of two-by-two about three feet long, he stopped to pick it up then continued toward the table.

"Carl?" he called when he got close. "Where's Carl?"

The men started looking around, then, one by one, looked at a large man walking from the latrine wiping his hands on his pants.

"You Carl?" Jim called.

The man squinted and kept approaching. "Yeah."

"You live with Jenny and Melissa?"

The man slowed down. "Yeah. So?"

"You the piece of shit who knocks around the woman you live with and her little girl?"

The man stopped, looking around at the crowd that was now looking at him. "You got no right to talk to me that way. Who the hell do you think you are?"

"I'm the man who owns the house you used to live in."

"What do you mean used too?"

"You don't live there anymore. I have your stuff tied up in a sheet. You can take it with you when you go."

"Go? Go where?"

Jim shrugged. "I don't care. Anywhere that's not here."

"I ain't goin' nowhere!" The man was becoming angry at being called out, especially in front of the crowd. "And you can't make me!"

Jim smiled. "You can leave in one piece or several pieces. It doesn't matter to me."

Carl nodded toward Christian, Eamon and Noel. "You talk pretty tough with them backin' you up. If they weren't here, I'd break you in half and show these people you're not the big man everybody thinks you are!"

Jim started walking toward the man. "I don't need help with a pissant like you, Carl." He stopped just far enough from the man so that he would have to take a long step to reach him. He could see that Carl was almost ready to crack. "You're nothing but a piece of shit who beats up on women and little girls because you're too much of a puss ... "

The man stepped with his left foot and threw a haymaker with his right fist, wanting to kill the man who was insulting him.

Jim had expected that. It seemed like the big loud ones always did the same thing, especially if you made them mad enough.

As Carl stepped forward with his left foot, Jim stepped to his right, planting his right foot outside Carl's left. As Carl's swing passed harmlessly to the left, Jim pulled his left foot back and swung the board at Carl's head.

The board made contact just above Carl's left ear and sounded like a wooden bat hitting a baseball. The momentum of the missed punch combined with the head strike caused the man to lose his balance, falling to the ground on his right side and rolling onto his back.

Moving in on the man, Jim waited for Carl to begin struggling to get back up and swung the board back-handed, this time striking him on the right side of his face below the eye.

Carl fell back to the ground, his legs working to get his knees under him and his hands trying to push his body up. The two strikes to the head had left him dazed and disoriented.

Jim walked around the man. "Come on, Carl, we're not done yet. You're going to break me in half, remember? Are you having some trouble because I'm not a six-year-old girl?"

Jim waited while Carl struggled to his feet, blood trailing down the left side of his head and the right side of his face.

"You're right handed, aren't you, Carl? I figured that out from the bruises on Jenny and Melissa's face. Guess what? So am I." He faked a swing with the board in his right hand, then drove a front kick into the man's stomach when he raised his arms to block.

Carl doubled over, falling to his hands and knees and gasping for breath.

Jim kept walking around the man. "How many times did you hit Jenny, Carl? How many times did you hit six-year-old Melissa? I've only hit you

THE REVIVAL

three times, Carl. We've got a ways to go before I catch up." He raised his right foot and stomped on the man's right hand with the heel of his boot.

Carl screamed and rolled to the ground, clutching his mangled hand to his stomach.

"Was that the hand you hit Jenny and Melissa with, Carl?" He continued walking around the man in a circle. Stopping and taking the board in both hands, he swung as hard as he could, bringing the board down on the back of the man's right thigh.

Carl screamed again, struggling to get to a knee while still holding his crippled hand to his stomach.

"Did Melissa scream when you whipped her legs, Carl?" He swung again, this time striking the back of the man's left thigh.

A guttural cry came from the man's throat.

Jim swung again, striking the right thigh just below the first impact point, then again on the left. "You're probably wishing I'd hit you in the head again to knock you out, aren't you Carl?" He shook his head. "Oh, no. Jenny and Melissa were awake for every punch, slap and whipping you gave them, weren't they?" He continued to circle the man who was now babbling and trying to burrow into the ground, swinging again and again, striking the man's thighs, shins, arms and back. After a minute, he stopped. The man was now limp and beyond comprehension.

He looked up at the crowd of people. "Cruelty to children will not be tolerated. If anyone abuses a child again, I'll kill them. Anyone who knows about a child being abused and doesn't speak up is no better."

He pointed at Carl with the board. "He is going to be driven out into the country far enough that he'll never come back. Should I do it or would you all like to do it?"

A man stepped forward. "We'll do it."

Jim nodded. "Take one of the trucks."

"What if he dies?" asked a woman.

Jim looked at the woman. "What if Jenny had died? What if Melissa had died?"

The woman was silent.

He looked around the crowd. "The safest person in the world should be a child living in this community. Each one of you is responsible for making sure of that." He looked at the man who had stepped forward. "Go ahead and get him out of here. I'd say twenty miles would be enough. Whoever goes with you continues to get full pay for the day."

The man nodded. "I'll go get a truck."

THE REVIVAL

Jim tossed the board aside and walked over to the serving line, spotting the overweight man who was watching with a look of disapproval. "What's your name?" he asked the man.

The look on the man's face changed immediately, his security of hiding among the women stripped away. "Kenneth," he answered hesitantly.

"Why are you over here with the women instead of on a building crew?"

The man looked around him, hoping for support from the women he felt he had become a part of. "I have a bad back. I can't lift anything heavy."

"I saw you lift a cooler of lemonade out of the truck. What's wrong with your back?"

The man seemed to shrivel as he saw that no support was coming from the women. "It goes out."

"What do you mean it goes out? Goes out where?"

"It just goes out. It hurts, and I have a hard time moving."

Jim nodded. "Mine used to do that. I lost weight and got in better shape. I suggest you do the same." He looked over to where a pickup was being backed up to the still-unmoving Carl. "That crew's short a man now. You're going to take his place."

The man stood stock-still, mouth hanging open in shock as his world changed.

"I don't mean tomorrow," said Jim, "I mean now. You can start by helping them lift him into the truck and driving him to his new future."

The man still didn't move. "Right now?" he whined.

Jim walked over to him. "Do you have kids?"

The man shook his head. "No."

"A wife?"

"No."

Jim nodded. "Good. You're useless here. I've watched you and you don't do as much work as the women. You put all your energy into trying to be top hen when you should be over with the roosters doing some man work. Get your ass on that truck. If you figure you want to work like a man you can come back in it. If you don't, you may as well stay out there with Carl, 'cause that's where you're headed if I ever see you sand-baggin' again."

27

"They're all fixed up," said Kelly, as she and Ann stepped up onto the veranda.

The truck that had taken Carl out had brought Jenny and Melissa to the compound later in the afternoon. They had very little in the way of clothing or personal items, so it didn't take long to get them situated in one of the cabins that had been vacated by a new Jamestown family. They put clean sheets, blankets and pillowcases on the bed and let Morgan and Melissa play for a bit before leaving the mother and daughter to get some sleep. Now it was dark, and the group was gathered on the veranda to hear the scout report from Mike.

"They doin' alright?" asked Jim.

Kelly nodded as she sat down. "They're wiped out. They've been pretty stressed living with that jerk, and I think the sudden change has just let them kind of collapse. I told Jenny we'd take them shopping tomorrow. I guess Carl spent most of his pay on himself. They're in pretty thin shape as far as clothes and essentials go."

Jim nodded. "Let's do them up nice. They've been through a lot."

"I thought the same thing," Kelly answered as she went to the sideboard to fill glasses of lemonade for herself and Ann. "Anybody need a refill?"

A chorus of no-thank-yous answered her.

She sat down next to Jim. "What did you do with Carl?"

Jim took a sip of his lemonade. "He left town."

"He just left?" she asked, her raised eyebrows asking for the rest of the story.

"Yep."

She looked around the table. Eamon and Noel had small smiles on their faces. Christian looked relaxed and noncommittal. "Christian?" she asked, pointedly.

Christian nodded. "Yep, he left." He smiled. "In a Jim sort of way."

It only took her a second to process that and she nodded. "Good. I bet that hurt."

Noel chuckled.

THE REVIVAL

Jim set his drink down on the table. "Mike has some things to tell us and I wanted the Moore's to hear it, too." He looked at Mike. "It's all yours."

Mike set his drink down. "The new courier program is already a success. Everyone was excited to have a regular communication system, and I even have a few quickly written notes here that they brought back - most of them just written for the fun of it and saying hello and such. What they're really excited about is being able to hop a ride to here or town and feel safe doing it.

"Someone at Hillmont asked a question that I've been thinking about, and that is could they go from there to School Center?" He looked at Jim. "We have been planning on sending the couriers out to each of those places at about noon and having them return directly here. That means four vehicles with eight scouts every day if we have two vehicles on each run. What I thought was, why not make it a circular route, instead? They could leave here, go to School Center, then to Church Crossing, then to town, then back here. The whole route would only take a few hours, including the stops, it would only take two vehicles and four scouts instead of four and eight, and, if someone wanted to go from School Center to Hillmont or town, they'd be able to do it in just a couple of hours instead if coming here, staying overnight, then getting on the other route the next day." He paused. "Of course, it wouldn't work the other way around."

"It would if we ran a route the other way around later in the day," said Kelly. "A person could leave from anywhere in the morning, go anywhere they wanted to, then return to wherever they wanted to in the afternoon. And it would still only take two vehicles and four scouts."

"That's a great idea," said Bill.

Jim looked back and forth between Mike and Kelly. ""You two are brilliant." He looked at Kelly. "No wonder I married you." Then he looked at Mike. "But we'll just stay friends."

Mike laughed.

"And that's not why he married me," said Kelly, cocking an eyebrow.

"She's right," said Jim. "It was her lemon cake." He looked at both of them. "You two figure out a schedule and start it as soon as you can."

Both nodded.

"May I make a suggestion?" asked Naomi. "There are kids at all of those places. How about if we have all of the kids here write letters to the kids in the other places? It would help them make friends all around, would increase the feeling of community and help them with their reading and writing."

"That's a wonderful idea!" Kelly exclaimed.

"And maybe we could have field trips to the different places for them," Naomi added. "That would let them see where the other kids live and what they do."

"That would be fantastic!" said Ann.

Jim looked at Naomi. "Do you bake lemon cake too?"

Naomi shook her head, self-conscious at the compliment. "Brownies?"

Christian laughed. "And boy, they're good."

"Would you be able to ram-rod that, Naomi? I mean, the letters and field trips, not the brownies."

Naomi nodded. "Sure thing."

"Thank you," he smiled, "though brownies are always welcome too." He looked back at Mike. "Go ahead."

"It took about half an hour each way for Booker's Crossing. The roads are clear, and we only saw one guy on a tractor. Mason and Bonnie were surprised and excited at the idea. Austin was out on road salvage, but Mason said the Vikings have come in closer together and are doing okay. They sent their best to everyone."

Jim nodded. "Good deal."

"The most interesting one," continued Mike, "was Sheriff Freelove. He said he was just about to come see you. The general at Fort Riley has set a date for the meeting. It's two weeks from Saturday at the fort. Freelove and McGregor haven't decided if they're going yet and want to know what you think."

Jim thought for a minute and looked at Declan. "The background on this is that Riley shut its gates when it happened. They didn't come out, wouldn't let anybody in, and didn't offer any help. A while back, they started running patrols - probes really - making contact with people and trying to identify groups but still not offering help. Now, their commanding general wants to have a big pow-wow, saying he wants to organize everyone for the good and safety of everyone in the area."

"Sounds like a man selling fire insurance after the house burned down," said Declan.

Jim nodded. "And wanting to put himself in the driver's seat after most of the risk is gone."

He nodded at Ann. "Ann's an electrical engineer and did some work on EMP and CME before all this happened. She thinks that most of their equipment, other than small arms and crew served, is nonfunctional. If that's true, I'm thinking that whoever is left in the fort has been cooped up eating

MREs for over a year and is trying to figure out a way to come into the new world now that they've figured out the old one isn't coming back."

Declan nodded. "How many do you figure are there?"

Jim shrugged. "Hard to know. Freelove or McGregor probably have a better idea." He looked at Tom. "What do you think? Do you have a sense of how things might have gone down?"

Tom thought for a moment. "That depends on the general, whether he had turned full politician or still had a bit of soldier in him." He paused. "I never made it to the stars, so I was never privy to the secret knowledge of those on high," he smiled sardonically, "but it starts with policy and COG - continuity of government." He looked around the table. "You see, the first priority of the government is to ensure its own survival."

"You mean it's not to serve the people?" Kelly asked in mock surprise.

Tom chuckled. "Your sense of humor must have come in second only to your lemon cake." He shook his head. "Sadly, no. From what I knew from my 'bird's' eye view, and remember, I spent most of my last years in the sandbox, not the Pentagon, was that an existential threat mandated a lock-down and re-call of all available personnel. That included civilian as well as military, but not necessarily off-base families."

"You mean they would leave families outside the base?" asked Ann.

Tom nodded. "Depending on the scenario, possibly. So, it would come down to what they knew, or thought they knew, and whether the general is a warrior or a rule-following, bureaucratic bean-counter." He looked at Jim. "The Geary County Sheriff out to be able to give us an idea."

Jim nodded. "We'll find out."

Tom continued. "I don't know what the manpower of the fort is, and it's impossible to know the base culture and morale without an inside source, but I would bet things are getting pretty frayed, and possibly fractured by now."

"What do you mean, fractured?"

"Any base, like any organization, has a number of different factions. In normal times, organizational discipline tends to conceal those fault lines, but when stress elevates, especially stress of an unfamiliar nature, those factions start to move like tectonic plates, threatening the integrity of the organizational and leadership structure. As the situation degrades, real leadership emerges which is often different from and at odds with the formal leadership, and the command structure can crumble, replaced by a new structure that may have different priorities and goals than the old one. In essence, the situation at the fort depends on quality of leadership and the makeup of the garrison."

THE REVIVAL

Jim looked at Declan. "Have you all dealt with anything like this down your way?"

Declan nodded. "I haven't directly, but Fort Hood initially shut its gates, then relaxed a bit. A lot of people deployed out of Hood, so there was a pretty tight feeling of community among the families. Also, Hood and Killeen are so intertwined it would have almost been an act of betrayal against the population if they had stayed locked down for too long."

"How long were their gates closed?" asked Tom.

"About a week, I think."

Tom looked at Jim. "If the posts were operating according to a general SOP, they would have locked down and re-opened at the same time. Same thing if they were receiving instructions from their command." He paused. "I think they're functioning autonomously. That means they're not receiving command communications." He paused again. "And that means there is probably no longer a national military or national government."

The table was silent for a minute. Finally, Jim spoke.

"We have suspected that. We've even been preparing for that eventuality. In a way, this is good for us."

He looked at Declan. "I don't know how you feel about this, but some time ago, with this in mind and after careful consideration, I declared Stonemont and its interests to be autonomous and sovereign, subordinate to no other governing authority. We knew that there might be a chance that vestiges of government might still exist and that, at some point in time, it might try to reassert its authority. I determined that, while we might work with such a government, we would no longer exist under the authority of strangers who did not always have our best interests in mind. Since then, we have been working to build our community to be able to sustain and defend that autonomy and sovereignty. So, if this is true, it's both good and bad for us. Good, in that we won't have to butt heads with a resurging national government sometime down the road, and bad in that we may be fighting a closer foe sooner if the leadership at Riley decides to assume a position of warlord or military government as Mike warned us about almost a year ago."

The group was silent for another minute, each thinking about the possible ramifications of what Jim had said. Finally, Declan leaned forward, resting his elbows on the table and cupping his right fist in his left hand.

"We started out as a Republic," he said, "winning our independence from Mexico and running our own country until we were annexed by the United States. Some have always maintained that the second part was a mistake, but that's a family argument.

"What you say makes a lot of sense, and the re-establishment of Texas as a republic is an idea that has broad support and is growing stronger. I support it myself. I don't see why it should be any different anywhere else. Men and women should live free, and sometimes you have to fight for it." He nodded. "I'm with you."

Jim nodded and looked at Mike. "Pick four scouts to go with you to tell Mark we'll be going to the meeting. Then go on from there to set up surveillance on the fort. I want to know everything you can find out before we go into the meeting. Send a scout back a couple of days before the meeting to give us a briefing and take us back to you the day before the meeting."

Mike nodded. "When do you want us to go?"

"As soon as you can."

28

"You've got a nice setup here," said Declan as he threw a saddle on the back of the large bay gelding he had picked. "And some darn good horses."

Jim adjusted his billet straps, ensuring the girth was tight. "Your daughter was a big part of that. She found the Morgans and finished off a lot of the green-broke stuff."

Declan looked over at Naomi where she was saddling her Arab in one of the front stalls next to Christian. "Yeah, she knows horses. Better than me, really. I was always fighting against them and she was always working with them. I think her way is better."

Jim dropped the stirrup and looked at Declan. "It's going to be hard, isn't it? Going back and leaving her here."

Declan nodded, still looking at his daughter. "Yeah, it will be. I always said I was sure she was okay, but I wasn't. A father tends to think the worst, you know?"

"Yeah, I know. It comes from seeing the worst too many times."

"That's a fact. But I know she's with a good man and a good family, and that makes all the difference." He looked at Jim and smiled. "And I know we'll be coming up to see our grandkids when the time comes."

Jim jerked the hitch from the stall rail and turned Ghost toward the stable door. "And I know they'll be heading down to see you when they can."

Declan tightened his girth strap and dropped the stirrup. "I hope so."

"You all ready?" Jim yelled to Christian.

"Waitin' on you!" Christian yelled back.

"Then you're fallin' behind! Let's go!"

They walked their horses out of the stable and mounted up. "You two go on in front where we can keep an eye you," said Jim, waving his hand forward.

Christian laughed and wheeled his horse to head toward the gate. "Did you ever see *The Quiet Man*, with John Wayne?" he asked Naomi as she fell in beside him.

"No. Why?"

THE REVIVAL

"It was one of my dad and Jim's favorite movies. We watched it every St. Patrick's Day. John Wayne plays a boxer who goes back to Ireland and falls in love with Maureen O'Hara. In her traditional village, the whole town follows them on their walks together before they get married to make sure there's no shenanigans." He hooked his thumb back toward Jim and Declan. "That's what this feels like."

"Shenanigans?" she giggled.

"Yep," he nodded, trying to look serious, "shenanigans. Shenanigans are an extremely serious business before you're married."

"And is that what we do at your place?" she laughed. "Shenanigans?"

He looked at her and chuckled. "Well, I never thought about it like that, but I guess so."

She smiled. "I like shenanigans."

They passed through the entry gate and onto the road. The sky was clear and blue with no clouds, making the fields look like an old postcard of Kansas, and they followed the road past the contact gate on their way to Church Crossing. They rode leisurely, enjoying the warmth of the day, the easy role of the horses and the quiet camaraderie only occasionally punctuated by a comment or a question and answer.

The white steeple of Redemption was the first thing they saw of the growing community, and they soon began passing the fields of crops from which workers smiled and waved their greetings. Just as around Stonemont, children played, running up and down the rows in which their parents worked, temporarily indulged in a communal recognition of the importance of the joy of childhood before being called back and reminded of their responsibility to pull weeds.

Reaching the crossroad, they turned left and headed up the hill to the church, passing a large cornfield which gave way to the church grounds where men were busy unloading an Associated Grocers trailer into a shipping container at the side of the church.

As the men saw them, one, a smiling, muscular man in a sweat-stained blue t-shirt, separated himself from the rest and walked purposefully toward them.

"Jim! Christian! Naomi!" called Pasquale Paoli as strode up to them. "How good it is to see you!"

"It looks like you've got them working hard," said Christian as he dismounted and held out his hand.

"Indeed!" said Pasquale. "One of your salvage teams just brought that in yesterday. It continues to amaze me how the Lord continues to provide." He laughed. "Through you, of course!"

He turned toward Jim, who had just dismounted. "And you, my friend. How are you?"

Jim took Pasquale's extended hand. "If I was any better, Pasquale, there would have to be two of me to hold all the happiness."

Pasquale laughed. "Then you are truly blessed." He turned to Naomi. "And I save you for last, so that your grace and beauty will linger with me throughout the day."

Naomi smiled, giving him a hug. "Hi, Pasquale. Can you teach Christian to talk like that?"

Pasquale laughed. "His love for you is different than mine and I'm sure he expresses it in different ways." He smiled and shrugged. "I must admit that I do not talk to Mrs. Paoli like that."

"Maybe you should. She might like it."

"Yes, she might," he nodded. "And that is the problem. If I started it, I would have to keep it up or she would think I was mad. Better to leave things as they are."

Naomi laughed. "Pasquale, I'd like you to meet my father, Declan Moore." She turned to Declan. "Dad, this Pastor Pasquale Paoli."

Declan stuck out his hand. "Pleased to meet you, padre."

Pasquale took Declan's hand in surprise. "From Texas?"

Declan nodded. "Yep."

Pasquale looked from Declan to Naomi. "What a wonderful surprise!" He looked back at Declan. "How did you get here?"

"The old-fashion way," Declan chuckled. "Pickup truck."

"But how ...?"

"Jim sent a scout team down to Lubbock to tell my parents I was getting married and they came right up," said Naomi. She smiled. "My brothers, too."

"That's wonderful!" He paused, a questioning look on his face. "You're getting married?" He gave a subtle nod toward Christian. "To, uh ... him?"

She laughed. "Yes, to, uh, him. And we would like you to officiate."

His smile widened, his eyes crinkling at the corners. "Well, it would be my pleasure and privilege!" He nodded toward the church. "Let's go in to my office. I should change my shirt for this!"

Pasquale came out of his changing room into his office buttoning a blue work shirt. "I can't say I'm exactly fresh," he smiled, "but the Lord performed miracles after walking around on dirt roads, so who am I to think I should do better?"

He sat in a chair angling toward two couches sitting at right angles to each other with Christian and Naomi sitting on one and Jim and Declan sitting on the other. "So," he said, smiling, "tell me all about this."

Christian and Naomi looked at each other. Christian shrugged. "Well, there's not much to tell, Pasquale. We want to get married and we'd like you to do it for us." He looked over at Jim. "Jim said he could do it with his on-line internet clergyfication through the church of something-or-other, but I want him to be my best man and I think God might prefer you do it."

Pasquale laughed and shrugged. "Oh, I don't know, a man of God is a man of God, no matter who else says so. It is your love and God's blessing that makes your marriage holy, not my little piece of paper, but I am honored you asked me." He paused. "You do love each other?" He looked hopefully from each to the other.

"You bet," said Christian, reaching to take Naomi's hand in his.

"Yes," said Naomi, almost shyly as she put her other hand on top of Christian's and squeezed it with both of hers.

Pasquale smiled. "Yes, I can see that. And I have to ask this. Are you both Christian?" He laughed, looking at Christian. "I mean, other than your name?"

"Yes," they both answered.

"Good, good. I had to ask. Now," he leaned forward, "before this all happened, I mean the collapse, not you two, we used to have couples go through a series of counseling sessions to prepare for marriage. I always thought that was a bit presumptuous of the church to think that it knew better than the ones undertaking this most sacred commitment, but we had to do it none-the-less because our bosses said we did. Thankfully, I'm no longer bound by that requirement and may allow couples to enter into their new lives as they did for thousands of years before counseling became a multi-billion-dollar industry. Still," he smiled and raised a finger, "I think that the advice and blessing of those who have gone before you can be important."

He looked at Jim and Declan. "May I ask if either of you have a piece of advice for these two fine young people?"

Jim and Declan looked at each other, each wondering if the other had something to say. Finally, Jim spoke.

"My father told me that a marriage and building a family is like a jigsaw puzzle and that the most important piece is the box with the picture on it because it shows you what the final result is supposed to look like. Then, you find and put together the edges because they became the boundaries of the

THE REVIVAL

puzzle. After that, it was just a matter of finding out for yourself where all the other pieces fit.

"When a person's parents have a good marriage," he continued, "that's the picture on the box. The principles and values passed on by those parents are the edge pieces that form the character of the person and the frame of their life and their marriage."

He looked at Christian. "Christian's parents gave him the picture, the principles and the values." He looked at Naomi. "And as I've gotten to know Naomi, there's no doubt that her parents did the same."

He looked back at Pasquale. "I have no doubt that they will put those pieces of their puzzle together just right and build a marriage that will be the picture their own children can look at for theirs."

He looked back at Christian and Naomi and smiled. "And I can't wait to see the family they build."

Pasquale stared at Jim for a moment and nodded. "I am going to steal your puzzle story for my homily." He looked at Declan. "And what would you tell them, Mr. Moore?"

Declan thought for a moment, looking at his daughter and Christian. "Marriage is like two people going down a river in a canoe, each with a paddle and an ice pick. Each one has to do their share of the paddling or they won't make much headway. Each must paddle in a way that will keep the canoe straight, or at least in the directions they want to go, or they'll be zig-zaggin' all over the place, not makin' much progress.

"Every now and then, someone's hand will slip off the paddle, grab their ice pick and poke a hole in the bottom. That's a careless word or a thoughtless act that hurts the other person and damages the relationship just a little bit. It can be patched up, but the canoe will never be new again unless God makes it so.

"Very few canoes make it down the river without a few patched-up holes. That's okay. It means the canoe got put in the water, used, and had a few experiences. It can still float just fine. But if too many holes get put in it, it won't be able to stay afloat. Eventually, it will break apart and sink."

He paused, looking at Christian, then at Naomi. "We each have a paddle and an ice pick. Love means you keep your paddle in your hand, your pick in your pocket, and, if somebody slips, you patch up the hole and try not to do it again. Then, you get back to paddling and forget it. "

Declan stretched his back and looked at his daughter. "Naomi always scared the hell out of the boys who took a liking to her ... , uh, excuse me, padre ... , but I've never doubted that one day she'd find the man she could put that puzzle of Jim's together with." He looked at Christian. "I have no doubt that Christian is that man."

He looked at Jim. "We have a saying about men who act like they're more than they really are. We say they're all hat and no cattle. Well, Christian is all cattle and no hat." He looked over at Christian and the camo cap he was wearing. "We've got to get him a hat."

29

The next two weeks were busy. Work on Jamestown continued at a brisk pace and the courier service grew quickly, carrying more letters, packages and passengers as word of it spread. Short notes, long letters, homemade bread and visitors made their way from one point to another, creating a forgotten feeling of greater community and improving the writing abilities of many. The main foci at Stonemont, however, were the preparations for the wedding and the meeting at Fort Riley.

Kelly, Ann and Cilla helped Naomi with the thousand things it took for a wedding; planning the ceremony, deciding on the food and entertainment for the after-party and inviting guests from outside Stonemont, while Jim, Christian, Bill and Tom had regular talks concerning the upcoming meeting at Riley as periodic reports came back from the scouts.

The wedding was the first major event in the area since the collapse, and everyone was invited. The entire communities of Stonemont and Jamestown attended, as did many from Church Crossing, School Center and Bookers Crossing. Sheriffs Freelove and McGregor brought groups from their counties, not only for the wedding but for the meeting to be held afterward

The ceremony was held outside on the steps of the main hall so that everyone could be a part of it. Declan walked Naomi to the makeshift altar through the throngs of attendees; Jim, Mike, Eamon and Noel stood up with Christian; Cilla, Kelly, Tracy and Brin stood up with Naomi; and Pasquale officiated, making good on his promise to steal Jim's puzzle story while also adding Declan's. Aedan and Brody acted as candle-lighters, and Morgan served as flower girl, sprinkling rose petals on the path in front of Naomi as she walked.

The party lasted throughout the night, Christian and Naomi leaving halfway through to go to the cabin Christian had thought he had built for only himself, Declan and Cilla joining those of the Stonemont core on the house veranda to relax and visit, and the rest enjoying the music, dancing and barbecue until the small hours of the morning.

THE REVIVAL

When the party finally ended, and the crowd began to disperse, the voice of the young woman who had sung *My Prayer* during the ceremony could be heard singing *At Last* from the now-dark altar.

Those who were leaving stopped, transfixed by the voice, and Naomi snuggled closer into Christian.

"That's the most beautiful thing I've ever heard," she said as she fell asleep.

30

Jim looked up from refilling Declan, Eamon and Noel's coffee cups. "Well, it looks like married life hasn't changed him any. He's still late for breakfast."

Christian chuckled as he stepped up onto the veranda. "Well, Jim, seeing a prettier face than yours to start my day made me linger a bit." He nodded at the Moores as he took a cup off the shelf and held it out to Jim. "Now that I see you I wish I'd lingered longer."

"Lingered longer?" Jim smirked as he filled Christian's cup. "You Dr. Seuss, now?" He nodded at the table. "Sit down. Naomi's dad and brothers want a word with you."

Christian raised his eyebrows as he sat down. "Do I need my rifle?"

Jim put the coffee pot down. "Well, if you do, it's too late now." He sat down. "A lesson in being prepared, I guess. Hope you live long enough to remember it."

Declan slid two boxes across the table to Christian. "A little something from me and the boys."

Christian put down his coffee cup and looked at the boxes. Both said Stetson on them in large, bold letters.

"I'd check and see which one's tickin' and which one's rattlin'," said Jim.

Christian looked at Declan, then at Eamon and Noel. The three men were leaning back in their chairs looking at him.

He lifted the top of the first box and looked inside, then smiled. Standing up he withdrew a silvery-white cowboy hat.

"That's a real deal 30X Silverbelly El Patron," said Declan.

"Seven hundred-dollar hat," said Eamon.

"Wish I had one," said Noel.

Christian took the hat gently by the crown as he had seen Jim and the Moores do and placed it carefully on his head, settling it till it felt just right. He smiled and nodded at the Moores in thanks, then turned to Jim. "How does it look?"

"The hat looks great," answered Jim. "You, however, look like a city dude dressed up for a Village People convention."

THE REVIVAL

Noel laughed. "You look great. But you can't wear that one in the summer time." He nodded at the other box. "That's your summer hat."

Christian took the hat off and examined it in appreciation, then placed it back in its box and opened the other one to see an ivory straw cowboy hat.

Again, he carefully took it out of the box and settled it on his head. Ignoring Jim this time, he looked at the Moores. "Is this right?" he asked.

"Right as rain," said Noel.

Declan and Eamon just nodded.

Christian took off the hat. "Thank you, guys. I really appreciate it." He set the hat on the table and put the lid back on the box.

"Now, we get to teach you hat etiquette," smiled Eamon. "I can't touch your hat, because that would be an insult, but you don't want to put your hat down on the brim like that." He nodded at Christian's hat. "It'll flatten it out."

"Plus," said Noel, "it won't catch any good luck that might be floating by."

Christian chuckled and turned the hat over to rest on its crown.

"And you don't want to set it on the table," said Eamon. "If there isn't a place to hang your hat, then set it in a chair next to you if possible. If not, keep it on. That way, you won't be showing the inside of your hat to people."

"I don't want to show the inside of my hat?" asked Christian.

"Nope," said Noel. "It's not polite."

"It would be like showing your underwear," said Eamon.

"You remove your hat whenever you enter a home or a church," said Eamon.

"But not necessarily in a business, unless you go into a private office or courtroom," added Noel.

"Are there a lot of rules?" asked Christian.

The brothers shrugged. "There's some," Eamon answered. "You might want to get a biscuit behind your buckle."

They had had breakfast and were walking to the central hall where they were meeting the others to discuss the upcoming trip to Fort Riley.

"You also remove your hat for the national anthem, the pledge of allegiance, and the passing of the flag," said Eamon, "in which case you can either hold it over your heart or in your left hand at your side with your hand over your heart."

"You take off your hat the first time you meet a woman," said Noel. "After that, just tip your hat when you see her."

"You do that by touching the brim of your hat while nodding," said Eamon.

THE REVIVAL

"But don't tip your hat to another man," said Noel. "That would be an insult."

"Why?" asked Christian.

"Because that's for women," said Eamon. "It would be like calling him a girly-man."

They mounted the steps and entered the hall, removing their hats as they stepped through the door. Standing there, they looked around, hats in hand.

"Guess I'd better put in some hat racks," said Jim.

The hall was empty except for the group of men sitting at a near table, making their footsteps and voices echo throughout the room.

"Where'd you get the hat?" Mike asked, smiling.

"My new in-laws," Christian answered, nodding toward the Moores, then stopped, looking at Declan. "Where did you get them?"

Declan smiled. "Better ask Mike."

Christian looked at Mike. "Yeah?"

Mike shrugged. "They said something about cattle and hats, said that you needed a hat and asked me if I thought our teams could find one. Kelly said we didn't have any in inventory, but there's a Sheplers up in Overland Park so we went up and snagged some. Got a bunch of them, too, in case you want to open up a hat store."

"Naomi measured your head while you were asleep," said Noel. "You lucked out, too. If your head was any bigger you would've missed out on that Patron."

"Hell, if his head was any bigger his hair wouldn't fit on it," said Jim, putting his hat on a side table with Freelove's and McGregor's.

"While I was asleep?" Christian asked, placing his hat next to Jim's and looking carefully at Declan.

Declan smiled back. "You must have dozed off in church."

"He usually does," said Jim as the others put their hats on the table. "That's why he never remembers the Thou shalt honor thy uncle part."

Christian laughed. "I've never heard that."

"Exactly."

Freelove looked at Declan as the men sat down. "You gettin' used to these two yet?"

Declan chuckled. "Gettin' there. They sure keep an edge on each other."

"They do at that," laughed McGregor.

"We'll be heading out to Riley tomorrow," said Jim as he sat down. "That will put us there two days before the meeting, so we can get a good look at things. Maybe even run a probe or two of our own."

He looked at Mike. "Mike has had scouts up around there, as you know, and was up there himself until the day before yesterday. He'll bring us up to speed after Mark tells us what he knows."

Mike nodded.

Jim looked at Freelove. "All yours."

Freelove nodded and looked around at those at the table. "The sheriff of Geary County is Tim Mullane. He's been kind of the conduit from the command staff at Riley to whatever law enforcement he can reach. He says that the meeting will be held at Marshall Army Airfield, which is at the entrance to the fort. That's good, because we were a bit hesitant to go into the fort itself in case we decided we needed to leave in a hurry. The airfield is right off I-70, so it's quick to get to and quick to get away from. The fort itself is beyond it across the river.

"The officer extending the invite is a Colonel Briggs. We had thought it was from the commanding general, but they say the general died sometime after the collapse."

"Do we know what from?" asked Tom.

Freelove shook his head. "Nope, they just say he died." He looked around at the others. "Tom's question is an important one. If the general didn't die of natural causes, it could mean there was a mutiny and we're dealing with someone who sees himself outside the normal army chain of command." He shrugged. "But we don't know."

He glanced at his notes. "Each community leader may bring two people with him. We don't know whether this is due to space constraints or to keep our numbers small."

"I'd bet on the latter," said Tom.

Freelove nodded. "We're leaning that way ourselves."

He looked at his notes again. "The official reason given for the meeting is, 'To assist, coordinate and facilitate local communities and other entities in establishing and maintaining coordinated efforts for continuing life-sustaining endeavors, and to reestablish competent governmental structure and authority for the recovery of the area in preparation for re-integration into the national framework'."

"Took a government office-boy to write that horse shit," scoffed McGregor.

Freelove nodded. "That's all of the information we've been given officially. However, from community sources, we have a little more of a picture.

"Like most military bases, pretty much everyone who could afford to live off-base, did. Local reports say that Riley called all personnel into the fort immediately after the event. They started allowing dependents in two days later but stopped two days after that. Locals say that looting and then fires erupted at some of the apartment complexes catering to base personnel, then spread into Junction City. Within a week, law enforcement had lost control of the town. Officers who lived out of town quit coming to work and those who lived in town either hunkered down with their families or left town to stay with family or friends in the country."

He looked around the table, sadness showing in his eyes. "Sheriff Mullane estimates a fifty percent die-off occurred in Junction City before winter and another twenty-five percent from winter to now. Nobody goes into town anymore, and small enclaves have developed among those who stayed there and survived. There are occasional flare-ups between the groups, but so far none have tried to wipe another one out or consolidate into larger groups. Interestingly, several of these groups have tried to pull raids on Riley. More interestingly, it looks like elements from Riley have pulled a couple of raids on the town."

"That seems odd," said Jim, looking at Tom. "To me, that would indicate that the fort needs things they think the town has and some in the town think the fort is weak enough to attack."

Tom nodded. "I'd say that's a fair assessment." He looked at Freelove. "Were any of the attacks on the fort successful?"

"They got in once and made off with a pallet of mustard."

"Mustard?"

"Apparently, it was on a skid unsecured behind the chow hall."

"Poor leadership, poor morale and possibly insufficient manpower," said Tom. He looked at Freelove. "Do you have any idea what their current manpower is, or why it would have dropped?"

Freelove shook his head. "Nope."

"I think I can answer that," said Mike.

Jim nodded for him to continue.

"There's kind of a trading post that's developed at an old Walmart on the highway west of the base. The area around it has been kept secure by locals as kind of a forward base to quell anything that looks like it might come out of the town and threaten the rural areas. It's manned by a bunch of hard-ass good old boys peppered with a few former soldiers and LEOs formed up into an area militia.

"During the week, there's not much going on, but they run their trading post on weekends when people come in from around the area with things to sell or trade or just to visit. It's become like a combination farmer's market, yard sale and country fair. Tracy and I went to it last weekend, covered by two other pairs of scouts."

He glanced at Bill to check for any sign of disapproval but saw none.

"We were able to talk to quite a few people, including some of the militia leadership." He looked at Bill again. "I think Tracy being there helped a lot with that. She's a natural."

Bill smiled.

"Their story," Mike continued, "is that a fight started in the fort after they started letting dependents in. One faction objected to the additional people, who they thought would use up needed resources. They say they heard that the commanding general was killed in the uprising and the colonel who is now in charge took over, expelling the dependents. This caused more fighting and many of the soldiers left with their families, followed by many of the non-aligned troops leaving over the next few months as the situation inside the fort deteriorated."

Mike looked around the table. "The militia thinks that the fort may be starting to run low on supplies and is using this meeting to try to develop alliances it can exploit to ensure its continued survival."

"Does the militia have any alliance with the fort?" asked Jim.

Mike shook his head. "They consider the fort to be hostile to the area. They've turned back patrols from the fort, and now Riley personnel don't travel west from their gate." He looked at Freelove. "I should add that the militia is at odds with the Sheriff. Some of the militia are former deputies who say he's just a politician siding with the fort in order to protect his own position."

"I'm not surprised," said McGregor.

Freelove shook his head. "Me neither. Disappointed, but not surprised."

McGregor leaned back in his chair and looked sideways at Freelove. "Could be Mullane is tryin' to snooker us - trying to pull us into this little game of his to back his play."

"Which would put us against the people," said Freelove.

"So, having betrayed their old friends, the fort has to make new friends in order to help them fight their old friends and survive," observed Bill.

Mike nodded. "That's about it."

"Does the militia have any idea of the current manpower at the fort?" asked Tom.

Mike shrugged. "They're not sure, but they estimate less than three hundred. I agree with that. We were able to set up a number of observation posts around the fort. We never met a patrol and saw no indications of any kind of counter-surveillance. The entire interior of the fort seems vacant, with all personnel seeming to be concentrated toward the front of the base. That may be why they want to meet at the airfield - so we don't see that. Patrols are predictable and sloppy. Sentries are few, and also sloppy. Discipline is situational at best."

He paused, waiting for questions.

"Does the militia share that opinion?" asked Jim.

Mike shook his head. "I don't think they've set up any surveillance of the fort. They've pretty much concentrated on just keeping the fort contained and out of they're lives."

"So, they haven't considered attacking the fort for the equipment and supplies it might have?"

"Not that I know of. Nobody said anything about it, anyway. Of course, we were outsiders, and I'm sure they didn't share all their thoughts with us. Plus, these are law-and-order type guys. Attacking an army base might not be at the front of their minds."

Jim leaned back and thought for a moment, then looked at Tom. "What would Riley still have that we could use? Or the people around there, for that matter?"

"A lot of things," Tom replied. "Small arms and ammo to start with, and plenty of both. They've been eating, but they haven't been doing a lot of shooting. Next, medical supplies. After that, uniforms and other personal gear. American taxpayers have always provided top-quality stuff for the troops. Then, everything else. A major military base is essentially a self-sufficient city. They have everything the town has except the dancers."

"Are you thinking of attacking an army post?" asked Declan, carefully.

Jim shook his head. "Nope. I'm thinking about liberating some equipment from a bunch of mutinous dirtbags who have taken over a former United States Army post and who prove a threat to the surrounding population."

He looked around the table. "I think this colonel is trying to scam us. He took over the fort by force but didn't have the juice to keep his game afloat. Now, he's trying to run a con where we back him in his move to take control of the area when, in reality, he's about to collapse." He nodded thoughtfully. "Typical sneaky punk move."

The table was silent for a moment until Freelove spoke.

"Are you thinking we ought to side with the militia?"

Jim looked at him. "Who are the militia?"

Freelove shrugged. "Just folks. Former cops, soldiers, ranchers, farmers, teachers, construction workers. You know, just normal folks."

Jim looked at Bill. "Bill, what did George Mason say the militia was?"

"He said the militia was the whole people, except for a few elected officials."

Jim nodded. "And we will be on the side of the people." He looked at Declan. "You still want to come with us?"

Declan looked at his two sons, then back at Jim and nodded. "Yep."

31

"How many can you have ready to go?"

They had spent the afternoon watching the scouts in training and taking a tour of Jamestown, both of which their visitors found interesting, and were now walking from the stable toward the house for supper.

The information from Mike had changed their understanding of the Fort Riley situation dramatically, and with it, their objective. They no longer saw the meeting as just an opportunity to assess a potential threat or ally, but, instead, as a larger opportunity to make contact with other citizen-led groups who might be securing and solidifying their areas. The fact that the normal governmental elements had themselves fractured brought a new dynamic into play, and an understanding that a return to basic principles was occurring at places other than Stonemont. The discovery that at least some sheriffs were siding with those trying to take control, while others were unaware of it, indicated a degree of separation between some pre-change government entities and the people they felt were under their authority - a separation that waited quietly, like a snow-covered glacial crevasse, ready to open up under pressure and expose the wider divide beneath.

"We have eleven teams that I feel comfortable having operational in the field right now," answered Mike. "Four more are almost ready and could function either as support or as replacement feeders to ops teams."

Jim took several steps before answering. "Good. We'll take eight ready teams and two of the support teams. That will give us a hundred and twenty with us while leaving three ready teams and the rest here with Christian."

"You want me to stay here?" asked Christian, the disappointment obvious in his voice.

THE REVIVAL

Jim nodded. "You have to. While I'm gone, you're in charge." He looked at his nephew and smiled. "I need to know the place will be in one piece when I get back."

Christian nodded his understanding. "I know."

They stepped up onto the veranda just as Kelly was coming out the door with Naomi, Cilla and two women they didn't know.

"Are you guys ready to eat?" asked Kelly as she started putting plates around the table.

"Does Jim whistle in his sleep?" Christian asked with a chuckle.

Kelly laughed. "My, you are ready!"

She set the last plate down as Cilla placed the silverware at each plate and Naomi placed the glasses. The other two women put platters of brisket, potatoes and several vegetables on the table, smiling as they did so.

"We have a surprise for you guys," said Kelly. She turned toward the two women. "This is Karen Calzone and her daughter, Jasmine. Jasmine is the one who sang those beautiful songs at the wedding."

"I fell asleep to *At Last*," smiled Naomi, giving Jasmine a hug as she passed behind her.

"But she's also the one who cooked all this for us tonight." She looked at Jasmine. "Would you like to explain everything to them?"

"Okay," the girl answered quietly. She pointed at the meat platter. "The brisket is in a raspberry-persimmon sauce with capers, peppercorns, chocolate basil and sweet peppers." She hesitated. "I've never used chocolate basil before, but Kelly had some in her herb garden and I thought it would go well."

She pointed at the other dishes. "Then, we have smashed potatoes with garlic, wild leeks and rosemary, asparagus with cranberries and shaved almonds, grilled carrots with a molasses and butter drizzle, and for dessert, chocolate cake with cherry sauce and rose petals."

"Rose petals?" asked Jim, his eyebrows raised in surprise. "Are we supposed to eat them?"

"Yes," she giggled shyly. "Roses are edible, and they're good."

The table stared at her in stunned silence.

Finally, Jim spoke. "Jasmine, I'm already married, but can I adopt you?"

"I think you've got a fan, Jasmine," laughed Kelly as she put pitchers of iced tea and lemonade on the table. She winked at the girl. "He doesn't offer to adopt just anybody."

Karen beamed at the compliment of her daughter.

"I just like to cook," Jasmine smiled, turning to go back to the kitchen.

"Is there more to bring out?" asked Jim.

Jasmine shook her head. "No. I'll bring out the cake when you're done with supper."

Jim looked at Kelly, confused. "Aren't they eating with us?"

"I asked them to, but they said they'd feel like they were intruding."

"Intruding on what, our eating this beautiful meal?" He pushed his plate away from him and looked at the two women. "I'm not eating unless you eat with us."

"Me neither," said Christian, pushing his plate away.

The others at the table pushed their plates away with similar declarations.

Jasmine looked at her mom. "Well, I don't know."

"It sure would be a shame to let all this food go to waste," said Jim, leaning back and crossing his arms over his chest. "And I'm stubborn." He nodded toward Kelly. "Just ask her."

Kelly nodded seriously.

Jim nodded to the other end of the table. "I see two empty spaces down there that need people sitting at them. Now, we can either sit here staring at our plates and starve to death or we can start eating as soon as you sit down." He looked pointedly at the two women. "Your choice."

Jasmine and Karen looked at each other and Karen shrugged. "I guess we'll join you."

Jim nodded. "Outstanding. Grab your plates and we'll say grace."

Kelly and Cilla brought settings to the table for Karen and Jasmine, who sat down, Jasmine smiling nervously.

"Karen, I don't suppose you are a minister?" asked Jim.

Karen laughed. "No, but I was a DJ."

Jim chuckled. "Well, I guess I'll say grace then."

He folded his hands, closed his eyes and bowed his head. "Father, we thank you for the many blessings you have bestowed upon us, for this food and for the friends with whom we are about to share it. Thank you again for bringing Declan, Cilla, Eamon and Noel to be with us, and for Karen and Jasmine to be with us tonight. Guide us in all that we do, blessing us, strengthening us and using us according to your will and for your purpose. Keep us ever mindful of those who are less fortunate than us and direct us in our proper duty to them. This we pray, in Jesus' name, amen."

"Amen," came the chorus of voices from around the table.

"Now," said Jim, taking several slices of brisket off the platter, passing it to Kelly, then looking at Jasmine, "to what do we owe this wonderful meal?"

THE REVIVAL

Jasmine looked nervously at Karen then back at Jim. "I just wanted to say thank you for helping us."

Jim looked at her closely, then at Karen. "Is it just the two of you?"

Karen shook her head. "My husband and our two boys are at home." She looked at her daughter. "Jasmine wanted to do this for you and I just came along to help."

Jim nodded as he spooned a large helping of smashed potatoes onto his plate. "And what do you all do?"

"Antonio and the boys work on the construction in Jamestown and Jasmine and I help with the food," answered Karen. "On Saturdays, we help unload trucks or with anything else that needs doing."

"It sounds like you keep busy." Jim took several spears of asparagus before passing it to Kelly.

Karen nodded. "We just moved into one of the new homes in Jamestown, but we're hoping to be able to stake our own place." She accepted the brisket platter from Cilla. "So, we're all working as much as we can."

Jim forked two carrots onto his plate. "What kind of a place do you hope to have?"

Karen passed the brisket to Jasmine and took the potatoes from Cilla. "We've always wanted a little farm. Even before this happened, we'd read all of the Mother Earth News and Backwoods Home Magazine stuff." She passed the potatoes and took the asparagus. "We had this dream about becoming self-reliant." She smiled. "I guess now is the time."

"You sound like us," said Kelly.

"We were heading in that direction, too" said Cilla. "So were a lot of our friends."

Karen nodded. "It seemed like a lot of people were feeling that pull. Not many of us took the steps to really get there, though."

"It sounds like your heads were in the right place," said Jim. "Were the kids on board with you?"

Karen shook her head. "Not really. They had all their activities and didn't really pay much attention to what was happening in the world around them." She shrugged. "You know kids."

She looked at her daughter. "The boys are starting to really get into it now, but Jasmine kind of had her world jerked out from under her."

"What were you going to do, Jasmine?" asked Naomi.

"I wanted to go to culinary school," said Jasmine quietly.

"We had hoped she would pursue music," said Karen, "but her heart was set on cooking."

"You have a beautiful voice, Jasmine," said Kelly. "Did you sing a lot?"

Jasmine nodded. "Yes, ma'am. I sang at church and in most of the groups at school."

"She had a music scholarship waiting for her at the university," said Karen.

"Really?" Kelly asked. "And you still wanted to go to culinary school?"

Jasmine nodded, a bit sadly. "Yes, ma'am. It's just what I love."

"Well, you certainly seem to know what you're doing," said Cilla.

"Have you thought about what you'd like to do now?" asked Jim.

Jasmine shrugged. "I guess I'll just keep helping out. I don't really know what else to do." She looked at Kelly. "Thank you for letting me cook for you tonight."

"Have you thought about opening your own restaurant?" Jim asked.

Jasmine looked confused. "There aren't any restaurants anymore."

"Sounds like a good reason to open one." He held up a fork of brisket and looked at it. "I'd pay for this."

He looked around the table. "Who else would pay for a meal like this?"

Raised hands and a chorus of 'I woulds' showed a unanimous response.

Jasmine looked from Jim to her mom and back at Jim. "How would I do that?"

Jim took a sip of tea. "We're building a town. The reason we're building a town is because people like to be around other people. Mrs. Hernandez opened the Jamestown Inn with credits she earned cooking for us. Right now, her restaurant is enough, but, as the town grows, there will undoubtedly be room for another one, maybe more."

He paused, looking at the girl. "I have a proposition for you, Jasmine. Since Mrs. Hernandez left, Kelly has had to do all the cooking, which keeps her from being able to give me all of the attention I deserve."

Kelly's swat on his arm barely beat Christian's laugh.

Jim side-nodded toward Kelly. "As you can see, she can't keep her hands off of me."

A second swat from Kelly.

"See?" he smiled.

Kelly rolled her eyes as the rest laughed.

"So, Jasmine, my offer is this," Jim continued. "If you would like to cook for Stonemont, I will pay you a wage that will allow you to open a restaurant in town, at a location I will rent to you, in one year, if that's what you still want to do."

Jasmine stared at him, then at her mom, who was also staring at him, then back at him.

"I have one condition," Jim continued, "and that is that you will sing in the church we will be building." He leaned forward and looked at her seriously. "Cooking may be your passion, but God blessed you with a beautiful voice. The proper use of his gifts to us is our gift back to him, and he uses that to bless others." He paused, watching her as she stared at him. "Is that a deal you'd like to make?"

Jasmine looked at Karen, then back at Jim. Her mind felt overloaded. Her family had struggled to survive for months before coming to Stonemont, and then they had all been working to save up to start a little place of their own where she knew her future would be farm work. Now, in the space of only a few minutes, her old dream had been resurrected and put back in front of her for her to grasp. "I ... I don't know what to say."

Jim smiled. "Say yes and eat up. I think we're all looking forward to that cake."

Jasmine smiled, tears forming in her eyes. "Okay. Yes."

32

They left mid-morning, taking the back roads to Highway 75, then north through Lyndon and Carbondale to catch the southern loop around Topeka onto westbound I-70. The roads were clear, and they only saw an occasional vehicle at crossroads or coming the other direction, even more rarely overtaking or being overtaken by vehicles also heading west.

Four scouts on dirt bikes ran point a mile ahead of the main body which was comprised of seven pickup trucks, three of which pulled horse trailers, two buses carrying the scout teams and two empty tractor-trailers that had been included in case they ran into any salvage opportunities. Four more scouts on dirt bikes ran drag, providing rear guard about a half mile behind the column.

They had concluded their discussions after dinner the night before, making several final decisions and adjustments to their plan until everyone felt they had covered what they could, but all of them knowing that reality could deal a blow to a plan at any time. Still, having a plan beat not having one, and sometimes they even worked like they were supposed to.

They kept their speed at around fifty and reached Clarks Creek, the first drop-off point, in the early afternoon where a scout team dropped off to follow the creek south, then head west cross-country to come up behind a berm on the eastern edge of I-70 where it turned south across from the airfield.

Several more miles brought them to the interchange of Highway 18, where four operational teams and one support team dropped off, keeping one bus, one tractor trailer and four motorcycles with them, which they parked under the overpass. The teams would remain there until dark, at which point the ops teams would move toward the fort, passing between the main base and Camp Funston to the northeast in order to establish surveillance. The support team would remain with the vehicles. Each group had an additional task scheduled for later that night.

The remainder of the convoy continued west on I-70. The highway curved to the south, taking them in front of the base on their right. They saw no activity as they passed, but they would review the video being taken by three digital cameras later.

THE REVIVAL

A brief stretch of vacant land gave way to businesses and apartment complexes on their right before a bridge over the Smokey Hill River swung them southwest again.

Taking an exit ramp, they passed a Cracker Barrel on their right then navigated a round-about onto Chestnut Street. Passing a Starbucks and a Freddy's on the right, they slowed as the approached a tall chain-link gate across the entrance to the Wal-Mart Super Center on the left and stopped about a hundred feet away.

Mike got out of Jim's lead truck and walked across the street, his rifle hanging at his right side. He stopped at the gate where he talked for a few minutes, then returned to the truck and got in.

"They say they weren't expecting this many. Most people haven't brought more than a dozen, so they're a bit leery of letting this many in."

"Do they want us to leave some of our people outside?" Jim asked.

Mike shook his head. "No. They checked with their boss. They just ask that our guys walk in and leave their rifles on the bus. Side arms are okay. Also, that we open the trailer, so they can take a peek as we go in."

Jim nodded. "No problem. They're just being careful." He cocked his head toward the back. "Go tell the others."

Mike got out and went back down the line with instructions. Within several minutes the scouts had exited the bus and formed up to follow it in, the scouts on the dirt bikes had stored their rifles in the bus and the driver of the semi had latched his trailer doors open.

Mike got back into the truck and nodded. "Good to go."

Jim tapped his horn for the point scouts to head to the gate.

The point scouts approached the gate and were waved through by the gate guards who put up a hand for Jim to stop. A well-muscled man wearing a black t-shirt, tactical vest and Wiley X sunglasses approached the truck.

"Mr. Wyatt?" the man asked, letting his rifle hang to his side.

Jim nodded. "Yep."

"Sorry for the inconvenience." The man pushed the three-percenter cap back on his forehead. "We weren't expecting such a large group." He looked over at Mike. "When Mike said you'd be coming up with some people, we figured a dozen or so like most of the others."

Jim shook his head. "No problem."

The man pointed down the fence-enclosed street to the large parking lot. "If you want to take your people down there and hang a left, you can set up in the northeast corner. Set up however you like. We keep things secure, but we won't be offended if you keep your own guard on your area too." He turned for a moment to wave at another guard at the other end of the street, then turned back. "Your guys can stay armed, but we'd appreciate it if you'd leave your rifles in the bus. We just don't want to make the place look like we're going to war."

Jim nodded again. "Sure thing."

The man nodded. "Thank you, sir. And when you get settled, Captain Dorser asks if you'd stop over to see him."

Jim nodded a third time. "Will do. Where can I find him?"

"His trailer is over by the west door. He's usually there. If not, just look for a guy with two little blonde girls buzzing around him like bumblebees. That'll be him."

Jim smiled and nodded a fourth time. "Thanks, buddy. What's your name?"

"Troy, sir."

"Well thanks for the welcome, Troy."

"You're welcome, sir. Good to have you."

Jim tapped the horn again and followed the lead scouts down the entrance road. Returning the wave of the second guard at the entry to the massive parking lot, they turned left toward the northeast corner where they circled the vehicles and shut off the engines.

Much of the lot was empty, with only a smattering of groups dotted around the perimeter, but a number of tents, tables and booths were set up closer to the building and had people milling around them.

Getting out of the truck, Jim looked around, then turned to Mike. "Have everybody get situated and stay close." He looked at the chain link fence separating them from the frontage road and the highway beyond. "Have the semi pull around to be between us and the rest of the lot and headed toward the fence. If we want to leave in a hurry, that's how we'll go. Then, have them put the bus on the other side of the semi so we can load and unload without being seen and fill in the back of the rectangle with the pickups."

Mike nodded. "Okay."

"Have them eat something and post sentries. I'll go talk to the captain and be back in a bit."

Mike nodded and left to organize their position.

"It looks like a regular afternoon at Wal-Mart," said Tom as he walked up behind Jim. "I wonder where the cardboard box of free kittens is?"

Jim chuckled as Declan, Eamon and Noel joined them. "You all want to come with us to meet their boss?"

Declan nodded. "May as well."

THE REVIVAL

They walked across the parking lot, nodding to those they passed and returning greetings to those who spoke to them. The crowd seemed relaxed and friendly, comfortable in the new reality and seeming to enjoy the community of the market. Children ran around playing and, as they got closer to the building, they began to smell aromas from the open-air food stalls.

"Two o'clock," said Tom.

Jim looked over and saw a tall man wearing a camo K-State ball cap carrying a blonde girl on his shoulders. Both were eating donuts.

Walking toward the man, they passed the stand from which a second little blonde girl ran with a donut in her hand yelling "Grandpa! Wait for me!"

The man turned and held out his hand to the little girl, then looked up and saw Jim and the others approaching.

"Captain Dorser?" Jim asked as the approached.

The man nodded. "That'd be me."

Jim extended his hand. "Jim Wyatt." He nodded to Tom and the Moores. "This is Tom Murphy, Declan Moore, Eamon Moore and Noel Moore."

Dorser shook the offered hands and smiled. "Well, you've got more Moores than I do. Stonemont, right?"

Jim nodded and smiled at the girls. "It looks like you've got your hands full."

Dorser chuckled and tousled the head of the little girl standing beside him. "Yep, they keep me hopping. Did you guys get a donut? They're the best in the parking lot."

Jim shook his head. "Not yet."

Dorser reached up and took the shoulder-rider by the waist, swinging her to the ground beside her sister. "Well, let me buy you one and we can chat. Follow me."

They followed Dorser through the growing crowd to the donut stand, watching how he interacted with those they passed. He seemed to have a smile and a friendly word for everyone, and everyone seemed to have one for him in return.

"April makes the best donuts around here," said Dorser as they arrived at the stand. He winked at them. "At least since Dunkin' Donuts closed down."

A pretty woman wearing an apron with a strawberry on the pocket whirled around. "Wade Dorser, I never saw your cruiser in front of the dunkster when I was open." She wiped her hands on her apron and smiled. "What can I get for you gentlemen?"

Jim smiled back. "I'll take one of whatever you've got, April."

"Me too," said Declan.

"Three," said Eamon.

"Four," said Noel

Tom just smiled.

April laughed. "Well, let's see what I have." She lifted the lid off a large plastic platter. "Looks like I have five apple spice, two chocolate, three blueberry and a glazed lemon cake." She smiled up at them. "Anything sound good?"

Jim patted his stomach. "They all sound good, but I'm partial to lemon. I'll have that one."

April picked up the lemon donut with a napkin and handed it to Jim. "How about you boys?" she asked, looking at Tom and the Moores.

Tom nodded to Declan to go ahead.

"I'll have an apple spice," said Declan.

"Me, too," said Eamon.

"Blueberry, ma'am," said Noel.

"And for the quiet one?" April smiled at Tom.

"I'll have the chocolate, please."

April handed the donuts out to a series of "Thank you"s and handed Wade a blueberry. "On your tab?" she asked him.

"Thanks," Dorser nodded with a smile.

"No problem." She looked at Jim and the others. "You guys come back as much as you want, and I'll put it on Wade's tab. I like having him in my debt." She smiled. "I learned that from watching The Godfather."

Dorser chuckled. "Let's go find somewhere to sit."

He led them to a picnic table under a sunshade with a Coleman cooler on it. "Have a seat. Paper cups are in the holder and the water ought to be cool."

He sat down at looked at Jim. "Troy says you brought an army."

Jim shrugged. "Just some of our scouts. We're a long ways from home and didn't know what to expect."

Dorser took a bite if his donut and nodded. "Don't blame you. I would have too if I had them." He looked at Tom and the Moores. "Are you all from Stonemont?"

"I am," said Tom. "Declan, Eamon and Noel are up from Texas. They're Rangers."

Dorser raised his eyebrows. "Lawmen or outfielders?"

Declan chuckled. "Lawmen."

"Well, I'll be," Dorser extended his hand to shake the three across the table. "I've never met any of you guys before. What brings you up here?"

"My daughter, their sister, married Jim's nephew," Declan answered. "We came up for the wedding and Jim invited us to come along."

Dorser looked surprised. "That's quite a trip, nowadays. What did you find on the way up? I mean, how is the country?"

"Pretty sparse," said Declan.

"Those who know how to work and pull together are doin' okay." said Eamon.

"Others, not so much," said Noel.

"Did you have any trouble?"

Declan shook his head. "None to speak of."

Jim looked around. "You seem pretty well set up."

Dorser looked around as if looking at what Jim had seen. "We're okay, but we're not where I think we need to be. I'll have a better idea after the meeting."

"What are you expecting?"

Dorser thought for a moment, looking out over the parking lot. "I don't know. To be honest, I wish the fort wasn't even here. They could have been a big help during the worst time, but they weren't. Now, they want to have this big pow-wow and act like they're the chief." He shook his head. "That's not going to fly. Not now." He shrugged. " It could cause trouble."

"Are all LEO on the same page?" asked Declan.

Dorser shook his head. "Not all. I'd say seventy-five percent. The sheriff, the JC chief and their inner circles, and some of the surrounding jurisdictions' leadership are on board with the Riley command staff. You know brass. They stick together to make sure they all keep their positions, no matter what else changes. There's going to be a split. No way around it that I can see."

"How many are you expecting for the meeting?" asked Tom.

"Hard to say. Freelove and McGregor are coming in tomorrow. We have about a dozen other sheriffs who sent word that they're coming, plus some town groups and a few militia groups. We even heard there may be a group coming from the Potawatomi reservation."

"What do you think is going to happen?" asked Declan.

Dorser squinted as he took his cap off, scratched his scalp and put the cap back on. "I think the colonel in charge is going to try to establish the base as the center of a new order of things. We have quite a few fort personnel out here who left because of the way things were going in there, and they say a lot of others left and went other places. That tells me that the atmosphere in there is autocratic, not cooperative." He looked at Declan. "Autocracies never become democracies on their own, and they don't try to organize cooperative groups they're willing to be an equal part of. They want to be in charge, and that means being in charge of us."

He looked around at the other men. "We made it through the bad times by working together, and now we're starting to build a community again. Not like what things had become, but the way we like it, and we don't have any interest in starting over again constructing a government that thinks it has a right to control things that ought to be left to us."

He looked at Jim. "I've heard a little about you guys, and I think you might feel the same way."

Jim looked at Tom and the Moores, then back at Dorser. "Yep."

THE REVIVAL

33

"It's empty."

Jim looked at Alex. "What do you mean it's empty?"

"Abandoned," replied Alex. "At least most of it. We cut the fence at the back and worked our way to the front. We didn't see anything but some raccoons until we got to the cavalry parade field. The only sign of life is in some of the buildings south of there."

"Cool place, though," said Aaron.

Alex nodded. "And big. Took us all night."

They had spent the rest of the previous day meeting others at the market and exchanging stories about their experiences since the collapse. Although everybody's stories were similar, the opportunity to talk with others from different areas was interesting to everyone and created not only a bond between groups but a sense of geographical continuity and support. The fact that sheriffs and militia groups were arriving from distant counties created an excitement among the locals exceeded only by the fact that Texas Rangers had come with some people from a place east of there.

That night, campfires and glowing grills had dotted the parking lot and a feeling of anticipation ran through the market area as people mingled, then slowly drifted off to their individual areas to sleep, unaware that Stonemont scouts were probing the fort in preparation for the upcoming meeting.

Now, the "Cools" were briefing Jim and the others sitting in a circle in their area.

Tom looked at Jim. "That confirms some of what we've heard." He looked back at Alex and Aaron. "No patrols, sentries, anything?"

Both shook their heads.

"We saw the first sentry near the cavalry museum," said Aaron.

"And he was asleep," added Alex.

Jim and Tom looked at each other.

"What do you think?" Jim asked.

Tom kept looking at Jim for a moment, then back at Alex and Aaron. "What happened when they heard the shots from across the highway?"

Alex shrugged. "Not much. Our guys opened up at o-three-hundred, right on time. Nothing happened for a couple of minutes, then some lights came on and some people started running between a few buildings. When the explosion from the bridge went off, a bunch more people came running out and looking around, then some ran back inside and came out again with rifles."

"They came out the first time without their rifles?" Tom asked in amazement.

Alex nodded.

"A bunch of them never even went back in to get theirs," said Aaron. "They just stood around asking each other what was going on."

"You were close enough to hear them?" asked Tom.

"Not everything," Aaron answered, "just when they yelled."

"Did there seem to be competent leadership?" asked Tom.

Alex scoffed. "The leadership of a chicken coop. One guy crowing and the rest running around like their heads were cut off."

"How did it play out?" asked Jim.

"Our guys discontinued fire as scheduled and the soldiers kept yelling and running around for a couple of minutes," said Alex. "We saw about a dozen take a truck down the road toward the airfield. They hadn't come back by the time we pulled out."

"We came back over the highway and touched base with the fire team across from the gate on our way here," said Aaron. "They said the sentries seemed confused and didn't return fire."

"How would you describe the ones you saw?" asked Tom.

The brothers looked at each other.

"Disorganized and confused," said Alex.

"Not ready to fight," said Aaron.

"How did the colonel act when he came out," Tom asked.

"He never came out that we saw," Alex answered.

Tom looked at Jim. "They're not soldiers anymore. They're a bunch of followers led by a punk."

Jim remained silent for a minute, then looked at the brothers. "Are you guys okay for another couple of hours before you get some sleep?"

"Sure," Alex nodded.

"Yes, sir," said Aaron.

Jim stood up. "Good. Let's go talk to Dorser.

34

Wade Dorser stared at Jim, silent. Freelove, McGregor and three other sheriffs had joined them at tables by the donut stand and they had just finished listening to the Cools' report.

"Sounds to me like we've got a back-stabber with a bunch of misfits thinking they're still the army," said the Dickenson County Sheriff, Tim Hersey, pushing his hat back on his head, "and trying to buffalo us into joining up with them."

Freelove nodded. "Yeah, it does."

"I say we go have a talk with him," said McGregor, glowering more than usual. "He's sittin' on land and who knows how much gear, paid for with taxpayers' money, and never offered a bit of help. Time for an accounting."

"Passed time," said another sheriff.

Hersey looked at Dorser. "How many men do you figure he's got?"

Dorser was still looking at Jim, trying to discern what Jim was thinking, but turned to Hersey. "We're guessing abound three hundred." He shrugged. "Could be more, could be less."

"Well, I brought about a dozen," said Hersey, looking around at the others. "How 'bout you guys?"

"About the same," said another sheriff.

"Me, too," nodded another.

"Eight," said Freelove.

"Five," said McGregor.

Hersey looked at Dorser. "How 'bout you, Wade? How many guys do you think you can get together?"

"About fifty, probably," Dorser answered. "Maybe more."

Hersey looked at Jim. "And you, Mr. Wyatt? Did you bring any people?"

Jim nodded. "About a hundred," he said, not wanting to give an exact count.

Hersey paused, staring at Jim. "A hundred?"

Jim nodded. "Yep."

"You brought a hundred people?" Hersey asked again. "From where?"

"Miami County," Jim answered.

Hersey looked confused. "I thought Bob Johnson was sheriff in Miami County."

"He is," Jim nodded.

"Jim has a spread in Miami County," said Freelove. "The guys he brought are his own guys."

Hersey pushed his hat back on his head. "You brought a hundred of your own guys, Mr. Wyatt?"

Jim smiled. "Yep. And call me Jim."

Hersey nodded. "You must have quite a spread, Jim."

"He does," growled McGregor.

Hersey nodded. "Well, Jim, you've got more people here than the rest of us put together but you're not saying much."

Jim shrugged. "I'm pretty much out of my neighborhood." He nodded at Freelove. "Mark invited us to the meeting and we came out to see what the deal was with the fort, but it's your backyard so you're the ones with the say." He looked around the group. "We'll be happy to help if it looks like we're on the same page."

Hersey looked around the group, himself. "To be honest, I'm not sure what page we're on."

McGregor leaned forward, placing his forearms on the picnic table in front of him. "I'll tell you what page I'm on. We've got a mostly empty fort, probably full of supplies and equipment we paid for with our tax dollars and could probably use, being held up by a mutinous jerk-off and his marginal morons who think they can con us into thinking they are in the driver's seat.

"And when I turn that page," he continued, "the next page in my book says we secure the fort and distribute whatever supplies it contains to whoever can use it."

"You mean attack the army and take government property from the fort?" asked one of the other sheriffs.

"Nope," McGregor shook his head. "There is no government and there is no army. A year of no-show when people needed help settles that for me." He looked around the group. "What always chapped my ass was how government workers always thought the stuff we gave them to serve us belonged to them. Didn't matter if it was a Learjet or a stapler. The feds were like that, the states were like that and a lot of our cities and counties were like that."

"Can't argue with that," said the other sheriff.

"I don't want any more of that," said McGregor. "It's time we stood up, fixed the things that need fixing and get back to the old 'of the people, by the people and for the people'."

THE REVIVAL

"I agree," nodded Freelove. "We've done it in our area and Jim has done it at Stonemont. They're even building a brand-new town over there."

He looked at Jim. "Would you mind telling them the proclamation you made about Stonemont?"

Jim thought for a moment. He had not come here to try to influence the actions of others, but simply to find out how others in the area were doing and how the situation at Riley might affect Stonemont. Still, Mark Freelove had asked him to share his position and it seemed only right that he do so.

He looked around the group, the proclamation he had committed to memory coming immediately to his mind. "Last Thanksgiving, after six months of surviving and re-building without any help or contact from any government, I said that from that time forward, Stonemont would be autonomous, independent and sovereign, apart from all others, subordinate to none, subject only to God and God's laws as we feel them written in our hearts."

McGregor nodded. "Damn right."

"I agree," said Freelove. "That's pretty much how we feel."

Dorser nodded thoughtfully and the Moores remained impassive.

Hersey looked at the other sheriffs, then at Jim. "That sounds good, but how are you going to back it up if part of the government is reestablished? Or if a larger group comes along and wants to make you a part of them?"

Jim looked at Hersey. "Your name sounds familiar. Your family has been out here a while, haven't they?"

Hersey looked surprised. "Yes, we have. My great, great, great grandfather put in a stagecoach stop called Mud Creek, which became Abilene."

"A name taken out of the Bible meaning city of the plains," said Jim.

Hersey nodded. "How did you know that?"

"Tom Smith was in one of our family lines."

Hersey looked even more surprised, then smiled. "'Bear River' Smith?"

Jim smiled. "Yep."

"Who's Tom Smith?" asked Freelove.

Hersey was still looking at Jim, smiling. "Marshall Tom Smith was the man who really cleaned up Abilene. Did it mostly with his fists, too."

"I thought Hickock cleaned up Abilene," said Noel, speaking for the first time.

Hersey looked at him. "Ol' Duck Bill? Nah. Hickock was there for about six months, accidentally killed his own deputy and got fired. Smith had it pretty much in hand before Hickock ever got there."

Jim looked at Noel. "He'd have lasted longer if he'd thought about going to his gun sooner and not relying so much on his fists. He went out to arrest a couple of guys, took a shot in the chest, his deputy ran out on him and the crooks cut his head off with an axe. There's a lesson there."

Hersey nodded. "That's a fact."

"You asked me how I'd back up my proclamation if some kind of government or other group came along," said Jim, thoughtfully. "I've had enough of people trying to tell me how to live and enforcing it with money they took from me. I don't intend to go back to that. I'll back it up now, and I'm preparing to back it up in the future."

He looked around the group. "Anybody who tries to make me be a part of something I don't want to be a part of is in for a long day. You all can do the same thing, and we can work together to keep the freedom we once had, lost, and now have again."

"I'm for that," said McGregor.

"Me too," nodded Freelove.

Hersey looked around the group, then at Declan. "We haven't heard from our Ranger friends. What do Texans think?"

Declan nodded soberly. "If Jim ain't right, then God's a possum."

35

The convoy left the market shortly after eight o'clock, moving out the entry street and east to I-70 into the sun. They kept their speed down to accommodate the over twenty vehicles in the caravan, a late arrival being a captain from the Riley County Sheriff Department with a professor from Kansas State University who fell in at the last minute.

Dorser had deferred to Hersey as the group's nominal leader, a nod to the sheriff's seniority among the local lawmen, and Hersey's group took the lead followed by Dorser, Freelove, McGregor and the other sheriffs with the Stonemont group bringing up the rear.

It only took a few minutes for them to reach the exit to Henry Drive, which went over the highway to the gate where six soldiers stopped them at Marshall Drive.

The vehicles stopped with room enough between them to maneuver, the bus turning right onto a road called Whisky Lake and stopping to off-load the scouts into a depression opposite the base. Signs identified the buildings on the right as the Visitors Control Center, beyond which sprawled the air field.

A soldier wearing the stripes of a staff sergeant and carrying an M-4 approached Hersey's truck. "You here for the meeting?"

Hersey nodded. "Yep."

The soldier pointed to Marshall Drive. "Turn there, pull into the parking lot and exit your vehicles. Leave any weapons you have in the vehicles. When you're all out, we'll have trucks come and take you to the meeting location."

Hersey noticed the lack of courtesy in the sergeant's instructions as well as several stains on the man's uniform. He looked at the other soldiers, who looked both lazy and nervous. "Where is the meeting?" he asked.

"It's down by the service hangars," the sergeant answered, sounding irritated. "Now, please pull over into the parking lot."

Hersey shook his head. "Nah, that's okay. We'd rather not be separated from our vehicles. We'll just follow the trucks when they get here."

The sergeant backed away from Hersey's door, his fingers flexing on the grip of the rifle and anger showing in his eyes. "Civilians are prohibited from bringing weapons on base. I need you to pull your vehicles into that parking area and secure them to await transport."

Hersey took off his sunglasses and looked the man in the eye. "Son, is that a grape jelly stain on your uniform?"

The sergeant looked down at his uniform to see a red dot flicking around his chest.

"My mistake," said Hersey. "That's where my chief deputy is going to put a couple of forty-five slugs if you don't get your hand away from that trigger and change your attitude."

The look on the sergeant's face changed from anger to angry confusion at the sudden change of control.

"I can see you thinking about it," said Hersey. "Don't. If you don't sling that weapon, and I mean right now, you're going to be dead in a minute and I won't be able to hear for a week."

The sergeant looked at the men behind him, trying to judge how much he could count on them.

"They can't help you, son. It's just you and us. Your attitude has brought you to within a few seconds of dying. Let's see if your brain can save you. Let that rifle hang and take your hands off it."

The sergeant looked at Hersey, then at the red dot dancing on his chest, then back at his men.

"This is the most important decision of your life, son. Make the right one."

The sergeant looked into the cold blue eyes of the chief deputy, then at the tanned steady hand that held the 1911, and finally at the large muzzle that seemed to grow in size as he looked into it. He could imagine the massive .45 slug resting in the darkness of the barrel waiting to be launched into his chest. Slowly, he lowered his rifle and took his hands off of it, allowing it to hang at his side.

Hersey nodded. "Good choice, son." He saw a truck coming down Marshall Drive toward them. "Who's that going to be?"

The sergeant didn't answer but backed away several steps and turned to walk quickly toward the approaching truck.

The truck turned off of Marshall and onto Henry, stopping for the sergeant to approach it.

The sergeant spoke with the driver for a minute, looking back at the convoy several times before the door opened and a man emerged.

The man stepped down, spoke with the sergeant for another minute, then walked toward the convoy. As he approached, Hersey could see black bars on his uniform.

THE REVIVAL

The man stopped about ten feet from Hersey's door. "Good morning. I'm Captain Benson. Is there a problem?"

Hersey nodded. "Morning, captain. I was telling the sergeant that we'd rather not be separated from our vehicles or our weapons. We'll be happy to follow you in to the meeting."

The captain shook his head. "I'm sorry, sir, it's just procedure. We're going into a secure area and civilians are prohibited from bringing in weapons or personal vehicles. I assure you they'll be safe in the lot over there."

Hersey ran his hand over his mouth and chin. "Captain, we were invited here with the understanding that you all wanted to talk about how to cooperate in this new world of ours. Asking us to relinquish our weapons and vehicles does not seem cooperative to me." He looked over at the air field. "The only time I was ever required to give up my weapon was when entering a jail or prison."

He looked at Benson. "Is that what this is, captain? A prison? Because if it is, we will call in more of our people and contain you within it. We will not have you operating a facility separate from the population and contrary to their interests."

The captain looked surprised at Hersey's response. "I'll have to contact the colonel about this."

"Do what you have to do, captain, but do it quick. We're getting tired of sittin' here."

The captain nodded, returned to his truck and drove back into the base.

"I don't like this, Tim," said Chief Deputy Loren Wills, re-holstering his gun. "They're sloppy, disorganized and pushy. Plus, they don't understand us if they think we'd give up our guns."

Hersey nodded. "Yep."

The truck returned several minutes later, and Captain Benson got out. "The colonel says to bring you in," he said, approaching Hersey's truck again. "I'll turn around and you can follow me."

"To the meeting location?" Hersey asked, watching Benson eyes.

"Yes, sir."

"And we'll be keeping our weapons," Hersey stated flatly.

Benson nodded. "Understood, sir."

"Okay, captain, lead on."

They watched as Benson returned to the truck and turned around, then followed him as he turned onto Marshall and entered the base.

They passed low buildings on both sides of the road, catching glimpses of helicopters lined up beyond the buildings to the left, and soon slowed to turn into a large parking area between two buildings. Seeing Benson park in front of one of the buildings, Hersey pulled around in a wide loop and stopped his truck in the middle of the lot facing the entrance, followed by the others.

The men in the convoy stepped out of their vehicles warily, rifles in hand, scanning the rooftops and the surrounding area for potential threats. Seeing none, most slung their rifles around their necks. Making visual checks with each other, they walked toward the large open sliding door where Benson stood.

"I don't suppose I could ask you to leave you rifles in your vehicles," said Benson.

Hersey shrugged. "You could ask, captain, but I wouldn't bet your next MRE on us doin' it."

Benson nodded. "Very well. Come on in."

The service hanger was set up with tables in a large U-shape, a separate table placed in the open end in front of another large open door. Soldiers with rifles stood at the door and others sat at the ends of the U, watching the lawmen and militia leaders as they entered but not speaking or getting up.

"Sit wherever you like," said Benson, looking at the group. "There are more of you than we expected, but I think there are more chairs in the other room if you need them."

Jim looked around and took a seat at one of the corners of the U, joined by Tom and the Moores. The others found seats around table, with some having to find chairs and set them up behind those at the table.

They sat mostly in silence, watching the soldiers for several minutes until Hersey asked, "Where is your colonel?"

One soldier turned in his direction. "He'll be here pretty soon."

"What's your name?" Hersey asked.

The soldier looked at Hersey for a moment before answering. "My name is Major Stafford."

The superior attitude grated on Hersey. "He's got five minutes."

Stafford looked at him without commenting.

Several more minutes passed before a group of soldiers walked through the large door, most of them fanning out across the doorway as several took places at the center table. One of them remained standing.

"I am Colonel Briggs," said the man. "I am glad that you all decided to come so that we can work together developing a plan to establish security and stability in the region."

He paused, seeming to expect a response that didn't come.

THE REVIVAL

"The past year has been a challenge for all of us," he continued. "In addition to the loss of technological assets and infrastructure, we have experienced a tremendous loss of human life. We have all suffered, but, by pulling together, we have made it through the toughest time."

He paused again, looking at the stoic lawmen and militia leaders, trying to judge their collective temperament. "Going forward, in order to provide for the safety, security and ongoing welfare of our country, it is important that we come together as one cohesive community, working under central leadership toward a common goal of rebuilding."

He nodded, as if to assure everyone of the importance of his statement. "That is what we are here for today - to let you know that we will be taking the lead and applying all of our resources in that effort."

The lawmen remained silent, watching Briggs.

"Our first step, today, will be to assess community needs and resources," Briggs continued. "To that end, my staff and I will be talking with each of you in order to develop a comprehensive supply and threat assessment and determine how resources may be distributed for maximal effect."

He looked around the still silent table. "Are the any questions so far?"

"Yeah, I have a question," said McGregor. "Where have you been?"

Briggs looked confused. "What do you mean?"

"You said that we made it through the last year by everybody pulling together. Well, we all pulled together," McGregor nodded around the table, "but nobody saw you out there helping. Where were you?"

Briggs nodded. "Yes, an understandable question." He glanced at some of the soldiers seated near him. "We have been busy keeping Fort Riley secure in order to preserve its ability to function as the hub of assistance for the region during this crisis. I am proud to say that we have been successful in that task."

"The initial crisis is pretty much over," said Freelove. "Seems to me the time for you to have been offering help was a year ago."

Briggs tried to stand taller. "Well, as I said, it was important for us to maintain base and command integrity so that we would be here to spearhead and support rebuilding. And, again, we have been successful in that. The important thing is that we now work together to re-establish community cohesion and development."

"And what kind of assistance are you offering now?" asked another sheriff.

Briggs looked relieved that the conversation seemed to be back on track. "Excellent question, and exactly the reason we are here."

He looked around the tables again, trying to adopt a look of strength and sincerity. "You all have done an exemplary job bringing your communities

THE REVIVAL

through this unprecedented catastrophe, and you should each be commended for it. Now, we must begin the post-incident phase and rebuild. We, the army, will provide command, control and logistical support for integrated rebuilding efforts, as well as providing the security that will enable those efforts to bear fruit." He tried to look even more sincere. "Naturally, we will want all of you to assume important leadership roles within the new structure."

The sheriff who had asked the question looked at Briggs closely, smelling the con. "And what would those leadership roles entail?"

"As leaders of your communities, you have the people's trust. As our direct representatives, you will be important links in the regional command structure as we centralize leadership and resources for rebuilding and general welfare, representing your constituencies to the central command and relaying directions from that command to your communities."

He paused, scanning the room for effect. "Total integration of resources is imperative if we are to reestablish an integrated regional social order. I am counting on each of you to be an important part of that process."

"And what resources will you be bringing to this effort?" asked Freelove.

Briggs nodded. "I'm glad you asked." He spread his arms as if to include the world around him. "As you can imagine, the resources of Fort Riley are immense. We will be bringing all of those resources to bear in this."

"Like what?" asked McGregor.

Briggs was irritated by McGregor's challenging tone but didn't want to break his carefully crafted message of cooperation. He shrugged. "The fort's resources are massive. Construction equipment, medical supplies, food, manpower ..."

"You have food?" Hersey asked.

"Yes," Briggs answered, seeing the interest of the sheriff. "We have stockpiles of emergency food we can distribute as necessary."

"Thousands of people have starved to death over the past year," said Hersey, coldly. "And you were sitting on emergency food?"

"Well," Briggs looked around nervously, "it was important that we kept it for a time like this, in order to rebuild."

"While fellow Americans who paid for it with their tax dollars starved to death around you," said Freelove, disgust evident in his voice.

Briggs shook his head. "It wasn't my choice. That decision was made by Homeland Security and FEMA as an SOP for large-scale catastrophes." He raised his hands, palms-up to indicate self-absolution. "There was nothing I could do."

THE REVIVAL

"And have you received authorization from your command to release those resources now?" asked Hersey.

Briggs didn't answer for a moment, looking at the other soldiers seated around him, then back at the lawmen. "We are not currently in communication with our command. It is not necessary that we be. Emergency directives are in place."

"Have you ever been in contact with your command since this thing started?" asked Freelove.

"That's classified," Briggs answered.

"How many people do you have left?" asked McGregor.

Briggs' face seemed to lose its color. "That's classified."

"How much of your equipment is operable?" asked Hersey.

Briggs seemed to be sweating. "That is also classified. He lifted his chin, attempting to appear taller. "The important thing is that we work together in order to re-establish a secure region until the federal government is able to re-integrate regions into a national collective again."

The lawmen looked at each other. Finally, Hersey laughed. "I haven't heard that much bullshit since the last federal task force meeting I went to."

He got to his feet, looking hard at Briggs. "You've got nothing of importance that works, three hundred or so undisciplined jerk-offs following you, and nothing we need that we can't take if we want to. You've hidden in here for over a year, afraid to come out and refusing help to those you could have saved."

He looked hard at Briggs. "As far as I'm concerned, you're guilty of murder, as are all of your officers. You're lucky I don't shoot you right here in front of your men, but you will go on trial so that everyone will hear what you all did."

Briggs started trembling, his face turning red. "How dare you ..."

Hersey raised the pistol he had drawn without anyone noticing and pointed it at Briggs. "You other men," he said addressing the soldiers, "there are fifty of us in here and another two hundred outside waiting to come in if they hear gunfire. So far, our only problem is with your colonel, who is now under arrest. But, if the ball starts rolling, none of you are going to make it out of here. That, I promise you. So, stay put. Raise a weapon and we'll punch your ticket right now."

The other lawmen got up and fanned out across the room, training their weapons on the soldiers.

"Your choice, colonel," said Hersey, lining his sights on Briggs' chest.

THE REVIVAL

"Excuse me, sheriff," said the captain from Riley County, stepping forward. "I think there is something everyone should know before we go any farther."

"Yeah, what's that?" Hersey asked, not taking his eyes or his gun off of Briggs, who stood perfectly still.

"I brought a professor from K-State with me." He motioned a small man forward to stand next to him.

"This is Dr. Vihaan Singh. He's a professor of physics and cosmology."

He nodded to the man. "Go ahead, Vihaan. Tell them."

The man took a tentative step forward, looking around almost apologetically. "What happened was caused by a massive coronal mass ejection, a CME. We knew it was coming thirty-six hours before it arrived, but the government would not allow us to announce it for fear of causing a panic."

He looked around again. "According to magnetohydrodynamic theory ..."

"Just the important parts, Vihaan," the captain said.

Singh nodded. "I'm sorry. Essentially, the sun ejected an enormous amount of magnetized plasma which disrupted our magnetosphere, resulting in the destruction of all unprotected electronics and electrical systems."

There was silence throughout the hanger. Finally, one of the militia leaders asked, "Do you mean everything's off over the entire country?"

Singh realized that they didn't understand what he was saying. But how could they? The enormity was almost too great to understand. He shook his head slowly, looking around at the group with sadness in his eyes. "No, I mean the entire world."

THE REVIVAL

THE REVIVAL

Coming in 2019!

The Renewal

With the revelation that a massive CME had taken out the electrical systems of the world, the people of Stonemont turn their energies to rebuilding a new society based on the foundational principles of freedom and liberty.

Across the continent and across the world, groups are forming to create new tribes, new city-states and new countries. For some, the catastrophe provided an opportunity to return to a better, simpler life celebrating the best of humankind; for others, a descent into the darkness, despair and depravity of a man-made hell.

The Stonemont group is growing and evolving, understanding and accepting the importance of their involvement in the new world dynamic, as are other groups around them with which they are already in contact - and others with which they will be – on both sides.

Follow the Stonemont series at
facebook.com/stonemont-series

Contact the author at
scsmith@integrativepreparedness.com

THE REVIVAL

Printed in Great Britain
by Amazon

46346398R00148